Baroness Orczy was born
of Baron Felix Orczy, a
composer and conductor. Orczy moved with her parents
Budapest to Brussels and Paris, where she was educated. She
studied art in London and exhibited work in the Royal
Academy.

Orczy married Montagu Barstow and together they worked
as illustrators and jointly published an edition of Hungarian
folk tales. Orczy became famous in 1905 with the publication
of *The Scarlet Pimpernel* (originally a play co-written with her
husband). Its background of the French Revolution and
swashbuckling hero, Sir Percy Blakeney, was to prove
immensely popular. Sequel books followed and film and TV
versions were later made. Orczy also wrote detective stories.

She died in 1947.

BY THE SAME AUTHOR
ALL PUBLISHED BY HOUSE OF STRATUS

LORD TONY'S WIFE

Baroness Orczy

HOUSE OF STRATUS

This edition published in 2002 by House of Stratus, an imprint of House of Stratus Ltd, Thirsk Industrial Park, York Road, Thirsk, North Yorkshire, YO7 3BX, UK.
Also at: House of Stratus Inc., 2 Neptune Road, Poughkeepsie, NY 12601, USA.

www.houseofstratus.com

Typeset, printed and bound by House of Stratus.

A catalogue record for this book is available from the British Library and the Library of Congress.

ISBN 0-7551-1116-8

To Dora Countess of Chesterfield
A Token of Friendship and Love

EMMUSKA ORCZY

Contents

PROLOGUE

Nantes, 1789

'Tyrant! tyrant! tyrant!'

It was Pierre who spoke, his voice was hardly raised above a murmur, but there was such an intensity of passion expressed in his face, in the fingers of his hand which closed slowly and convulsively as if they were clutching the throat of a struggling viper, there was so much hate in those muttered words, so much power, such compelling and awesome determination that an ominous silence fell upon the village lads and the men who sat with him in the low narrow room of the auberge des Trois Vertus.

Even the man in the tattered coat and threadbare breeches, who – perched upon the centre table – had been haranguing the company on the subject of the Rights of Man, paused in his peroration and looked down on Pierre half afraid of that fierce flame of passionate hate which his own words had helped to kindle.

The silence, however, had only lasted a few moments, the next Pierre was on his feet, and a cry like that of a bull in a slaughter-house escaped his throat.

'In the name of God!' he shouted, 'let us cease all that senseless talking. Haven't we planned enough and talked enough to satisfy our puling consciences? The time has come to strike, mes amis, to strike I say, to strike at those cursed aristocrats, who have made us what we are – ignorant, wretched, downtrodden – senseless clods to work our fingers to the bone, our bodies till they break so that they may wallow in their pleasures and their luxuries! Strike, I say!' he reiterated while his eyes glowed and his breath came and went through his throat with a hissing sound. 'Strike! as the men and women struck in Paris on that great day in July. To them the Bastille stood for tyranny, and they struck at it as they would at the head of a tyrant – and the tyrant cowered, cringed, made terms – he was frightened at the wrath of the people! That is what happened in Paris! That is what must happen in Nantes. The château of the duc de Kernogan is our Bastille! Let us strike at it tonight, and if the arrogant aristocrat resists, we'll raze his house to the ground. The hour, the day, the darkness are all propitious. The arrangements hold good. The neighbours are ready. Strike, I say!'

He brought his hard fist crashing down upon the table, so that mugs and bottles rattled: his enthusiasm had fired all his hearers: his hatred and his lust of revenge had done more in five minutes than all the tirades of the agitators sent down from Paris to instil revolutionary ideas into the slow-moving brains of village lads.

'Who will give the signal?' queried one of the older men quietly.

'I will!' came in lusty response from Pierre.

He strode to the door, and all the men jumped to their feet, ready to follow him, dragged into this hot-headed venture by the mere force of one man's towering passion. They followed Pierre like sheep – sheep that have momentarily become intoxicated – sheep that have become fierce – a strange sight truly – and yet one that the man in the tattered coat who had done so much speechifying lately watched with eager interest and presently related with great wealth of detail to M. de Mirabeau the champion of the people.

2

'It all came about through the death of a pair of pigeons,' he said.

The death of the pigeons, however, was only the spark which set all these turbulent passions ablaze. They had been smouldering for half a century, and had been ready to burst into flames for the past decade.

Antoine Melun, the wheelwright, who was to have married Louise, Pierre's sister, had trapped a pair of pigeons in the woods of M. le duc de Kernogan. He had done it to assert his rights as a man – he did not want the pigeons. Though he was a poor man, he was no poorer than hundreds of peasants for miles around: but he paid imposts and taxes until every particle of profit which he gleaned from his miserable little plot of land went into the hands of the collectors, whilst M. le duc de Kernogan paid not one sou towards the costs of the State, and he had to live on what was left of his own rye and wheat after M. le duc's pigeons had had their fill of them.

Antoine Melun did not want to eat the pigeons which he had trapped, but he desired to let M. le duc de Kernogan know that God and Nature had never intended all the beasts and birds of the woods to be the exclusive property of one man, rather than another. So he trapped and killed two pigeons and M. le duc's head-bailiff caught him in the act of carrying those pigeons home.

Whereupon Antoine was arrested for poaching and thieving: he was tried at Nantes under the presidency of M. le duc de Kernogan, and ten minutes ago while the man in the tattered coat was declaiming to a number of peasant lads in the coffee-room of the auberge des Trois Vertus on the subject of their rights as men and citizens, someone brought the news that Antoine Melun had just been condemned to death and would be hanged on the morrow.

That was the spark which had fanned Pierre Adet's hatred of the aristocrats to a veritable conflagration: the news of Antoine Melun's fate was the bleat which rallied all those human sheep

3

around their leader. For Pierre had naturally become their leader because his hatred of M. le duc was more tangible, more powerful than theirs. Pierre had had more education than they. His father, Jean Adet the miller, had sent him to a school in Nantes, and when Pierre came home M. le *curé* of Vertou took an interest in him and taught him all he knew himself – which was not much – in the way of philosophy and the classics. But later on Pierre took to reading the writings of M. Jean-Jacques Rousseau and soon knew the *Contrat Social* almost by heart. He had also read the articles in M. Marat's newspaper *L'ami du Peuple*! and like Antoine Melun, the wheelwright, he had got it into his head that it was not God, nor yet Nature who had intended one man to starve while another gorged himself on all the good things of this world.

He did not, however, speak of these matters, either to his father or to his sister or to M. le *curé*, but he brooded over them, and when the price of bread rose to four sous he muttered curses against M. le duc de Kernogan, and when famine prices ruled throughout the district those curses became overt threats; and by the time that the pinch of hunger was felt in Vertou Pierre's passion of fury against the duc de Kernogan had turned to a frenzy of hate against the entire noblesse of France.

Still he said nothing to his father, nothing to his mother and sister. But his father knew. Old Jean would watch the storm-clouds which gathered on Pierre's lowering brow; he heard the muttered curses which escaped from Pierre's lips whilst he worked for the liege-lord whom he hated. But Jean was a wise man and knew how useless it is to put out a feeble hand in order to stem the onrush of a torrent. He knew how useless are the words of wisdom from an old man to quell the rebellious spirit of the young.

Jean was on the watch. And evening after evening when the work on the farm was done, Pierre would sit in the small low room of the auberge with other lads from the village talking,

talking of their wrongs, of the arrogance of the aristocrats, the sins of M. le duc and his family, the evil conduct of the King and the immorality of the Queen: and men in ragged coats and tattered breeches came in from Nantes, and even from Paris, in order to harangue these village lads and told them yet further tales of innumerable wrongs suffered by the people at the hands of the aristos, and stuffed their heads full of schemes for getting even once and for all with those men and women who fattened on the sweat of the poor and drew their luxury from the hunger and the toil of the peasantry.

Pierre sucked in these harangues through every pore: they were meat and drink to him. His hate and passions fed upon these effusions till his whole being was consumed by a maddening desire for reprisals, for vengeance – for the lust of triumph over those whom he had been taught to fear.

And in the low, narrow room of the auberge the fevered heads of village lads were bent together in conclave, and the ravings and shoutings of a while ago were changed to whisperings and low murmurings behind barred doors and shuttered windows. Men exchanged cryptic greetings when they met in the village street, enigmatical signs passed between them while they worked: strangers came and went at dead of night to and from the neighbouring villages. M. le duc's overseers saw nothing, heard nothing, guessed nothing. M. le *curé* saw much and old Jean Adet guessed a great deal, but they said nothing, for nothing then would have availed.

Then came the catastrophe.

2

Pierre pushed open the outer door of the auberge des Trois Vertus and stepped out under the porch. A gust of wind caught him in the face. The night, so the chronicles of the time tell us, was as dark as pitch: on ahead lay the lights of the city flickering in the gale: to the left the wide tawny ribbon of the river wound its turbulent course toward the ocean, the booming of the waters swollen by the recent melting of the snows sounded like the weird echoes of invisible cannons far away.

Without hesitation Pierre advanced. His little troop followed him in silence. They were a little sobered now that they came out into the open and that the fumes of cider and of hot, perspiring humanity no longer obscured their vision or inflamed their brain.

They knew whither Pierre was going. It had all been pre-arranged – throughout this past summer, in the musty parlour of the auberge, behind barred doors and shuttered windows – all they had to do was to follow Pierre, whom they had tacitly chosen as their leader. They walked on behind him, their hands buried in the pockets of their thin, tattered breeches, their heads bent forward against the fury of the gale.

Pierre made straight for the mill – his home – where his father lived and where Louise was even now crying her eyes out because Antoine Melun, her sweetheart, had been condemned to be hanged for killing two pigeons.

At the back of the mill was the dwelling house and beyond it a small farmery, for Jean Adet owned a little bit of land and would have been fairly well off if the taxes had not swallowed up all the money that he made out of the sale of his rye and his hay. Just here the ground rose sharply to a little hillock which dominated the flat valley of the Loire and commanded a fine view over the more distant villages.

Pierre skirted the mill and without looking round to see if the others followed him he struck squarely to the right up a narrow lane bordered by tall poplars, and which led upwards to the summit of the little hillock around which clustered the tumble-down barns of his father's farmery. The gale lashed the straight, tall stems of the poplars until they bent nearly double, and each tiny bare twig sighed and whispered as if in pain. Pierre strode on and the others followed in silence. They were chilled to the bone under their scanty clothes, but they followed on with grim determination, set teeth, and anger and hate seething in their hearts.

The top of the rising ground was reached. It was pitch dark, and the men when they halted fell up against one another trying to get a foothold on the sodden ground. But Pierre seemed to have eyes like a cat. He only paused one moment to get his bearings, then – still with out a word – he set to work. A large barn and a group of small circular straw-ricks loomed like solid masses out of the darkness – black, silhouetted against the black of the stormy sky. Pierre turned toward the barn: those of his comrades who were in the forefront of the small crowd saw him disappearing inside one of those solid shadowy masses that looked so ghostlike in the night.

Anon those who watched and who happened to be facing the interior of the barn saw sparks from a tinder flying in every direction: the next moment they could see Pierre himself quite clearly. He was standing in the middle of the barn and intent on lighting a roughly-fashioned torch with his tinder: soon the resin caught a spark and Pierre held the torch inclined toward the ground so that the flames could lick their way up the shaft. The flickering light cast a weird glow and deep grotesque shadows upon the face and figure of the young man. His hair, lanky and dishevelled, fell over his eyes; his mouth and jaw, illumined from below by the torch, looked unnaturally large, and showed his teeth gleaming white, like the fangs of a beast of prey. His shirt was torn open at the neck and the sleeves of his coat were rolled up to the elbow. He seemed not to feel either the cold from without or the scorching heat of the flaming torch in his hand. But he worked deliberately and calmly, without haste or febrile movements: grim determination held his excitement in check.

At last his work was done. The men who had pressed forward, in order to watch him, fell back as he advanced torch in hand. They knew exactly what he was going to do, they had thought it all out, planned it, spoken of it till even their unimaginative minds had visualized this coming scene with absolutely realistic perception. And yet now that the supreme hour had come, now that they saw Pierre – torch in hand – prepared to give the signal which would set ablaze the seething revolt of the countryside, their heart seemed to stop its beating within their body; they held their breath, their toil-worn hands went up to their throats as if to repress that awful choking sensation which was so like fear.

But Pierre had no such hesitations; if his breath seemed to choke him as it reached his throat, if it escaped through his set teeth with a strange whistling sound, it was because his excitement was that of a hungry beast who has sighted his prey and is ready to spring and devour. His hand did not shake, his step was firm: the gusts of wind caught the flame of his torch till the sparks flew in every direction and scorched his hair and his hands, and while the others recoiled he strode on, to the straw-rick that was nearest.

For one moment he held the torch aloft. There was triumph now in his eyes, in his whole attitude. He looked out into the darkness far away which seemed all the more impenetrable beyond the restricted circle of flickering torch-light. It seemed as if he would wrest from that inky blackness all the secrets which it hid – all the enthusiasm, the excitement, the passions, the hatred which he would have liked to set ablaze as he would the straw-ricks anon.

'Are you ready, mes amis?' he called.

'Aye! aye!' they replied – not gaily, not lustily, but calmly and under their breath.

One touch of the torch and the dry straw began to crackle; a gust of wind caught the flame and whipped it into energy; it crept up the side of the little rick like a glowing python that wraps its prey in its embrace. Another gust of wind and the flame leapt joyously up to the pinnacle of the rick, and sent forth other tongues to lick and to lick, to enfold the straw, to devour, to consume.

But Pierre did not wait to see the consummation of his work of destruction. Already with a few rapid strides he had reached his father's second straw-rick and this too he set alight, and then another and another, until six blazing furnaces sent their lurid tongues of flames, twisting and twirling, writhing and hissing through the stormy night.

Within the space of two minutes the whole summit of the hillock seemed to be ablaze and Pierre, like a god of fire, torch in hand seemed to preside over and command a multitude of ever-spreading flames to his will. Excitement had overmastered him now, the lust to destroy was upon him, and excitement had seized all the others too.

There was shouting and cursing, and laughter that sounded mirthless and forced, and calls to Pierre and oaths of revenge. Memory like an evil-intentioned witch was riding invisibly in the darkness and she touched each seething brain with her fever-giving wand. Every man had an outrage to remember, an injustice to recall, and strong, brown fists were shaken aloft in the direction of the château de Kernogan whose lights glimmered feebly in the distance beyond the Loire.

'Death to the tyrant! A la lanterne les aristos! The people's hour has come at last! No more starvation! No more injustice! Equality! Liberty! A mort les aristos!'

The shouts, the curses, the crackling flames, the howling of the wind, the soughing of the trees made up a confusion of sounds which seemed hardly of this earth; the blazing ricks, the flickering, red light of the flames had finally transformed the little hillock behind the mill into another Brocken on whose summit witches and devils do of a truth hold their revels.

'A moi!' shouted Pierre again, and he threw his torch down upon the ground and once more made for the barn. The others followed him. In the barn were such weapons as these wretched penniless peasants had managed to collect – scythes, poles, axes, saws, anything that would prove useful for the destruction of the château de Kernogan and the proposed brow-beating of

M. le duc and his family. All the men trooped in in the wake of Pierre. The entire hillock was now a blaze of light – lurid and red and flickering – alternately teased and fanned and subdued by the gale, so that at times every object stood out clearly cut, every blade of grass, every stone in bold relief, and in the ruts and fissures, every tiny pool of muddy water shimmered like strings of fire-opals: whilst at others a pall of inky darkness, smoke-laden and impenetrable would lie over the ground and erase the outline of farm-buildings and distant mill and of the pushing and struggling mass of humanity inside the barn. But Pierre, heedless of light and darkness, of heat or of cold, proceeded quietly and methodically to distribute the primitive implements of warfare to this crowd of ignorant men who were by now over ready for mischief: and with every weapon which he placed in willing hands he found the right words for willing ears – words which would kindle passion and lust of vengeance most readily where they lay dormant, or would fan them into greater vigour where they smouldered.

'For thee this scythe, Hector Lebrun,' he would say to a tall, lanky youth whose emaciated arms and bony hands were stretched with longing toward the bright piece of steel; 'remember last year's harvest, the heavy tax thou wert forced to pay, so that not one sou of profit went into thy pocket, and thy mother starved whilst M. le duc and his brood feasted and danced and shiploads of corn were sunk in the Loire lest abundance made bread too cheap for the poor!'

'For thee this pick-axe, Henri Meunier! Remember the new roof on thy hut, which thou didst build to keep the wet off thy wife's bed who was crippled with ague – and the heavy impost levied on thee by the tax-collector for this improvement to thy miserable hovel.'

'This pole for thee, Charles Blanc! Remember the beating administered to thee by the duc's bailiff for daring to keep a tame rabbit to amuse thy children!'

'Remember! Remember, mes amis!' he added exultantly, 'remember every wrong you have endured, every injustice, every blow! remember your poverty and his wealth, your crusts of dry bread and his succulent meals, your rags and his silks and velvets, remember your starving children and ailing mother, your care-laden wife and toil-worn daughters! Forget nothing, mes amis, tonight, and at the gates of the château de Kernogan demand of its arrogant owner wrong for wrong and outrage for outrage.'

A deafening cry of triumph greeted this peroration, scythes and sickles and axes and poles were brandished in the air and several scores of hands were stretched out to Pierre and clasped in this newly-formed bond of vengeful fraternity.

3

Then it was that with vigorous play of the elbows Jean Adet, the miller, forced his way through the crowd till he stood face to face with his son.

'Unfortunate!' he cried, 'what is all this? What dost thou propose to do? Whither are ye all going?'

'To Kernogan!' they all shouted in response.

'En avant, Pierre! we follow!' cried some of them impatiently.

But Jean Adet – who was a powerful man despite his years – had seized Pierre by the arm and dragged him to a distant corner of the barn: 'Pierre!' he said in tones of command, 'I forbid thee in the name of thy duty and the obedience which thou dost owe to me and to thy mother, to move another step in this hot-headed adventure. I was on the high-road, walking homewards, when that conflagration and the senseless cries of these poor lads warned me that some awful mischief was afoot. Pierre! my son! I command thee to lay that weapon down.'

But Pierre – who in his normal state was a dutiful son and sincerely fond of his father – shook himself free from Jean Adet's grasp.

'Father!' he said loudly and firmly, 'this is no time for interference. We are all of us men here and know our own minds. What we mean to do tonight we have thought on and planned for weeks and months. I pray you, father, let me be! I am not a child and I have work to do.'

'Not a child?' exclaimed the old man as he turned appealingly to the lads who had stood by, silent and sullen during this little scene. 'Not a child? But you are all only children, my lads. You don't know what you are doing. You don't know what terrible consequences this mad escapade will bring upon us all, upon the whole village, aye! and the country-side. Do you suppose for one moment that the château of Kernogan will fall at the mercy of a few ignorant unarmed lads like yourselves? Why! four hundred of you would not succeed in forcing your way even as far as the courtyard of the palace. M. le duc has had wind for some time of your turbulent meetings at the auberge: he has kept an armed guard inside his castle yard for weeks past, a company of artillery with two guns hoisted upon his walls. My poor lads! you are running straight to ruin! Go home, I beg of you! Forget this night's escapade! Nothing but misery to you and yours can result from it.'

They listened quietly, if surlily, to Jean Adet's impassioned words. Far be it from their thoughts to flout or to mock him. Paternal authority commanded respect even among the most rough; but they all felt that they had gone too far now to draw back: the savour of anticipated revenge had been too sweet to be foregone quite so readily, and Pierre with his vigorous personality, his glowing eloquence, his compelling power had more influence over them than the sober counsels of prudence and the wise admonitions of old Jean Adet. Not one word was spoken, but with an instinctive gesture every man grasped his weapon more firmly and then turned to Pierre, thus electing him their spokesman.

Pierre too had listened in silence to all that his father said, striving to bide the burning anxiety which was gnawing at his heart, lest his comrades allowed themselves to be persuaded by the old man's counsels and their ardour be cooled by the wise dictates of prudence. But when Jean Adet had finished speaking and Pierre saw each man thus grasping his weapon all the more firmly and in silence, a cry of triumph escaped his lips.

'It is all in vain, father,' he cried, 'our minds are made up. A host of angels from heaven would not bar our way now to victory and to vengeance.'

'Pierre!' admonished the old man.

'It is too late, my father,' said Pierre firmly, 'en avant, lads!'

'Yes! en avant! en avant!' assented some, 'we have wasted too much time as it is.'

'But, unfortunate lads,' admonished the old man, 'what are you going to do? – a handful of you – where are you going?'

'We go straight to the cross-roads now, father,' said Pierre firmly. 'The fixing of your ricks – for which I humbly crave your pardon – is the preconcerted signal which will bring the lads from all the neighbouring villages – from Goulaine and les Sorinières and Doulon and Tourne-Bride – to our meeting place. Never you fear! There will be more than four hundred of us and a company of paid soldiers is not like to frighten us. Eh, lads?'

'No! no! en evant!' they shouted and murmured impatiently, 'there has been too much talking already and we have wasted precious time.'

'Pierre!' entreated the miller.

But no one listened to the old man now. A general movement down the hillock had already begun and Pierre turning his back on his father had pushed his way to the front of the crowd and was now leading the way down the slope. Up on the summit the fire was already burning low: only from time to time an imprisoned tongue of flame would dart out of the dying embers and leap fitfully up into the night. A dull red glow illumined the small farmery and the mill and the slowly moving mass of men along the narrow road, whilst clouds of black, dense smoke were tossed about by the gale. Pierre walked with head erect. He ceased to think of his father and he never looked back to see if the others followed him. He knew that they did: like the straw-ricks a while ago, they had become the prey of a consuming fire: the fire of their own passion which had caught them and held them and would not leave them now until their ardour was consumed in victory or defeat.

4

M. le duc de Kernogan had just finished dinner when Jacques Labrunière his head-bailiff came to him with the news that a rabble crowd composed of the peasantry of Goulaine and Vertou and the neighbouring villages had assembled at the cross-roads, there held revolutionary speeches, and was even now marching toward the castle still shouting and singing and brandishing a miscellaneous collection of weapons chiefly consisting of scythes and axes.

'The guard is under arms, I imagine,' was M. le duc's comment on this not altogether unforeseen piece of news.

'Everything is in perfect order," replied the head-bailiff coolly,' for the defence of M. le duc and his property – and of Mademoiselle.'

M. le duc who had been lounging in one of the big armchairs in the stately hall of Kernogan jumped to his feet at these words: his cheeks suddenly pallid, and a look of deadly fear in his eyes.

'Mademoiselle,' he said hurriedly, 'by G–d, Labrunière, I had forgotten – momentarily – '

'M. le duc?' stammered the bailiff in anxious inquiry. 'Mademoiselle de Kernogan is on her way home – even now – she spent the day with Mme. la Marquise d'Herbignac – she was to return at about eight o'clock. If those devils meet her carriage on the road...'

'There is no cause for anxiety, M. le duc,' broke in Labrunière hurriedly. 'I will see that half a dozen men get to horse at once and go and meet Mademoiselle and escort her home...'

'Yes,...yes...Labrunière,' murmured the duc, who seemed very much overcome with terror now that his daughter's safety was in jeopardy, 'see to it at once. Quick! quick! I shall wax crazy with anxiety.'

While Labrunière ran to make the necessary arrangements for an efficient escort for Mademoiselle de Kernogan and gave the sergeant in charge of the posse the necessary directions, M. le duc remained motionless, huddled up in the capacious armchair, his head buried in his hand, shivering in front of the huge fire which burned in the monumental hearth, himself the prey of nameless, overwhelming terror.

He knew – none better – the appalling hatred wherewith he and all his family and belongings were regarded by the local peasantry. Astride upon his manifold rights – feudal, territorial, seigniorial rights – he had all his life ridden roughshod over the prejudices, the miseries, the undoubted rights of the poor people, who were little better than serfs in the possession of the high and mighty duc de Kernogan. He also knew – none better – that gradually, very gradually it is true, but with unerring certainty, those same down-trodden, ignorant, miserable and half-starved peasants were turning against their oppressors, that riots and outrages had occurred in many rural districts in the North and that the insidious poison of social revolution was gradually creeping toward the South and West, and had already infected the villages and small townships which were situated quite unpleasantly close to Nantes and to Kernogan.

For this reason he had kept a company of artillery at his own expense inside the precincts of his château, and with the aristocrat's open contempt for this peasantry which it had not yet learned to fear, he had disdained to take further measures for the repression of local gatherings, and would not pay the village rabble the compliment of being afraid of them in any way.

But with his daughter Yvonne in the open roadway on the very night when an assembly of that same rabble was obviously bent on mischief, matters became very serious. Insult, outrage or worse might befall the proud aristocrat's only child, and knowing that from these people, whom she had been taught to look upon as little better than beasts, she could expect neither mercy nor chivalry, the duc de Kernogan within his unassailable castle felt for his daughter's safety the most abject, the most deadly fear which hath ever unnerved any man.

Labrunière a few minutes later did his best to reassure his master.

'I have ordered the men to take the best horses out of the stables, M. le duc,' he said, 'and to cut across the fields toward la Gramoire so as to intercept Mademoiselle's coach ere it reach the cross-roads. I feel confident that there is no cause for alarm,' he added emphatically.

'Pray God you are right, Labrunière,' murmured the duc feebly. 'Do you know how strong the rabble crowd is?'

'No, Monseigneur, not exactly. Camille the under-bailiff, who brought me the news, was riding homewards across the meadows about an hour ago when he saw a huge conflagration which seemed to come from the back of Adet's mill: the whole sky has been lit up by a lurid light for the past hour, and I fancied myself that Adet's straw must be on fire. But Camille pushed his horse up the rising ground which culminates at Adet's farmery. It seems that he heard a great deal of shouting which did not seem to be accompanied by any attempt at putting out the fire. So he dismounted and led his horse round the hillock skirting Adet's farm buildings so that he should not be seen. Under cover of darkness he heard and saw the old miller with his son Pierre engaged in distributing scythes, poles and axes to a crowd of youngsters and haranguing them wildly all the time. He also heard Pierre Adet speak of the conflagration as a preconcerted signal, and say that he and his mates would meet the lads of the neighbouring villages at the cross-roads and that four hundred of them would then march on Kernogan and pillage the castle.'

'Bah!' quoth M. le duc in a voice hoarse with execration and contempt, 'a lot of oafs who will give the hangman plenty of trouble tomorrow. As for that Adet and his son, they shall suffer for this... I can promise them that... If only Mademoiselle were home!' he added with a heartrending sigh.

5

Indeed, had M. le duc de Kernogan been gifted with second sight, the agony of mind which he was enduring would have been aggravated an hundredfold. At the very moment when the head-bailiff was doing his best to reassure his liege-lord as to the safety of Mlle. de Kernogan, her coach was speeding along from the château of Herbignac toward those same cross-roads where a couple of hundred hot-headed peasant lads were planning as much mischief as their unimaginative minds could conceive.

The fury of the gale had in no way abated, and now a heavy rain was falling – a drenching, sopping rain which in the space of half an hour had added five centimetres to the depth of the mud on the roads, and had in that same space of time considerably damped the enthusiasm of some of the poor lads. Three score or so had assembled from Goulaine, two score from les Sorinières, some three dozen from Doulon: they had rallied to the signal in hot haste, gathered their scythes and spades, very eager and excited, and had reached the cross-roads which were much nearer to their respective villages than to Jean Adet's farm and the mill, even while the old man was admonishing his son and the lads of Vertou on the summit of the blazing hillock. Here they had spent half an hour in cooling their heels and their tempers under the drenching rain – wet to the skin – fuming and fretting at the delay.

But even so – damped in ardour and chilled to the marrow – they were still a dangerous crowd and prudence ought to have dictated to Mademoiselle de Kernogan the wiser course of ordering her coachman Jean-Marie to head his horses back toward Herbignac, the moment that the outrider reported that a mob, armed with scythes, spades and axes, held the cross-roads and that it would be dangerous for the coach to advance any further.

Already for the past few minutes the sound of loud shouting had been heard even above the tramp of the horses and the clatter of the coach. Jean-Marie had pulled up and sent one of the outriders on ahead to see what was amiss: the man returned with very unpleasant tidings – in his opinion it certainly would be dangerous to go any further. The mob appeared bent on mischief: he had heard threats and curses all levelled against M. le duc de Kernogan – the conflagration up at Vertou was evidently a signal which would bring along a crowd of malcontents from all the neighbouring villages. He was for turning back forthwith. But Mademoiselle put her head out of the window just then and asked what was amiss. On hearing that Jean-Marie and the postilion and outriders were inclined to be afraid of a mob of peasant lads who had assembled at the cross-roads and were apparently threatening to do mischief, she chided them for their cowardice.

'Jean-Marie,' she called scornfully to the old coachman, who had been in her father's service for close on half a century, 'do you really mean to tell me that you are afraid of that rabble!'

'Why no! Mademoiselle, so please you,' replied the old man, nettled in his pride by the taunt, 'but the temper of the peasantry round here has been ugly of late, and 'tis your safety I have got to guard.'

' 'Tis my commands you have got to obey,' retorted Mademoiselle with a gay little laugh which mitigated the peremptoriness of her tone. 'If my father should hear that there's trouble on the road he will die of anxiety if I do not return: so whip up the horses Jean-Marie. No one will dare to attack the coach.'

'But Mademoiselle – ' remonstrated the old man.

'Ah çà!' she broke in more impatiently, 'am I to be openly disobeyed? Best join that rabble, Jean-Marie, if you have no respect for my commands.'

Thus twitted by Mademoiselle's sharp tongue Jean-Marie could not help but obey. He tried to peer into the distance through the veil of blinding rain which beat against his face and stung the horses to restlessness. But the light from the coach lanthorns prevented his seeing clearly into the darkness beyond. Still it seemed to him that on ahead a dense and solid mass was moving toward the coach, also that the sound of shouting and of excited humanity was considerably nearer than it had been before. No doubt the mob had perceived the lights of the coach and was even now making towards it, with what intent Jean-Marie divined all too accurately.

But he had his orders, and though he was an old and trusted servant disobedience these days was not even to be thought of. So he did as he was bid. He whipped up his horses, which were high-spirited and answered to the lash with a bound and a plunge forward. Mlle de Kernogan leaned back on the cushions of the coach. She was satisfied that Jean-Marie had done as he was told, and she was not in the least afraid.

But less than five minutes later she had a rude awakening. The coach gave a terrific lurch. The horses reared and plunged, there was a deafening clamour all around: men were shouting and cursing: there was the clash of wood and iron and the cracking of whips: the tramp of horses' hoofs in the soft ground, and the dull thud of human bodies falling in the mud followed by loud cries of pain. There was the sudden crash of broken glass, the coach lanthorns had been seized and broken: it seemed to Yvonne de Kernogan that out of the darkness faces distorted with fury were peering at her through the window-panes. But through all the confusion the coach kept moving on.

Jean-Marie stuck to his post as did also the postilion and the four outriders, and with whip and tongue they urged their horses to break through the crowd regardless of human lives, knocking and trampling down men and lads heedless of curses and blasphemies which were hurled on them and on the occupants of the coach, whoever they might be.

The next moment, however, the coach came to a sudden halt and a wild cry of triumph drowned the groans of the injured and the dying.

'Kernogan! Kernogan! 'was shouted from every side. 'Adet! Adet!'

'You limbs of Satan,' cried Jean-Marie, 'you'll rue this night's work and weep tears of blood for the rest of your lives Let me tell you that! Mademoiselle is in the coach. When M. le duc hears of this, there will be work for the hangman...'

'Mademoiselle in the coach,' broke in a hoarse voice with a rough tone of command. 'Let's look at her...'

'Aye! Aye! let's have a look at Mademoiselle,' came with a volley of objurgations and curses from the crowd.

'You devils – you would dare?' protested Jean-Marie. Within the coach Yvonne de Kernogan hardly dared to breathe. She sat bolt upright, her cape held tightly round her shoulders: her eyes – dilated now with excitement, if not with fear, were fixed upon the darkness beyond the window panes. She could see nothing, but she *felt* the presence of that hostile crowd who had succeeded in overpowering Jean-Marie and were intent on doing her harm.

But she belonged to a caste which never reckoned cowardice amongst its many faults. During these few moments when she knew that her life hung on the merest thread of chance, she neither screamed nor fainted but sat rigidly still, her heart beating in unison with the agonizing seconds which went so fatefully by. And even now when the carriage door was torn violently open and even through the darkness she discerned vaguely the forms of these avowed enemies close beside her, and anon felt a rough hand seize her wrist, she did not move, but said quite calmly, with hardly a tremor in her voice:

'Who are you? and what do you want?'

An outburst of harsh and ironical laughter came in response.

'Who are we, my fine lady?' said the foremost man in the crowd, he who had seized her wrist and was half in and half out of the coach at this moment, 'we are the men who throughout our lives have toiled and starved whilst you and such as you travel in fine coaches and eat your fill. What we want? Why just the spectacle of such a fine lady as you are being knocked down into the mud just as our wives and daughters are if they happen to be in the way when your coach is passing. Isn't that it, mes amis?'

'Aye! aye!' they replied, shouting lustily. 'Into the mud with the fine lady. Out with her, Adet. Let's have a look at Mademoiselle how she will look with her face in the mud. Out with her, quick!'

But the man who was still half in and half out of the coach and who had hold of Mademoiselle's wrist did not obey his mates immediately. He drew her nearer to him and suddenly threw his rough, begrimed arms round her, and with one hand pulled back her hood, then placing two fingers under her chin, he jerked it up till her face was level with his own.

Yvonne de Kernogan was certainly no coward, but at the loathsome contact of this infuriated and vengeful creature, she was overcome with such a hideous sense of fear that for the moment consciousness almost left her: not completely alas! for though she could not distinguish his face she could feel his hot breath upon her cheeks, she could smell the nauseating odour of his damp clothes and she could hear his hoarse mutterings as for the space of a few seconds he held her thus close to him in an embrace which to her was far more awesome than that of death.

'And just to punish you, my fine lady,' he said in a whisper which sent a shudder of horror right through her, 'to punish you for what you are, the brood of tyrants, proud, disdainful, a budding tyrant yourself, to punish you for every misery my mother and sister have had to endure, for every luxury which you have enjoyed, I will kiss you on the lips and the cheeks and just between your white throat and chin and never as long as you live if you die this night or live to be an hundred will you be able to wash off those kisses showered upon you by one who hates and loathes you – a miserable peasant whom you despise and who in your sight is lower far than your dogs.'

Yvonne with eyes closed hardly breathed, but through the veil of semi-consciousness which mercifully wrapped her senses she could still hear those awful words, and feel the pollution of those loathsome kisses with which – true to his threat – this creature – half man, wholly devil, whom she could not see but whom she hated and feared as she would Satan himself – now covered her face and throat.

After that she remembered nothing more. Consciousness mercifully forsook her altogether. When she recovered her senses, she was within the precincts of the castle: a confused murmur of voices reached her ears, and her father's arms were round her. Gradually she distinguished what was being said: she gathered the threads of the story which Jean-Marie and the postilion and outriders were hastily unravelling in response to M. le duc's commands.

These men of course knew nothing of the poignant little drama which had been enacted inside the coach. All they knew was that they had been surrounded by a rough crowd – a hundred or so strong – who brandished scythes and spades, that they had made valiant efforts to break through the crowd by whipping up their horses, but that suddenly some of those devils more plucky than the others seized the horses by their bits and rendered poor Jean-Marie quite helpless. He thought then that all would be up with the lot of them and was thinking of scrambling down from his box in order to protect Mademoiselle with his body, and the pistols which he had in the boot, when happily for everyone concerned he heard in the distance – above the clatter which that abominable rabble was making, the hurried tramp of horses. At once he jumped to the conclusion that these could be none other than a company of soldiers sent by M. le duc. This spurred him to a fresh effort and gave him a new idea. To Carmail the postilion who had a pistol in his holster he gave the peremptory order to fire a shot into the air or into the crowd, Jean-Marie cared not which. This Carmail did and at once the horses, already maddened by the crowd, plunged and reared wildly, shaking themselves free. Jean-Marie, however, had them well in hand, and from far away there came the cries of encouragement from the advancing horsemen who were bearing down on them full tilt. The next moment there was a general mêlée. Jean-Marie saw nothing save his horses' heads, but the outriders declared that men were trampled down like flies all around while others vanished into the night.

What happened after that none of the men knew or cared. Jean-Marie galloped his horses all the way to the castle and never drew rein until the precincts were reached.

6

Had M. de Kernogan had his way and a free hand to mete out retributive justice in the proportion that he desired, there is no doubt that the hangman of Nantes would have been kept exceedingly busy. As it was a number of arrests were effected the following day – half the manhood of the countryside was implicated in the aborted *jacquerie* and the city prison was not large enough to hold it all.

A court of justice presided over by M. le duc and composed of half a dozen men who were directly or indirectly in his employ pronounced summary sentences on the rioters which were to have been carried out as soon as the necessary arrangements for such wholesale executions could be made.

Nantes was turned into a city of wailing; peasant-women – mothers, sisters, daughters, wives of the condemned, trooped from their villages into the city, loudly calling on M. le duc for mercy, besieging the improvised court-house, the prison gates, the town residence of M. le duc, the palace of the bishop: they pushed their way into the courtyards and the very corridors of those buildings – flunkeys could not cope with them – they fought with fists and elbows for the right to make a direct appeal to the liege-lord who had power of life and death over their men.

The municipality of Nantes held aloof from this distressful state of things and the town councillors, the city functionaries and their families shut themselves up in their houses in order to avoid being a witness to the heartrending scenes which took place uninterruptedly round the court-house and the prison. The mayor himself was powerless to interfere, but it is averred that he sent a secret courier to Paris to M. de Mirabeau, who was known to be a personal friend of his, with a detailed account of the *jacquerie* and of the terrible measures of reprisal contemplated by M. le duc de Kernogan, together with an earnest request that pressure from the highest possible quarters be brought to bear upon His Grace so that he should abate something of his vengeful rigours.

Poor King Louis, who in these days was being terrorized by the National Assembly and swept off his feet by the eloquence of M. de Mirabeau, was only too ready to make concessions to the democratic spirit of the day. He also desired his noblesse to be equally ready with such concessions. He sent a personal letter to M. le duc, not only asking him but commanding him to show grace and mercy to a lot of misguided peasant lads whose loyalty and adherence – he urged – might be won by a gracious and unexpected act of clemency.

The King's commands could not in the nature of things be disobeyed: the same stroke of the pen which was about to send half a hundred young countrymen to the gallows granted them

M. le duc's gracious pardon and their liberty: the only exception to this general amnesty being Pierre Adet, the son of the miller. M. le duc's servants had deposed to seeing him pull open the door of the coach and stand for some time half in and half out of the carriage, obviously trying to terrorize Mademoiselle. Mademoiselle refused either to corroborate or to deny this statement, but she had arrived fainting at the gate of the château, and she had been very ill ever since. She had sustained a serious shock to her nerves, so the doctor hastily summoned from Paris had averred, and it was supposed that she had lost all recollection of the terrible incidents of that night.

But M. le duc was satisfied that it was Pierre Adet's presence inside the coach which had brought about his daughter's mysterious illness and that heartrending look of nameless horror which had dwelt in her eyes ever since. Therefore with regard to that man M. le duc remained implacable and as a concession to a father's outraged feelings both the mayor of Nantes and the city functionaries accepted Adet's condemnation without a murmur of dissent.

The sentence of death finally passed upon Pierre, the son of Jean Adet, miller of Vertou, could not, however, be executed, for the simple reason that Pierre had disappeared and that the most rigorous search instituted in the neighbourhood and for miles around failed to bring him to justice. One of the outriders who had been in attendance on Mademoiselle on that fateful night declared that when Jean-Marie finally whipped up his horses at the approach of the party of soldiers, Adet fell backwards from the step of the carriage and was run over by the hind wheels and instantly killed. But his body was never found among the score or so which were left lying there in the mud of the road until the women and old men came to seek their loved ones among the dead.

Pierre Adet had disappeared. But M. le duc's vengeance had need of a prey. The outrage which he was quite convinced had been perpetrated against his daughter must be punished by death – if not by the death of the chief offender, then by that of the one who stood nearest to him. Thus was Jean Adet the miller dragged from his home and cast into prison. Was he not implicated himself in the riots? Camille the bailiff had seen and heard him among the insurgents on the hillock that night. At first it was stated that he would be held as hostage for the reappearance of his son. But Pierre Adet had evidently fled the countryside: he was obviously ignorant of the terrible fate which his own folly had brought upon his father. Many thought that he had gone to seek his fortune in Paris where his talents and erudition would ensure him a good place in the present mad rush for equality amongst all men. Certain it is that he did not return and that with merciless hate and vengeful relentlessness M. le duc de Kernogan had Jean Adet hanged for a supposed crime said to be committed by his son.

Jean Adet died protesting his innocence. But the outburst of indignation and revolt aroused by this crying injustice was swamped by the torrent of the revolution which, gathering force by these very acts of tyranny and of injustice, soon swept innocent and guilty alike into a vast whirlpool of blood and shame and tears.

BOOK ONE
Bath, 1793

Bath to Weston road. It had been quite a good secondary road once. The accounts of the county administration under date 1725 go to prove that it was completed in that year at considerable expense and with stone brought over for the purpose all the way from Draycott quarries, and for twenty years after that a coach used to ply along it between Chelwood and Redhill as well as two or three carriers, and of course there was all the traffic in connection with the Stanton markets and the Norton Fairs. But that was nigh on fifty years ago now, and somehow – once the mail-coach was discontinued – it had never seemed worthwhile to keep the road in decent repair. It had gone from bad to worse since then, and travelling on it these days either ahorse or afoot had become very unpleasant. It was full of ruts and crevasses and knee-deep in mud, as the stranger had very appositely remarked, and the stone parapet which bordered it on either side, and which had once given it such an air of solidity and of value, was broken down in very many places and threatened soon to disappear altogether.

The country round was as lonely and desolate as the road. And that sense of desolation seemed to pervade the very atmosphere right through the darkness which had descended on upland and valley and hill. Though nothing now could be seen through the gloom and the mist, the senses were conscious that even in broad daylight there would be nothing to see. Loneliness dwelt in the air as well as upon the moor. There were no homesteads for miles around, no cattle grazing, no pastures, no hedges, nothing – just and, waste land with here and there a group of stunted trees or an isolated yew, and tracts of rough, coarse grass not nearly good enough for cattle to eat.

There are vast stretches of upland equally desolate in many parts of Europe – notably in Northern Spain – but in England, where they are rare, they seem to gain an additional air of loneliness through the very life which dulsates in their vicinity. This bit of Somersetshire was one of them in this year of grace 1793. Despite the proximity of Bath and its fashionable life, its gaieties and vitality, distant only a little over twenty miles, and of Bristol distant less than thirty, it had remained wild and forlorn, almost savage in its grim isolation, primitive in the grandeur of its solitude.

3

The road at the point now reached by the travellers begins to slope in a gentle gradient down to the level of the Chew, a couple of miles further on: it was midway down this slope that the only sign of living humanity could be perceived in that tiny light which glimmered persistently. The air itself under its mantle of fog had become very still, only the water of some tiny moorland stream murmured feebly in its stony bed ere it lost its entity in the bosom of the river far away.

'Five more minutes and we be at th' Bottom Inn,' quoth the man who was ahead, in response to another impatient ejaculation from his companion.

'If we don't break our necks meanwhile in this confounded darkness,' retorted the other, for his horse had just stumbled and the inexperienced rider had been very nearly pitched over into the mud.

'I be as anxious to arrive as you are, Mounzeer,' observed the countryman laconically.

'I thought you knew the way,' muttered the stranger.

''Ave I not brought you safely through the darkness?' retorted the other; 'you was pretty well ztranded at Chelwood, Mounzeer, or I be much mistaken. Who else would 'ave brought you out 'ere at this time o' night, I'd like to know – and in this weather too? You wanted to get to th' Bottom Inn and didn't know 'ow to zet about it: none o' the gaffers up to Chelwood 'peared eager to 'elp you when I come along. Well, I've brought you to th' Bottom Inn and... Whoa! Whoa! my beauty! Whoa, confound you! Whoa!'

And for the next moment or two the whole of his attention had perforce to be concentrated on the business of sticking to his saddle whilst he brought his fagged-out, ill-conditioned nag to a standstill.

The little glimmer of light had suddenly revealed itself in the shape of a lanthorn hung inside the wooden porch of a small house which had loomed out of the darkness and the fog. It stood at an angle of the road where a narrow lane had its beginnings ere it plunged into the moor beyond and was swallowed up by the all-enveloping gloom. The house was small and ugly; square like a box and built of grey stone, its front flush with the road, its rear flanked by several small outbuildings. Above the porch hung a plain sign-board bearing the legend: 'The Bottom Inn' in white letters upon a black ground: to right and left of the porch there was a window with closed shutters, and on the floor above two more windows – also shuttered – completed the architectural features of the Bottom Inn.

It was uncompromisingly ugly and uninviting, for beyond the faint glimmer of the lanthorn only one or two narrow streaks of light filtrated through the chinks of the shutters.

4

The travellers, after some difference of opinion with their respective horses, contrived to pull up and to dismount without any untoward accident. The stranger looked about him, peering into the darkness. The place indeed appeared dismal and inhospitable enough: its solitary aspect suggested footpads and the abode of cut-throats. The silence of the moor, the pall of mist and gloom that hung over upland and valley sent a shiver through his spine.

'You are sure this is the place?' he queried.

'Can't ye zee the zign?' retorted the other gruffly.

'Can you hold the horses while I go in?'

'I doan't know as 'ow I can, Mounzeer. I've never 'eld two 'orzes all at once. Suppose they was to start kickin' or thought o' runnin' away.'

'Running away, you fool!' muttered the stranger, whose temper had evidently suffered grievously during the weary, cold journey from Chelwood. 'I'll break your *satané* head if anything happens to the beasts. How can I get back to Bath save the way I came? Do you think I want to spend the night in this God-forsaken hole?'

Without waiting to hear any further protests from the lout, he turned into the porch and with his riding whip gave three consecutive raps against the door of the inn, followed by two more. The next moment there was the sound of a rattling of bolts and chains, the door was cautiously opened and a timid voice queried: 'Is it Mounzeer?'

'Pardieu! Who else?' growled the stranger. 'Open the door, woman. I am perished with cold.'

With an unceremonious kick he pushed the door further open and strode in. A woman was standing in the dimly lighted passage. As the stranger walked in she bobbed him a respectful curtsey.

'It is all right, Mounzeer,' she said; 'the Captain's in the coffee-room. He came over from Bristol early this afternoon.'

'No one else here, I hope,' he queried curtly.

'No one, zir. It ain't their hour not yet. You'll 'ave the 'ouse to yourself till after midnight. After that there'll be a bustle, I reckon. Two shiploads come into Watchet last night – brandy and cloth, Mounzeer, so the Captain says, and worth a mint o' money. The pack 'orzes will be through yere in the small hours.'

'That's all right, then. Send me in a bite and a mug of hot ale.'

'I'll see to it, Mounzeer.'

'And stay – have you some sort of stabling where the man can put the two horses up for an hour's rest?'

'Aye, aye, zir.'

'Very well then, see to that too: and see that the horses get a feed and a drink and give the man something to eat.'

'Very good, Mounzeer. This way, zir. I'll see the man presently. Straight down the passage, zir. The coffee-room is on the right. The Captain's there, waiting for ye.'

She closed the front door carefully, then followed the stranger to the door of the coffee-room. Outside an anxious voice was heard muttering a string of inconsequent and wholly superfluous 'Whoa's!' Of a truth the two wearied nags were only too anxious for a little rest.

2

The Bottom Inn

A man was sitting, huddled up in the ingle-nook of the small coffee-room, sipping hot ale from a tankard which he had in his hand.

Anything less suggestive of a rough sea-faring life than his appearance it would be difficult to conceive; and how he came by the appellation 'the Captain' must for ever remain a mystery. He was small and spare, with thin delicate face and slender hands: though dressed in very rough garments, he was obviously ill at ease in them; his narrow shoulders scarcely appeared able to bear the weight of the coarsely made coat and his thin legs did not begin to fill the big fisherman's boots which reached midway up his lean thighs. His hair was lank and plentifully sprinkled with grey: he wore it tied at the nape of the neck with a silk bow which certainly did not harmonize with the rest of his clothing. A wide-brimmed felt hat something the shape of a sailor's, but with higher crown – of the shape worn by the peasantry in Brittany – lay on the bench beside him.

When the stranger entered he had greeted him curtly, speaking in French.

The room was inexpressibly stuffy, and reeked of the fumes of stale tobacco, stale victuals and stale beer; but it was warm, and the stranger, stiff to the marrow and wet to the skin, uttered an exclamation of well-being as he turned to the hearth, wherein a bright fire burned cheerily. He had put his hat down when first he entered and had divested himself of his big coat: now he held one foot and then the other to the blaze and tried to infuse new life into his numbed hands.

'The Captain' took scant notice of his comings and goings. He did not attempt to help him off with his coat, nor did he make an effort to add another log to the fire. He sat silent and practically motionless, save when from time to time he took a sip out of his mug of ale. But whenever the new-comer came within his immediate circle of vision he shot a glance at the latter's elegant attire – the well-cut coat, the striped waistcoat, the boots of fine leather – the glance was quick and comprehensive and full of scorn, a flash that lasted only an instant and was at once veiled again by the droop of the flaccid lids which hid the pale, keen eyes.

'When the woman has brought me something to eat and drink,' the stranger said after a while, 'we can talk. I have a good hour to spare, as those miserable nags must have some rest.'

He too spoke in French and with an air of authority, not to say arrogance, which caused 'the Captain's' glance of scorn to light up with an added gleam of hate and almost of cruelty. But he made no remark and continued to sip his ale in silence, and for the next half-hour the two men took no more notice of one another, just as if they had never travelled all those miles and come to this desolate spot for the sole purpose of speaking with one another. During the course of that half-hour the woman brought in a dish of mutton stew, a chunk of bread, a piece of cheese and a jug of spiced ale, and placed them on the table: all of these good things the stranger consumed with an obviously keen appetite. When he had eaten and drunk his fill, he rose from the table, drew a bench into the ingle-nook and sat down so that his profile only was visible to his friend 'the Captain.'

'Now, citizen Chauvelin,' he said with an attempt at ease and familiarity not unmixed with condescension, 'I am ready for your news.'

2

Chauvelin had winced perceptibly both at the condescension and the familiarity. It was such a very little while ago that men had trembled at a look, a word from him: his silence had been wont to strike terror in quaking hearts. It was such a very little while ago that he had been president of the Committee of Public Safety, all-powerful, the right hand of citizen Robespierre, the master sleuth-hound who could track an unfortunate 'suspect' down to his most hidden lair, before whose keen, pale eyes the innermost secrets of a soul stood revealed, who guessed at treason ere it was wholly born, who scented treachery ere it was formulated. A year ago he had with a word sent scores of men, women and children to the guillotine – he had with a sign brought the whole machinery of the ruthless Committee to work against innocent or guilty alike on mere suspicion, or to gratify his own hatred against all those whom he considered to be the enemies of that bloody revolution which he had helped to make. Now his presence, his silence, had not even the power to ruffle the self-assurance of an upstart.

But in the hard school both of success and of failure through which he had passed during the last decade, there was one lesson which Armand once Marquis de Chauvelin had learned to the last letter, and that was the lesson of self-control. He had winced at the other's familiarity, but neither by word nor gesture did he betray what he felt.

'I can tell you,' he merely said quite curtly, 'all I have to say in far less time than it has taken you to eat and drink, citizen Adet...'

But suddenly, at sound of that name, the other had put a warning hand on Chauvelin's arm, even as he cast a rapid, anxious look all round the narrow room.

'Hush, man!' he murmured hurriedly, 'you know quite well that that name must never be pronounced here in England. I am Martin-Roget now,' he added, as he shook off his momentary fright with equal suddenness, and once more resumed his tone of easy condescension, 'and try not to forget it.'

Chauvelin without any haste quietly freed his arm from the other's grasp. His pale face was quite expressionless, only the thin lips were drawn tightly over the teeth now, and a curious hissing sound escaped faintly from them as he said: 'I'll try and remember, citizen, that here in England you are an aristo, the same as all these confounded English whom may the devil sweep into a bottomless sea.'

Martin-Roget gave a short, complacent laugh.

'Ah,' he said lightly, 'no wonder you hate them, citizen Chauvelin. You too were an aristo here in England once – not so very long ago, I am thinking – special envoy to His Majesty King George, what? – until failure to bring one of these *satané* Britishers to book made you...er...well, made you what you are now.'

He drew up his tall, broad figure as he spoke and squared his massive shoulders as he looked down with a fatuous smile and no small measure of scorn on the hunched-up little figure beside him. It had seemed to him that something in the nature of a threat had crept into Chauvelin's attitude, and he, still flushed with his own importance, his immeasurable belief in himself, at once chose to measure his strength against this man who was the personification of failure and disgrace – this man whom so many people had feared for so long and whom it might not be wise to defy even now.

'No offence meant, citizen Chauvelin,' he added with an air of patronage which once more made the other wince. 'I had no wish to wound your susceptibilities. I only desired to give you timely warning that what I do here is no one's concern, and that I will brook interference and criticism from no man.'

And Chauvelin, who in the past had oft with a nod sent a man to the guillotine, made no reply to this arrogant taunt. His small figure seemed to shrink still further within itself: and anon he passed his thin, claw-like hand over his face as if to obliterate from its surface any expression which might war with the utter humility wherewith he now spoke.

'Nor was there any offence meant on my part, citizen Martin-Roget,' he said suavely. 'Do we not both labour for the same end? The glory of the Republic and the destruction of her foes?'

Martin-Roget gave a sigh of satisfaction. The battle had been won: he felt himself strong again – stronger than before through that very act of deference paid to him by the once all-powerful Chauvelin. Now he was quite prepared to be condescending and jovial once again: 'Of course, of course,' he said pleasantly, as he once more bent his tall figure to the fire. 'We are both servants of the Republic, and I may yet help you to retrieve your past failures, citizen, by giving you an active part in the work I have in hand. And now,' he added in a calm, business-like manner, the manner of a master addressing a servant who has been found at fault and is taken into favour again, 'let me hear your news.'

'I have made all the arrangements about the ship,' said Chauvelin quietly.

'Ah! that is good news indeed. What is she?'

'She is a Dutch ship. Her master and crew are all Dutch...'

'That's a pity. A Danish master and crew would have been safer.'

'I could not come across any Danish ship willing to take the risks,' said Chauvelin dryly.

'Well! And what about this Dutch ship then?'

'She is called the *Hollandia* and is habitually engaged in the sugar trade: but her master does a lot of contraband – more that than fair trading, I imagine: anyway, he is willing for the sum you originally named to take every risk and incidentally to hold his tongue about the whole business.'

'For two thousand francs?'

'Yes.'

'And he will run the *Hollandia* into Le Croisic?'

'When you command.'

'And there is suitable accommodation on board her for a lady and her woman?'

'I don't know what you call suitable,' said Chauvelin with a sarcastic tone, which the other failed or was unwilling to note, 'and I don't know what you call a lady. The accommodation available on board the *Hollandia* will be sufficient for two men and two women.'

'And her master's name?' queried Martin-Roget.

'Some outlandish Dutch name,' replied Chauvelin. 'It is spelt K U Y P E R. The devil only knows how it is pronounced.'

'Well! And does Captain K U Y P E R understand exactly what I want?'

'He says he does. The *Hollandia* will put into Portishead on the last day of this month. You and your guests can get aboard her any day after that you choose. She will be there at your disposal, and can start within an hour of your getting aboard. Her master will have all his papers ready. He will have a cargo of West Indian sugar on board – destination Amsterdam, consignee Mynheer van Smeer – everything perfectly straight and square. French aristos, *émigrés* on board on their way to join the army of the Princes. There will be no difficulty in England.'

'And none in Le Croisic. The man is running no risks.'

'He thinks he is. France does not make Dutch ships and Dutch crews exactly welcome just now, does she?'

'Certainly not. But in Le Croisic and with citizen Adet on board…'

'I thought that name was not to be mentioned here,' retorted Chauvelin dryly.

'You are right, citizen,' whispered the other, 'it escaped me and…'

Already he had jumped to his feet: his face suddenly pale, his whole manner changed from easy, arrogant self-assurance to uncertainty and obvious dread. He moved to the window, trying to subdue the sound of his footsteps upon the uneven floor.

3

'Are you afraid of eavesdroppers, citizen Martin-Roget?' queried Chauvelin with a shrug of his narrow shoulders.

'No. There is no one there. Only a lout from Chelwood who brought me here. The people of the house are safe enough. They have plenty of secrets of their own to keep.'

He was obviously saying all this in order to reassure himself, for there was no doubt that his fears were on the alert. With a febrile gesture he unfastened the shutters, and pushed them open, peering out into the night.

'Hallo!' he called.

But he received no answer.

'It has started to rain,' he said more calmly. 'I imagine that lout has found shelter in an outhouse with the horses.'

'Very likely,' commented Chauvelin laconically. 'Then if you have nothing more to tell me,' quoth Martin-Roget, 'I may as well think about getting back. Rain or no rain, I want to be in Bath before midnight.'

'Ball or supper-party at one of your duchesses?' queried the other with a sneer. 'I know them.'

To this Martin-Roget vouchsafed no reply.

'How are things at Nantes?' he asked.

'Splendid! Carrier is like a wild beast let loose. The prisons are over-full: the surplus of accused, condemned and suspect fills the cellars and warehouses along the wharf. Priests and such like trash are kept on disused galliots up stream. The guillotine is never idle, and friend Carrier fearing that she might give out

– get tired, what? – or break down – has invented a wonderful way of getting rid of shoals of undesirable people at one magnificent swoop. You have heard tell of it no doubt.'

'Yes. I have heard of it,' remarked the other curtly.

'He began with a load of priests. Requisitioned an old barge. Ordered Baudet the shipbuilder to construct half a dozen portholes in her bottom. Baudet demurred: he could not understand what the order could possibly mean. But Foucaud and Lamberty – Carrier's agents – you know them – explained that the barge would be towed down the Loire and then up one of the smaller navigable streams which it was feared the royalists were preparing to use as a way for making a descent upon Nantes, and that the idea was to sink the barge in midstream in order to obstruct the passage of their army. Baudet, satisfied, put five of his men to the task. Everything was ready on the 16th of last month. I know the woman Pichot, who keeps a small tavern opposite La Sécherie. She saw the barge glide up the river toward the galliot where twenty-five priests of the diocese of Nantes had been living for the past two months in the company of rats and other vermin as noxious as themselves. Most lovely moon-light there was that night. The Loire looked like a living ribbon of silver. Foucaud and Lamberty directed operations, and Carrier had given them full instructions. They tied the calotins up two and two and transferred them from the galliot to the barge. It seems they were quite pleased to go. Had enough of the rats, I presume. The only thing they didn't like was being searched. Some had managed to secrete silver ornaments about their person when they were arrested. Crucifixes and such like. They didn't like to part with these, it seems. But Foucaud and Lamberty relieved them of everything but the necessary clothing, and they didn't want much of that seeing whither they were going. Foucaud made a good pile, so they say. Self-seeking, avaricious brute! He'll learn the way to one of Carrier's barges too one day, I'll bet.'

He rose and with quick footsteps moved to the table. There was some ale left in the jug which the woman had brought for Martin-Roget a while ago. Chauvelin poured the contents of it down his throat. He had talked uninterruptedly, in short, jerky sentences, without the slightest expression of horror at the atrocities which he recounted. His whole appearance had become transfigured while he spoke. Gone was the urbane manner which he had learnt at courts long ago, gone was the last instinct of the gentleman sunk to proletarianism through stress of circumstances, or financial straits or even political convictions. The erstwhile Marquis de Chauvelin – envoy of the Republic at the Court of St James' – had become citizen Chauvelin in deed and in fact, a part of that rabble which he had elected to serve, one of that vile crowd of bloodthirsty revolutionaries who had sullied the pure robes of Liberty and of Fraternity by spattering them with blood. Now he smacked his lips, wiped his mouth with his sleeve, and burying his hands in the pockets of his breeches he stood with legs wide apart and a look of savage satisfaction settled upon his pale face. Martin-Roget had made no comment upon the narrative. He had resumed his seat by the fire and was listening attentively. Now while the other drank and paused, he showed no sign of impatience, but there was something in the look of the bent shoulders, in the rigidity of the attitude, in the large, square hands tightly clasped together which suggested the deepest interest and an intentness that was almost painful.

'I was at the woman Pichot's tavern that night,' resumed Chauvelin after a while. 'I saw the barge – a moving coffin, what? – gliding down stream towed by the galliot and escorted by a small boat. The floating battery at La Samaritaine challenged her as she passed, for Carrier had prohibited all navigation up or down the Loire until further notice. Foucaud, Lamberty, Fouquet and O'Sullivan the armourer were in the boat: they rowed up to the pontoon and Vailly the chief gunner of the battery challenged them once more. However, they had some sort of written authorization from Carrier, for they were allowed to pass. Vailly remained on guard. He saw the barge glide further down stream. It seems that the moon at that time was hidden by a cloud. But the night was not dark and Vailly watched the barge till she was out of sight. She was towed past Trentemoult and Chantenay into the wide reach of the river just below Cheviré where, as you know, the Loire is nearly two thousand feet wide.'

Once more he paused, looking down with grim amusement on the bent shoulders of the other man.

'Well?'

Chauvelin laughed. The query sounded choked and hoarse, whether through horror, excitement or mere impatient curiosity it were impossible to say.

'Well!' he retorted with a careless shrug of the shoulders. 'I was too far up stream to see anything and Vailly saw nothing either. But he heard. So did others who happened to be on the shore close by.'

'What did they hear?'

'The hammering,' replied Chauvelin curtly, 'when the portholes were knocked open to let in the flood of water. And the screams and yells of five and twenty drowning priests.'

'Not one of them escaped, I suppose?'

'Not one.'

Once more Chauvelin laughed. He had a way of laughing – just like that – in a peculiar mirthless, derisive manner, as if with joy at another man's discomfiture, at another's material or moral downfall. There is only one language in the world which has a word to express that type of mirth; the word is *Schadenfreude*.

It was Chauvelin's turn to triumph now. He had distinctly perceived the signs of an inward shudder which had gone right through Martin-Roget's spine: he had also perceived through the man's bent shoulders, his silence, his rigidity that his soul was filled with horror at the story of that abominable crime which he – Chauvelin – had so blandly retailed and that he was afraid to show the horror which he felt. And the man who is afraid can never climb the ladder of success above the man who is fearless.

4

There was silence in the low-raftered room for awhile: silence only broken by the crackling and sizzling of damp logs in the hearth, and the tap-tapping of a loosely fastened shutter which sounded weird and ghoulish like the knocking of ghosts against the window-frame. Martin-Roget bending still closer to the fire knew that Chauvelin was watching him and that Chauvelin had triumphed, for – despite failure, despite humiliation and disgrace – that man's heart and will had never softened: he had remained as merciless, as fanatical, as before and still looked upon every sign of pity and humanity for a victim of that bloody revolution – which was his child, the thing of his creation, yet worshipped by him, its creator – as a crime against patriotism and against the Republic.

And Martin-Roget fought within himself lest something he might say or do, a look, a gesture should give the other man an indication that the horrible account of a hideous crime perpetrated against twenty-five defenceless men had roused a feeling of unspeakable horror in his heart. That was the punishment of these callous makers of a ruthless revolution – that was their hell upon earth, that they were doomed to hate and to fear one another; every man feeling that the other's hand was up against him as it had been against law and order, against the guilty and the innocent, the rebel and the defenceless; every man knowing that the other was always there on the alert ready to pounce like a beast of prey upon any victim – friend, comrade, brother – who came within reach of his hand.

Like many men stronger than himself, Pierre Adet – or Martin-Roget as he now called himself – had been drawn into the vortex of bloodshed and of tyranny out of which now he no longer had the power to extricate himself. Nor had he any wish to extricate himself. He had too many past wrongs to avenge, too much injustice on the part of Fate and Circumstance to make good, to wish to draw back now that a newly-found power had been placed in the hands of men such as he through the revolt of an entire people. The sickening sense of horror which a moment ago had caused him to shudder and to turn away in loathing from Chauvelin was only like the feeble flicker of a light before it wholly dies down – the light of something purer, early lessons of childhood, former ideals, earlier aspirations, now smothered beneath the passions of revenge and of hate.

And he would not give Chauvelin the satisfaction of seeing him wince. He was himself ashamed of his own weakness. He had deliberately thrown in his lot with these men and he was determined not to fall a victim to their denunciations and to their jealousies. So now he made a great effort to pull himself together, to bring back before his mind those memory-pictures of past tyranny and oppression which had effectually killed all sense of pity in his heart, and it was in a tone of perfect indifference which gave no loophole to Chauvelin's sneers that he asked after awhile:

'And was citizen Carrier altogether pleased with the result of his patriotic efforts?'

'Oh, quite!' replied the other. 'He has no one's orders to take. He is proconsul – virtual dictator in Nantes: and he has vowed that he will purge the city from all save its most deserving citizens. The cargo of priests was followed by one of malefactors, night-birds, cut-throats and such like. That is where Carrier's patriotism shines out in all its glory. It is not only priests and aristos, you see – other miscreants are treated with equal fairness.'

'Yes! I see he is quite impartial,' remarked Martin-Roget coolly.

'Quite,' retorted Chauvelin, as he once more sat down in the ingle-nook. And, leaning his elbows upon his knees he looked straight and deliberately into the other man's face, and added slowly: 'You will have no cause to complain of Carrier's want of patriotism when you hand over your bag of birds to him.'

This time Martin-Roget had obviously winced, and Chauvelin had the satisfaction of seeing that his thrust had gone home: though Martin-Roget's face was in shadow, there was something now in his whole attitude, in the clasping and unclasping of his large, square hands which indicated that the man was labouring under the stress of a violent emotion. In spite of this he managed to say quite coolly: 'What do you mean exactly by that, citizen Chauvelin?'

'Oh!' replied the other, 'you know well enough what I mean – I am no fool, what?...or the Revolution would have no use for me. If after my many failures she still commands my services and employs me to keep my eyes and ears open, it is because she knows that she can count on me. I do keep my eyes and ears open, citizen Adet or Martin-Roget, whatever you like to call yourself, and also my mind – and I have a way of putting two and two together to make four. There are few people in Nantes who do not know that old Jean Adet, the miller, was hanged four years ago, because his son Pierre had taken part in some kind of open revolt against the tyranny of the ci-devant duc de Kernogan, and was not there to take his punishment himself. I knew old Jean Adet... I was on the Place du Bouffay at Nantes when he was hanged...'

But already Martin-Roget had jumped to his feet with a muttered blasphemy.

'Have done, man,' he said roughly, 'have done!' And he started pacing up and down the narrow room like a caged panther, snarling and showing his teeth, whilst his rough, toil-worn hands quivered with the desire to clutch an unseen enemy by the throat and to squeeze the life out of him. 'Think you,' he added hoarsely, 'that I need reminding of that?'

'No. I do not think that, citizen,' replied Chauvelin calmly, 'I only desired to warn you.'

'Warn me? Of what?'

Nervous, agitated, restless, Martin-Roget had once more gone back to his seat: his hands were trembling as he held them up mechanically to the blaze and his face was the colour of lead. In contrast with his restlessness Chauvelin appeared the more calm and bland.

'Why should you wish to warn me?' asked the other querulously, but with an attempt at his former overbearing manner. 'What are my affairs to you – what do you know about them?'

'Oh, nothing, nothing, citizen Martin-Roget,' replied Chauvelin pleasantly, 'I was only indulging the fancy I spoke to you about just now of putting two and two together in order to make four. The chartering of a smuggler's craft – aristos on board her – her ostensible destination Holland – her real objective Le Croisic… Le Croisic is now the port for Nantes and we don't bring aristos into Nantes these days for the object of providing them with a feather-bed and a competence, what?'

'And,' retorted Martin-Roget quietly, 'if your surmises are correct, citizen Chauvelin, what then?'

'Oh, nothing!' replied the other indifferently. 'Only…take care, citizen…that is all.'

'Take care of what?'

'Of the man who brought me, Chauvelin, to ruin and disgrace.'

'Oh! I have heard of that legend before now,' said Martin-Roget with a contemptuous shrug of the shoulders. 'The man they call the Scarlet Pimpernel you mean?'

'Why, yes!'

'What have I to do with him?'

'I don't know. But remember that I myself have twice been after that man here in England; that twice he slipped through my fingers when I thought I held him so tightly that he could not possibly escape and that twice in consequence I was brought to humiliation and to shame. I am a marked man now – the guillotine will soon claim me for her future use. Your affairs, citizen, are no concern of mine, but I have marked that Scarlet Pimpernel for mine own. I won't have any blunderings on your part give him yet another triumph over us all.'

Once more Martin-Roget swore one of his favourite oaths.

'By Satan and all his brood, man,' he cried in a passion of fury, 'have done with this interference. Have done, I say. I have nothing to do, I tell you, with your *satané* Scarlet Pimpernel. My concern is with...'

'With the duc de Kernogan,' broke in Chauvelin calmly, 'and with his daughter; I know that well enough. You want to be even with them over the murder of your father. I know that too. All that is your affair. But beware, I tell you. To begin with, the secrecy of your identity is absolutely essential to the success of your plan. What?'

'Of course it is. But...'

'But nevertheless, your identity is known to the most astute, the keenest enemy of the Republic.'

'Impossible,' asserted Martin-Roget hotly.

'The duc de Kernogan...?'

'Bah! He had never the slightest suspicion of me. Think you his High and Mightiness in those far-off days ever looked twice at a village lad so that he would know him again four years later? I came into this country as an *émigré* stowed away in a smuggler's ship like a bundle of contraband goods. I have papers to prove that my name is Martin-Roget and that I am a banker from Brest. The worthy Bishop of Brest – denounced to the Committee of Public Safety for treason against the Republic – was given his life and a safe conduct into Spain on the condition that he gave me – Martin-Roget – letters of personal introduction to various high-born *émigrés* in Holland, in Germany and in England. Armed with these I am invulnerable. I have been presented to His Royal Highness the Regent, and to the élite of English society in Bath. I am the friend of M. le duc de Kernogan now and the accredited suitor for his daughter's hand.'

'His daughter!' broke in Chauvelin with a sneer, and his pale, keen eyes had in them a spark of malicious mockery.

Martin-Roget made no immediate retort to the sneer. A curious hot flush had spread over his forehead and his ears, leaving his cheeks wan and livid.

'What about the daughter?' reiterated Chauvelin.

'Yvonne de Kernogan has never seen Pierre Adet the miller's son,' replied the other curtly. 'She is now the affianced wife of Martin-Roget the millionaire banker of Brest. Tonight I shall persuade M. le duc to allow my marriage with his daughter to take place within the week. I shall plead pressing business in Holland and my desire that my wife shall accompany me thither. The duke will consent and Yvonne de Kernogan will not be consulted. The day after my wedding I shall be on board the *Hollandia* with my wife and father-in-law, and together we will be on our way to Nantes where Carrier will deal with them both.'

'You are quite satisfied that this plan of yours is known to no one, that no one at the present moment is aware of the fact that Pierre Adet, the miller's son, and Martin-Roget, banker of Brest, are one and the same?'

'Quite satisfied,' replied Martin-Roget emphatically. 'Very well, then, let me tell you this, citizen,' rejoined Chauvelin slowly and deliberately, 'that in spite of what you say I am as convinced as that I am here, alive, that your real identity will be known – if it is not known already – to a gentleman who is at this present moment in Bath, and who is known to you, to me, to the whole of France as the Scarlet Pimpernel.'

Martin-Roget laughed and shrugged his shoulders.

'Impossible!' he retorted. 'Pierre Adet no longer exists... he never existed...much... Anyhow, he ceased to be on that stormy day in September, 1789. Unless your pet enemy is a wizard he cannot know.'

'There is nothing that my pet enemy – as you call him – cannot ferret out if he has a mind to. Beware of him, citizen Martin-Roget. Beware, I tell you.'

'How can I,' laughed the other contemptuously, 'if I don't know who he is?'

'If you did,' retorted Chauvelin, 'it wouldn't help you...much. But beware of every man you don't know; beware of every stranger you meet; trust no one; above all, follow no one. He is there where you least expect him under a disguise you would scarcely dream of.'

'Tell me who he is then – since you know him – so that I may duly beware of him.'

'No,' rejoined Chauvein with the same slow deliberation, 'I will not tell you who he is. Knowledge in this case would be a very dangerous thing.'

'Dangerous? To whom?'

'To yourself probably. To me and to the Republic most undoubtedly. No! I will not tell you who the Scarlet Pimpernel is. But take my advice, citizen Martin-Roget,' he added emphatically, 'go back to Paris or to Nantes and strive there to serve your country rather than run your head into a noose by meddling with things here in England, and running after your own schemes of revenge.'

'My own schemes of revenge!' exclaimed Martin-Roget with a hoarse cry that was like a snarl... It seemed as if he wanted to say something more, but that the words choked him even before they reached his lips. The hot flush died down from his forehead and his face was once more the colour of lead. He took up a log from the corner of the hearth and threw it with a savage, defiant gesture into the fire.

Somewhere in the house a clock struck nine.

5

Martin-Roget waited until the last echo of the gong had died away, then he said very slowly and very quietly:

'Forego my own schemes of revenge? Can you even remotely guess, citizen Chauvelin, what it would mean to a man of my temperament and of my calibre to give up that for which I have toiled and striven for the past four years? Think of what I was on that day when a conglomeration of adverse circumstances turned our proposed expedition against the château de Kernogan into a disaster for our village lads, and a triumph for the duc. I was knocked down and crushed all but to death by the wheels of Mlle. de Kernogan's coach. I managed to crawl in the mud and the cold and the rain, on my hands and knees, hurt, bleeding, half dead, as far as the presbytery of Vertou where the *curé* kept me hidden at risk of his own life for two days until I was able to crawl farther away out of sight. The *curé* did not know, I did not know then of the devilish revenge which the duc de Kernogan meant to wreak against my father. The news reached me when it was all over and I had worked my way to Paris with the few sous in my pocket which that good *curé* had given me, earning bed and bread as I went along. I was an ignorant lout when I arrived in Paris. I had been one of the ci-devant Kernogan's labourers – his chattel, what? – little better or somewhat worse off than a slave. There I heard that my father had been foully murdered – hung for a crime which I was supposed to have committed, for which I had not even been tried. Then the change in me began. For four years I starved in a garret, toiling like a galley-slave with my hands and muscles by day and at my books by night. And what am I now? I have worked at books, at philosophy, at science: I am a man of education. I can talk and discuss with the best of those d–d aristos who flaunt their caprices and their mincing manners in the face of the outraged democracy of two continents. I speak English – almost like a native – and Danish and German too. I can quote English poets and criticize M. de Voltaire. I am an aristo, what? For this I have worked, citizen Chauvelin – day and night – oh! those nights! how I have slaved to make myself what I now am! And all for the one object – the sole object without which existence would have been absolutely unendurable. That object guided me, helped me to bear and to toil, it cheered and comforted me! To be even one day with the duc de Kernogan and with his daughter! to be their master! to hold them at my mercy!...to destroy or pardon as I choose!...to be the arbiter of their fate!... I have worked for four years: now my goal is in sight, and you talk glibly of foregoing my own schemes of revenge! Believe me, citizen Chauvelin,' he concluded, 'it would be easier for me to hold my right hand into those flames until it hath burned to a cinder than to forego the hope of that vengeance which has eaten into my soul. It would hurt much less.'

He had spoken thus at great length, but with extraordinary restraint. Never once did he raise his voice or indulge in gesture. He spoke in even, monotonous tones, like one who is reciting a lesson; and he sat straight in front of the fire, his elbow on his knee, his chin resting in his hand and his eyes fixed upon the flames.

Chauvelin had listened in perfect silence. The scorn, the resentful anger, the ill-concealed envy of the fallen man for the successful upstart had died out of his glance. Martin-Roget's story, the intensity of feeling betrayed in that absolute, outward calm had caused a chord of sympathy to vibrate in the other's atrophied heart. How well he understood that vibrant passion of hate, that longing to exact an eye for an eye, an outrage for an outrage! Was not his own life given over now to just such a longing? – a mad aching desire to be even once with that hated enemy, that maddening, mocking, elusive Scarlet Pimpernel who had fooled and baffled him so often?

6

Some few moments had gone by since Martin-Roget's harsh, monotonous voice had ceased to echo through the low-raftered room: silence had fallen between the two men – there was indeed nothing more to say; the one had unburthened his overfull heart and the other had understood. They were of a truth made to understand one another, and the silence between them betokened sympathy.

Around them all was still, the stillness of a mist-laden night; in the house no one stirred: the shutter even had ceased to creak; only the crackling of the wood fire broke that silence which soon became oppressive.

Martin-Roget was the first to rouse himself from this trance-like state wherein memory was holding such ruthless sway: he brought his hands sharply down on his knees, turned to look for a moment on his companion, gave a short laugh and finally rose, saying briskly the while: 'And now, citizen, I shall have to bid you adieu and make my way back to Bath. The nags have had the rest they needed and I cannot spend the night here.'

He went to the door and opening it called a loud 'Hallo, there!'

The same woman who had waited on him on his arrival came slowly down the stairs in response.

'The man with the horses,' commanded Martin-Roget peremptorily. 'Tell him I'll be ready in two minutes.'

He returned to the room and proceeded to struggle into his heavy coat, Chauvelin as before making no attempt to help him. He sat once more huddled up in the ingle-nook hugging his elbows with his thin white hands. There was a smile half scornful, but not wholly dissatisfied around his bloodless lips. When Martin-Roget was ready to go he called out quietly after him: 'The *Hollandia* remember! At Portishead on the last day of the month. Captain K U Y P E R.'

'Quite right,' replied Martin-Roget laconically. 'I'm not like to forget.'

He then picked up his hat and riding whip and went out.

7

Outside in the porch he found the woman bending over the recumbent figure of his guide.

'He be azleep, Mounzeer,' she said placidly, 'fast azleep, I do believe.'

'Asleep?' cried Martin-Roget roughly, 'we'll soon see about waking him up.'

He gave the man a violent kick with the toe of his boot. The man groaned, stretched himself, turned over and rubbed his eyes. The light of the swinging lanthorn showed him the wrathful face of his employer. He struggled to his feet very quickly after that.

'Stir yourself, man,' cried Martin-Roget savagely, as he gripped the fellow by the shoulder and gave him a vigorous shaking. 'Bring the horses along now, and don't keep me waiting, or there'll be trouble.'

'All right, Mounzeer, all right,' muttered the man placidly, as he shook himself free from the uncomfortable clutch on his shoulder and leisurely made his way out of the porch.

'Haven't you got a boy or a man who can give that lout a hand with those *sacré* horses?' queried Martin-Roget impatiently. 'He hardly knows a horse's head from its tail.'

'No, zir, I've no one tonight,' replied the woman gently. 'My man and my son they be gone down to Watchet to 'elp with the cargo and the pack-'orzes. They won't be 'ere neither till after midnight. But,' she added more cheerfully, 'I can straighten a saddle if you want it.'

'That's all right then – but...'

He paused suddenly, for a loud cry of 'Hallo! Well! I'm...' rang through the night from the direction of the rear of the house. The cry expressed both surprise and dismay.

'What the – is it?' called Martin-Roget loudly in response.

'The 'orzes!'

'What about them?'

To this there was no reply, and with a savage oath and calling to the woman to show him the way Martin-Roget ran out in the direction whence had come the cry of dismay. He fell straight into the arms of his guide, who promptly set up another cry, more dismal, more expressive of bewilderment than the first.

'They be gone,' he shouted excitedly.

'Who have gone?' queried the Frenchman.

'The 'orzes!'

'The horses? What in – do you mean?'

The 'orzes have gone, Mounzeer. There was no door to the ztables and they be gone.'

'You're a fool,' growled Martin-Roget, who of a truth had not taken in as yet the full significance of the man's jerky sentences. 'Horses don't walk out of the stables like that. They can't have done if you tied them up properly.'

'I didn't tie them up,' protested the man. 'I didn't know 'ow to tie the beastly nags up, and there was no one to 'elp me. I didn't think they'd walk out like that.'

'Well! if they're gone you'll have to go and get them back somehow, that's all,' said Martin-Roget, whose temper by now was beyond his control, and who was quite ready to give the lout a furious thrashing.

'Get them back, Mounzeer,' wailed the man, "ow can I? In the dark, too. Besides, if I did come nose to nose wi' 'em I shouldn't know 'ow to get 'em. Would you, Mounzeer?' he added with bland impertinence.

'I shall know how to lay you out, you *satané* idiot,' growled Martin-Roget, 'if I have to spend the night in this hole.'

He strode on in the darkness in the direction where a little glimmer of light showed the entrance to a wide barn which obviously was used as a rough stabling. He stumbled through a yard and over a miscellaneous lot of rubbish. It was hardly possible to see one's hand before one's eyes in the darkness and the fog. The woman followed him, offering consolation in the shape of a seat in the coffee-room whereon to pass the night, for indeed she had no bed to spare, and the man from Chelwood brought up the rear – still ejaculating cries of astonishment rather than distress.

'You are that careless, man!' the woman admonished him placidly, 'and I give you a lanthorn and all for to look after your 'orzes properly.'

'But you didn't give me a 'and for to tie 'em up in their stalls, and give 'em their feed. Drat 'em! I 'ate 'orzes and all to do with 'em.'

'Didn't you give 'em the feed I give you for 'em then?'

'No, I didn't. Think you I'd go into one o' them narrow stalls and get kicked for my pains.'

'Then they was 'ungry, pore things,' she concluded, 'and went out after the 'ay what's just outside. I don't know 'ow you'll ever get 'em back in this fog.'

There was indeed no doubt that the nags had made their way out of the stables, in that irresponsible fashion peculiar to animals, and that they had gone astray in the dark. There certainly was no sound in the night to denote their presence anywhere near.

'We'll get 'em all right in the morning,' remarked the woman with her exasperating placidity.

'Tomorrow morning!' exclaimed Martin-Roget in a passion of fury. 'And what the d–l am I going to do in the meanwhile?'

The woman reiterated her offer of a seat by the fire in the coffee-room.

'The men won't mind ye, zir,' she said, 'heaps of 'em are Frenchies like yourself, and I'll tell 'em you ain't a spying on 'em.'

'It's no more than five mile to Chelwood,' said the man blandly, 'and maybe you get a better shakedown there.'

'A five-mile tramp,' growled Martin-Roget, whose wrath seemed to have spent itself before the hopelessness of his situation, 'in this fog and gloom, and knee-deep in mud... There'll be a sovereign for you, woman,' he added curtly, 'if you can give me a clean bed for the night.'

The woman hesitated for a second or two.

'Well! a zovereign is tempting, zir,' she said at last. 'You shall 'ave my son's bed. I know 'e'd rather 'ave the zovereign if 'e was ever zo tired. This way, zir,' she added, as she once more turned toward the house, 'mind them 'urdles there.'

'And where am I goin' to zleep?' called the man from Chelwood after the two retreating figures.

'I'll look after the man for you, zir,' said the woman; 'for a matter of a shillin' 'e can sleep in the coffee-room, and I'll give 'im 'is breakfast too.'

'Not one farthing will I pay for the idiot,' retorted Martin-Roget savagely. 'Let him look after himself.'

He had once more reached the porch. Without another word, and not heeding the protests and curses of the unfortunate man whom he had left standing shelterless in the middle of the yard, he pushed open the front door of the house and once more found himself in the passage outside the coffee-room.

But the woman had turned back a little before she followed her guest into the house, and she called out to the man the darkness: 'You may zleep in any of them outhouses and welcome, and zure there'll be a bit o' porridge for ye in the mornin'!'

'Think ye I'll stop,' came in a furious growl out of the gloom, 'and conduct that d–d frogeater back to Chelwood? No fear. Five miles ain't nothin' to me, and 'e can keep the miserable shillin' 'e'd 'ave give me for my pains. Let 'im get 'is 'orzes back 'izelf and get to Chelwood as best 'e can. I'm off, and you can tell 'im zo from me. It'll make 'im sleep all the better, I reckon.'

The woman was obviously not of a disposition that would ever argue a matter of this sort out. She had done her best, she reckoned, both for master and man, and if they chose to quarrel between themselves that was their business and not hers.

So she quietly went into the house again; barred and bolted the door, and finding the stranger still waiting for her in the passage she conducted him to a tiny room on the floor above.

'My son's room, Mounzeer,' she said; 'I 'ope as 'ow ye'll be comfortable.'

'It will do all right,' assented Martin-Roget. 'Is "the Captain" sleeping in the house tonight?' he added as with an afterthought.

'Only in the coffee-room, Mounzeer. I couldn't give 'im a bed. "The Captain" will be leaving with the pack 'orzes a couple of hours before dawn. Shall I tell 'im you be 'ere.'

'No, no,' he replied promptly. 'Don't tell him anything. I don't want to see him again: and he'll be gone before I'm awake, I reckon.'

'That 'e will, zir, most like. Good night, zir.'

'Good night. And – mind – that lout gets the two horses back again for my use in the morning. I shall have to make my way to Chelwood as early as may be.'

'Aye, aye, zir,' assented the woman placidly. It were no use, she thought, to upset the Mounzeer's temper once more by telling him that his guide had decamped. Time enough in the morning, when she would be less busy.

'And my John can see 'im as far as Chelwood,' she thought to herself, as she finally closed the door on the stranger and made her way slowly down the creaking stairs.

3

The Assembly Rooms

The sigh of satisfaction was quite unmistakable.

It could be heard from end to end, from corner to corner of the building. It sounded above the din of the orchestra who had just attacked with vigour the opening bars of a schottische, above the brouhaha of moving dancers and the frou-frou of skirts: it travelled from the small octagon hall, through the central salon to the tea-room, the ball-room and the card-room: it reverberated from the gallery in the ball-room to the maids' gallery: it distracted the ladies from their gossip and the gentlemen from their cards.

It was a universal, heartfelt 'Ah!' of intense and pleasurable satisfaction.

Sir Percy Blakeney and his lady had just arrived. It was close on midnight, and the ball had positively languished. What was a ball without the presence of Sir Percy? His Royal Highness too had been expected earlier than this. But it was not thought that he would come at all, despite his promise, if the spoilt pet of Bath society remained unaccountably absent; and the Assembly Rooms had worn an air of woe even in the face of the gaily dressed throng which filled every vast room in its remotest angle.

But now Sir Percy Blakeney had arrived, just before the clocks had struck midnight, and exactly one minute before His

Royal Highness drove up himself from the Royal Apartments. Lady Blakeney was looking more radiant and beautiful than ever before, so everyone remarked when a few moments later she appeared in the crowded ball-room on the arm of His Royal Highness and closely followed by my lord Anthony Dewhurst and by Sir Percy himself, who had the young Duchess of Flintshire on his arm.

'What do you mean, you incorrigible rogue,' her Grace was saying with playful severity to her cavalier, 'by coming so late to the ball? Another two minutes and you would have arrived after His Royal Highness himself: and how would you have justified such solecism, I would like to know.'

'By swearing that thoughts of your Grace had completely addled my poor brain,' he retorted gaily, 'and that in the mental contemplation of such charms I forgot time, place, social duties, everything.'

'Even the homage due to truth,' she laughed. 'Cannot you for once in your life be serious, Sir Percy?'

'Impossible, dear lady, whilst your dainty hand rests upon mine arm.'

2

It was not often that His Royal Highness graced Bath with his presence, and the occasion was made the excuse for quite exceptional gaiety and brilliancy. The new fashions of this memorable year of 1793 had defied the declaration of war and filtrated through from Paris: London milliners had not been backward in taking the hint, and though most of the more starchy dowagers obstinately adhered to the pre-war fashions – the huge hooped skirts, stiff stomachers, pointed waists, voluminous panniers and monumental head erections – the young and smart matrons were everywhere to be seen in the new gracefully flowing skirts innocent of steel constructions, the high waist line, the pouter pigeon-like draperies over their pretty bosoms.

Her Grace of Flintshire looked ravishing with her curly fair hair entirely free from powder, and Lady Betty Draitune's waist seemed to be nestling under her arm-pits. Of course Lady Blakeney wore the very latest thing in striped silks and gossamer-like muslin and lace, and it were hard to enumerate all the pretty débutantes and young brides who fluttered about the Assembly Rooms this night.

And gliding through that motley throng, bright-plumaged like a swarm of butterflies, there were a few figures dressed in sober blacks and greys – the *émigrés* over from France – men, women, young girls and gilded youth from out that seething cauldron of revolutionary France – who had shaken the dust of that rampant demagogism from off their buckled shoes, taking away with them little else but their lives. Mostly chary of speech, grave in their demeanour, bearing upon their wan faces traces of that horror which had seized them when they saw all the traditions of their past tottering around them, the proletariat whom they had despised turning against them with all the fury of caged beasts let loose, their kindred and friends massacred, their King and Queen murdered. The shelter and security which hospitable England had extended to them, had not altogether removed from their hearts the awful sense of terror and of gloom.

Many of them had come to Bath because the more genial climate of the West of England consoled them for the inclemencies of London's fogs. Received with open arms and with that lavish hospitality which the refugees and the oppressed had already learned to look for in England, they had gradually allowed themselves to be drawn into the fashionable life of the gay little city. The Comtesse de Tournai was here and her daughter, Lady Ffoulkes, Sir Andrew's charming and happy bride, and M. Paul Déroulède and his wife – beautiful Juliette Déroulède with the strange, haunted look in her large eyes, as of one who has looked closely on death; and M. le duc de Kernogan with his exquisite daughter, whose pretty air of seriousness and of repose sat so quaintly upon her young face. But everyone remarked as soon as M. le duc entered the rooms that M. Martin-Roget was not in attendance upon Mademoiselle, which was quite against the order of things; also that M. le duc appeared to keep a more sharp eye than usual upon his daughter in consequence, and that he asked somewhat anxiously if milor Anthony Dewhurst was in the room, and looked obviously relieved when the reply was in the negative.

At which trifling incident everyone who was in the know smiled and whispered, for M. le duc made it no secret that he favoured his own compatriot's suit for Mademoiselle Yvonne's hand rather than that of my lord Tony – which – as old Euclid has it – is absurd.

3

But with the arrival of the royal party M. de Kernogan's troubles began. To begin with, though M. Martin-Roget had not arrived, my lord Tony undoubtedly had. He had come in, in the wake of Lady Blakeney, but very soon he began wandering round the room obviously in search of someone. Immediately there appeared to be quite a conspiracy among the young folk in the ball-room to keep both Lord Tony's and Mlle. Yvonne's movements hidden from the prying eyes of M. le duc: and anon His Royal Highness, after a comprehensive survey of the ball-room and a few gracious words to his more intimate circle, wandered away to the card-room, and as luck would have it he claimed M. le duc de Kernogan for a partner at faro.

Now M. le duc was a courtier of the old régime: to have disobeyed the royal summons would in his eyes have been nothing short of a crime. He followed the royal party to the card-room, and on his way thither had one gleam of comfort in that he saw Lady Blakeney sitting on a sofa in the octagon hall engaged in conversation with his daughter, whilst Lord Anthony Dewhurst was nowhere in sight.

However, the gleam of comfort was very brief, for less than a quarter of an hour after he had sat down at His Highness' table, Lady Blakeney came into the card-room and stood thereafter for some little while close beside the Prince's chair. The next hour after that was one of special martyrdom for the anxious father, for he knew that his daughter was in all probability sitting out in a specially secluded corner in the company of my lord Tony.

If only Martin-Roget were here!

4

Martin-Roget with the eagle eyes and the airs of an accredited suitor would surely have intervened when my lord Tony in the face of the whole brilliant assembly in the ball-room, drew Mlle. de Kernogan into the seclusion of the recess underneath the gallery.

My lord Tony was never very glib of tongue. That peculiar dignified shyness which is one of the chief characteristics of well-bred Englishmen caused him to be tongue-tied when he had most to say. It was just with gesture and an appealing pressure of his hand upon her arm that he persuaded Yvonne de Kernogan to sit down beside him on the sofa in the remotest and darkest corner of the recess, and there she remained beside him silent and grave for a moment or two, and stole timid glances from time to time through the veil of her lashes at the finely-chiselled, expressive face of her young English lover.

He was pining to put a question to her, and so great was his excitement that his tongue refused him service, and she, knowing what was hovering on his lips, would not help him out, but a humorous twinkle in her dark eyes, and a faint smile round her lips lit up the habitual seriousness of her young face.

'Mademoiselle…' he managed to stammer at last. 'Mademoiselle Yvonne…you have seen Lady Blakeney?'

'Yes,' she replied demurely, 'I have seen Lady Blakeney.'

'And... and...she told you?'

'Yes. Lady Blakeney told me many things.'

'She told you that...that... In God's name, Mademoiselle Yvonne,' he added desperately, 'do help me out – it is cruel to tease me! Can't you see that I'm nearly crazy with anxiety.'

Then she looked up at him, her dark eyes glowing and brilliant, her face shining with the light of a great tenderness.

'Nay, milor,' she said earnestly, 'I had no wish to tease you. But you will own 'tis a grave and serious step which Lady Blakeney suggested that I should take. I have had no time to think...as yet.'

'But there is no time for thinking, Mademoiselle Yvonne,' he said naïvely. 'If you will consent... Oh! you will consent, will you not?' he pleaded.

She made no immediate reply, but gradually her hand which rested upon the sofa stole nearer and then nearer to his: and with a quiver of exquisite happiness his hand closed upon hers. The tips of his fingers touched the smooth warm palm and poor Lord Tony had to close his eyes for a moment as his sense of superlative ecstasy threatened to make him faint. Slowly he lifted that soft white hand to his lips.

'Upon my word, Yvonne,' he said with quiet fervour, 'you will never have cause to regret that you have trusted me.'

'I know that well, milor,' she replied demurely.

She settled down a shade or two closer to him still.

They were now like two birds in a cosy nest – secluded from the rest of the assembly, who appeared to them like dream-figures flitting in some other world that had nothing to do with their happiness. The strains of the orchestra who had struck the measure of the first figure of a contredanse sounded like fairy-music, distant, unreal in their ears. Only their love was real, their joy in one another's company, their hands clasped closely together!

'Tell me,' she said after awhile, 'how it all came about. It is all so terribly sudden...so exquisitely sudden. I was prepared of course...but not so soon...and certainly not tonight. Tell me just how it happened.'

She spoke English quite fluently, with just a charming slight accent, which he thought the most adorable thing he had ever heard.

'You see, dear heart,' he replied, and there was a quiver of intense feeling in his voice as he spoke, 'there is a man who not only is the friend whom I love best in all the world, but is also the one whom I trust absolutely, more than myself. Two hours ago he sent for me and told me that grave danger threatened you – threatened our love and our happiness, and he begged me to urge you to consent to a secret marriage...at once...tonight.'

'And you think this...this friend knew?'

'I know,' he replied earnestly, 'that he knew, or he would not have spoken to me as he did. He knows that my whole life is in your exquisite hands – he knows that our happiness is somehow threatened by that man Martin-Roget. How he obtained that information I could not guess...he had not the time or the inclination to tell me. I flew to make all arrangements for our marriage tonight and prayed to God – as I have never prayed in my life before – that you, dear heart, would deign to consent.'

'How could I refuse when Lady Blakeney advised? She is the kindest and dearest friend I possess. She and your friend ought to know one another. Will you not tell me who he is?'

'I will present him to you, dear heart, as soon as we are married,' he replied with awkward evasiveness. Then suddenly he exclaimed with boyish enthusiasm: 'I can't believe it! I can't believe it! It is the most extraordinary thing in the world...'

'What is that, milor?' she asked.

'That you should have cared for me at all. For of course you must care, or you wouldn't be sitting here with me now... you would not have consented...would you?'

'You know that I do care, milor,' she said in her grave quiet way. 'How could it be otherwise?'

'But I am so stupid and so slow,' he said naïvely. 'Why! look at me now. My heart is simply bursting with all that I want to say to you, but I just can't find the words, and I do nothing but talk rubbish and feel how you must despise me.'

Once more that humorous little smile played for a moment round Yvonne de Kernogan's serious mouth. She didn't say anything just then, but her delicate fingers gave his hand an expressive squeeze.

'You are not frightened?' he asked abruptly.

'Frightened? Of what?' she rejoined.

'At the step you are going to take?'

'Would I take it,' she retorted gently, 'if I had any misgivings?'

'Oh! if you had... Do you know that even now...' he continued clumsily and haltingly, 'now that I have realized just what it will mean to have you...and just what it would mean to me, God help me – if I were to lose you...well!...that even now I would rather go through that hell than that you should feel the least bit doubtful or unhappy about it all.'

Again she smiled, gently, tenderly up into his eager, boyish face.

'The only unhappiness,' she said gravely, 'that could ever overtake me in the future would be parting from you, milor.'

'Oh! God bless you for that, my dear! God bless you for that! But for pity's sake turn your dear eyes away from me or I vow I shall go crazy with joy. Men do go crazy with joy sometimes, you know, and I feel that in another moment I shall stand up and shout at the top of my voice to all the people in the room that within the next few hours the loveliest girl in all the world is going to be my wife.'

'She certainly won't be that, if you do shout it at the top of your voice, milor, for father would hear you and there would be an end to our beautiful adventure.'

'It will be a beautiful adventure, won't it? 'he sighed with unconcealed ecstasy.

'So beautiful, my dear lord,' she replied with gentle earnestness, 'so perfect, in fact, that I am almost afraid something must happen presently to upset it all.'

'Nothing can happen,' he assured her. 'M. Martin-Roget is not here, and His Royal Highness is even now monopolizing M. le duc de Kernogan so that he cannot get away.'

'Your friend must be very clever to manipulate so many strings on our behalf!'

'It is long past midnight now, sweetheart,' he said with sudden irrelevance.

'Yes, I know. I have been watching the time: and I have already thought everything out for the best. I very often go home from balls and routs in the company of Lady Ffoulkes and sleep in her house those nights. Father is always quite satisfied, when I do that, and tonight he will be doubly satisfied feeling that I shall be taken away from your society. Lady Ffoulkes is in the secret, of course, so Lady Blakeney told me, and she will be ready for me in a few minutes now: she'll take me home with her and there I will change my dress and rest for awhile, waiting for the happy hour. She will come to the church with me and then…oh then! Oh! my dear milor!' she added suddenly with a deep sigh whilst her whole face became irradiated with a light of intense happiness, 'as you say it is the most wonderful thing in all the world – this – our beautiful adventure together.'

'The parson will be ready at half-past six, dear heart, it was the earliest hour that I could secure…after that we go at once to your church and the priest will tie up any loose threads which our English parson failed to make tight. After those two ceremonies we shall be very much married, shan't we?…and nothing can come between us, dear heart, can it?' he queried with a look of intense anxiety on his young face.

'Nothing,' she replied. Then she added with a short sigh: 'Poor father!'

'Dear heart, he will only fret for a little while. I don't believe he can really want you to marry that man Martin-Roget. It is just obstinacy on his part. He can't have anything against me really...save of course that I am not clever and that I shall never do anything very big in the world...except to love you, Yvonne, with my whole heart and soul and with every fibre and muscle in me... Oh! I'll do that,' he added with boyish enthusiasm, 'better than anyone else in all the world could do! And your father will, I'll be bound, forgive me for stealing you, when he sees that you are happy, and contented, and have everything you want and...and...'

As usual Lord Tony's eloquence was not equal to all that it should have expressed. He blushed furiously and with a quaint, shy gesture, passed his large, well-shaped hand over his smooth, brown hair. 'I am not much, I know,' he continued with a winning air of self-deprecation, 'and you are far above me as the stars – you are so wonderful, so clever, so accomplished and I am nothing at all...but...but I have plenty of high-born connections, and I have plenty of money and influential friends...and...and Sir Percy Blakeney, who is the most accomplished and finest gentleman in England, calls me his friend.'

She smiled at his eagerness. She loved him for his clumsy little ways, his halting speech, that big, loving heart of his which was too full of fine and noble feelings to find vent in mere words.

'Have you ever met a finer man in all the world?' he added enthusiastically.

Yvonne de Kernogan smiled once more. Her recollections of Sir Percy Blakeney showed her an elegant man of the world, whose mind seemed chiefly occupied on the devising and the wearing of exquisite clothes, in the uttering of lively witticisms for the entertainment of his royal friend and the ladies of his entourage: it showed her a man of great wealth and vast possessions who seemed willing to spend both in the mere pursuit of pleasures. She liked Sir Percy Blakeney well enough, but she could not understand clever and charming Marguerite Blakeney's adoration for her inane and foppish husband, nor the whole-hearted admiration openly lavished upon him by men like Sir Andrew Ffoulkes, my lord Hastings, and others. She would gladly have seen her own dear milor choose a more sober and intellectual friend. But then she loved him for his marvellous power of whole-hearted friendship, for his loyalty to those he cared for, for everything in fact that made up the sum total of his winning personality, and she pinned her faith on that other mysterious friend whose individuality vastly intrigued her.

'I am more interested in your anonymous friend,' she said quaintly, 'than in Sir Percy Blakeney. But he too is kindness itself and Lady Blakeney is an angel. I like to think that the happiest days of my life – our honeymoon, my dear lord – will be spent in their house.'

'Blakeney has lent me Combwich Hall for as long as we like to stay there. We'll drive thither directly after the service, dear heart, and then we'll send a courier to your father and ask for his blessing and his forgiveness.'

'Poor father!' sighed Yvonne again. But evidently compassion for the father whom she had elected to deceive did not weigh over heavily in the balance of her happiness. Her little hand once more stole like a timid and confiding bird into the shelter of his firm grasp.

5

In the card-room at His Highness' table Sir Percy Blakeney was holding the bank and seemingly luck was dead against him. Around the various tables the ladies stood about, chattering and hindering the players. Nothing appeared serious tonight, not even the capricious chances of hazard.

His Royal Highness was in rare good humour, for he was winning prodigiously.

Her Grace of Flintshire placed her perfumed and beringed hand upon Sir Percy Blakeney's shoulder; she stood behind his chair, chattering incessantly in a high flutey treble just like a canary. Blakeney vowed that she was so ravishing that she had put Dame Fortune to flight.

'You have not yet told us, Sir Percy,' she said roguishly, 'how you came to arrive so late at the ball.'

'Alas, madam,' he sighed dolefully, ''twas the fault of my cravat.'

'Your cravat?'

'Aye indeed! You see I spent the whole of today in perfecting my new method for tying a butterfly bow, so as to give the neck an appearance of utmost elegance with a minimum of discomfort. Lady Blakeney will bear me out when I say that I set my whole mind to my task. Was I not busy all day m'dear?' he added, making a formal appeal to Marguerite, who stood immediately behind His Highness' chair, and with her luminous eyes, full of merriment and shining with happiness, fixed upon her husband.

'You certainly spent a considerable time in front of the looking-glass,' she said gaily, 'with two valets in attendance and my lord Tony an interested spectator in the proceedings.'

'There now!' rejoined Sir Percy triumphantly, 'her ladyship's testimony thoroughly bears me out. And now you shall see what Tony says on the matter. Tony! Where's Tony!' he added as his lazy grey eyes sought the brilliant crowd in the card-room. 'Tony, where the devil are you?'

There was no reply, and anon Sir Percy's merry gaze encountered that of M. le duc de Kernogan who, dressed in sober black, looked strangely conspicuous in the midst of this throng of bright-coloured butterflies, and whose grave eyes, as they rested on the gorgeous figure of the English exquisite, held a world of contempt in their glance.

'Ah! M. le duc,' continued Blakeney, returning that scornful look with his habitual good-humoured one, 'I had not noticed that Mademoiselle Yvonne was not with you, else I had not thought of inquiring so loudly for my friend Tony.'

'My lord Antoine is dancing with my daughter, Sir Percy,' said the other man gravely, in excellent if somewhat laboured English, 'he had my permission to ask her.'

'And is a thrice happy man in consequence,' retorted Blakeney lightly, 'though I fear me M. Martin-Roget's wrath will descend upon my poor Tony's head with unexampled vigour in consequence.'

'M. Martin-Roget is not here this evening,' broke in the Duchess, 'and methought,' she added in a discreet whisper, 'that my lord Tony was all the happier for his absence. The two young people have spent a considerable time together under the shadow of the gallery in the ball-room, and, if I mistake not, Lord Tony is making the most of his time.'

She talked very volubly and with a slight North-country brogue which no doubt made it a little difficult for the stranger to catch her every word. But evidently M. le duc had understood the drift of what she said, for now he rejoined with some acerbity: 'Mlle. de Kernogan is too well educated, I hope, to allow the attentions of any gentleman, against her father's will.'

'Come, come, M. de Kernogan,' here interposed His Royal Highness with easy familiarity, 'Lord Anthony Dewhurst is the son of my old friend the Marquis of Atiltone: one of our most distinguished families in this country, who have helped to make English history. He has moreover inherited a large fortune from his mother, who was a Cruche of Crewkerne and one of the richest heiresses in the land. He is a splendid fellow – a fine sportsman, a loyal gentleman. His attentions to any young lady, however high-born, can be but flattering – and I should say welcome – to those who have her future welfare at heart.'

But in response to this gracious tirade, M. le duc de Kernogan bowed gravely, and his stern features did not relax as he said coldly: 'Your Royal Highness is pleased to take an interest in the affairs of my daughter. I am deeply grateful.'

There was a second's awkward pause, for everyone felt that despite his obvious respect and deference M. le duc de Kernogan had endeavoured to inflict a snub upon the royal personage, and one or two hot-headed young fops in the immediate entourage even muttered the word: 'Impertinence!' inaudibly through their teeth. Only His Royal Highness appeared not to notice anything unusual or disrespectful in M. le duc's attitude. It seemed as if he was determined to remain good-humoured and pleasant. At any rate he chose to ignore the remark which had offended the ears of his entourage. Only those who stood opposite to His Highness, on the other side of the card table, declared afterwards that the Prince had frowned and that a haughty rejoinder undoubtedly hovered on his lips.

Be that as it may, he certainly did not show the slightest sign of ill-humour: quite gaily and unconcernedly he scooped up his winnings which Sir Percy Blakeney, who held the Bank, was at this moment pushing towards him.

'Don't go yet, M. de Kernogan,' he said as the Frenchman made a movement to work his way out of the crowd, feeling no doubt that the atmosphere round him had become somewhat frigid if not exactly inimical, 'don't go yet, I beg of you. *Pardi!* Can't you see that you have been bringing me luck? As a rule Blakeney, who can so well afford to lose, has the devil's own good fortune, but tonight I have succeeded in getting some of my own back from him. Do not, I entreat you, break the run of my luck by going.'

'Oh, Monseigneur,' rejoined the old courtier suavely, 'how can my poor presence influence the gods, who of a surety always preside over your Highness' fortunes?'

'Don't attempt to explain it, my dear sir,' quoth the Prince gaily. 'I only know that if you go now, my luck may go with you and I shall blame you for my losses.'

'Oh! in that case, Monseigneur...'

'And with all that, Blakeney,' continued His Highness, once more taking up the cards and turning to his friend, 'remember that we still await your explanation as to your coming so late to the ball.'

'An omission, your Royal Highness,' rejoined Blakeney, 'an absence of mind brought about by your severity, and that of Her Grace. The trouble was that all my calculations with regard to the exact adjustment of the butterfly bow were upset when I realized that the set of the present day waistcoat would not harmonize with it. Less than two hours before I was due to appear at this ball my mind had to make a complete *volte-face* in the matter of cravats. I became bewildered, lost, utterly confused. I have only just recovered, and one word of criticism on my final efforts would plunge me now into the depths of despair.'

'Blakeney, you are absolutely incorrigible,' retorted His Highness with a laugh. 'M. le duc,' he added, once more turning to the grave Frenchman with his wonted graciousness, 'I pray you do not form your judgement on the gilded youth of England by the example of my friend Blakeney. Some of us can be serious when occasion demands, you know.'

'Your Highness is pleased to jest,' said M. de Kernogan stiffly. 'What greater occasion for seriousness can there be than the present one. True, England has never suffered as France is suffering now, but she has engaged in a conflict against the most powerful democracy the world has ever known, she has thrown down the gauntlet to a set of human beasts of prey who are as determined as they are ferocious. England will not emerge victorious from this conflict, Monseigneur, if her sons do not realize that war is not mere sport and that victory can only be attained by the sacrifice of levity and of pleasure.'

He had dropped into French in response to His Highness' remark, in order to express his thoughts more accurately. The Prince – a little bored no doubt – seemed disinclined to pursue the subject. Nevertheless, it seemed as if once again he made a decided effort not to show ill-humour. He even gave a knowing wink – a wink! – in the direction of his friend Blakeney and of Her Grace as if to beg them to set the ball of conversation rolling once more along a smoother – a less boring – path. He was obviously quite determined not to release M. de Kernogan from attendance near his royal person.

6

As usual Sir Percy threw himself in the breach, filling the sudden pause with his infectious laugh: 'La!' he said gaily, 'how beautifully M. le duc does talk. Ffoulkes,' he added, addressing Sir Andrew, who was standing close by, 'I'll wager you ten pounds to a pinch of snuff that you couldn't deliver yourself of such splendid sentiments, even in your own native lingo.'

'I won't take you, Blakeney,' retorted Sir Andrew with a laugh. 'I'm no good at peroration.'

'You should hear our distinguished guest M. Martin-Roget on the same subject,' continued Sir Percy with mock gravity. 'By Gad! can't he talk? I feel a d–d worm when he talks about our national levity, our insane worship of sport, our...our...M. le duc,' he added with becoming seriousness and in atrocious French, 'I appeal to you. Does not M. Martin-Roget talk beautifully?'

'M. Martin-Roget,' replied the duc gravely, 'is a man of marvellous eloquence, fired by overwhelming patriotism. He is a man who must command respect wherever he goes.'

'You have known him long, M. le duc?' queried His Royal Highness graciously.

'Indeed not very long, Monseigneur. He came over as an émigré from Brest some three months ago, hidden in a smuggler's ship. He had been denounced as an aristocrat who was furthering the cause of the royalists in Brittany by helping them plentifully with money, but he succeeded in escaping, not only with his life, but also with the bulk of his fortune.'

'Ah! M. Martin-Roget is rich?'

'He is sole owner of a rich banking business in Brest, Monseigneur, which has an important branch in America and correspondents all over Europe. Monseigneur the Bishop of Brest recommended him specially to my notice in a very warm letter of introduction, wherein he speaks of M. Martin-Roget as a gentleman of the highest patriotism and integrity. Were I not quite satisfied as to M. Martin-Roget's antecedents and present connections I would not have ventured to present him to your Highness.'

'Nor would you have accepted him as a suitor for your daughter, M. le duc, *c'est entendu!* 'concluded His Highness urbanely. 'M. Martin-Roget's wealth will no doubt cover his lack of birth.'

'There are plenty of high-born gentlemen devoted to the royalist cause, Monseigneur,' rejoined the duc in his grave, formal manner. 'But the most just and purest of causes must at times be helped with money. The Vendéens in Brittany, the Princes at Coblentz are all sorely in need of funds...'

'And M. Martin-Roget son-in-law of M. le duc de Kernogan is more likely to feed those funds than M. Martin-Roget the plain businessman who has no aristocratic connections,' concluded His Royal Highness dryly. 'But even so, M. le duc,' he added more gravely, 'surely you cannot be so absolutely certain as you would wish that M. Martin-Roget's antecedents are just as he has told you. Monseigneur the Bishop of Brest may have acted in perfect good faith...'

'Monseigneur the Bishop of Brest, your Highness, is a man who has our cause, the cause of our King and of our Faith, as much at heart as I have myself. He would know that on his recommendation I would trust any man absolutely. He was not like to make careless use of such knowledge.'

'And you are quite satisfied that the worthy Bishop did not act under some dire pressure...?'

'Quite satisfied, Monseigneur,' replied the duc firmly. What pressure could there be that would influence a prelate of such high integrity as Monseigneur the Bishop of Brest?'

7

There was silence for a moment or two, during which the heavy bracket clock over the door struck the first hour after midnight. His Royal Highness looked round at Lady Blakeney, and she gave him a smile and an almost imperceptible nod. Sir Andrew Ffoulkes had in the meanwhile quietly slipped away.

'I understand,' said His Royal Highness quite gravely, turning back to M. le duc, 'and I must crave your pardon, sir, for what must have seemed to you an indiscretion. You have given me a very clear exposé of the situation. I confess that until tonight it had seemed to me – and to all your friends, Monsieur, a trifle obscure. In fact, it had been my intention to intercede with you in favour of my young friend Lord Anthony Dewhurst, who of a truth is deeply enamoured of your daughter.'

'Though your Highness' wishes are tantamount to a command, yet would I humbly assert that my wishes with regard to my daughter are based upon my loyalty and my duty to my Sovereign King Louis XVII, whom may God guard and protect, and that therefore it is beyond my power now to modify them.'

'May God trounce you for an obstinate fool,' murmured His Highness in English, and turning his head away so that the other should not hear him. But aloud and with studied graciousness he said: 'M. le duc, will you not take a hand at hazard? My luck is turning, and I have faith in yours. We must fleece Blakeney tonight. He has had Satan's own luck these past few weeks. Such good fortune becomes positively revolting.'

There was no more talk of Mlle. de Kernogan after that. Indeed her father felt that her future had already been discussed far too freely by all these well-wishers who of a truth were not a little indiscreet. He thought that the manners and customs of good society were very peculiar here in this fog-ridden England. What business was it of all these high-born ladies and gentlemen – of His Royal Highness himself for that matter – what plans he had made for Yvonne's future? Martin-Roget was *bourgeois* by birth, but he was vastly rich and had promised to pour a couple of millions into the coffers of the royalist army if Mlle. de Kernogan became his wife. A couple of millions with more to follow, no doubt, and a loyal adherence to the royalist cause was worth these days all the blue blood that flowed in my lord Anthony Dewhurst's veins.

So at any rate thought M. le duc this night, while His Royal Highness kept him at cards until the late hours of the morning.

4

The Father

It was close on ten o'clock now in the morning on the following day, and M. le duc de Kernogan was at breakfast in his lodgings in Laura Place, when a courier was announced who was the bearer of a letter for M. le duc.

He thought the man must have been sent by Martin-Roget, who mayhap was sick, seeing that he had not been present at the Assembly Rooms last night, and the duc took the letter and opened it without misgivings. He read the address on the top of the letter: 'Combwich Hall' – a place unknown to him, and the first words of the letter: 'Dear father!' And even then he had no misgivings.

In fact he had to read the letter through three times before the full meaning of its contents had penetrated into his brain. Whilst he read, he sat quite still, and even the hand which held the paper had not the slightest tremor. When he had finished he spoke quite quietly to his valet: 'Give the courier a glass of ale, Frédérick,' he said, 'and tell him he can go; there is no answer. And – stay,' he added, 'I want you to go round at once to M. Martin-Roget's lodgings and ask him to come and speak with me as early as possible.'

The valet left the room, and M. le duc deliberately read through the letter from end to end for the fourth time. There was no doubt, no possible misapprehension. His daughter

Yvonne de Kernogan had eloped clandestinely with my lord Anthony Dewhurst and had been secretly married to him in the small hours of the morning in the Protestant church of St James, and subsequently before a priest of her own religion in the Priory Church of St John the Evangelist.

She apprised her father of this fact in a few sentences which purported to be dictated by profound affection and filial respect, but in which M. de Kernogan failed to detect the slightest trace of contrition. Yvonne! his Yvonne! the sole representative now of the old race – eloped like a kitchen-wench! Yvonne! his daughter! his asset for the future! his thing! his fortune! that which he meant with perfect egoism to sacrifice on the altar of his own beliefs and his own loyalty to the kingship of France! Yvonne had taken her future in her own hands! She knew that her hand, her person, were the purchase price of so many millions to be poured into the coffers of the royalist cause, and she had disposed of both, in direct defiance of her father's will and of her duty to her King and to his cause!

Yvonne de Kernogan was false to her traditions, false to her father! false to her King and country! In the years to come when the chroniclers of the time came to write the histories of the great families that had rallied round their King in the hour of his deadly peril, the name of Kernogan would be erased from those glorious pages. The Kernogans will have failed in their duty, failed in their loyalty! Oh! the shame of it all! The shame!!

The duc was far too proud a gentleman to allow his valet to see him under the stress of violent emotion, but now that he was alone his thin, hard face – with that air of gravity which he had transmitted to his daughter – became distorted with the passion of unbridled fury; he tore the letter up into a thousand little pieces and threw the fragments into the fire. On the bureau beside him there stood a miniature of Yvonne de Kernogan painted by Hall three years ago, and framed in a circlet of brilliants. M. le duc's eyes casually fell upon it; he picked it up and with a violent gesture of rage threw it on the floor and stamped upon it with his heel, destroying in this paroxysm of silent fury a work of art worth many hundred pounds.

His daughter had deceived him. She had also upset all his plans whereby the army of M. le Prince de Condé would have been enriched by a couple of million francs. In addition to the shame upon her father, she had also brought disgrace upon herself and her good name, for she was a minor and this clandestine marriage, contracted without her father's consent, was illegal in France, illegal everywhere: save perhaps in England – of this M. de Kernogan was not quite sure, but he certainly didn't care. And in this solemn moment he registered a vow that never as long as he lived would he be reconciled to that English nincompoop who had dared to filch his daughter from him, and never – as long as he lived – would he by his consent render the marriage legal, and the children born of that wedlock legitimate in the eyes of his country's laws.

A calm akin to apathy had followed his first outbreak of fury. He sat down in front of the fire, and buried his chin in his hand. Something of course must be done to get his daughter back. If only Martin-Roget were here, he would know better how to act. Would Martin-Roget stick to his bargain and accept the girl for wife, now that her fame and honour had been irretrievably tarnished? There was the question which the next half-hour would decide. M. de Kernogan cast a feverish, anxious look on the clock. Half an hour had gone by since Frédérick went to seek Martin-Roget, and the latter had not yet appeared.

Until he had seen Martin-Roget and spoken with Martin-Roget M. de Kernogan could decide nothing. For one brief, mad moment, the project had formed itself in his disordered brain to rush down to Combwich Hall and provoke that impudent Englishman who had stolen his daughter: to kill him or be killed by him; in either case Yvonne would then be parted from him for ever. But even then, the thought of Martin-Roget brought more sober reflection. Martin-Roget would see to it. Martin-Roget would know what to do. After all, the outrage had hit the accredited lover just as hard as the father.

But why in the name of – did Martin-Roget not come?

2

It was past midday when at last Martin-Roget knocked at the door of M. le duc's lodgings in Laura Place. The older man had in the meanwhile gone through every phase of overwhelming emotions. The outbreak of unreasoning fury – when like a maddened beast that bites and tears he had broken his daughter's miniature and trampled it underfoot – had been followed by a kind of dull apathy, when for close upon an hour he had sat staring into the flames, trying to grapple with an awful reality which seemed to elude him all the time. He could not believe that this thing had really happened: that Yvonne, his well-bred dutiful daughter, who had shown such marvellous courage and presence of mind when the necessity of flight and of exile had first presented itself in the wake of the awful massacres and wholesale executions of her own friends and kindred, that she should have eloped – like some flirtatious wench – and outraged her father in this monstrous fashion, by a clandestine marriage with a man of alien race and of a heretical religion! M. de Kernogan could not realize it. It passed the bounds of possibility. The very flames in the hearth seemed to dance and to mock the bare suggestion of such an atrocious transgression.

To this gloomy numbing of the senses had succeeded the inevitable morbid restlessness: the pacing up and down the narrow room, the furtive glances at the clock, the frequent orders to Frédérick to go out and see if M. Martin-Roget was not yet home. For Frédérick had come back after his first errand with the astounding news that M. Martin-Roget had left his lodgings the previous day at about four o'clock, and had not been seen or heard of since. In fact his landlady was very anxious about him and was sorely tempted to see the town-crier on the subject.

Four times did Frédérick have to go from Laura Place to the Bear Inn in Union Street, where M. Martin-Roget lodged, and three times he returned with the news that nothing had been heard of Mounzeer yet. The fourth time – it was then close on midday – he came back running – thankful to bring back the good tidings, since he was tired of that walk from Laura Place to the Bear Inn. M. Martin-Roget had come home. He appeared very tired and in rare ill-humour: but Frédérick had delivered the message from M. le duc, whereupon M. Martin-Roget had become most affable and promised that he would come round immediately. In fact he was even then treading hard on Frédérick's heels.

3

'My daughter has gone! She left the ball clandestinely last night, and was married to Lord Anthony Dewhurst in the small hours of the morning. She is now at a place called Combwich Hall – with him!'

M. le duc de Kernogan literally threw these words in Martin-Roget's face, the moment the latter had entered the room, and Frédérick had discreetly closed the door.

'What? What?' stammered the other vaguely. 'I don't understand. What do you mean?' he added, bewildered at the duc's violence, tired after his night's adventure and the long ride in the early morning, irritable with want of sleep and decent food. He stared, uncomprehending, at the duc, who had once more started pacing up and down the room, like a caged beast, with hands tightly clenched behind his back, his eyes glowering both at the new-comer and at the imaginary presence of his most bitter enemy – the man who had dared to come between him and his projects for his daughter.

Martin-Roget passed his hand across his brow like a man who is not yet fully awake.

'What do you mean?' he reiterated hazily.

'Just what I say,' retorted the other roughly. 'Yvonne has eloped with that nincompoop Lord Anthony Dewhurst. They have gone through some sort of marriage ceremony together. And she writes me a letter this morning to tell me that she is quite happy and contented and spending her honeymoon at a place called Combwich Hall. Honeymoon!' he repeated savagely, as if to lash his fury up anew, 'Tsha!'

Martin-Roget on the other hand was not the man to allow himself to fall into a state of frenzy, which would necessarily interfere with calm consideration.

He had taken the fact in now. Yvonne's elopement with his English rival, the clandestine marriage, everything. But he was not going to allow his inward rage to obscure his vision of the future. He did not spend the next precious seconds – as men of his race are wont to do – in smashing things around him, in raving and fuming and gesticulating. No. That was not the temper M. Martin-Roget was in at this moment when Fate and a girl's folly were ranging themselves against his plans. His friend, citizen Chauvelin, would have envied him his calm in the face of this disaster.

Whilst M. le duc still stormed and raved, Martin-Roget sat down quietly in front of the fire, rested his chin in his hand and waited for a lull in the other man's paroxysm ere he spoke.

'From your attitude, M. le duc,' he then said quietly, hiding obvious sarcasm behind a veil of studied deference, 'from your attitude I gather that your wishes with regard to Mlle. de Kernogan have undergone no modification. You would still honour me by desiring that she should become my wife?'

'I am not in the habit of changing my mind,' said M. le duc gruffly. He desired the marriage, he coveted Martin-Roget's millions for the royalist cause, but he had no love for the man. All the pride of the Kernogans. their long line of ancestry, rebelled against the thought of a fair descendant of this glorious race being allied to a *roturier* – a *bourgeois* – a tradesman, what? and the cause of King and country counted few greater martyrdoms than that of the duc de Kernogan whenever he met the banker Martin-Roget on an equal social footing.

'Then there is not much harm done,' rejoined the latter coolly; 'the marriage is not a legal one. It need not even be dissolved – Mademoiselle de Kernogan is still Mademoiselle de Kernogan and I her humble and faithful adorer.'

M. le duc paused in his restless walk.

'You would...' he stammered, then checked himself, turning abruptly away. He had some difficulty in hiding the scorn wherewith he regarded the other's coolness. Bourgeois blood was not to be gainsaid. The tradesman – or banker, whatever he was – who hankered after an alliance with Mademoiselle de Kernogan, and was ready to lay down a couple of millions for the privilege – was not to be deterred from his purpose by any considerations of pride or of honour. M. le duc was satisfied and re-assured, but he despised the man for his leniency for all that.

'The marriage is no marriage at all according to the laws of France,' reiterated Martin-Roget calmly.

'No, it is not,' assented the Duke roughly.

For a while there was silence: Martin-Roget seemed immersed in his own thoughts and not to notice the febrile comings and goings of the other man.

'What we have to do, M. le duc,' he said after a while, 'is to induce Mlle. de Kernogan to return here immediately.'

'How are you going to accomplish that?' sneered the Duke.

'Oh! I was not suggesting that I should appear in the matter at all,' rejoined Martin-Roget with a shrug of the shoulders.

'Then how can I...?'

'Surely...' argued the younger man tentatively.

'You mean...?'

Martin-Roget nodded. Despite these ambiguous half-spoken sentences the two men had understood one another.

'We must get her back, of course,' assented the Duke, who had suddenly become as calm as the other man.

'There is no harm done,' reiterated Martin-Roget with slow and earnest emphasis.

Whereupon the Duke, completely pacified, drew a chair close to the hearth and sat down, leaning his elbows on his knees and holding his fine, aristocratic hands to the blaze.

Frédérick came in half an hour later to ask if M. le duc would have his luncheon. He found the two gentlemen sitting quite close together over the dying embers of a fire that had not been fed for close upon an hour: and that prince of valets was glad to note that M. le duc's temper had quite cooled down and that he was talking calmly and very affably to M. Martin-Roget

5

The Nest

There are lovely days in England sometimes in November or December, days when the departing year strives to make us forget that winter is nigh, and autumn smiles, gentle and benignant, caressing with a still tender kiss the last leaves of the scarlet oak which linger on the boughs, and touching up with a vivid brush the evergreen verdure of bay trees, of ilex and of yew. The sky is of that pale, translucent blue which dwellers in the South never see, with the soft transparency of an aquamarine as it fades into the misty horizon at midday. And at dusk the thrushes sing: 'Kiss me quick! kiss me quick! kiss me quick' in the naked branches of old acacias and chestnuts, and the robins don their crimson waistcoats and dart in and out among the coppice and through the feathery arms of larch and pine. And the sun which tips the prickly points of holly leaves with gold, joins in this merry make-believe that winter is still a very, very long way off, and that mayhap he has lost his way altogether, and is never coming to this balmy beautiful land again.

Just such a day was the penultimate one of November, 1793, when Lady Anthony Dewhurst sat at a desk in the wide bay window of the drawing-room in Combwich Hall, trying to put into a letter to Lady Blakeney all that her heart would have wished to express of love and gratitude and happiness.

Three whole days had gone by since that exciting night, when before break of day in the dimly-lighted old church, in the presence of two or three faithful friends, she had plighted her troth to Lord Anthony: even whilst other kind friends – including His Royal Highness – formed part of the little conspiracy which kept her father occupied and, if necessary, would have kept M. Martin-Roget out of the way. Since then her life had been one continuous dream of perfect bliss. From the moment when after the second religious ceremony in the Roman Catholic church she found herself alone in the carriage with milor, and felt his arms – so strong and yet so tender – closing round her and his lips pressed to hers in the first masterful kiss of complete possession, until this hour when she saw his tall, elegant figure hurrying across the garden toward the gate and suddenly turning toward the window whence he knew that she was watching him, every hour and every minute had been nothing but unalloyed happiness.

Even there where she had looked for sorrow and difficulty her path had been made smooth for her. Her father, who she had feared would prove hard and irreconcilable had been tender and forgiving to such an extent that tears almost of shame would gather in her eyes whenever she thought of him.

As soon as she arrived at Combwich Hall she had written a long and deeply affectionate letter to her father, imploring his forgiveness for the deception and unfilial conduct which on her part must so deeply have grieved him. She pleaded for her right to happiness in words of impassioned eloquence, she pleaded for her right to love and to be loved, for her right to a home, which a husband's devotion would make a paradise for her.

This letter she had sent by special courier to her father and the very next day she had his reply. She had opened the letter with trembling fingers, fearful lest her father's harshness should mar the perfect serenity of her life. She was afraid of what he would say, for she knew her father well: knew his faults as well as his qualities, his pride, his obstinacy, his unswerving

89

determination and his loyalty to the King's cause – all of which must have been deeply outraged by his daughter's high-handed action. But as she began to read, astonishment, amazement at once filled her soul: she could hardly trust her comprehension, hardly believe that what she read could indeed be reality, and not just the continuance of the happy dream wherein she was dwelling these days.

Her father – gently reproachful – had not one single harsh word to utter. He would not, he said, at the close of his life, after so many bitter disappointments, stand in the way of his daughter's happiness: 'You should have trusted me, my child,' he wrote: and indeed Yvonne could not believe her eyes. 'I had no idea that your happiness was at stake in this marriage, or I should never have pressed the claims of my own wishes in the matter. I have only you in the world left, now that misery and exile are to be my portion! Is it likely that I would allow any personal desires to weigh against my love for you?'

Happy as she was Yvonne cried – cried bitterly with remorse and shame when she read that letter. How could she have been so blind, so senseless as to misjudge her father so? Her young husband found her in tears, and had much ado to console her: he too read the letter and was deeply touched by the kind reference to himself contained therein: 'My lord Anthony is a gallant gentleman,' wrote M. le duc de Kernogan, 'he will make you happy, my child, and your old father will be more than satisfied. All that grieves me is that you did not trust me sooner. A clandestine marriage is not worthy of a daughter of the Kernogans.'

'I did speak most earnestly to M. le duc,' said Lord Tony reflectively, 'when I begged him to allow me to pay my addresses to you. But then,' he added cheerfully, 'I am such a clumsy lout when I have to talk at any length – and especially clumsy when I have to plead my own cause. I suppose I put my case so badly before your father, m'dear, that he thought me three parts an idiot and would not listen to me.'

'I too begged and entreated him, dear,' she said with a smile, 'but he was very determined then and vowed that I should marry M. Martin-Roget despite my tears and protestations. Dear father! I suppose he didn't realize that I was in earnest.'

'He has certainly accepted the inevitable very gracefully,' was my lord Tony's final comment.

2

Then they read the letter through once more, sitting close together, he with one arm round her shoulder, she nestling against his chest, her hair brushing against his lips and with the letter in her hands which she could scarcely read for the tears of joy which filled her eyes.

'I don't feel very well today,' the letter concluded; 'the dampness and the cold have got into my bones: moreover you two young love birds will not desire company just yet, but tomorrow if the weather is more genial I will drive over to Combwich in the afternoon, and perhaps you will give me supper and a bed for the night. Send me word by the courier who will forthwith return to Bath if this will be agreeable to you both.'

Could anything be more adorable, more delightful? It was just the last drop that filled Yvonne's cup of happiness right up to the brim.

3

The next afternoon she sat at her desk in order to tell Lady Blakeney all about it. She made out a copy of her father's letter and put that in with her own, and begged dear Lady Blakeney to see Lady Ffoulkes forthwith and tell her all that had happened. She herself was expecting her father every minute and milor Tony had gone as far as the gate to see if the barouche was in sight.

Half an hour later M. de Kernogan had arrived and his daughter lay in his arms, happy, beyond the dreams of men. He looked rather tired and wan and still complained that the cold had got into his bones: evidently he was not very well and Yvonne after the excitement of the meeting felt not a little anxious about him. As the evening wore on he became more and more silent; he hardly would eat anything and soon after eight o'clock he announced his desire to retire to bed.

'I am not ill,' he said as he kissed his daughter and bade her a fond 'Good night,' 'only a little wearied...with emotion no doubt. I shall be better after a night's rest.'

He had been quite cordial with my lord Tony, though not effusive, which was only natural – he was at all times a very reserved man, and – unlike those of his race – never demonstrative in his manner: but with his daughter he had been singularly tender, with a wistful affection which almost suggested remorse, even though it was she who, on his arrival, had knelt down before him and had begged for his blessing and his forgiveness.

4

But the following morning he appeared to be really ill: his cheeks looked sunken, almost livid, his eyes dim and hollow. Nevertheless he would not hear of staying on another day or so.

'No, no,' he declared emphatically, 'I shall be better in Bath. It is more sheltered there, here the north winds would drive me to my bed very quickly. I shall take a course of baths at once. They did me a great deal of good before, you remember, Yvonne – in September, when I caught a chill...they soon put me right. That is all that ails me now... I've caught a chill.'

He did his best to reassure his daughter, but she was far from satisfied: more especially as he hardly would touch the cup of chocolate which she had prepared for him with her own hands.

'I shall be quite myself again in Bath,' he declared, 'and in a day or two when you can spare the time – or when milor can spare you – perhaps you will drive over to see how the old father is getting on, eh?'

'Indeed,' she said firmly, 'I shall not allow you to go to Bath alone. If you will go, I shall accompany you.'

'Nay!' he protested, 'that is foolishness, my child. The barouche will take me back quite comfortably. It is less than two hours' drive and I shall be quite safe and comfortable.'

'You will be quite safe and comfortable in my company,' she retorted with a tender, anxious glance at his pale face and the nervous tremor of his hands. 'I have consulted with my dear husband and he has given his consent that I should accompany you.'

'But you can't leave milor like that, my child,' he protested once more. 'He will be lonely and miserable without you.'

'Yes. I think he will,' she said wistfully. 'But he will be all the happier when you are well again, and I can return to Combwich satisfied.'

Whereupon M. le duc yielded. He kissed and thanked his daughter and seemed even relieved at the prospect of her company. The barouche was ordered for eleven o'clock, and a quarter of an hour before that time Lord Tony had his young wife in his arms, bidding her a sad farewell.

'I hate your going from me, sweetheart,' he said as he kissed her eyes, her hair, her lips. 'I cannot bear you out of my sight even for an hour…let alone a couple of days.'

'Yet I must go, dear heart,' she retorted, looking up with that sweet, grave smile of hers into his eager young face. 'I could not let him travel alone…could I?'

'No, no,' he assented somewhat dubiously, 'but remember, dear heart, that you are infinitely precious and that I shall scarce live for sheer anxiety until I have you here, safe, once more in my arms.'

'I'll send you a courier this evening,' she rejoined, as she extricated herself gently from his embrace, 'and if I can come back tomorrow...'

'I'll ride over to Bath in any case in the morning so that I may escort you back if you really can come.'

'I will come if I am reassured about father. Oh, my dear lord,' she added with a wistful little sigh, 'I knew yesterday morning that I was too happy, and that something would happen to mar the perfect felicity of these last few days.'

'You are not seriously anxious about M. le duc's health, dear heart?'

'No, not seriously anxious. Farewell, milor. It is *au revoir*...a few hours and we'll resume our dream.'

5

There was nothing in all that to arouse my lord Tony's suspicions. All day he was miserable and forlorn because Yvonne was not there – but he was not suspicious.

Fate had a blow in store for him, from which he was destined never wholly to recover, but she gave him no warning, no premonition. He spent the day in making up arrears of correspondence, for he had a large private fortune to administer – trust funds on behalf of brothers and sisters who were minors – and he always did it conscientiously and to the best of his ability. The last few days he had lived in a dream and there was an accumulation of business to go through. In the evening he expected the promised courier, who did not arrive: but his was not the sort of disposition that would fret and fume because of a contretemps which might be attributable to the weather – it had rained heavily since afternoon – or to sundry trifling causes which he at Combwich, ten or a dozen miles from Bath, could not estimate. He had no suspicions even then. How could he have? How could he guess? Nevertheless when he ultimately went to bed, it was with the firm resolve that he would in any case go over to Bath in the morning and remain there until Yvonne was able to come back with him.

Combwich without her was anyhow unendurable.

6

He started for Bath at nine o'clock in the morning. It was still raining hard. It had rained all night and the roads were very muddy. He started out without a groom. A little after half-past ten, he drew rein outside his house in Chandos Buildings, and having changed his clothes he started to walk to Laura Place. The rain had momentarily left off, and a pale wintry sun peeped out through rolling banks of grey clouds. He went round by way of Saw Close and the Upper Borough Walls, as he wanted to avoid the fashionable throng that crowded the neighbourhood of the Pump Room and the Baths. His intention was to seek out the Blakeneys at their residence in the Circus after he had seen Yvonne and obtained news of M. le duc.

He had no suspicions. Why should he have?

The Abbey clock struck a quarter-past eleven when finally he knocked at the house in Laura Place. Long afterwards he remembered how just at that moment a dense grey mist descended into the valley. He had not noticed it before, now he saw that it had enveloped this part of the city so that he could not even see clearly across the Place.

A woman came to open the door. Lord Tony then thought this strange considering how particular M. le duc always was about everything pertaining to the management of his household:

'The house of a poor exile,' he was wont to say, 'but nevertheless that of a gentleman.'

'Can I go straight up?' he asked the woman, who he thought was standing ostentatiously in the hall as if to bar his way. 'I desire to see M. le duc.'

'Ye can walk upstairs, zir,' said the woman, speaking with a broad Somersetshire accent, 'but I doubt me if ye'll see 'is Grace the Duke. 'Es been gone these two days.'

Tony had paid no heed to her at first; he had walked across the narrow hall to the oak staircase, and was halfway up the first flight when her last words struck upon his ear...quite without meaning for the moment...but nevertheless he paused, one foot on one tread, and the other two treads below...and he turned round to look at the woman, a swift frown across his smooth forehead.

'Gone these two days,' he repeated mechanically; 'what do you mean?'

'Well! 'Is Grace left the day afore yesterday – Thursday it was... 'Is man went yesterday afternoon with luggage and sich...'e went by coach 'e did... Leave off,' she cried suddenly; 'what are ye doin'? Ye're 'urtin' me.'

For Lord Tony had rushed down the stairs again and was across the hall, gripping the unoffending woman by the wrist and glaring into her expressionless face until she screamed with fright.

'I beg your pardon,' he said humbly as he released her wrist: all the instincts of the courteous gentleman arrayed against his loss of control. 'I... I forgot myself for the moment,' he stammered; 'would you mind telling me again...what...what you said just now?'

The woman was prepared to put on the airs of outraged dignity, she even glanced up at the malapert with scorn expressed in her small beady eyes. But at sight of his face her anger and her fears both fell away from her. Lord Tony was white to the lips, his cheeks were the colour of dead ashes, his mouth trembled, his eyes alone glowed with ill-repressed anxiety.

' 'Is Grace,' she said with slow emphasis, for of a truth she thought that the young gentleman was either sick or daft, ' 'Is Grace left this 'ouse the day afore yesterday in a hired barouche. 'Is man – Frèdèrick – went yesterday afternoon with the liggage. 'E caught the Bristol coach at two o'clock. I was 'Is Grace's 'ousekeeper and I am to look after the 'ouse and the zervants until I 'ear from 'Is Grace again. Them's my orders. I know no more than I'm tellin' ye.'

'But His Grace returned here yesterday forenoon,' argued Lord Tony calmly, mechanically, as one who would wish to convince an obstinate child. 'And my lady... Mademoiselle Yvonne, you know...was with him.'

'Noa! Noa!' said the woman placidly. ' 'Is Grace 'asn't been near this 'ouse come Thursday afternoon, and 'is man left yesterday wi' th' liggage. Why!' she added confidentially, ' 'e ain't gone far. It was all zettled that zuddint I didn't know nothing about it myzelf till I zeed Mr Frèdèrick start off wi' th' liggage. Not much liggage neither it wasn't. Sure but 'Is Grace'll be 'ome zoon. 'E can't 'ave gone far. Not wi' that bit o' liggage. Zure.'

'But my lady... Mademoiselle Yvonne...'

'Lor, zir, didn't ye know? Why 'twas all over th' town o' Tuesday as 'ow Mademozell 'ad eloped with my lord Anthony Dew'urst, and...'

'Yes! yes! But you have seen my lady since?'

'Not clapped eyes on 'er, zir, since she went to the ball come Monday evenin'. An' a picture she looked in 'er white gown...'

'And...did His Grace leave no message...for...for anyone?...no letter?'

'Ah, yes, now you come to mention it, zir. Mr Frèdèrick 'e give me a letter yesterday. " 'Is Grace," sez 'e, "left this yere letter on 'is desk. I just found it," sez 'e. "If my lord Anthony Dew'urst calls," sez 'e, "give it to 'im." I've got the letter zomewhere, zir. What may your name be?'

'I am Lord Anthony Dewhurst,' replied the young man mechanically.

'Your pardon, my lord, I'll go fetch th' letter.'

7

Lord Tony never moved while the woman shuffled across the passage and down the back stairs. He was like a man who has received a knock-out blow and has not yet had time to recover his scattered senses. At first when the woman spoke, his mind had jumped to fears of some awful accident...runaway horses... a broken barouche...or a sudden aggravation of the duc's ill-health. But soon he was forced to reject what now would have seemed a consoling thought: had there been an accident, he would have heard – a rumour would have reached him – Yvonne would have sent a courier. He did not know yet what to think, his mind was like a slate over which a clumsy hand had passed a wet sponge – impressions, recollections, above all a hideous, nameless fear, were all blurred and confused within his brain.

The woman came back carrying a letter which was crumpled and greasy from a prolonged sojourn in the pocket of her apron. Lord Tony took the letter and broke its heavy seal. The woman watched him, curiously, pityingly now, for he was good to look on, and she scented the significance of the tragedy which she had been the means of revealing to him. But he had become quite unconscious of her presence, of everything in fact save those few sentences, written in French, in a cramped hand, and which seemed to dance a wild saraband before his eyes:

'MILOR, --
'You tried to steal my daughter from me, but I have taken her from you now. By the time this reaches you we shall

be on the high seas on our way to Holland, thence to Coblentz, where Mademoiselle de Kernogan will in accordance with my wishes be united in lawful marriage to M. Martin-Roget whom I have chosen to be her husband. She is not and never was your wife. As far as one may look into the future, I can assure you that you will never in life see her again.'

And to this monstrous document of appalling callousness and cold-blooded cruelty there was appended the signature of André Dieudonné Duc de Kernogan.

But unlike the writer thereof Lord Anthony Dewhurst neither stormed nor raged: he did not even tear the execrable letter into an hundred fragments. His firm hand closed over it with one convulsive clutch, and that was all. Then he slipped the crumpled paper into his pocket. Quite deliberately he took out some money and gave a piece of silver to the woman.

I thank you very much,' he said somewhat haltingly. 'I quite understand everything now.'

The woman curtseyed and thanked him; tears were in her eyes, for it seemed to her that never had she seen such grief depicted upon any human face. She preceded him to the hall door and held it open for him, while he passed out. After the brief gleam of sunshine it had started to rain again, but he didn't seem to care. The woman suggested fetching a hackney coach, but he refused quite politely, quite gently: he even lifted his hat as he went out. Obviously he did not know what he was doing. Then he went out into the rain and strode slowly across the Place.

6

The Scarlet Pimpernel

Instinct kept him away from the more frequented streets – and instinct after awhile drew him in the direction of his friend's house at the corner of The Circus. Sir Percy Blakeney had not gone out fortunately: the lacquey who opened the door to my lord Tony stared astonished and almost paralyzed for the moment at the extraordinary appearance of his lordship. Rain dropped down from the brim of his hat onto his shoulders: his boots were muddy to the knees, his clothes wringing wet. His eyes were wild and hazy and there was a curious tremor round his mouth.

The lacquey declared with a knowing wink afterwards that his lordship must 'ave been drinkin'!

But at the moment his sense of duty urged him to show my lord – who was his master's friend – into the library, whatever condition he was in. He took his dripping coat and hat from him and marshalled him across the large, square hall.

Sir Percy Blakeney was sitting at his desk, writing, when Lord Tony was shown in. He looked up and at once rose and went to his friend.

'Sit down, Tony,' he said quietly, 'while I get you some brandy.'

He forced the young man down gently into a chair in front of the fire and threw another log into the blaze. Then from a cupboard he fetched a flask of brandy and a glass, poured some out and held it to Tony's lips. The latter drank – unresisting – like a child. Then as some warmth penetrated into his bones, he leaned forward, resting his elbows on his knees and buried his face in his hands. Blakeney waited quietly, sitting down opposite to him, until his friend should be able to speak.

'And after all that you told me on Monday night!' were the first words which came from Tony's quivering lips, 'and the letter you sent me over on Tuesday! Oh! I was prepared to mistrust Martin-Roget. Why! I never allowed her out of my sight!... But her father!... How could I guess?'

'Can you tell me exactly what happened?'

Lord Tony drew himself up, and staring vacantly into the fire told his friend the events of the past four days. On Wednesday the courier with M. de Kernogan's letter, breathing kindness and forgiveness. On Thursday his arrival and seeming ill-health, on Friday his departure with Yvonne. Tony spoke quite calmly. He had never been anything but calm since first, in the house in Laura Place, he had received that awful blow.

'I ought to have known,' he concluded dully, 'I ought to have guessed. Especially since you warned me.'

'I warned you that Martin-Roget was not the man he pretended to be,' said Blakeney gently, 'I warned you against him. But I too failed to suspect the duc de Kernogan. We are Britishers, you and I, my dear Tony,' he added with a quaint little laugh, 'our minds will never be quite equal to the tortuous ways of these Latin races. But we are not going to waste time now talking about the past. We have got to find your wife before those brutes have time to wreak their devilries against her.'

'On the high seas...on the way to Holland...thence to Coblentz...' murmured Tony, 'I have not yet shown you the duc's letter to me.'

He drew from his pocket the crumpled, damp piece of paper on which the ink had run into patches and blotches, and which had become almost undecipherable now. Sir Percy took it from him and read it through:

'The duc de Kernogan and Lady Anthony Dewhurst are not on their way to Holland and to Coblentz,' he said quietly as he handed the letter back to Lord Tony.

'Not on their way to Holland?' queried the young man with a puzzled frown. 'What do you mean?'

Blakeney drew his chair closer to his friend: a marvellous and subtle change had suddenly taken place in his individuality. Only a few moments ago he was the polished, elegant man of the world, then the kindly and understanding friend – self-contained, reserved, with a perfect manner redolent of sympathy and dignity. Suddenly all that was changed. His manner was still perfect and outwardly calm, his gestures scarce, his speech deliberate, but the compelling power of the leader – which is the birthright of such men – glowed and sparkled now in his deep-set eyes: the spirit of adventure and reckless daring was awake – insistent and rampant – and subtle effluvia of enthusiasm and audacity emanated from his entire personality.

Sir Percy Blakeney had sunk his individuality in that of the Scarlet Pimpernel.

'I mean,' he said, returning his friend's anxious look with one that was inspiring in its unshakeable confidence, 'I mean that on Monday last, the night before your wedding – when I urged you to obtain Yvonne de Kernogan's consent to an immediate marriage – I had followed Martin-Roget to a place called 'The Bottom Inn' on Goblin Combe – a place well known to every smuggler in the county.'

'You, Percy!' exclaimed Tony in amazement.

'Yes, I,' laughed the other lightly. 'Why not? I had had my suspicions of him for some time. As luck would have it he started off on the Monday afternoon by hired coach to Chelwood. I followed. From Chelwood he wanted to go on to Redhill: but the roads were axle deep in mud, and evening was gathering in very fast. Nobody would take him. He wanted a horse and a guide. I was on the spot – as disreputable a bar-loafer as you ever saw in your life. I offered to take him. He had no choice. He had to take me. No one else had offered. I took him to the Bottom Inn. There he met our esteemed friend M. Chauvelin...'

'Chauvelin!' cried Tony, suddenly roused from the dull apathy of his immeasurable grief, at sound of that name which recalled so many exciting adventures, such mad, wild, hair-breadth escapes. 'Chauvelin! What in the world is he doing here in England?'

'Brewing mischief, of course,' replied Blakeney dryly. 'In disgrace, discredited, a marked man – what you will – my friend M. Chauvelin has still an infinite capacity for mischief. Through the interstices of a badly fastened shutter I heard two blackguards devising infinite devilry. That is why, Tony,' he added, 'I urged an immediate marriage as the only real protection for Yvonne de Kernogan against those blackguards.'

'Would to God you had been more explicit!' exclaimed Tony with a bitter sigh.

'Would to God I had,' rejoined the other, 'but there was so little time, with licences and what not all to arrange for, and less than an hour to do it in. And would you have suspected the duc himself of such execrable duplicity even if you had known, as I did then, that the so-called Martin-Roget hath name Adet, and that he matures thoughts of deadly revenge against the duc de Kernogan and his daughter?'

'Martin-Roget? the banker – the exiled royalist who...'

'He may be a banker now...but he certainly is no royalist – he is the son of a peasant who was unjustly put to death four years ago by the duc de Kernogan.'

'Ye gods!'

'He came over to England plentifully supplied with money – I could not gather if the money is his or if it has been entrusted to him by the revolutionary government for purposes of spying and corruption – but he came to England in order to ingratiate himself with the duc de Kernogan and his daughter, and then to lure them back to France, for what purpose you may well imagine.'

'Good God, man…you can't mean…?'

'He has chartered a smuggler's craft – or rather Chauvelin has done it for him. Her name is the *Hollandia*, her master hath name Kuyper. She was to be in Portishead harbour on the last day of November: all her papers in order. Cargo of West India sugar, destination Amsterdam, consignee some Mynheer over there. But Martin-Roget, or whatever his name may be, and no doubt our friend Chauvelin too, were to be aboard her, and also M. le duc de Kernogan and his daughter. And the *Hollandia* is to put into Le Croisic for Nantes, whose revolutionary proconsul, that infamous Carrier, is of course Chauvelin's bosom friend.'

Sir Percy Blakeney finished speaking. Lord Tony had listened to him quietly and in silence: now he rose and turned resolutely to his friend. There was no longer any trace in him of that stunned apathy which had been the primary result of the terrible blow. His young face was still almost unrecognizable from the lines of grief and horror which marred its habitual fresh, boyish look. He looked twenty years older than he had done a few hours ago, but there was also in his whole attitude now the virility of more mature manhood, its determination and unswerving purpose.

'And what can I do now?' he asked simply, knowing that he could trust his friend and leader with what he held dearest in all the world. 'Without you, Blakeney, I am of course impotent and lost. I haven't the head to think. I haven't sufficient brains to pit against those cunning devils. But if you will help me…'

Then he checked himself abruptly, and the look of hopeless despair once more crept into his eyes.

'I am mad, Percy,' he said with a self-deprecating shrug of the shoulders, 'gone crazy with grief, I suppose, or I shouldn't talk of asking your help, of risking your life in my cause.'

'Tony, if you talk that rubbish, I shall be forced to punch your head,' retorted Blakeney with his light laugh. 'Why man,' he added gaily, 'can't you see that I am aching to have at my old friend Chauvelin again.'

And indeed the zest of adventure, the zest to fight, never dormant, was glowing with compelling vigour now in those lazy eyes of his which were resting with such kindliness upon his stricken friend. 'Go home, Tony!' he added, 'go, you rascal, and collect what things you want, while I send for Hastings and Ffoulkes, and see that four good horses are ready for us within the hour. Tonight we sleep at Portishead, Tony. The *Day Dream* is lying off there, ready to sail at any hour of the day or night. The *Hollandia* has twenty-four hours' start of us, alas! and we cannot overtake her now: but we'll be in Nantes ere those devils can do much mischief: and once in Nantes!... Why, Tony man! think of the glorious escapes we've had together, you and I! Think of the gay, mad rides across the north of France, with half-fainting women and swooning children across our saddlebows! Think of the day when we smuggled the de Tournais out of Calais harbour, the day we snatched Juliette Déroulède and her Paul out of the tumbril and tore across Paris with that howling mob at our heels! Think! think, Tony! of all the happiest, merriest moments of your life and they will seem dull and lifeless beside what is in store for you, when with your dear wife's arms clinging round your neck, we'll fly along the quays of Nantes on the road to liberty! Ah, Tony lad! were it not for the anxiety which I know is gnawing at your heart, I would count this one of the happiest hours of my happy life!'

He was so full of enthusiasm, so full of vitality, that life itself seemed to emanate from him and to communicate itself to the very atmosphere around. Hope lit up my lord Tony's wan face:

he believed in his friend as mediaeval ascetics believed in the saints whom they adored. Enthusiasm had crept into his veins, dull despair fell away from him like a mantle.

'God bless you, Percy,' he exclaimed as his firm and loyal hand grasped that of the leader whom he revered.

'Nay!' retorted Blakeney with sudden gravity. 'He hath done that already. Pray for His help today, lad, as you have never prayed before.'

7

Marguerite

Lord Tony had gone, and for the space of five minutes Sir Percy Blakeney stood in front of the hearth staring into the fire. Something lay before him, something had to be done now, which represented the heavy price that had to be paid for those mad and happy adventures, for that reckless daring, aye for that selfless supreme sacrifice which was as the very breath of life to the Scarlet Pimpernel.

And in the dancing flames he could see Marguerite's blue eyes, her ardent hair, her tender smile all pleading with him not to go. She had so much to give him – so much happiness, such an infinity of love, and he was all that she had in the world! It seemed to him as if he could feel her arms around him even now, as if he could hear her voice whispering appealingly: 'Do not go! Am I nothing to you that thoughts of others should triumph over my pleading? that the need of others should outweigh mine own most pressing need? I want you, Percy! aye! even I! You have done so much for others – it is my turn now.'

But even as in a kind of trance those words seemed to reach his strained senses, he knew that he must go, that he must tear himself away once more from the clinging embrace of her dear arms and shut his eyes to the tears which anon would fill her own. Destiny demanded that he should go. He had chosen his path in life himself, at first only in a spirit of wild recklessness, a mad tossing of his life into the scales of Fate. But now that same destiny which he had chosen had become his master: he no longer could draw back. What he had done once, twenty times, an hundred times, that he must do again, all the while that the weak and the defenceless called mutely to him from across the seas, all the while that innocent women suffered and orphaned children cried.

And today it was his friend, his comrade, who had come to him in his distress: the young wife whom he idolized was in the most dire peril that could possibly threaten any woman: she was at the mercy of a man who, driven by the passion of revenge, meant to show her no mercy, and the devil alone knew these days to what lengths of infamy a man so driven would go.

The minutes sped on. Blakeney's eyes grew hot and wearied from staring into the fire. He closed them for a moment and then quietly turned to go.

2

All those who knew Marguerite Blakeney these days marvelled if she was ever unhappy. Lady Ffoulkes, who was her most trusted friend, vowed that she was not. She had moments – days – sometimes weeks of intense anxiety, which amounted to acute agony. Whenever she saw her husband start on one of those expeditions to France wherein every minute, every hour, he risked his life and more in order to snatch yet another threatened victim from the awful clutches of those merciless Terrorists, she endured soul-torture such as few women could have withstood who had not her splendid courage and her boundless faith. But against such crushing sorrow she had to set off the happiness of those reunions with the man whom she loved so passionately – happiness which was so great, that it overrode and conquered the very memory of past anxieties.

Marguerite Blakeney suffered terribly at times – at others she was overwhelmingly happy – the measure of her life was made up of the bitter dregs of sorrow and the sparkling wine of joy! No! she was not altogether unhappy: and gradually that enthusiasm which irradiated from the whole personality of the valiant Scarlet Pimpernel, which dominated his every action, entered into Marguerite Blakeney's blood too. His vitality was so compelling, those impulses which carried him headlong into unknown dangers were so generous and were actuated by such pure selflessness, that the noble-hearted woman whose very soul was wrapped up in the idolized husband, allowed herself to ride by his side on the buoyant waves of his enthusiasm and of his desires: she smothered every expression of anxiety, she swallowed her tears, she learned to say the word 'Goodbye' and forgot the word 'Stay!'

3

It was half an hour after midday when Percy knocked at the door of her boudoir. She had just come in from a walk in the meadows round the town and along the bank of the river: the rain had overtaken her and she had come in very wet, but none the less exhilarated by the movement and the keen, damp, salt-laden air which came straight over the hills from the Channel. She had taken off her hat and her mantle and was laughing gaily with her maid who was shaking the wet out of a feather. She looked round at her husband when he entered, and with a quick gesture ordered the maid out of the room.

She had learned to read every line on Percy's face, every expression of his lazy, heavy-lidded eyes. She saw that he was dressed with more than his usual fastidiousness, but in dark clothes and travelling mantle. She knew, moreover, by that subtle instinct which had become a second nature and which warned her whenever he meant to go.

Nor did he announce his departure to her in so many words. As soon as the maid had gone, he took his beloved in his arms.

109

'They have stolen Tony's wife from him,' he said with that light, quaint laugh of his. 'I told you that the man Martin-Roget had planned some devilish mischief – well! he has succeeded so far, thanks to that unspeakable fool the duc de Kernogan.

He told her briefly the history of the past few days. 'Tony did not take my warning seriously enough,' he concluded with a sigh; 'he ought never to have allowed his wife out of his sight.'

Marguerite had not interrupted him while he spoke. At first she just lay in his arms, quiescent and listening, nerving herself by a supreme effort not to utter one sigh of misery or one word of appeal. Then, as her knees shook under her, she sank back into a chair by the hearth and he knelt beside her with his arms clasped tightly round her shoulders, his cheek pressed against hers. He had no need to tell her that duty and friendship called, that the call of honour was once again – as it so often has been in the world – louder than that of love.

She understood and she knew, and he, with that supersensitive instinct of his, understood the heroic effort which she made.

'Your love, dear heart,' he whispered, 'will draw me back safely home as it hath so often done before. You believe that, do you not?'

And she had the supreme courage to murmur: 'Yes!'

8

The Road to Portishead

It was not until Bath had very obviously been left behind that Yvonne de Kernogan – Lady Anthony Dewhurst – realized that she had been trapped.

During the first half-hour of the journey her father had lain back against the cushions of the carriage with eyes closed, his face pale and wan as if with great suffering. Yvonne, her mind a prey to the gravest anxiety sat beside him, holding his limp cold hand in hers. Once or twice she ventured on a timid question as to his health and he invariably murmured a feeble assurance that he felt well, only very tired and disinclined to talk. Anon she suggested – diffidently, for she did not mean to disturb him – that the driver did not appear to know his way into Bath, he had turned into a side road which she felt sure was not the right one. M. le duc then roused himself for a moment from his lethargy. He leaned forward and gazed out of the window.

'The man is quite right, Yvonne,' he said quietly, 'he knows his way. He brought me along this road yesterday. He gets into Bath by a slight détour but it is pleasanter driving.'

This reply satisfied her. She was a stranger in the land, and knew little or nothing of the environs of Bath. True, last Monday morning after the ceremony of her marriage she had driven out to Combwich, but dawn was only just breaking then, and she had lain for the most part – wearied and happy – in her young husband's arms. She had taken scant note of roads and signposts.

A few minutes later the coach came to a halt and Yvonne, looking through the window, saw a man who was muffled up to the chin and enveloped in a huge travelling cape, mount swiftly up beside the driver.

'Who is that man?' she queried sharply.

'Some friend of the coachman's, no doubt,' murmured her father in reply, 'to whom he is giving a lift as far as Bath.'

The barouche had moved on again.

Yvonne could not have told you why, but at her father's last words she had felt a sudden cold grip at her heart – the first since she started. It was neither fear nor yet suspicion, but a chill seemed to go right through her. She gazed anxiously through the window, and then looked at her father with eyes that challenged and that doubted. But M. le duc would not meet her gaze. He had once more closed his eyes and sat quite still, pale and haggard, like a man who is suffering acutely.

2

'Father we are going back to Bath, are we not ?'

The query came out trenchant and hard from her throat which now felt hoarse and choked. Her whole being was suddenly pervaded by a vast and nameless fear. Time had gone on, and there was no sign in the distance of the great city. M. de Kernogan made no reply, but he opened his eyes and a curious glance shot from them at the terror-stricken face of his daughter.

Then she knew – knew that she had been tricked and trapped – that her father had played a hideous and complicated role of hypocrisy and duplicity in order to take her away from the husband whom she idolized.

Fear and her love for the man of her choice gave her initiative and strength. Before M. de Kernogan could realize

what she was doing, before he could make a movement to stop
her, she had seized the handle of the carriage door, wrenched
the door open and jumped out into the road. She fell on her
face in the mud, but the next moment she picked herself up
again and started to run – down the road which the carriage had
just traversed, on and on as fast as she could go. She ran on
blindly, unreasoningly, impelled by a purely physical instinct to
escape, not thinking how childish, how futile such an attempt
was bound to be.

Already after the first few minutes of this swift career over
the muddy road, she heard quick, heavy footsteps behind her.
Her father could not run like that – the coachman could not
have thus left his horses – but still she could hear those
footsteps at a run – a quicker run than hers – and they were
gaining on her – every minute, every second. The next, she felt
two powerful arms suddenly seizing her by the shoulders. She
stumbled and would once more have fallen, but for those same
strong arms which held her close.

'Let me go! Let me go!' she cried, panting.

But she was held and could no longer move. She looked up
into the face of Martin-Roget, who without any hesitation or
compunction lifted her up as if she had been a bale of light
goods and carried her back toward the coach. She had forgotten
the man who had been picked up on the road awhile ago, and
had been sitting beside the coachman since.

He deposited her in the barouche beside her father, then
quietly closed the door and once more mounted to his seat on
the box, The carriage moved on again. M. de Kernogan was no
longer lethargic, he looked down on his daughter's inert form
beside him, and not one look of tenderness or compassion
softened the hard callousness of his face.

'Any resistance, my child,' he said coldly, 'will as you see be
useless as well as undignified. I deplore this necessary violence, but
I should be forced once more to requisition M. Martin-Roget's

help if you attempted such foolish tricks again. When you are a little more calm, we will talk openly together.'

For the moment she was lying back against the cushions of the carriage; her nerves having momentarily given way before this appalling catastrophe which had overtaken her and the hideous outrage to which she was being subjected by her own father. She was sobbing convulsively. But in the face of his abominable callousness, she made a great effort to regain her self-control. Her pride, her dignity came to the rescue. She had had time in those few seconds to realize that she was indeed more helpless than any bird in a fowler's net, and that only absolute calm and presence of mind could possibly save her now.

If indeed there was the slightest hope of salvation.

She drew herself up and resolutely dried her eyes and re-adjusted her hair and her hood and mantle.

'We can talk openly at once, sir,' she said coldly. 'I am ready to hear what explanation you can offer for this monstrous outrage.'

'I owe you no explanation, my child,' he retorted calmly. 'Presently when you are restored to your own sense of dignity and of self-respect you will remember that a lady of the house of Kernogan does not elope in the night with a stranger and a heretic like some kitchen-wench. Having so far forgotten herself my daughter must, alas! take the consequences, which I deplore, of her own sins and lack of honour.'

'And no doubt, father,' she retorted, stung to the quick by his insults, 'that you too will anon be restored to your own sense of self-respect and remember that hitherto no gentleman of the house of Kernogan has acted the part of a liar and of a hypocrite!'

'Silence!' he commanded sternly.

'Yes!' she reiterated wildly, 'it was the role of a liar and of a hypocrite that you played from the moment when you sat down to pen that letter full of protestations of affection and forgiveness, until like a veritable Judas you betrayed your own daughter with a kiss. Shame on you, father!' she cried. 'Shame!'

'Enough!' he said, as he seized her wrist so roughly that the cry of pain which involuntarily escaped her effectually checked the words in her mouth. 'You are mad, beside yourself, a thoughtless, senseless creature whom I shall have to coerce more effectually if you do not cease your ravings. Do not force me to have recourse once again to M. Martin-Roget's assistance to keep your undignified outbursts in check.'

The name of the man whom she had learned to hate and fear more than any other human being in the world was sufficient to restore to her that measure of self-control which had again threatened to leave her.

'Enough indeed,' she said more calmly; 'the brain that could devise and carry out such infamy in cold blood is not like to be influenced by a defenceless woman's tears. Will you at least tell me whither you are taking me?'

'We go to a place on the coast now,' he replied coldly, 'the outlandish name of which has escaped me. There we embark for Holland, from whence we shall join their Royal Highnesses at Coblentz. It is at Coblentz that your marriage with M. Martin-Roget will take place, and...'

'Stay, father,' she broke in, speaking quite as calmly as he did, 'ere you go any further. Understand me clearly, for I mean every word that I say. In the sight of God – if not in that of the laws of France – I am the wife of Lord Anthony Dewhurst. By everything that I hold most sacred and most dear I swear to you that I will never become Martin-Roget's wife. I would die first,' she added with burning but resolutely suppressed passion.

He shrugged his shoulders.

'Pshaw, my child,' he said quietly, 'many a time since the world began have women registered such solemn and sacred

115

vows, only to break them when force of circumstance and their own good sense made them ashamed of their own folly.'

'How little you know me, father,' was all that she said in reply.

3

Indeed, Yvonne de Kernogan – Yvonne Dewhurst as she was now in sight of God and men – had far too much innate dignity and self-respect to continue this discussion, seeing that in any case she was physically the weaker, and that she was absolutely helpless and defenceless in the hands of two men, one of whom – her own father – who should have been her protector, was leagued with her bitterest enemy against her.

That Martin-Roget was her enemy – aye and her father's too – she had absolutely no doubt. Some obscure yet keen instinct was working in her heart, urging her to mistrust him even more wholly than she had done before. Just now, when he laid ruthless hands on her and carried her, inert and half-swooning, back into the coach, and she lay with closed eyes, her very soul in revolt against this contact with him, against the feel of his arms around her, a vague memory surcharged with horror and with dread stirred within her brain: and over the vista of the past few years she looked back upon an evening in the autumn – a rough night with the wind from the Atlantic blowing across the lowlands of Poitou and soughing in the willow trees that bordered the Loire – she seemed to hear the tumultuous cries of enraged human creatures dominating the sound of the gale, she felt the crowd of evil-intentioned men around the closed carriage wherein she sat, calm and unafraid. Darkness then was all around her. She could not see. She could only hear and feel. And she heard the carriage door being wrenched open, and she felt the cold breath of the wind upon her cheek, and also the hot breath of a man in a passion of fury and of hate.

She had seen nothing then, and mercifully semi-unconsciousness had dulled her aching senses, but even now her soul shrunk with horror at the vague remembrance of that ghost-like form – the spirit of hate and of revenge – of its rough arms encircling her shoulders, its fingers under her chin – and then that awful, loathsome, contaminating kiss which she thought then would have smirched her for ever. It had taken all the pure, sweet kisses of a brave and loyal man whom she loved and revered, to make her forget that hideous, indelible stain: and in the arms of her dear milor she had forgotten that one terrible moment, when she had felt that the embrace of death must be more endurable than that of this unknown and hated man.

It was the memory of that awful night which had come back to her as in a flash while she lay passive and broken in Martin-Roget's arms. Of course for the moment she had no thought of connecting the rich banker from Brest, the enthusiastic royalist and *émigrè*, with one of those turbulent, uneducated peasant lads who had attacked her carriage that night: all that she was conscious of was that she was outraged by his presence, just as she had been outraged then, and that the contact of his hands of his arms, was absolutely unendurable.

To fight against the physical power which held her a helpless prisoner in the hands of the enemy was sheer impossibility. She knew that, and was too proud to make feeble and futile efforts which could only end in defeat and further humiliation. She felt hideously wretched and lonely – thoughts of her husband, who at this hour was still serenely unconscious of the terrible catastrophe which had befallen him, brought tears of acute misery to her eyes. What would he do when – tomorrow, perhaps – he realized that his bride had been stolen from him, that he had been fooled and duped as she had been too. What could he do when he knew?

She tried to solace her own soul-agony by thinking of his influential friends who, of course, would help him as soon as they knew. There was that mysterious and potent friend of

117

whom he spoke so little, who already had warned him of coming danger and urged on the secret marriage which should have proved a protection. There was Sir Percy Blakeney, of whom he spoke much, who was enormously rich, independent, the most intimate friend of the Regent himself. There was...

But what was the use of clinging even for one instant to those feeble cords of Hope's broken lyre. By the time her dear lord knew that she was gone, she would be on the high seas, far out of his reach.

And she had not even the solace of tears – heart-broken sobs rose in her throat, but she resolutely kept them back. Her father's cold, impassive face, the callous glitter in his eyes told her that every tear would be in vain, her most earnest appeal an object for his sneers.

4

As to how long the journey in the coach lasted after that Yvonne Dewhurst could not have said. It may have been a few hours, it may have been a cycle of years. She had been young – a happy bride, a dutiful daughter – when she left Combwich Hall. She was an old woman now, a supremely unhappy one, parted from the man she loved without hope of ever seeing him again in life, and feeling nothing but hatred and contempt for the father who had planned such infamy against her.

She offered no resistance whatever to any of her father's commands. After the first outburst of revolt and indignation she had not even spoken to him.

There was a halt somewhere on the way, when in the low-raftered room of a posting-inn, she had to sit at table with the two men who had compassed her misery. She was thirsty, feverish and weak: she drank some milk in silence. She felt ill physically as well as mentally, and the constant effort not to break down had helped to shatter her nerves. As she had stepped out of the barouche without a word, so she stepped into it again when it stood outside, ready with a fresh relay of horses to take her further, still further, away from the cosy little nest where even now her young husband was waiting longingly for her return. The people of the inn – a kindly-looking woman, a portly middle-aged man, one or two young ostlers and serving-maids were standing about in the yard when her father led her to the coach. For a moment the wild idea rushed to her mind to run to these people and demand their protection, to proclaim at the top of her voice the infamous act which was dragging her away from her husband and her home, and lead her a helpless prisoner to a fate that was infinitely worse than death. She even ran to the woman who looked so benevolent and so kind, she placed her small quivering hand on the other's rough toil-worn one and in hurried, appealing words begged for her help and the shelter of a home till she could communicate with her husband.

The woman listened with a look of kindly pity upon her homely face, she patted the small, trembling hand and stroked it gently, tears of compassion gathered in her eyes:

'Yes, yes, my dear,' she said soothingly, speaking as she would to a sick woman or to a child, 'I quite understand. I wouldna' fret if I was you. I would jess go quietly with your pore father: 'e knows what's best for you, that 'e do. You come 'long wi' me,' she added as she drew Yvonne's hand through her arm, 'I'll see ye're comfortable in the coach.'

Yvonne, bewildered, could not at first understand either the woman's sympathy or her obvious indifference to the pitiable tale, until – Oh! the shame of it! – she saw the two young serving-maids looking on her with equal pity expressed in their round eyes, and heard one of them whispering to the other: 'Pore lady! so zad ain't it? I'm that zorry for the pore father!'

And the girl with a significant gesture indicated her own forehead and glanced knowingly at her companion. Yvonne felt a hot flush rise to the very roots of her hair. So her father and Martin-Roget had thought of everything, and had taken every

119

precaution to cut the ground from under her feet. Wherever a halt was necessary, wherever the party might come in contact with the curious or the indifferent, it would be given out that the poor young lady was crazed, that she talked wildly, and had to be kept under restraint.

Yvonne as she turned away from that last faint glimmer of hope, encountered Martin-Roget's glance of triumph and saw the sneer which curled his full lips. Her father came up to her just then and took her over from the kindly hostess, with the ostentatious manner of one who has charge of a sick person, and must take every precaution for her welfare.

'Another loss of dignity, my child,' he said to her in French, so that none but Martin-Roget could catch what he said. 'I guessed that you would commit some indiscretion, you see, so M. Martin-Roget and myself warned all the people at the inn the moment we arrived. We told them that I was travelling with a sick daughter who had become crazed through the death of her lover, and believed herself – like most crazed persons do – to be persecuted and oppressed. You have seen the result. They pitied you. Even the serving-maids smiled. It would have been wiser to remain silent.'

Whereupon he handed her into the barouche with loving care, a crowd of sympathetic onlookers gazing with obvious compassion on the poor crazed lady and her sorely tried father.

After this episode Yvonne gave up the struggle.

No one but God could help her, if He chose to perform a miracle.

5

The rest of the journey was accomplished in silence. Yvonne gazed, unseeing, through the carriage window as the barouche rattled on the cobble-stones of the streets of Bristol. She marvelled at the number of people who went gaily by along the streets, unheeding, unknowing that the greatest depths of misery to which any human being could sink had been probed by the unfortunate young girl who wide-eyed, mute and broken-hearted gazed out upon the busy world without.

Portishead was reached just when the grey light of day turned to a gloomy twilight. Yvonne unresisting, insentient, went whither she was bidden to go. Better that, than to feel Martin-Roget's coercive grip on her arm, or to hear her father's curt words of command.

She walked along the pier and anon stepped into a boat, hardly knowing what she was doing the twilight was welcome to her, for it hid much from her view and her eyes – hot with unshed tears – ached for the restful gloom. She realized that the boat was being rowed along for some little way down the stream, that Frédérick, who had come she knew not how or whence, was in the boat too with some luggage which she recognized as being familiar that another woman was there whom she did not know, but who appeared to look after her comforts, wrapped a shawl closer round her knees and drew the hood of her mantle closer round her neck. But it was all like an ugly dream the voices of her father and of Martin-Roget, who were talking in monosyllables, the sound of the oars as they struck the water, or creaked in their rowlocks, came to her as from an ever-receding distance.

A couple of hours later she came back to complete consciousness. She was in a narrow place, which at first appeared to her like a cupboard: the atmosphere was both cold and stuffy and reeked of tar and of oil. She was lying on a hard bed with her mantle and a shawl wrapped round her. It was very dark save where the feeble glimmer of a lamp threw a circle of light around. Above her head there was a constant and heavy tramping of feet, and the sound of incessant and varied creakings and groanings of wood, cordage and metal filled the night air with their weird and dismal sounds. A slow feeling of movement coupled with a gentle oscillation confirmed the unfortunate girl's first waking impression that she was on board a ship. How she had got there she did not know. She must ultimately have fainted in the small boat and been carried aboard. She raised herself slightly on her elbow and peered round her into the dark corners of the cabin: opposite to her upon a bench, also wrapped up in shawl and mantle, lay the woman who had been in attendance on her in the boat.

The woman's heavy breathing indicated that she was fast asleep.

Loneliness! Misery! Desolation encompassed the happy bride of yesterday. With a moan of exquisite soul-agony she fell back against the hard cushions, and for the first time this day a convulsive flow of tears eased the super-acuteness of her misery.

9

The Coast of France

The whole of that wretched mournful day Yvonne Dewhurst spent upon the deck of the ship which was bearing her away every hour, every minute, further and still further from home and happiness. She seldom spoke: she ate and drank when food was brought to her: she was conscious neither of cold nor of wet, of well-being or ill. She sat upon a pile of cordages in the stern of the ship leaning against the taff-rail and in imagination seeing the coast of England fade into illimitable space.

Part of the time it rained, and then she sat huddled up in the shawls and tarpaulins which the woman placed about her: then, when the sun came out, she still sat huddled up, closing her eyes against the glare.

When daylight faded into dusk, and then twilight into night she gazed into nothingness as she had gazed on water and sky before, thinking, thinking, thinking! This could not be the end – it could not. So much happiness, such pure love, such perfect companionship as she had had with the young husband whom she idolized could not all be wrenched from her like that, without previous foreboding and without some warning from Fate. This miserable, sordid, wretched journey to an unknown land could not be the epilogue to the exquisite romance which had suddenly changed the dreary monotony of her life into one long, glowing dream of joy and of happiness! This could not be the end!

And gazing into the immensity of the far horizon she thought and thought and racked her memory for every word, every look which she had had from her dear milor. And upon the grey background of sea and sky she seemed to perceive the vague and dim outline of that mysterious friend – the man who knew everything – who foresaw everything, even and above all the dangers that threatened those whom he loved. He had foreseen this awful danger too! Oh! if only milor and she herself had realized its full extent! But now surely! surely! he would help, he would know what to do. Milor was wont to speak of him as being omniscient and having marvellous powers.

Once or twice during the day M. le duc de Kernogan came to sit beside his daughter and tried to speak a few words of comfort and of sympathy. Of a truth – here on the open sea – far both from home and kindred and from the new friends he had found in hospitable England – his heart smote him for all the wrong he had done to his only child. He dared not think of the gentle and patient wife who lay at rest in the churchyard of Kernogan, for he feared that with his thoughts he would conjure up her pale, avenging ghost who would demand an account of what he had done with her child.

Cold and exposure – the discomfort of the long sea-journey in this rough, trading ship had somewhat damped M. de Kernogan's pride and obstinacy: his loyalty to the cause of his King had paled before the demands of a father's duty toward his helpless daughter.

2

It was close on six o'clock and the night, after the turbulent and capricious alternations of rain and sunshine, promised to be beautifully clear, though very cold. The pale crescent of the moon had just emerged from behind the thick veil of cloud and mist which still hung threateningly upon the horizon: a fitful sheen of silver danced upon the waves.

M. le duc stood beside his daughter. He had inquired after her health and well-being and received her monosyllabic reply with an impatient sigh. M. Martin-Roget was pacing up and down the deck with restless and vigorous strides: he had just gone by and made a loud and cheery comment on the weather and the beauty of the night.

Could Yvonne Dewhurst have seen her father's face now, or had she cared to study it, she would have perceived that he was gazing out to sea in the direction to which the schooner was heading with an intent look of puzzlement, and that there was a deep furrow between his brows. Half an hour went by and he still stood there, silent and absorbed: then suddenly a curious exclamation escaped his lips: he stooped and seized his daughter by the wrist.

'Yvonne!' he said excitedly, 'tell me! am I dreaming, or am I crazed?'

'What is it?' she asked coldly.

'Out there! Look! Just tell me what you see?' He appeared so excited and his pressure on her wrist was so insistent that she dragged herself to her feet and looked out to sea in the direction to which he was pointing.

'Tell me what you see,' he reiterated with ever-growing excitement, and she felt that the hand which held her wrist trembled violently.

'The light from a lighthouse, I think,' she said.

'And besides that?'

'Another light – a much smaller one – considerably higher up. It must be perched up on some cliffs.'

'Anything else?'

'Yes. There are lights dotted about here and there. Some village on the coast.'

'On the coast?' he murmured hoarsely, 'and we are heading towards it.'

'So it appears,' she said indifferently. What cared she to what shore she was being taken: every land save England was exile to her now.

Just at this moment M. Martin-Roget in his restless wanderings once more passed by.

'M. Martin-Roget!' called the duc.

And vaguely Yvonne wondered why his voice trembled so.

'At your service, M. le duc,' replied the other as he came to a halt, and then stood with legs wide apart firmly planted upon the deck, his hands buried in the pockets of his heavy mantle, his head thrown back, as if defiantly, his whole attitude that of a master condescending to talk with slaves.

'What are those lights over there, ahead of us?' asked M. le duc quietly.

'The lighthouse of Le Croisic, M. le duc,' replied Martin-Roget dryly, 'and of the guard-house above and the harbour below. All at your service,' he added, with a sneer.

'Monsieur...' exclaimed the duc.

'Eh? what?' queried the other blandly.

'What does this mean?'

In the vague, dim light of the moon Yvonne could just distinguish the two men as they stood confronting one another. Martin-Roget, tall, massive, with arms now folded across his breast, shrugging his broad shoulders at the duc's impassioned query – and her father who suddenly appeared to have shrunk within himself, who raised one trembling hand to his forehead and with the other sought with pathetic entreaty the support of his daughter's arm.

'What does this mean?' he murmured again.

'Only,' replied Martin-Roget with a laugh, 'that we are close to the coast of France and that with this unpleasant but useful north-westerly wind we shall be in Nantes two hours before midnight.'

'In Nantes?' queried the duc vaguely, not understanding, speaking tonelessly like a somnambulist or a man in a trance. He was leaning heavily now on his daughter's arm, and she with that motherly instinct which is ever present in a good woman's heart even in the presence of her most cruel enemy, drew him tenderly towards her, gave him the support he needed, not quite understanding herself yet what it was that had befallen them both.

'Yes, in Nantes, M. le duc,' reiterated Martin-Roget with a sneer.

'But 'twas to Holland we were going.'

'To Nantes, M. le duc,' retorted the other with a ringing note of triumph in his voice, 'to Nantes, from which you fled like a coward when you realized that the vengeance of an outraged people had at last overtaken you and your kind.'

'I do not understand,' stammered the duc, and mechanically now – instinctively – father and daughter clung to one another as if each was striving to protect the other from the raving fury of this madman. Never for a moment did they believe that he was sane. Excitement, they thought, had turned his brain: he was acting and speaking like one possessed.

'I dare say it would take far longer than the next four hours while we glide gently along the Loire, to make such as you understand that your arrogance and your pride are destined to be humbled at last and that you are now in the power of those men who awhile ago you did not deem worthy to lick your boots. I dare say,' he continued calmly, 'you think that I am crazed. Well! perhaps I am, but sane enough anyhow, M. le duc, to enjoy the full flavour of revenge.'

'Revenge?...what have we done?...what has my daughter done?...' stammered the duc incoherently. 'You swore you loved her...desired to make her your wife... I consented...she... Martin-Roget's harsh laugh broke in on his vague murmurings.

'And like an arrogant fool you fell into the trap,' he said with calm irony, 'and you were too blind to see in Martin-Roget, suitor for your daughter's hand, Pierre Adet, the son of the

127

victim of your execrable tyranny, the innocent man murdered at
your bidding.'

'Pierre Adet... I don't understand.'

' 'Tis but little meseems that you do understand, M. le duc,'
sneered the other. 'But turn your memory back, I pray you, to
the night four years ago when a few hot-headed peasant lads
planned to give you a fright in your castle of Kernogan...the
plan failed and Pierre Adet, the leader of that unfortunate band,
managed to fly the country, whilst you, like a crazed and blind
tyrant, administered punishment right and left for the fright
which you had had. Just think of it! those boors! those louts!
that swinish herd of human cattle had dared to raise a cry of
revolt against you! To death with them all! to death! Where is
Pierre Adet, the leader of those hogs? to him an exemplary
punishment must be meted! a deterrent against any other
attempt at revolt. Well, M. le duc, do you remember what
happened then? Pierre Adet, severely injured in the mélée, had
managed to crawl away into safety. While he lay betwixt life and
death, first in the presbytery of Vertou, then in various ditches
on his way to Paris, he knew nothing of what happened at
Nantes. When he returned to consciousness and to active life he
heard that his father, Jean Adet the miller, who was innocent of
any share in the revolt, had been hanged by order of M. le duc
de Kernogan.'

He paused awhile and a curious laugh – half-convulsive
and not unmixed with sobs – shook his broad shoulders.
Neither the duc nor Yvonne made any comment on what
they heard: the duc felt like a fly caught in a death-dealing
web. He was dazed with the horror of his position, dazed
above all with the rush of bitter remorse which had surged
up in his heart and mind, when he realized that it was his
own folly, his obstinacy – aye! and his heartlessness which
had brought this awful fate upon his daughter. And Yvonne
felt that whatever she might endure of misery and hopelessness

was nothing in comparison with what her father must feel with the addition of bitter self-reproach.

'Are you beginning to understand the position better now, M. le duc?' queried Martin-Roget after awhile.

The duc sank back nerveless upon the pile of cordages close by. Yvonne was leaning with her back against the taffrail, her two arms outstretched, the north-west wind blowing her soft brown hair about her face whilst her eyes sought through the gloom to read the lines of cruelty and hatred which must be distorting Martin-Roget's face now.

'And,' she said quietly after awhile, 'you have waited all these years, Monsieur, nursing thoughts of revenge and of hate against us. Ah! believe me,' she added earnestly, 'though God knows my heart is full of misery at this moment, and though I know that at your bidding death will so soon claim me and my father as his own, yet would I not change my wretchedness for yours.'

'And I, citizeness,' he said roughly, addressing her for the first time in the manner prescribed by the revolutionary government, 'would not change places with any king or other tyrant on earth. Yes,' he added as he came a step or two closer to her, 'I have waited all these years. For four years I have thought and striven and planned, planned to be even with your father and with you one day. You had fled the country – like cowards, bah! – ready to lend your arms to the foreigner against your own country in order to re-establish a tyrant upon the throne whom the whole of the people of France loathed and detested. You had fled, but soon I learned whither you had gone. Then I set to work to gain access to you... I learned English... I too went to England...under an assumed name...with the necessary introductions so as to gain a footing in the circles in which you moved. I won your father's condescension – almost his friendship!... The rich banker from Brest should be fleeced in order to provide funds for the armies that were to devastate France – and the rich banker of Brest refused to be fleeced unless he was lured by the promise of Mlle. de Kernogan's hand in marriage.'

'You need not, Monsieur,' rejoined Yvonne coldly, while Martin-Roget paused in order to draw breath, 'you need not, believe me, take the trouble to recount all the machinations which you carried through in order to gain your ends. Enough that my father was so foolish as to trust you, and that we are now completely in your power, but...'

'There is no "but," ' he broke in gruffly, 'you are in my power and will be made to learn the law of the talion which demands an eye for an eye, a life for a life: that is the law which the people are applying to that herd of aristos who were arrogant tyrants once and are shrinking, cowering slaves now. Oh! you were very proud that night, Mademoiselle Yvonne de Kernogan, when a few peasant lads told you some home truths while you sat disdainful and callous in your carriage, but there is one fact that you can never efface from your memory, strive how you may, and that is that for a few minutes I held you in my arms and that I kissed you, my fine lady, aye! kissed you like I would any pert kitchen-wench, even I, Pierre Adet, the miller's son.'

He drew nearer and nearer to her as he spoke; she, leaning against the taffrail, could not retreat any further from him. He laughed.

'If you fall over into the water, I shall not complain,' he said, 'it will save our proconsul the trouble, and the guillotine some work. But you need not fear. I am not trying to kiss you again. You are nothing to me, you and your father, less than nothing. Your death in misery and wretchedness is all I want, whether you find a dishonoured grave in the Loire or by suicide I care less than nothing. But let me tell you this,' he added, and his voice came now like a hissing sound through his set teeth, 'that there is no intention on my part to make glorious martyrs of you both. I dare say you have heard some pretty stories over in England of aristos climbing the steps of the guillotine with an ecstatic look of martyrdom upon their face: and tales of the

tumbrils of Paris laden with men and women going to their
death and shouting "God save the King" all the way. That is not
the sort of paltry revenge which would satisfy me. My father
was hanged by yours as a malefactor – hanged, I say, like a
common thief! he, a man who had never wronged a single soul
in the whole course of his life, who had been an example of fine
living, of hard work, of noble courage through many adversities.
My mother was left a widow – not the honoured widow of
an honourable man – but a pariah, the relict of a malefactor
who had died of the hangman's rope – my sister was left an
orphan – dishonoured – without hope of gaining the love of a
respectable man. All that I and my family owe to ci-devant M.
le duc de Kernogan, and therefore I tell you, that both he and
his daughter shall not die like martyrs but like malefactors too
– shamed – dishonoured – loathed and execrated even by their
own kindred! Take note of that, M. le duc de Kernogan! You
have sown shame, shame shall you reap! and the name of which
you are so proud will be dragged in the mire until it has become
a by-word in the land for all that is despicable and base.'

Perhaps at no time of his life had Martin-Roget, erstwhile
Pierre Adet, spoken with such an intensity of passion, even
though he was at all times turbulent and a ready prey to his
own emotions. But all that he had kept hidden in the inmost
recesses of his heart, ever since as a young stripling he had
chafed at the social conditions of his country, now welled forth
in that wild harangue. For the first time in his life he felt that
he was really master of those who had once despised and
oppressed him. He held them and was the arbiter of their fate.
The sense of possession and of power had gone to his head like
wine: he was intoxicated with his own feeling of triumphant
revenge, and this impassioned rhetoric flowed from his mouth
like the insentient babble of a drunken man.

The duc de Kernogan, sitting on the coil of cordages with his
elbows on his knees and his head buried in his hands, had
no thought of breaking in on the other man's ravings. The

bitterness of remorse paralyzed his thinking faculties. Martin-Roget's savage words struck upon his senses like blows from a sledge-hammer. He knew that nothing but his own folly was the cause of Yvonne's and his own misfortune. Yvonne had been safe from all evil fortune under the protection of her fine young English husband; he – the father who should have been her chief protector – had dragged her by brute force away from that husband's care and had landed her...where?... A shudder like acute ague went through the unfortunate man's whole body as he thought of the future.

Nor did Yvonne Dewhurst attempt to make reply to her enemy's delirious talk. She would not give him even the paltry satisfaction of feeling that he had stung her into a retort. She did not fear him – she hated him too much for that – but like her father she had no illusions as to his power over them both. While he stormed and raved she kept her eyes steadily fixed upon him. She could only just barely distinguish him in the gloom, and he no doubt failed to see the expression of lofty indifference wherewith she contrived to regard him: but he felt her contempt, and but for the presence of the sailors on the deck he probably would have struck her.

As it was when, from sheer lack of breath, he had to pause, he gave one last look of hate on the huddled figure of the duc, and the proud, upstanding one of Yvonne, then with a laugh which sounded like that of a fiend – so cruel, so callous was it, he turned on his heel, and as he strode away towards the bow his tall figure was soon absorbed in the surrounding gloom.

3

The duc de Kernogan and his daughter saw little or nothing of Martin-Roget after that. For awhile longer they caught sight of him from time to time as he walked up and down the deck with ceaseless restlessness and in the company of another man, who was much shorter and slimmer than himself and whom they had not noticed hitherto. Martin-Roget talked most of the time in a loud and excited voice, the other appearing to listen to him with a certain air of deference. Whether the conversation between these two was actually intended for the ears of the two unfortunates, or whether it was merely chance which brought certain phrases to their ears when the two men passed closely by, it were impossible to say. Certain it is that from such chance phrases they gathered that the barque would not put into Nantes, as the navigation of the Loire was suspended for the nonce by order of Proconsul Carrier. He had need of the river for his awesome and nefarious deeds. Yvonne's ears were regaled with tales – told with loud ostentation – of the terrible *noyades*, the wholesale drowning of men, women and children, malefactors and traitors, so as to ease the burden of the guillotine.

After three bells it got so bitterly cold that Yvonne, fearing that her father would become seriously ill, suggested their going down to their stuffy cabins together. After all, even the foul and shut-up atmosphere of these close, airless cupboards was preferable to the propinquity of those two human fiends up on deck and the tales of horror and brutality which they loved to tell.

And for two hours after that, father and daughter sat in the narrow cell-like place, locked in each other's arms. She had everything to forgive, and he everything to atone for: but Yvonne suffered so acutely, her misery was so great that she found it in her heart to pity the father whose misery must have been even greater than hers. The supreme solace of bestowing love and forgiveness and of easing the racking paroxysms of remorse which brought the unfortunate man to the verge of dementia, warmed her heart towards him and brought surcease to her own sorrow.

133

BOOK TWO
Nantes, December, 1793

1

The Tiger's Lair

Nantes is in the grip of the tiger.

Representative Carrier – with powers as of a proconsul – has been sent down to stamp out the lingering remnants of the counter-revolution. La Vendée is temporarily subdued; the army of the royalists driven back across the Loire; but traitors still abound – this the National Convention in Paris hath decreed – there are traitors everywhere. They were not *all* massacred at Cholet and Savenay. Disbanded, yes! but not exterminated, and wolves must not be allowed to run loose, lest they band again, and try to devour the flocks.

Therefore extermination is the order of the day. Every traitor or would-be traitor – every son and daughter and father and mother of traitors must be destroyed ere they do more mischief. And Carrier – Carrier the coward who turned tail and bolted at Cholet – is sent to Nantes to carry on the work of destruction. Wolves and wolflings all! Let none survive. Give them fair trial, of course. As traitors they have deserved death – have they not taken up arms against the Republic and against the Will and the Reign of the People? But let a court of justice sit in Nantes town; let the whole nation know how traitors are dealt with: let the nation see that her rulers are both wise and just. Let wolves and wolflings be brought up for trial, and set up the guillotine on Place du Bouffay with four executioners appointed to do her work. There would be too much work for two, or even three. Let there be four – and let the work of extermination be complete.

And Carrier – with powers as of a proconsul – arrives in Nantes town and sets to work to organize his household. Civil and military – with pomp and circumstance – for the son of a small farmer, destined originally for the Church and for obscurity is now virtual autocrat in one of the great cities of France. He has power of life and death over thousands of citizens – under the direction of justice, of course! So now he has citizens of the bedchamber, and citizens of the household, he has a guard of honour and a company of citizens of the guard. And above all he has a crowd of spies around him – servants of the Committee of Public Safety so they are called – they style themselves "La Compagnie Marat" in honour of the great patriot who was foully murdered by a female wolfling.

So la Compagnie Marat is formed – they wear red bonnets on their heads – no stockings on their feet – short breeches to display their bare shins: their captain, Fleury, has access at all times to the person of the proconsul, to make report on the raids which his company effect at all hours of the day or night. Their powers are supreme too. In and out of houses – however private – up and down the streets – through shops, taverns and warehouses, along the quays and the yards – everywhere they go. Everywhere they have the right to go! to ferret and to spy, to listen, to search, to interrogate – the red-capped Company is paid for what it can find. Piece-work, what? Work for the guillotine!

And they it is who keep the guillotine busy. Too busy in fact. And the court of justice sitting in the Hôtel du Département is overworked too. Carrier gets impatient. Why waste the time of patriots by so much paraphernalia of justice? Wolves and wolflings can be exterminated so much more quickly, more easily than that. It only needs a stroke of genius, one stroke, and Carrier has it.

He invents the *Noyades*!

The Drownages we may call them!

They are so simple! An old flat-bottomed barge. The work of two or three ship's carpenters! Portholes below the water-line and made to open at a given moment. All so very, very simple. Then a journey downstream as far as Belle Isle or la Maréchale, and "sentence of deportation" executed without any trouble on a whole crowd of traitors – "vertical deportation" Carrier calls it facetiously and is mightily proud of his invention and of his witticism too.

The first attempt was highly successful. Ninety priests, and not one escaped. Think of the work it would have entailed on the guillotine – and on the friends of Carrier who sit in justice in the Hôtel du Département! Ninety heads! Bah! That old flat-bottomed barge is the most wonderful labour-saving machine.

After that the "Drownages" become the order of the day. The red-capped Company recruits victims for the hecatomb, and over Nantes Town there hangs a pall of unspeakable horror. The prisons are not vast enough to hold all the victims, so the huge entrepôt, the bonded warehouse on the quay, is converted: instead of chests of coffee it is now encumbered with human freight: into it pell-mell are thrown all those who are destined to assuage Carrier's passion for killing: ten thousand of them: men, women, and young children, counter-revolutionists, innocent tradesmen, thieves, aristocrats, criminals and women of evil fame – they are herded together like cattle, without straw whereon to lie, without water, without fire, with barely food enough to keep up the last attenuated thread of a miserable existence.

And when the warehouse gets over full, to the Loire with them! – a hundred or two at a time! Pestilence, dysentery decimates their numbers. Under pretence of hygienic require-ments two hundred are flung into the river on the 14th day of December. Two hundred – many of them women – crowds of children and a batch of parish priests.

Some there are among Carrier's colleagues – those up in Paris – who protest! Such wholesale butchery will not redound to the credit of any revolutionary government – it even savours of treachery – it is unpatriotic! There are the emissaries of the National Convention, deputed from Paris to supervise and control – they protest as much as they dare – but such men are swept off their feet by the torrent of Carrier's gluttony for blood. Carrier's mission is to "purge the political body of every evil that infests it." Vague and yet precise! He reckons that he has full powers and thinks he can flaunt those powers in the face of those sent to control him. He does it too for three whole months ere he in his turn meets his doom. But for the moment he is omnipotent. He has to make report every week to the Committee of Public Safety, and he sends brief, garbled versions of his doings. 'He is pacifying La Vendée! he is stamping out the remnants of the rebellion! he is purging the political body of every evil that infests it.' Anon he succeeds in getting the emissaries of the National Convention recalled. He is impatient of control. 'They are weak, pusillanimous, unpatriotic! He must have freedom to act for the best.'

After that he remains virtual dictator, with none but obsequious, terrified myrmidons around him: these are too weak to oppose him in any way. And the municipality dare not protest either – nor the district council – nor the departmental. They are merely sheep who watch others of their flock being sent to the slaughter.

After that from within his lair the man-tiger decides that it is a pity to waste good barges on the cattle: 'Fling them out!' he cries. 'Fling them out! Tie two and two together. Man and woman! criminal and aristo! the thief with the ci-devant duke's daughter! the ci-devant marquis with the slut from the streets! Fling them all out together into the Loire and pour a hail of grape shot above them until the last struggler has disappeared! Equality!' he cries, 'Equality for all! Fraternity! Unity in death!'

His friends call this new invention of his: 'Marriage Républicain!' and he is pleased with the *môt*.

And Republican marriages become the order of the day.

2

Nantes itself now is akin to a desert – a desert wherein the air is filled with weird sounds of cries and of moans, of furtive footsteps scurrying away into dark and secluded byways, of musketry and confused noises, of sorrow and of lamentations.

Nantes is a city of the dead – a city of sleepers. Only Carrier is awake – thinking and devising and planning shorter ways and swifter, for the extermination of traitors.

In the Hôtel de la Villestreux the tiger has built his lair: at the apex of the island of Feydeau, with the windows of the hotel facing straight down the Loire. From here there is a magnificent view downstream upon the quays which are now deserted and upon the once prosperous port of Nantes.

The staircase of the hotel which leads up to the apartments of the proconsul is crowded every day and all day with suppliants and with petitioners, with the citizens of the household and the members of the Compagnie Marat.

But no one has access to the person of the dictator. He stands aloof, apart, hidden from the eyes of the world, a mysterious personality whose word sends hundreds to their death, whose arbitrary will has reduced a once flourishing city to abject poverty and squalor. No tyrant has ever surrounded himself with a greater paraphernalia of pomp and circumstance – no aristo has ever dwelt in greater luxury: the spoils of churches and chateaux fill the Hôtel de la Villestreux from attic to cellar, gold and silver plate adorn his table, priceless works of art hang upon his walls, he lolls on couches and chairs which have been the resting-place of kings. The wholesale spoliation of the entire countryside has filled the demagogue's abode with all that is most sumptuous in the land.

And he himself is far more inaccessible than was le *Roi Soleil* in the days of his most towering arrogance, than were the Popes in the glorious days of mediaeval Rome. Jean-Baptiste Carrier, the son of a small farmer, the obscure deputy for Cantal in the National Convention, dwells in the Hôtel de la Villestreux as in a stronghold. No one is allowed near him save a few – a very few – intimates: his valet, two or three women, Fleury the commander of the Marats, and that strange and abominable youngster, Jacques Lalouët, about whom the chroniclers of that tragic epoch can tell us so little – a cynical young braggart, said to be a cousin of Robespierre and the son of a midwife of Nantes, beardless, handsome and vicious: the only human being – so we are told – who had any influence over the sinister proconsul: mere hanger-on of Carrier or spy of the National Convention, no one can say – a malignant personality which has remained an enigma and mystery to this hour.

None but these few are ever allowed now inside the inner sanctuary wherein dwells and schemes the dictator. Even Lamberty, Fouquet and the others of the staff are kept at arm's length. Martin-Roget, Chauvelin and other strangers are only allowed as far as the ante-room. The door of the inner chamber is left open and they hear the proconsul's voice and see his silhouette pass and repass in front of them, but that is all.

Fear of assassination – the inevitable destiny of the tyrant – haunts the man-tiger even within the fastnesses of his lair. Day and night a carriage with four horses stands in readiness on La Petite Hollande, the great, open, tree-bordered Place at the extreme end of the Isle Feydeau and on which give the windows of the Hôtel de la Villestreux. Day and night the carriage is ready – with coachman on the box and postilion in the saddle, who are relieved every two hours lest they get sleepy or slack – with luggage in the boot and provisions always kept fresh inside the coach; everything always ready lest something – a warning from a friend or a threat from an enemy, or merely a sudden access of unreasoning terror, the haunting memory of a bloody act – should decide the tyrant at a moment's notice to fly from the scenes of his brutalities.

3

Carrier in the small room which he has fitted up for himself as a sumptuous boudoir, paces up and down just like a wild beast in its cage: and he rubs his large bony hands together with the excitement engendered by his own cruelties, by the success of this wholesale butchery which he has invented and carried through.

There never was an uglier man than Carrier, with that long hatchet-face of his, those abnormally high cheek bones, that stiff, lanky hair, that drooping, flaccid mouth and protruding underlip. Nature seemed to have set herself the task of making the face a true mirror of the soul – the dark and hideous soul on which of a surety Satan had already set his stamp. But he is dressed with scrupulous care – not to say elegance – and with a display of jewellery the provenance of which is as unjustifiable as that of the works of art which fill his private sanctum in every nook and cranny.

In front of the tall window, heavy curtains of crimson damask are drawn closely together, in order to shut out the light of day: the room is in all but total darkness: for that is the proconsul's latest caprice: that no one shall see him save in semi-obscurity.

Captain Fleury has stumbled into the room, swearing lustily as he barks his shins against the angle of a priceless Louis XV bureau. He has to make report on the work done by the Compagnie Marat. Fifty-three priests from the department of Anjou who have refused to take the new oath of obedience to the government of the Republic. The red-capped Company who tracked them down and arrested them, vow that all these *calotins* have precious objects – money, jewellery, gold plate – concealed about their persons. What is to be done about these things? Are the *calotins* to be allowed to keep them or to dispose of them for their own profit?

Carrier is highly delighted. What a haul!

'Confiscate everything,' he cries, 'then ship the whole crowd of that pestilential rabble, and don't let me hear another word about them.'

Fleury goes. And that same night fifty-three priests are 'shipped' in accordance with the orders of the proconsul, and Carrier, still rubbing his large bony hands contentedly together, exclaims with glee:

'What a torrent, eh! What a torrent! What a revolution!'

And he sends a letter to Robespierre. And to the Committee of Public Safety he makes report:

'Public spirit in Nantes,' he writes, 'is magnificent: it has risen to the most sublime heights of revolutionary ideals.'

4

After the departure of Fleury, Carrier suddenly turned to a slender youth, who was standing close by the window, gazing out through the folds of the curtain on the fine vista of the Loire and the quays which stretched out before him.

'Introduce citizen Martin-Roget into the ante-room now, Lalouët,' he said loftily. 'I will hear what he has to say, and citizen Chauvelin may present himself at the same time.'

Young Lalouët lolled across the room, smothering a yawn.

'Why should you trouble about all that rabble?' he said roughly, 'it is nearly dinner-time and you know that the chef hates the soup to be kept waiting.'

'I shall not trouble about them very long,' replied Carrier, who had just started picking his teeth with a tiny gold tool. 'Open the door, boy, and let the two men come.'

Lalouët did as he was told. The door through which he passed he left wide open, he then crossed the ante-room to a further door, threw it open and called in a loud voice:

'Citizen Chauvelin! Citizen Martin-Roget!'

For all the world like the ceremonious audiences at Versailles in the days of the great Louis.

There was sound of eager whisperings, of shuffling of feet, of chairs dragged across the polished floor. Young Lalouët had already and quite unconcernedly turned his back on the two men who, at his call, had entered the room.

Two chairs were placed in front of the door which led to the private sanctuary – still wrapped in religious obscurity – where Carrier sat enthroned. The youth curtly pointed to the two chairs, then went back to the inner room. The two men advanced. The full light of midday fell upon them from the tall window on their right – the pale, grey, colourless light of December. They bowed slightly in the direction of the audience chamber where the vague silhouette of the proconsul was alone visible.

The whole thing was a farce. Martin-Roget held his lips tightly closed together lest a curse or a sneer escaped them. Chauvelin's face was impenetrable – but it is worthy of note that just one year later when the half-demented tyrant was in his turn brought before the bar of the Convention and sentenced to the guillotine, it was citizen Chauvelin's testimony which weighed most heavily against him.

There was silence for a time: Martin-Roget and Chauvelin were waiting for the dictator's word. He sat at his desk with the scanty light, which filtrated between the curtains, immediately behind him, his ungainly form with the high shoulders and mop-like, shaggy hair half swallowed up by the surrounding gloom. He was deliberately keeping the other two men waiting and busied himself with turning over desultorily the papers and writing tools upon his desk, in the intervals of picking at his teeth and muttering to himself all the time as was his wont. Young Lalouët had resumed his post beside the curtained window and he was giving sundry signs of his growing impatience.

At last Carrier spoke:

'And now, citizen Martin-Roget,' he said in tones of that lofty condescension which he loved to affect, 'I am prepared to hear what you have to tell me with regard to the cattle which you brought into our city the other day. Where are the aristos now? and why have they not been handed over to Commandant Fleury?'

'The girl,' replied Martin-Roget, who had much ado to keep his vehement temper in check, and who chose for the moment to ignore the second of Carrier's peremptory queries, 'the girl is in lodgings in the Carrefour de la Poissonnerie. The house is kept by my sister, whose lover was hanged four years ago by the ci-devant duc de Kernogan for trapping two pigeons. A dozen or so lads from our old village – men who worked with my father and others who were my friends – lodge in my sister's house. They keep a watchful eye over the wench for the sake of the past, for my sake and for the sake of my sister Louise. The ci-devant Kernogan woman is well-guarded. I am satisfied as to that.'

'And where is the ci-devant duc?'

'In the house next door – a tavern at the sign of the Rat Mort – a place which is none too reputable, but the landlord – Lemoine – is a good patriot and he is keeping a close eye on the aristo for me.'

'And now will you tell me, citizen,' rejoined Carrier with that unctuous suavity which always veiled a threat, 'will you tell me how it comes that you are keeping a couple of traitors alive all this while at the country's expense?'

'At mine,' broke in Martin-Roget curtly.

'At the country's expense,' reiterated the proconsul inflexibly. 'Bread is scarce in Nantes. What traitors eat is stolen from good patriots. If you can afford to fill two mouths at your expense, I can supply you with some that have never done aught but proclaim their adherence to the Republic. You have had those two aristos inside the city nearly a week and – '

'Only three days,' interposed Martin-Roget, 'and you must have patience with me, citizen Carrier. Remember I have done well by you, by bringing such high game to your bag – '

'Your high game will be no use to me,' retorted the other with a harsh laugh, 'if I am not to have the cooking of it. You have talked of disgrace for the rabble and of your own desire for vengeance over them, but – '

'Wait, citizen,' broke in Martin-Roget firmly, 'let us understand one another. Before I embarked on this business you gave me your promise that no one – not even you – would interfere between me and my booty.'

'And no one has done so hitherto to my knowledge, citizen,' rejoined Carrier blandly. 'The Kernogan rabble has been yours to do with what you like – er – so far,' he added significantly. 'I said that I would not interfere and I have not done so up to now, even though the pestilential crowd stinks in the nostrils of every good patriot in Nantes. But I don't deny that it was a bargain that you should have a free hand with them...for a time, and Jean-Baptiste Carrier has never yet gone back on a given word.'

Martin-Roget made no comment on this peroration. He shrugged his broad shoulders and suddenly fell to contemplating the distant landscape. He had turned his head away in order to hide the sneer which curled his lips at the recollection of that 'bargain' struck with the imperious proconsul. It was a matter of five thousand francs which had passed from one pocket to the other and had bound Carrier down to a definite promise.

After a brief while Carrier resumed: 'At the same time,' he said, 'my promise was conditional, remember. I want that cattle out of Nantes – I want the bread they eat – I want the room they occupy. I can't allow you to play fast and loose with them indefinitely – a week is quite long enough – '

'Three days,' corrected Martin-Roget once more.

'Well! three days or eight,' rejoined the other roughly. 'Too long in any case. I must be rid of them out of this city or I shall

have all the spies of the Convention about mine ears. I am beset
with spies, citizen Martin-Roget, yes, even I – Jean-Baptiste
Carrier – the most selfless, the most devoted patriot the
Republic has ever known! Mine enemies up in Paris send spies
to dog my footsteps, to watch mine every action. They are ready
to pounce upon me at the slightest slip, to denounce me, to drag
me to their bar – they have already whetted the knife of the
guillotine which is to lay low the head of the finest patriot in
France – '

'Hold on! hold on, Jean-Baptiste my friend,' here broke in
young Lalouët with a sneer, 'we don't want protestations of
your patriotism just now. It is nearly dinner-time.'

Carrier had been carried away by his own eloquence. At
Lalouët's mocking words he pulled himself together: murmured:
'You young viper!' in tones of tigerish affection, and then turned
back to Martin-Roget and resumed more calmly:

'They'll be saying that I harbour aristos in Nantes if I keep
that Kernogan rabble here any longer. So I must be rid of them,
citizen Martin-Roget...say within the next four-and-twenty
hours...' He paused for a moment or two, then added drily:
'That is my last word, and you must see to it. What is it you do
want to do with them enfin?'

'I want their death,' replied Martin-Roget with a curse, and
he brought his heavy fist crashing down upon the arm of his
chair, 'but not a martyr's death, understand? I don't want the
pathetic figure of Yvonne Kernogan and her father to remain
as a picture of patient resignation in the hearts and minds of
every other aristo in the land. I don't want it to excite pity or
admiration. Death is nothing for such as they! they glory in it!
they are proud to die. The guillotine is their final triumph!
What I want for them is shame...degradation...a sensational
trial that will cover them with dishonour... I want their name
dragged in the mire – themselves an object of derision or of
loathing. I want articles in the *Moniteur* giving account of the
trial of the ci-devant duc de Kernogan and his daughter for

something that is ignominious and base. I want shame and mud slung at them – noise and beating of drums to proclaim their dishonour. Noise! noise! that will reach every corner of the land, aye that will reach Coblentz and Germany and England. It is that which they would resent – the shame of it – the disgrace to their name!'

'Tshaw!' exclaimed Carrier. 'Why don't you marry the wench, citizen Martin-Roget? That would be disgrace enough for her, I'll warrant,' he added with a loud laugh, enchanted at his witticism.

'I would tomorrow,' replied the other, who chose to ignore the coarse insult, 'if she would consent. That is why I have kept her at my sister's house these three days.'

'Bah! you have no need of a traitor's consent. My consent is sufficient... I'll give it if you like. The laws of the Republic permit, nay desire every good patriot to ally himself with an aristo, if he have a mind. And the Kernogan wench face to face with the guillotine – or worse – would surely prefer your embraces, citizen, what?'

A deep frown settled between Martin-Roget's glowering eyes, and gave his face a sinister expression.

'I wonder...' he muttered between his teeth.

'Then cease wondering, citizen,' retorted Carrier cynically, 'and try our Republican marriage on your Kernogans...thief linked to aristo, cut-throat to a proud wench...and then the Loire! Shame? Dishonour? Fal lal I say! Death, swift and sure and unerring. Nothing better has yet been invented for traitors.'

Martin-Roget shrugged his shoulders.

'You have never known,' he said quietly, 'what it is to hate.'

Carrier uttered an exclamation of impatience.

'Bah!' he said, 'that is all talk and nonsense. Theories, what? Citizen Chauvelin is a living example of the futility of all that rubbish. He too has an enemy it seems whom he hates more thoroughly than any good patriot has ever hated the enemies of the Republic. And hath this deadly hatred availed him, forsooth? He too wanted the disgrace and dishonour of that confounded Englishman whom I would simply have tossed into the Loire long ago, without further process. What is the result? The Englishman is over in England, safe and sound, making long noses at citizen Chauvelin, who has much ado to keep his own head out of the guillotine.'

Martin-Roget once more was silent: a look of sullen obstinacy had settled upon his face.

'You may be right, citizen Carrier,' he muttered after awhile.

'I am always right,' broke in Carrier curtly.

'Exactly...but I have your promise.'

'And I'll keep it, as I have said, for another four-and-twenty hours. Curse you for a mulish fool,' added the proconsul with a snarl, 'what in the d–l's name do you want to do? You have talked a vast deal of rubbish but you have told me nothing of your plans. Have you any...that are worthy of my attention?'

5

Martin-Roget rose from his seat and began pacing up and down the narrow room. His nerves were obviously on edge. It was difficult for any man – let alone one of his temperament and half-tutored disposition – to remain calm and deferential in face of the overbearance of this brutal Jack-in-office, Martin-Roget – himself an upstart – loathed the offensive self-assertion of that uneducated and bestial parvenu, who had become all-powerful through the sole might of his savagery, and it cost him a mighty effort to keep a violent retort from escaping his lips – a retort which probably would have cost him his head.

Chauvelin, on the other hand, appeared perfectly unconcerned. He possessed the art of outward placidity to a masterly degree. Throughout all this while he had taken no part in the discussion. He sat silent and all but motionless, facing the darkened room in front of him, as if he had done nothing else in all his life but interview great dictators who chose to keep their sacred persons in the dark. Only from time to time did his slender fingers drum a tattoo on the arm of his chair.

Carrier had resumed his interesting occupation of picking his teeth: his long, thin legs were stretched out before him; from beneath his flaccid lids he shot swift glances upwards, whenever Martin-Roget in his restless pacing crossed and recrossed in front of the open door. But anon, when the latter came to a halt under the lintel and with his foot almost across the threshold, young Lalouët was upon him in an instant, barring the way to the inner sanctum.

'Keep your distance, citizen,' he said drily, 'no one is allowed to enter here.'

Instinctively Martin-Roget had drawn back – suddenly awed despite himself by the air of mystery which hung over that darkened room, and by the dim silhouette of the sinister tyrant who at his approach had with equal suddenness cowered in his lair, drawing his limbs together and thrusting his head forward, low down over the desk, like a leopard crouching for a spring. But this spell of awe only lasted a few seconds, during which Martin-Roget's unsteady gaze encountered the half-mocking, wholly supercilious glance of young Lalouët.

The next, he had recovered his presence of mind. But this crowning act of audacious insolence broke the barrier of his self-restraint. An angry oath escaped him.

'Are we,' he exclaimed roughly, 'back in the days of Capet, the tyrant, and of Versailles, that patriots and citizens are treated like menials and obtrusive slaves? Pardieu, citizen Carrier, let me tell you this...'

'Pardieu, citizen Martin-Roget,' retorted Carrier with a growl like that of a savage dog, 'let me tell you that for less than two pins I'll throw you into the next barge that will float with open portholes down the Loire. Get out of my presence, you swine, ere I call Fleury to throw you out.'

Martin-Roget at the insult and the threat had become as pale as the linen at his throat: a cold sweat broke out upon his forehead and he passed his hand two or three times across his brow like a man dazed with a sudden and violent blow. His nerves, already overstrained and very much on edge, gave way completely. He staggered and would have measured his length across the floor, but that his hand encountered the back of his chair and he just contrived to sink into it, sick and faint, horror-struck and pallid.

A low cackle – something like a laugh – broke from Chauvelin's thin lips. As usual he had witnessed the scene quite unmoved.

'My friend Martin-Roget forgot himself for the moment, citizen Carrier,' he said suavely, 'already he is ready to make amends.'

Jacques Lalouët looked down for a moment with infinite scorn expressed in his fine eyes, on the presumptuous creature who had dared to defy the omnipotent representative of the People. Then he turned on his heel, but he did not go far this time: he remained standing close beside the door – the terrier guarding his master.

Carrier laughed loud and long. It was a hideous, strident laugh which had not a tone of merriment in it.

'Wake up, friend Martin-Roget,' he said harshly, 'I bear no malice: I am a good dog when I am treated the right way. But if anyone pulls my tail or treads on my paws, why! I snarl and growl of course. If the offence is repeated... I bite...remember that; and now let us resume our discourse, though I confess I am getting tired of your Kernogan rabble.'

While the great man spoke, Martin-Roget had succeeded in pulling himself together. His throat felt parched, his hands hot and moist: he was like a man who had been stumbling along a road in the dark and been suddenly pulled up on the edge of a yawning abyss into which he had all but fallen. With a few harsh words, with a monstrous insult Carrier had made him feel the gigantic power which could hurl any man from the heights of self-assurance and of ambition to the lowest depths of degradation: he had shown him the glint of steel upon the guillotine.

He had been hit as with a sledge-hammer – the blow hurt terribly, for it had knocked all his self-esteem into nothingness and pulverized his self-conceit. It had in one moment turned him into a humble and cringing sycophant.

'I had no mind,' he began tentatively, 'to give offence. My thoughts were bent on the Kernogans. They are a fine haul for us both, citizen Carrier, and I worked hard and long to obtain their confidence over in England and to induce them to come with me to Nantes.'

'No one denies that you have done well,' retorted Carrier gruffly and not yet wholly pacified. 'If the haul had not been worth having you would have received no help from me.'

'I have shown my gratitude for your help, citizen Carrier. I would show it again...more substantially if you desire...'

He spoke slowly and quite deferentially but the suggestion was obvious. Carrier looked up into his face: the light of measureless cupidity – the cupidity of the coarse-grained, enriched peasant – glittered in his pale eyes. It was by a great effort of will that he succeeded in concealing his eagerness beneath his habitual air of lofty condescension:

'Eh? What?' he queried airily.

'If another five thousand francs is of any use to you...'

'You seem passing rich, citizen Martin-Roget,' sneered Carrier.

'I have slaved and saved for four years. What I have amassed I will sacrifice for the completion of my revenge.'

'Well!' rejoined Carrier with an expressive wave of the hand, 'it certainly is not good for a pure-minded republican to own too much wealth. Have we not fought,' he continued with a grandiloquent gesture, 'for equality of fortune as well as of privileges...'

A sardonic laugh from young Lalouët broke in on the proconsul's eloquent effusion.

Carrier swore as was his wont, but after a second or two he began again more quietly:

'I will accept a further six thousand francs from you, citizen Martin-Roget, in the name of the Republic and all her needs. The Republic of France is up in arms against the entire world. She hath need of men, of arms, of...'

'Oh! cut that,' interposed young Lalouët roughly.

But the over-vain, high and mighty despot who was ready to lash out with unbridled fury against the slightest show of disrespect on the part of any other man, only laughed at the boy's impudence.

'Curse you, you young viper,' he said with that rude familiarity which he seemed to reserve for the boy, 'you presume too much on my forebearance. These children you know, citizen... Name of a dog!' he added roughly, 'we are wasting time! What was I saying...?'

'That you would take six thousand francs,' replied Martin-Roget curtly, 'in return for further help in the matter of the Kernogans.'

'Why, yes!' rejoined Carrier blandly, 'I was forgetting. But I'll show you what a good dog I am. I'll help you with those Kernogans...but you mistook my words, citizen: 'tis ten thousand francs you must pour into the coffers of the Republic, for her servants will have to be placed at the disposal of your private schemes of vengeance.'

'Ten thousand francs is a large sum,' said Martin-Roget. 'Let me hear what you will do for me for that.'

He had regained something of his former complacency. The man who buys – be it goods, consciences or services -- is always for the moment master of the man who sells. Carrier, despite his dictatorial ways, felt this disadvantage, no doubt, for his tone was more bland, his manner less curt. Only young Jacques Lalouët stood by – like a snarling terrier – still arrogant and still disdainful – the master of the situation – seeing that neither schemes of vengeance nor those of corruption had ruffled his self-assurance. He remained beside the door, ready to pounce on either of the two intruders if they showed the slightest sign of forgetting the majesty of the great proconsul.

6

'I told you just now, citizen Martin-Roget,' resumed Carrier after a brief pause, 'and I suppose you knew it already, that I am surrounded with spies.'

'Spies, citizen?' murmured Martin-Roget, somewhat taken aback by this sudden irrelevance. 'I didn't know... I imagine... Anyone in your position...'

'That's just it,' broke in Carrier roughly. 'My position is envied by those who are less competent, less patriotic than I am. Nantes is swarming with spies. Mine enemies in Paris are working against me. They want to undermine the confidence which the National Convention reposes in her accredited representative.'

'Preposterous,' ejaculated young Lalouët solemnly.

'Well!' rejoined Carrier with a savage oath, 'you would have thought that the Convention would be only too thankful to get a strong man at the head of affairs in this hotbed of treason and of rebellion. You would have thought that it was no one's affair to interfere with the manner in which I administer the powers that have been given me. I command in Nantes, what? Yet some busy-bodies up in Paris, some fools, seem to think that we are going too fast in Nantes. They have become weaklings over there since Marat has gone. It seems that they have heard rumours of our flat-bottomed barges and of our fine Republican marriages: apparently they disapprove of both. They don't realize that we have to purge an entire city of every kind of rabble – traitors as well as criminals. They don't understand my aspirations, my ideals,' he added loftily and with a wide, sweeping gesture of his arm, 'which is to make Nantes a model city, to free her from the taint of crime and of treachery, and...'

An impatient exclamation from young Lalouët once again broke in on Carrier's rhetoric, and Martin-Roget was able to slip in the query which had been hovering on his lips:

'And is this relevant, citizen Carrier,' he asked, 'to the subject which we have been discussing?'

'It is,' replied Carrier drily, 'as you will see in a moment. Learn then, that it has been my purpose for some time to silence mine enemies by sending to the National Convention a tangible reply to all the accusations which have been levelled against me. It is my purpose to explain to the Assembly my reasons for mine actions in Nantes, my Drownages, my Republican marriages, all the coercive measures which I have been forced to take in order to purge the city from all that is undesirable.'

'And think you, citizen Carrier,' queried Martin-Roget without the slightest trace of a sneer, 'that up in Paris they will understand your explanations?'

'Yes! they will – they must when they realize that everything that I have done has been necessitated by the exigencies of public safety.'

'They will be slow to realize that,' mused the other. 'The National Convention today is not what the Constitutional Assembly was in '92. It has become soft and sentimental. Many there are who will disapprove of your doings... Robespierre talks loftily of the dignity of the Republic...her impartial justice... The Girondins...'

Carrier interposed with a coarse imprecation. He suddenly leaned forward, sprawling right across the desk. A shaft of light from between the damask curtains caught the end of his nose and the tip of his protruding chin, distorting his face and making it seem grotesque as well as hideous in the dim light. He appeared excited and inflated with vanity. He always gloried in the atrocities which he committed, and though he professed to look with contempt on everyone of his colleagues, he was always glad of an opportunity to display his inventive powers before them, and to obtain their fulsome eulogy.

'I know well enough what they talk about in Paris,' he said, 'but I have an answer – a substantial, definite answer for all their rubbish. Dignity of the Republic? Bah! Impartial justice? 'Tis force, strength, Spartan vigour that we want...and I'll show them... Listen to my plan, citizen Martin-Roget, and see how it will work in with yours. My idea is to collect together all the most disreputable and notorious evil-doers of this city...there are plenty in the entrepôt at the present moment, and there are plenty more still at large in the streets of Nantes – thieves, malefactors, forgers of State bonds, assassins and women of evil fame...and to send them in a batch to Paris to appear before the Committee of Public Safety, whilst I will send to my colleagues there a letter couched in terms of gentle reproach: "See!" I shall say, "what I have to contend with in Nantes. See! the moral pestilence that infests the city. These evil-doers are but a few among the hundreds and thousands of whom I am vainly trying to purge this city which you have entrusted to my care!" They won't know how to deal with the rabble, he continued with his harsh strident laugh. 'They may send them to the guillotine wholesale or deport them to Cayenne, and they will have to give them some semblance of a trial in any case. But they will have to admit that my severe measures are justified, and in future, I imagine, they will leave me more severely alone.'

'If as you say,' urged Martin-Roget, 'the National Convention give your crowd a trial, you will have to produce some witnesses.'

'So I will,' retorted Carrier cynically. 'So I will. Have I not said that I will round up all the most noted evil-doers in the town. There are plenty of them I assure you. Lately, my Company Marat have not greatly troubled about them. After Savenay there was such a crowd of rebels to deal with, there was no room in our prisons for malefactors as well. But we can easily lay our hands on a couple of hundred or so, and members of the municipality or of the district council, or tradespeople of substance in the city will only be too glad to be rid of them, and will testify against those that were actually caught red-handed. Not one but has suffered from the pestilential rabble that has infested the streets at night, and lately I have been pestered with complaints of all these night-birds – men and women and...'

Suddenly he paused. He had caught Martin-Roget's feverish gaze fixed excitedly upon him. Whereupon he leaned back in his chair, threw his head back and broke into loud and immoderate laughter.

'By the devil and all his myrmidons, citizen!' he said, as soon as he had recovered his breath, 'meseems you have tumbled to my meaning as a pig into a heap of garbage. Is not ten thousand francs far too small a sum to pay for such a perfect realization of all your dreams? We'll send the Kernogan girl and her father to Paris with the herd, what?... I promise you that such filth and mud will be thrown on them and on their precious name that no one will care to bear it for centuries to come.'

Martin-Roget of a truth had much ado to control his own excitement. As the proconsul unfolded his infamous plan, he had at once seen as in a vision the realization of all his hopes. What more awful humiliation, what more dire disgrace could be devised for proud Kernogan and his daughter than being herded together with the vilest scum that could be gathered together among the flotsam and jetsam of the population of a seaport town. What more perfect retaliation could there be for the ignominious death of Jean Adet the miller?

Martin-Roget leaned forward in his chair. The hideous figure of Carrier was no longer hideous to him. He saw in that misshapen, gawky form the very embodiment of the god of vengeance, the wielder of the flail of retributive justice which was about to strike the guilty at last.

'You are right, citizen Carrier,' he said, and his voice was thick and hoarse with excitement. He rested his elbow on his knee and his chin in his hand. He hammered his nails against his teeth. 'That was exactly in my mind while you spoke.'

'I am always right,' retorted Carrier loftily. 'No one knows better than I do how to deal with traitors.'

'And how is the whole thing to be accomplished? The wench is in my sister's house at present...the father is in the Rat Mort...'

'And the Rat Mort is an excellent place... I know of none better. It is one of the worst-famed houses in the whole of Nantes...the meeting-place of all the vagabonds, the thieves and the cut-throats of the city.'

'Yes! I know that to my cost. My sister's house is next door to it. At night the street is not safe for decent females to be abroad: and though there is a platoon of Marats on guard at Le Bouffay close by, they do nothing to free the neighbourhood of that pest.'

'Bah!' retorted Carrier with cynical indifference, 'they have more important quarry to net. Rebels and traitors swarm in Nantes, what? Commandant Fleury has had no time hitherto to waste on mere cut-throats, although I had thoughts before now of razing the place to the ground. Citizen Lamberty has his lodgings on the other side and he does nothing but complain of the brawls that go on there o' nights. Sure it is that while a stone of the Rat Mort remains standing all the night-hawks of Nantes will congregate around it and brew mischief there which is no good to me and no good to the Republic.'

'Yes! I know all about the Rat Mort. I found a night's shelter there four years ago when...'

'When the ci-devant duc de Kernogan was busy hanging your father – the miller – for a crime which he never committed. Well then, citizen Martin-Roget,' continued Carrier with one of his hideous leers, 'since you know the Rat Mort so well what say you to your fair and stately Yvonne de Kernogan and her father being captured there in the company of the lowest scum of the population of Nantes?

'You mean...?' murmured Martin-Roget, who had become livid with excitement.

'I mean that my Marats have orders to raid some of the haunts of our Nantese cut-throats, and that they may as well begin tonight and with the Rat Mort. They will make a descent on the house and a thorough perquisition, and every person – man, woman and child – found on the premises will be arrested and sent with a batch of malefactors to Paris, there to be tried as felons and criminals and deported to Cayenne where they will, I trust, rot as convicts in that pestilential climate. Think you,' concluded the odious creature with a sneer, 'that when put face to face with the alternative, your Kernogan wench will still refuse to become the wife of a fine patriot like yourself?'

'I don't know,' murmured Martin-Roget. 'I... I...'

'But I do know,' broke in Carrier roughly, 'that ten thousand francs is far too little to pay for so brilliant a realization of all one's hopes. Ten thousand francs? 'Tis an hundred thousand you should give to show your gratitude.'

Martin-Roget rose and stretched his large, heavy figure to its full height. He was at great pains to conceal the utter contempt which he felt for the abominable wretch before whom he was forced to cringe.

'You shall have ten thousand francs, citizen Carrier,' he said slowly; 'it is all that I possess in the world now – the last remaining fragment of a sum of twenty-five thousand francs which I earned and scraped together for the past four years. You have had five thousand francs already. And you shall have the other ten. I do not grudge it. If twenty years of my life were any use to you, I would give you that, in exchange for the help you are giving me in what means far more than life to me.'

The proconsul laughed and shrugged his shoulders – of a truth he thought citizen Martin-Roget an awful fool.

'Very well then,' he said, 'we will call the matter settled. I confess that it amuses me, although remember that I have warned you. With all these aristos, I believe in the potency of my barges rather than in your elaborate schemes. Still! it shall never be said that Jean-Baptiste Carrier has left a friend in the lurch.'

'I am grateful for your help, citizen Carrier,' said Martin-Roget coldly. Then he added slowly, as if reviewing the situation in his own mind: 'Tonight, you say?'

'Yes. Tonight. My Marats under the command of citizen Fleury will make a descent upon the Rat Mort. Those shall be my orders. The place will be swept clean of every man, woman and child who is inside. If your two Kernogans are there...well!' he said with a cynical laugh and a shrug of his shoulders, 'they can be sent up to Paris with the rest of the herd.'

'The dinner bell has gone long ago,' here interposed young Lalouët drily, 'the soup will be stone-cold and the chef red-hot with anger.'

'You are right, citizen Lalouët,' said Carrier as he leaned back in his chair once more and stretched out his long legs at his ease. 'We have wasted far too much time already over the affairs of a couple of aristos, who ought to have been at the bottom of the Loire a week ago. The audience is ended,' he added airily, and he made a gesture of overweening condescension, for all the world like the one wherewith the *Grand Monarque* was wont to dismiss his courtiers.

Chauvelin rose too and quietly turned to the door. He had not spoken a word for the past half-hour, ever since in fact he had put in a conciliatory word on behalf of his impetuous colleague. Whether he had taken an active interest in the conversation or not it were impossible to say. But now, just as he was ready to go, and young Lalouët prepared to close the doors of the audience chamber, something seemed suddenly to occur to him and he called somewhat peremptorily to the young man.

'One moment, citizen,' he said.

161

'What is it now?' queried the youth insolently, and from his fine eyes there shot a glance of contempt on the meagre figure of the once powerful Terrorist.

'About the Kernogan wench,' continued Chauvelin. 'She will have to be conveyed some time before night to the tavern next door. There may be agencies at work on her behalf...'

'Agencies?' broke in the boy gruffly. 'What agencies?'

'Oh!' said Chauvelin vaguely, 'we all know that aristos have powerful friends these days. It will not be over safe to take the girl across after dark from one house to another...the alley is badly lighted: the wench will not go willingly. She might scream and create a disturbance and draw...er...those same unknown agencies to her rescue. I think a body of Marats should be told off to convey her to the Rat Mort...'

Young Lalouët shrugged his shoulders.

'That's your affair,' he said curtly, 'Eh, Carrier?' And he glanced over his shoulder at the proconsul, who at once assented.

Martin-Roget – struck by his colleague's argument – would have interposed, but Carrier broke in with one of his uncontrolled outbursts of fury.

'Ah ça,' he exclaimed, 'enough of this now. Citizen Lalouët is right and I have done enough for you already. If you want the Kernogan wench to be at the Rat Mort, you must see to getting her there yourself. She is next door, what? I won't have anything to do with it and I won't have my Marats implicated in the affair either. Name of a dog! have I not told you that I am beset with spies. It would of a truth be a climax if I was denounced as having dragged aristos to a house of ill-fame and then had them arrested there as malefactors! Now out with you! I have had enough of this! If your rabble is at the Rat Mort tonight, they shall be arrested with all the other cut-throats. That is my last word. The rest is your affair. Lalouët! the door!'

And without another word, and without listening to further protests from Martin-Roget or Chauvelin, Jacques Lalouët closed the doors of the audience chamber in their face.

7

Outside on the landing, Martin-Roget swore a violent, all comprehensive oath.

'To think that we are under the heel of that skunk!' he said.

'And that in the pursuit of our own ends we have need of his help!' added Chauvelin with a sigh.

'If it were not for that... And even now,' continued Martin-Roget moodily, 'I doubt what I can do. Yvonne de Kernogan will not follow me willingly either to the Rat Mort or elsewhere, and if I am not to have her conveyed by the guard...'

He paused and swore again. His companion's silence appeared to irritate him.

'What do you advise me to do, citizen Chauvelin?' he asked.

'For the moment,' replied Chauvelin imperturbably, 'I should advise you to join me in a walk along the quay as far as Le Bouffay. I have work to see to inside the building and the north-westerly wind is sure to be of good counsel.'

An angry retort hovered on Martin-Roget's lips, but after a second or two he succeeded in holding his irascible temper in check. He gave a quick sigh of impatience.

'Very well,' he said curtly. 'Let us to Le Bouffay by all means. I have much to think on, and as you say the north-westerly wind may blow away the cobwebs which for the nonce do o'ercloud my brain.'

And the two men wrapped their mantles closely round their shoulders, for the air was keen. Then they descended the staircase of the hotel and went out into the street.

2

Le Bouffay

In the centre of the Place the guillotine stood idle – the paint had worn off her sides – she looked weather-beaten and forlorn – stern and forbidding still, but in a kind of sullen loneliness, with the ugly stains of crimson on her, turned to rust and grime.

The Place itself was deserted, in strange contrast to the bustle and the movement which characterized it in the days when the death of men, women and children was a daily spectacle here for the crowd. Then a constant stream of traffic, of carts and of tumbrils, of soldiers and gaffers encumbered it in every corner, now a few tumble-down booths set up against the frontage of the grim edifice – once the stronghold of the Dukes of Brittany, now little else but a huge prison – a few vendors and still fewer purchasers of the scanty wares displayed under their ragged awnings, one or two idlers loafing against the mud-stained walls, one or two urchins playing in the gutters were the only signs of life. Martin-Roget with his colleague Chauvelin turned into the Place from the quay – they walked rapidly and kept their mantles closely wrapped under their chin, for the afternoon had turned bitterly cold. It was then close upon five o'clock – a dark, moonless, starless night had set in with only a suspicion of frost in the damp air; but a blustering north-westerly wind blowing down the river and tearing round the narrow streets and the open Place, caused passers-by to muffle themselves, shivering, yet tighter in their cloaks.

Martin-Roget was talking volubly and excitedly, his tall, broad figure towering above the slender form of his companion. From time to time he tossed his mantle aside with an impatient, febrile gesture and then paused in the middle of the Place, with one hand on the other man's shoulder, marking a point in his discourse or emphasizing his argument with short staccato sentences and brief, emphatic words. Chauvelin – placid and impenetrable as usual – listened much and talked little. He was ready to stand still or to walk along just as his colleague's mood demanded; in the darkness, and with the collar of a large mantle pulled tightly up to his ears, it was impossible to guess by any sign in his face what was going on in his mind.

They were a strange contrast these two men – temperamentally as well as physically – even though they had so much in common and were both the direct products of that same social upheaval which was shaking the archaic dominion of France to its very foundations. Martin-Roget, tall, broad-shouldered, bull-necked, the typical self-educated peasant, with square jaw and flat head, with wide bony hands and spatulated fingers: and Chauvelin – the aristocrat turned demagogue, thin and frail-looking, bland of manner and suave of speech, with delicate hands and pale, almost ascetic face.

The one represented all that was most brutish and sensual in this fight of one caste against the other, the thirst for the other's blood, the human beast that has been brought to bay through wrongs perpetrated against it by others and has turned upon its oppressors, lashing out right and left with blind and lustful fury at the crowd of tyrants that had kept him in subjection for so long. Whilst Chauvelin was the personification of the spiritual side of this bloody Revolution – the spirit of cool and calculating reprisals that would demand an eye for an eye and see that it got two. The idealist who dreams of the righteousness of his own cause and the destruction of its enemies, but who leaves to others the accomplishment of all the carnage and the bloodshed which his idealism has demanded, and which his reason has appraised as necessary for the triumph of which he dreams. Chauvelin was the man of thought and Martin-Roget the man of action. With the one, revenge and reprisals were selfish desires, the avenging of wrongs done to himself or to his caste, hatred for those who had injured him or his kindred. The other had no personal feelings of hatred: he had no personal wrongs to avenge: his enemies were the enemies of his party, the erstwhile tyrants who in the past had oppressed an entire people. Every man, woman or child who was not satisfied with the present Reign of Terror, who plotted or planned for its overthrow, who was not ready so see husband, father, wife or child sacrificed for the ultimate triumph of the Revolution was in Chauvelin's sight a noxious creature, fit only to be trodden under heel and ground into subjection or annihilation as a danger to the State.

Martin-Roget was the personification of sans-culottism, of rough manners and foul speech – he chafed against the conventions which forced him to wear decent clothes and boots on his feet – he would gladly have seen everyone go about the streets half-naked, unwashed, a living sign of that downward levelling of castes which he and his friends stood for, and for which they had fought and striven and committed every crime which human passions let loose could invent. Chauvelin, on the other hand, was one of those who wore fine linen and buckled shoes and whose hands were delicately washed and perfumed whilst they signed decrees which sent hundreds of women and children to a violent and cruel death.

The one trod in the paths of Danton: the other followed in the footsteps of Robespierre.

2

Together the two men mounted the outside staircase which leads up past the lodge of the concierge and through the clerk's office to the interior of the stronghold. Outside the monumental doors they had to wait a moment or two while the clerk examined their permits to enter.

'Will you come into my office with me?' asked Chauvelin of his companion; 'I have a word or two to add to my report for the Paris courier tonight. I won't be long.'

'You are still in touch with the Committee of Public Safety then?' asked Martin-Roget.

'Always,' replied the other curtly.

Martin-Roget threw a quick, suspicious glance on his companion. Darkness and the broad brim of his sugar-loaf hat effectually concealed even the outlines of Chauvelin's face, and Martin-Roget fell to musing over one or two things which Carrier had blurted out awhile ago. The whole of France was overrun with spies these days – everyone was under suspicion, everyone had to be on his guard. Every word was overheard, every glance seen, every sign noted.

What was this man Chauvelin doing here in Nantes? what reports did he send up to Paris by special courier? He, the miserable failure who had ceased to count was nevertheless in constant touch with that awful Committee of Public Safety which was wont to strike at all times and unexpectedly in the dark. Martin-Roget shivered beneath his mantle. For the first time since his schemes of vengeance had wholly absorbed his mind he regretted the freedom and safety which he had enjoyed in England, and he marvelled if the miserable game which he was playing would be worth the winning in the end. Nevertheless he had followed Chauvelin without comment. The man appeared to exercise a fascination over him – a kind of subtle power, which emanated from his small shrunken figure, from his pale keen eyes and his well-modulated, suave mode of speech.

3

The clerk had handed the two men their permits back. They were allowed to pass through the gates.

In the hall some half-dozen men were nominally on guard – nominally, because discipline was not over strict these days, and the men sat or lolled about the place; two of them were intent on a game of dominoes, another was watching them, whilst the other three were settling some sort of quarrel among themselves which necessitated vigorous and emphatic gestures and the copious use of expletives. One man, who appeared to be in command, divided his time impartially between the domino-players and those who were quarrelling.

The vast place was insufficiently lighted by a chandelier which hung from the ceiling and a couple of small oil-lamps placed in the circular niches in the wall opposite the front door.

No one took any notice of Martin-Roget or of Chauvelin as they crossed the hall, and presently the latter pushed open a door on the left of the main gates and held it open for his colleague to pass through.

'You are sure that I shall not be disturbing you?' queried Martin-Roget.

'Quite sure,' replied the other curtly. 'And there is something which I must say to you...where I know that I shall not be overheard.'

Then he followed Martin-Roget into the room and closed the door behind him. The room was scantily furnished with a square deal table in the centre, two or three chairs, a broken-down bureau leaning against one wall and an iron stove wherein a meagre fire sent a stream of malodorous smoke through sundry cracks in its chimney-pipe. From the ceiling there hung an oil-lamp the light of which was thrown down upon the table, by a large green shade made of cardboard.

Chauvelin drew a chair to the bureau and sat down; he pointed to another and Martin-Roget took a seat beside the table. He felt restless and excited – his nerves all on the jar: his colleague's calm, sardonic glance acted as a further irritant to his temper.

'What is it that you wished to say to me, citizen Chauvelin?' he asked at last.

'Just a word, citizen,' replied the other in his quiet urbane manner. 'I have accompanied you faithfully on your journey to England: I have placed my feeble powers at your disposal: awhile ago I stood between you and the proconsul's wrath. This, I think, has earned me the right of asking what you intend to do.'

'I don't know about the right,' retorted Martin-Roget gruffly, 'but I don't mind telling you. As you remarked awhile ago the north-west wind is wont to be of good counsel. I have thought the matter over whilst I walked with you along the quay and I have decided to act on Carrier's suggestion. Our eminent proconsul said just now that it was the duty of every true patriot to marry an aristo, an he be free and Chance puts a comely wench in his way. I mean,' he added with a cynical laugh, 'to act on that advice and marry Yvonne de Kernogan…if I can.'

'She has refused you up to now?'

'Yes…up to now.'

'You have threatened her – and her father?'

'Yes – both. Not only with death but with shame.'

'And still she refuses?'

'Apparently,' said Martin-Roget with ever-growing irritation.

'It is often difficult,' rejoined Chauvelin meditatively, 'to compel these aristos. They are obstinate…'

'Oh! don't forget that I am in a position now to bring additional pressure on the wench. That lout Carrier has splendid ideas – a brute, what? but clever and full of resource. That suggestion of his about the Rat Mort is splendid…'

'You mean to try and act on it?'

'Of course I do,' said Martin-Roget roughly. 'I am going over presently to my sister's house to see the Kernogan wench again, and to have another talk with her. Then if she still refuses, if she still chooses to scorn the honourable position which I offer her, I shall act on Carrier's suggestion. It will be at the Rat Mort tonight that she and I will have our final interview, and there when I dangle the prospect of Cayenne and the convict's brand before her, she may not prove so obdurate as she has been up to now.'

'H'm! That is as may be,' was Chauvelin's dry comment. 'Personally I am inclined to agree with Carrier. Death, swift and sure – the Loire or the guillotine – is the best that has yet been invented for traitors and aristos. But we won't discuss that again. I know your feelings in the matter and in a measure I respect them. But if you will allow me I would like to be present at your interview with the *soi-disant* Lady Anthony Dewhurst. I won't disturb you and I won't say a word…but there is something I would like to make sure of…'

'What is that?'

'Whether the wench has any hopes…' said Chauvelin slowly, 'whether she has received a message or has any premonition… whether in short she thinks that outside agencies are at work on her behalf.'

'Tshaw!' exclaimed Martin-Roget impatiently, 'you are still harping on that Scarlet Pimpernel idea.'

'I am,' retorted the other drily.

'As you please. But understand, citizen Chauvelin, that I will not allow you to interfere with my plans, whilst you go off on one of those wild-goose chases which have already twice brought you into disrepute.'

'I will not interfere with your plans, citizen,' rejoined Chauvelin with unwonted gentleness, 'but let me in my turn impress one thing upon you, and that is that unless you are as wary as the serpent, as cunning as the fox, all your precious plans will be upset by that interfering Englishman whom you choose to disregard.'

'What do you mean?'

'I mean that I know him – to my cost – and you do not. But you will, an I am not gravely mistaken, make acquaintance with him ere your great adventure with these Kernogan people is successfully at an end. Believe me, citizen Martin-Roget,' he added impressively, 'you would have been far wiser to accept Carrier's suggestion and let him fling that rabble into the Loire for you.'

'Pshaw! you are not childish enough to imagine, citizen Chauvelin, that your Englishman can spirit away that wench from under my sister's eyes? Do you know what my sister suffered at the hands of the Kernogans? Do you think that she is like to forget my father's ignominious death any more than I am? And she mourns a lover as well as a father – she mourns her youth, her happiness, the mother whom she worshipped. Think you a better gaoler could be found anywhere? And there are friends of mine – lads of our own village, men who hate the Kernogans as bitterly as I do myself – who are only too ready to lend Louise a hand in case of violence. And after that – suppose your magnificent Scarlet Pimpernel succeeded in hoodwinking my sister and in evading the vigilance of a score of determined village lads, who would sooner die one by one than see the Kernogan escape – suppose all that, I say, there would still be the guard at every city gate to challenge. No! no! it couldn't be done, citizen Chauvelin,' he added with a complacent laugh. 'Your Englishman would need the help of a legion of angels, what? to get the wench out of Nantes this time.'

Chauvelin made no comment on his colleague's impassioned harangue. Memory had taken him back to that one day in September in Boulogne when he too had set one prisoner to guard a precious hostage: it brought back to his mind a vision of a strangely picturesque figure as it appeared to him in the window-embrasure of the old castle-hall:[1] it brought back to his ears the echo of that quaint, irresponsible laughter, of that lazy, drawling speech, of all that had acted as an irritant on his nerves ere he found himself baffled, foiled, eating out his heart with vain reproach at his own folly.

'I see you are unconvinced, citizen Martin-Roget,' he said quietly, 'and I know that it is the fashion nowadays among young politicians to sneer at Chauvelin – the living embodiment of failure. But let me just add this. When you and I talked matters over together at the Bottom Inn, in the wilds of Somersetshire, I warned you that not only was your identity known to the man who calls himself the Scarlet Pimpernel, but also that he knew everyone of your plans with regard to the Kernogan wench and her father. You laughed at me then...do you remember?...you shrugged your shoulders and jeered at what you called my far-fetched ideas...just as you do now. Well! will you let me remind you of what happened within four-and-twenty hours of that warning which you chose to disregard?... Yvonne de Kernogan was married to Lord Anthony Dewhurst and...'

'I know all that, man,' broke in Martin-Roget impatiently. 'It was all a mere coincidence...the marriage must have been planned long before that...your Scarlet Pimpernel could not possibly have had anything to do with it.'

'Perhaps not,' rejoined Chauvelin drily. 'But mark what has happened since. Just now when we crossed the Place I saw in the distance a figure flitting past – the gorgeous figure of an exquisite who of a surety is a stranger in Nantes: and carried upon the wings of the north-westerly wind there came to me the sound of a voice which, of late, I have only heard in my dreams. On my soul, citizen Martin-Roget,' he added with earnest emphasis, 'I assure you that the Scarlet Pimpernel is in

1 This adventure is recorded in *The Elusive Pimpernel*.

Nantes at the present moment, that he is scheming, plotting, planning to rescue the Kernogan wench, out of your clutches. He will not leave her in your power, on this I would stake my life; she is the wife of one of his dearest friends: he will not abandon her, not while he keeps that resourceful head of his on his shoulders. Unless you are desperately careful he will outwit you; of that I am as convinced as that I am alive.'

'Bah! you have been dreaming citizen Chauvelin,' rejoined Martin-Roget with a laugh and shrugging his broad shoulders; 'your mysterious Englishman in Nantes? Why man! the navigation of the Loire has been totally prohibited these last fourteen days – no carriage, van or vehicle of any kind is allowed to enter the city – no man, woman or child to pass the barriers without special permit signed either by the proconsul himself or by Fleury the captain of the Marats. Why! even I, when I brought the Kernogans in overland from Le Croisic, I was detained two hours outside Nantes while my papers were sent in to Carrier for inspection. You know that, you were with me.'

'I know it,' replied Chauvelin drily, 'and yet...'

He paused, with one claw-like finger held erect to demand attention. The door of the small room in which they sat gave on the big hall where the half-dozen Marats were stationed, the single window at right angles to the door looked out upon the Place below. It was from there that suddenly there came the sound of a loud peal of laughter – quaint and merry – somewhat inane and affected, and at the sound Chauvelin's pale face took on the hue of ashes and even Martin-Roget felt a strange sensation of cold creeping down his spine.

For a few seconds the two men remained quite still, as if a spell had been cast over them through that light-hearted peal of rippling laughter. Then equally suddenly the younger man shook himself free of the spell; with a few long strides he was already at the door and out in the vast hall: Chauvelin following closely on his heels.

173

4

The clock in the tower of the edifice was even then striking five. The Marats in the hall looked up with lazy indifference at the two men who had come rushing out in such an abrupt and excited manner.

'Any stranger been through here?' queried Chauvelin peremptorily of the sergeant in command.

'No,' replied the latter curtly. 'How could they, without a permit?'

He shrugged his shoulders and the men resumed their game and their argument. Martin-Roget would have parleyed with them but Chauvelin had already crossed the hall and was striding past the clerk's office and the lodge of the concierge out toward the open. Martin-Roget, after a moment's hesitation, followed him.

The Place was wrapped in gloom. From the platform of the guillotine an oil-lamp hoisted on a post threw a small circle of light around. Small pieces of tallow candle, set in pewter sconces, glimmered feebly under the awnings of the booths, and there was a street-lamp affixed to the wall of the old château immediately below the parapet of the staircase, and others at the angles of the Rue de la Monnaye and the narrow Ruelle des Jacobins.

Chauvelin's keen eyes tried to pierce the surrounding darkness. He leaned over the parapet and peered into the remote angles of the building and round the booths below him.

There were a few people on the Place, some walking rapidly across from one end to the other, intent on business, others pausing in order to make purchases at the booths. Up and down the steps of the guillotine a group of street urchins were playing hide-and-seek. Round the angles of the narrow streets the vague figures of passers-by flitted to and fro, now easily discernible in the light of the street lanthorns, anon swallowed up again in the darkness beyond. Whilst immediately below the parapet two or three men of the Company Marat were lounging against the walls. Their red bonnets showed up clearly in the flickering light of the street lamps, as did their bare shins and the polished points of their sabots. But of an elegant, picturesque figure such as Chauvelin had described awhile ago there was not a sign.

Martin-Roget leaned over the parapet and called peremptorily:

'Hey there! citizens of the Company Marat!' One of the red-capped men looked up leisurely. 'Your desire, citizen?' he queried with insolent deliberation, for they were mighty men, this bodyguard of the great proconsul, his spies and tools in the awesome work of frightfulness which he carried on so ruthlessly.

'Is that you Paul Friche?' queried Martin-Roget in response.

'At your service, citizen,' came the glib reply, delivered not without mock deference.

'Then come up here. I wish to speak with you.'

'I can't leave my post, nor can my mates,' retorted the man who had answered to the name of Paul Friche. 'Come down, citizen, an you desire to speak with us.'

Martin-Roget swore lustily.

'The insolence of that rabble…' he murmured. 'Hush! I'll go,' interposed Chauvelin quickly. 'Do you know that man Friche? Is he trustworthy?'

'Yes, I know him. As for being trustworthy…added Martin-Roget with a shrug of the shoulders. 'He is a corporal in the Marats and high in favour with Commandant Fleury.'

Every second was of value, and Chauvelin was not the man to waste time in useless parleyings. He ran down the stairs at the foot of which one of the red-capped gentry deigned to speak with him.

'Have you seen any strangers across the Place just now?' he queried in a whisper.

'Yes,' replied the man Friche. 'Two!'

Then he spat upon the ground and added spitefully:

Aristos, what? In fine clothes – like yourself citizen…'

'Which way did they go?'

'Down the Ruelle des Jacobins.'

'When?'

'Two minutes ago.'

'Why did you not follow them?... Aristos and...'

'I would have followed,' retorted Paul Friche with studied insolence; ' 'twas you called me away from my duty.'

'After them then!' urged Chauvelin peremptorily. 'They cannot have gone far. They are English spies, and remember, citizen, that there's a reward for their apprehension.'

The man grunted an eager assent. The word 'reward' had fired his zeal. In a trice he had called to his mates and the three Marats soon sped across the Place and down the Ruelle des Jacobins where the surrounding gloom quickly swallowed them up.

Chauvelin watched them till they were out of sight, then he rejoined his colleague on the landing at the top of the stairs. For a second or two longer the click of the men's sabots upon the stones resounded on the adjoining streets and across the Place, and suddenly that same quaint, merry, somewhat inane laugh woke the echoes of the grim buildings around and caused many a head to turn inquiringly, marvelling who it could be that had the heart to laugh these days in the streets of Nantes.

5

Five minutes or so later the three Marats could vaguely be seen recrossing the Place and making their way back to Le Bouffay, where Martin-Roget and Chauvelin still stood on the top of the stairs excited and expectant. At sight of the men Chauvelin ran down the steps to meet them.

'Well?' he queried in an eager whisper.

'We never saw them,' replied Paul Friche gruffly, though we could hear them clearly enough, talking, laughing and walking very rapidly toward the quay. Then suddenly the earth or the river swallowed them up. We saw and heard nothing more.'

Chauvelin swore and a curious hissing sound escaped his thin lips.

'Don't be too disappointed, citizen,' added the man with a coarse laugh, 'my mate picked this up at the corner of the Ruelle, when, I fancy, we were pressing the aristos pretty closely.'

He held out a small bundle of papers tied together with a piece of red ribbon: the bundle had evidently rolled in the mud, for the papers were covered with grime. Chauvelin's thin, claw-like fingers had at once closed over them.

'You must give me back those papers, citizen,' said the man, 'they are my booty. I can only give them up to citizen-captain Fleury.'

'I'll give them to the citizen-captain myself,' retorted Chauvelin. 'For the moment you had best not leave your post of duty,' he added more peremptorily, seeing that the man made as he would follow him.

'I take orders from no one except...' protested the man gruffly.

'You will take them from me now,' broke in Chauvelin with a sudden assumption of command and authority which sat with weird strangeness upon his thin shrunken figure. 'Go back to your post at once, ere I lodge a complaint against you for neglect of duty, with the citizen proconsul.'

He turned on his heel and, without paying further heed to the man and his mutterings, he remounted the stone stairs.

'No success, I suppose?' queried Martin-Roget.

'None,' replied Chauvelin curtly.

He had the packet of papers tightly clasped in his hand. He was debating in his mind whether he would speak of them to his colleague or not.

'What did Friche say?' asked the latter impatiently. 'Oh! very little. He and his mates caught sight of the strangers and followed them as far as the quays. But they were walking very fast and suddenly the Marats lost their trace in the darkness. It seemed, according to Paul Friche, as if the earth or the night had swallowed them up.'

'And was that all?'

'Yes. That was all.'

'I wonder,' added Martin-Roget with a light laugh and a careless shrug of his wide shoulders, 'I wonder if you and I, citizen Chauvelin – and Paul Friche too for that matter – have been the victims of our nerves.'

'I wonder,' assented Chauvelin drily. And – quite quietly – he slipped the packet of papers in the pocket of his coat.

'Then we may as well adjourn. There is nothing else you wish to say to me about that enigmatic Scarlet Pimpernel of yours?'

'No – nothing.'

'And you still would like to hear what the Kernogan wench will say and see how she will look when I put my final proposal before her?'

'If you will allow me.'

'Then come,' said Martin-Roget. 'My sister's house is close by.'

3

The Fowlers

In order to reach the Carrefour de la Poissonnerie the two men had to skirt the whole edifice of Le Bouffay, walk a little along the quay and turn up the narrow alley opposite the bridge. They walked on in silence, each absorbed in his own thoughts.

The house occupied by the citizeness Adet lay back a little from the others in the street. It was one of an irregular row of mean, squalid, tumble-down houses, some of them little more than lean-to sheds built into the walls of Le Bouffay. Most of them had overhanging roofs which stretched out like awnings more than halfway across the road, and even at midday shut out any little ray of sunshine which might have a tendency to peep into the street below.

In this year 11 of the Republic the Carrefour de la Poissonnerie was unpaved, dark and evil-smelling. For two-thirds of the year it was ankle-deep in mud: the rest of the time the mud was baked into cakes and emitted clouds of sticky dust under the shuffling feet of the passers-by. At night it was dimly lighted by one or two broken-down lanthorns which were hung on transverse chains overhead from house to house. These lanthorns only made a very small circle of light immediately below them: the rest of the street was left in darkness save for the faint glimmer which filtrated through an occasional ill-fitting doorway or through the chinks of some insecurely fastened shutter.

The Carrefour de la Poissonnerie was practically deserted in the daytime; only a few children – miserable little atoms of humanity showing their meagre, emaciated bodies through the scanty rags which failed to cover their nakedness – played weird, mirthless games in the mud and filth of the street. But at night it became strangely peopled with vague and furtive forms that were wont to glide swiftly by, beneath the hanging lanthorns, in order to lose themselves again in the welcome obscurity beyond: men and women – ill-clothed and unshod, with hands buried in pockets or beneath scanty shawls – their feet, oft-times bare, making no sound as they went squishing through the mud. A perpetual silence used to reign in this kingdom of squalor and of darkness, where night-hawks alone fluttered their wings; only from time to time a joyless greeting of boon-companions, or the hoarse cough of some wretched consumptive would wake the dormant echoes that lingered in the gloom.

2

Martin-Roget knew his way about the murky street well enough. He went up to the house which lay a little back from the others. It appeared even more squalid than the rest, not a sound came from within – hardly a light – only a narrow glimmer found its way through the chink of a shutter on the floor above. To right and left of it the houses were tall, with walls that reeked of damp and of filth: from one of these – the one on the left – an iron sign dangled and creaked dismally as it swung in the wind. Just above the sign there was a window with partially closed shutters: through it came the sound of two husky voices raised in heated argument.

In the open space in front of Louise Adet's house vague forms standing about or lounging against the walls of the neighbouring houses were vaguely discernible in the gloom. Martin-Roget and Chauvelin as they approached were challenged by a raucous voice which came to them out of the inky blackness around.

'Halt! who goes there?'

'Friends!' replied Martin-Roget promptly. 'Is citizeness Adet within?'

'Yes! she is!' retorted the man bluntly; 'excuse me, friend Adet – I did not know you in this confounded darkness.'

'No harm done,' said Martin-Roget. 'And it is I who am grateful to you all for your vigilance.'

'Oh!' said the other with a laugh, 'there's not much fear of your bird getting out of its cage. Have no fear, friend Adet! That Kernogan rabble is well looked after.'

The small group dispersed in the darkness and Martin-Roget rapped against the door of his sister's house with his knuckles.

'That is the Rat Mort,' he said, indicating the building on his left with a nod of the head. 'A very unpleasant neighbourhood for my sister, and she has oft complained of it – but name of a dog! won't it prove useful this night?'

Chauvelin had as usual followed his colleague in silence, but his keen eyes had not failed to note the presence of the village lads of whom Martin-Roget had spoken. There are no eyes so watchful as those of hate, nor is there aught so incorruptible. Everyone of these men here had an old wrong to avenge, an old score to settle with those ci-devant Kernogans who had once been their masters and who were so completely in their power now. Louise Adet had gathered round her a far more efficient bodyguard than even the proconsul could hope to have.

A moment or two later the door was opened, softly and cautiously, and Martin-Roget asked: 'Is that you, Louise?' for of a truth the darkness was almost deeper within than without, and he could not see who it was that was standing by the door.

'Yes! it is,' replied a weary and querulous voice. 'Enter quickly. The wind is cruel, and I can't keep myself warm. Who is with you, Pierre?'

'A friend,' said Martin-Roget drily. 'We want to see the aristo.'

The woman without further comment closed the door behind the new-comers. The place now was as dark as pitch, but she seemed to know her way about like a cat, for her shuffling footsteps were heard moving about unerringly. A moment or two later she opened another door opposite the front entrance, revealing an inner room – a sort of kitchen – which was lighted by a small lamp.

'You can go straight up,' she called curtly to the two men.

The narrow, winding staircase was divided from this kitchen by a wooden partition. Martin-Roget, closely followed by Chauvelin, went up the stairs. On the top of these there was a tiny landing with a door on either side of it. Martin-Roget without any ceremony pushed open the door on his right with his foot.

A tallow candle fixed in a bottle and placed in the centre of a table in the middle of the room flickered in the draught as the door flew open. It was bare of everything save a table and a chair, and a bundle of straw in one corner. The tiny window at right angles to the door was innocent of glass, and the north-westerly wind came in an icy stream through the aperture. On the table, in addition to the candle, there was a broken pitcher half-filled with water, and a small chunk of brown bread blotched with stains of mould.

On the chair beside the table and immediately facing the door sat Yvonne Lady Dewhurst. On the wall above her head a hand unused to calligraphy had traced in clumsy characters the words: 'Liberté! Fraternité! Egalite!' and below that 'ou la Mort.'

3

The men entered the narrow room and Chauvelin carefully closed the door behind him. He at once withdrew into a remote corner of the room and stood there quite still, wrapped in his mantle, a small, silent, mysterious figure on which Yvonne fixed dark, inquiring eyes.

Martin-Roget, restless and excited, paced up and down the small space like a wild animal in a cage. From time to time exclamations of impatience escaped him and he struck one fist repeatedly against his open palm. Yvonne followed his movements with a quiet, uninterested glance, but Chauvelin paid no heed whatever to him.

He was watching Yvonne ceaselessly, and closely.

Three days' incarceration in this wind-swept attic, the lack of decent food and of warmth, the want of sleep and the horror of her present position all following upon the soul-agony which she had endured when she was forcibly torn away from her dear milor, had left their mark on Yvonne Dewhurst's fresh young face. The look of gravity which had always sat so quaintly on her piquant features had now changed to one of deep and abiding sorrow: her large dark eyes were circled and sunk: they had in them the unnatural glow of fever, as well as the settled look of horror and of pathetic resignation. Her soft brown hair had lost its lustre; her cheeks were drawn and absolutely colourless.

Martin-Roget paused in his restless walk. For a moment he stood silent and absorbed, contemplating by the flickering light of the candle all the havoc which his brutality had wrought upon Yvonne's dainty face.

But Yvonne after a while ceased to look at him – she appeared to be unconscious of the gaze of these two men, each of whom was at this moment only thinking of the evil which he meant to inflict upon her – each of whom only thought of her as a helpless bird whom he had at last ensnared and whom he could crush to death as soon as he felt so inclined.

She kept her lips tightly closed and her head averted. She was gazing across at the unglazed window into the obscurity beyond, marvelling in what direction lay the sea and the shores of England.

Martin-Roget crossed his arms over his broad chest and clutched his elbows with his hands with an obvious effort to keep control over his movements and his temper in check. The quiet, almost indifferent attitude of the girl was exasperating to his over-strung nerves.

'Look here, my girl,' he said at last, roughly and peremptorily, 'I had an interview with the proconsul this afternoon. He chides me for my leniency toward you. Three days he thinks is far too long to keep traitors eating the bread of honest citizens and taking up valuable space in our city. Yesterday I made a proposal to you. Have you thought on it?'

Yvonne made no reply. She was still gazing out into nothingness and just at that moment she was very far away from the narrow, squalid room and the company of these two inhuman brutes. She was thinking of her dear milor and of that lovely home at Combwich wherein she had spent three such unforgettable days. She was remembering how beautiful had been the colour of the bare twigs in the chestnut coppice when the wintry sun danced through and in-between them and drew fantastic patterns of living gold upon the carpet of dead leaves; and she remembered too how exquisite were the tints of russet and blue on the distant hills, and how quaintly the thrushes had called: 'Kiss me quick!' She saw again those trembling leaves of a delicious faintly crimson hue which still hung upon the branches of the scarlet oak, and the early flowering heath which clothed the moors with a gorgeous mantle of rosy amethyst.

Martin-Roget's harsh voice brought her abruptly back to the hideous reality of the moment.

'Your obstinacy will avail you nothing,' he said, speaking quietly, even though a note of intense irritation was distinctly perceptible in his voice. 'The proconsul has given me a further delay wherein to deal leniently with you and with your father if I am so minded. You know what I have proposed to you: Life with me as my wife – in which case your father will be free to return to England or to go to the devil as he pleases – or the death of a malefactor for you both in the company of all the thieves and evil-doers who are mouldering in the prisons of Nantes at this moment. Another delay wherein to choose between an honourable life and a shameful death. The proconsul waits. But tonight he must have his answer.'

Then Yvonne turned her head slowly and looked calmly on her enemy.

'The tyrant who murders innocent men, women and children,' she said, 'can have his answer now. I choose death which is inevitable in preference to a life of shame.'

'You seem,' he retorted, 'to have lost sight of the fact that the law gives me the right to take by force that which you so obstinately refuse.'

'Have I not said,' she replied, 'that death is my choice? Life with you would be a life of shame.'

'I can get a priest to marry us without your consent and your religion forbids you to take your own life,' he said with a sneer.

To this she made no reply, but he knew that he had his answer. Smothering a curse, he resumed after a while:

'So you prefer to drag your father to death with you? Yet he has begged you to consider your decision and to listen to reason. He has given his consent to our marriage.'

'Let me see my father,' she retorted firmly, 'and hear him say that with his own lips.'

'Ah!' she added quickly, for at her words Martin-Roget had turned his head away and shrugged his shoulders with well-assumed indifference, 'you cannot and dare not let me see him. For three days now you have kept us apart and no doubt fed us both up with your lies. My father is duc de Kernogan, Marquis de Trentemoult,' she added proudly, 'he would far rather die side by side with his daughter than see her wedded to a criminal.'

'And you, my girl,' rejoined Martin-Roget coldly, 'would you see your father branded as a malefactor, linked to a thief and sent to perish in the Loire?

'My father,' she retorted, 'will die as he has lived, a brave and honourable gentleman. The brand of a malefactor cannot cling to his name. Sorrow we are ready to endure – death is less than nothing to us – we will but follow in the footsteps of our King and of our Queen and of many whom we care for and whom you and your proconsul and your colleagues have brutally murdered. Shame cannot touch us, and our honour and our pride are so far beyond your reach that your impious and blood-stained hands can never sully them.'

She had spoken very slowly and very quietly. There were no heroics about her attitude. Even Martin-Roget – callous brute though he was – felt that she had only spoken just as she felt, and that nothing that he might say, no plea that he might urge, would ever shake her determination.

'Then it seems to me,' he said, 'that I am only wasting my time by trying to make you see reason and common sense. You look upon me as a brute. Well! perhaps I am. At any rate I am that which your father and you have made me. Four years ago, when you had power over me and over mine, you brutalized us. Today we – the people – are your masters and we make you suffer, not for all – that were impossible – but for part of what you made us suffer. That, after all, is only bare justice. By making you my wife I would have saved you from death – not from humiliation, for that you must endure, and at my hands in a full measure – but I would have made you my wife because I still have pleasant recollections of that kiss which I snatched from you on that never-to-be-forgotten night and in the darkness – a kiss for which you would gladly have seen me hang then, if you could have laid hands on me.'

He paused, trying to read what was going on behind those fine eyes of hers, with their vacant, far-seeing gaze which seemed like another barrier between her and him. At this rough allusion to that moment of horror and of shame, she had not moved a muscle, nor did her gaze lose its fixity.

He laughed.

'It is an unpleasant recollection, eh, my proud lady? The first kiss of passion was not implanted on your exquisite lips by that fine gentleman whom you deemed worthy of your hand and your love, but by Pierre Adet, the miller's son, what? a creature not quite so human as your horse or your pet dog. Neither you nor I are like to forget that methinks...'

Yvonne vouchsafed no reply to the taunt, and for a moment there was silence in the room, until Chauvelin's thin, suave voice broke in quite gently:

'Do not lose your patience with the wench, citizen Martin-Roget. Your time is too precious to be wasted in useless recriminations.'

'I have finished with her,' retorted the other sullenly. 'She shall be dealt with now as I think best. I agree with citizen Carrier. He is right after all. To the Loire with the lot of that foul brood!'

'Nay!' here rejoined Chauvelin with placid urbanity, 'are you not a little harsh, citizen, with our fair Yvonne? Remember! Women have moods and megrims. What they indignantly refuse to yield to us one day, they will grant with a smile the next. Our beautiful Yvonne is no exception to this rule, I'll warrant.'

Even while he spoke he threw a glance of warning on his colleague. There was something enigmatic in his manner at this moment, in the strange suavity wherewith he spoke these words of conciliation and of gentleness. Martin-Roget was as usual ready with an impatient retort. He was in a mood to bully and to brutalize, to heap threat upon threat, to win by frightfulness that which he could not gain by persuasion. Perhaps that at this moment he desired Yvonne de Kernogan for wife, more even than he desired her death. At any rate his headstrong temper was ready to chafe against any warning or advice. But once again Chauvelin's stronger mentality dominated over his less resolute colleague. Martin-Roget – the fowler – was in his turn caught in the net of a keener snarer than himself, and whilst – with the obstinacy of the weak – he was making mental resolutions to rebuke Chauvelin for his interference later on, he had already fallen in with the latter's attitude.

'The wench has had three whole days wherein to alter her present mood,' he said more quietly, 'and you know yourself, citizen, that the proconsul will not wait after today.'

'The day is young yet,' rejoined Chauvelin. 'It still hath six hours to its credit… Six hours… Three hundred and sixty minutes!' he continued with a pleasant little laugh; 'time enough for a woman to change her mind three hundred and sixty times. Let me advise you, citizen, to leave the wench to her own meditations for the present, and I trust that she will accept the advice of a man who has a sincere regard for her beauty and her charms and who is old enough to be her father, and seriously think the situation over in a conciliatory spirit. M. le duc de Kernogan will be grateful to her, for of a truth he is not over happy either at the moment…and will be still less happy in the dépôt tomorrow: it is over-crowded, and typhus, I fear me, is rampant among the prisoners. He has, I am convinced – in spite of what the citizeness says to the contrary – a rooted objection to being hurled into the Loire, or to be arraigned before the bar of the Convention, not as an aristocrat and a traitor but as an unit of an undesirable herd of criminals sent up to Paris for trial, by an anxious and harried proconsul. There! There!' he added benignly, 'we will not worry our fair Yvonne any longer, will we, citizen? I think she has grasped the alternative and will soon realize that marriage with an honourable patriot is not such an untoward fate after all.'

'And now, citizen Martin-Roget,' he concluded, 'I pray you allow me to take my leave of the fair lady and to give you the wise recommendation to do likewise She will be far better alone for awhile. Night brings good counsel, so they say.'

He watched the girl keenly while he spoke. Her impassivity had not deserted her for a single moment: but whether her calmness was of hope or of despair he was unable to decide. On the whole he thought it must be the latter: hope would have kindled a spark in those dark, purple-rimmed eyes, it would have brought moisture to the lips, a tremor to the hand.

The Scarlet Pimpernel was in Nantes – that fact was established beyond a doubt – but Chauvelin had come to the conclusion that so far as Yvonne Dewhurst herself was concerned, she knew nothing of the mysterious agencies that were working on her behalf.

Chauvelin's hand closed with a nervous contraction over the packet of papers in his pocket. Something of the secret of that enigmatic English adventurer lay revealed within its folds. Chauvelin had not yet had the opportunity of examining them: the interview with Yvonne had been the most important business for the moment.

From somewhere in the distance a city clock struck six. The afternoon was wearing on. The keenest brain in Europe was on the watch to drag one woman and one man from the deadly trap which had been so successfully set for them. A few hours more and Chauvelin in his turn would be pitting his wits against the resources of that intricate brain, and he felt like a war-horse scenting blood and battle. He was aching to get to work – aching to form his plans – to lay his snares – to dispose his trap so that the noble English quarry should not fail to be caught within its meshes.

He gave a last look to Yvonne, who was still sitting quite impassive, gazing through the squalid walls into some beautiful distance, the reflection of which gave to her pale, wan face an added beauty.

'Let us go, citizen Martin-Roget,' he said peremptorily. 'There is nothing else that we can do here.'

And Martin-Roget, the weaker morally of the two, yielded to the stronger personality of his colleague. He would have liked to stay on for awhile, to gloat for a few moments longer over the helplessness of the woman who to him represented the root of every evil which had ever befallen him and his family. But Chauvelin commanded and he felt impelled to obey. He gave one long, last look on Yvonne – a look that was as full of triumph as of mockery – he looked round the four dank walls, the unglazed window, the broken pitcher, the mouldy bread. Revenge was of a truth the sweetest emotion of the human heart. Pierre Adet – son of the miller who had been hanged by orders of the Duc de Kernogan for a crime which he had never committed – would not at this moment have changed places with Fortune's Benjamin.

4

Downstairs in Louise Adet's kitchen, Martin-Roget seized his colleague by the arm.

'Sit down a moment, citizen,' he said persuasively, 'and tell me what you think of it all.'

Chauvelin sat down at the other's invitation. All his movements were slow, deliberate, perfectly calm.

'I think,' he said drily, 'as far as your marriage with the wench is concerned, that you are beaten, my friend.'

'Tshaw!' The exclamation, raucous and surcharged with hate came from Louise Adet. She, too, like Pierre – more so than Pierre mayhap – had cause to hate the Kernogans. She, too, like Pierre had lived the last three days in the full enjoyment of the thought that Fate and Chance were about to level things at last between herself and those detested aristos. Silent and sullen she was shuffling about in the room, among her pots and pans, but she kept an eye upon her brother's movements and an ear on what he said. Men were apt to lose grit where a pretty wench was concerned. It takes a woman's rancour and a woman's determination to carry a scheme of vengeance against another to a successful end.

Martin-Roget rejoined more calmly:

'I knew that she would still be obstinate,' he said. 'If I forced her into a marriage, which I have the right to do, she might take her own life and make me look a fool. So I don't want to do that. I believe in the persuasiveness of the Rat Mort tonight,' he added with a cynical laugh, 'and if that fails... Well! I was never really in love with the fair Yvonne, and now she has even ceased to be desirable... If the Rat Mort fails to act on her sensibilities as I would wish, I can easily console myself by following Carrier's herd to Paris. Louise shall come with me – eh, little sister? – and we'll give ourselves the satisfaction of seeing M. le duc de Kernogan and his exquisite daughter stand in the felon's dock – tried for malpractices and for evil living. We'll see them branded as convicts and packed off like so much cattle to Cayenne. That will be a sight,' he concluded with a deep sigh of satisfaction, 'which will bring rest to my soul.'

He paused: his face looked sullen and evil under the domination of that passion which tortured him.

Louise Adet had shuffled up close to her brother. In one hand she held the wooden spoon wherewith she had been stirring the soup: with the other she brushed away the dark, lank hair which hung in strands over her high, pale forehead. In appearance she was a woman immeasurably older than her years. Her face had the colour of yellow parchment, her skin was stretched tightly over her high cheekbones – her lips were colourless and her eyes large, wide-open, were pale in hue and circled with red. Just now a deep frown of puzzlement between her brows added a sinister expression to her cadaverous face:

'The Rat Mort?' she queried in that tired voice of hers, 'Cayenne? What is all that about?'

'A splendid scheme of Carrier's, my Louise,' replied Martin-Roget airily. 'We convey the Kernogan woman to the Rat Mort. Tonight a descent will be made on that tavern of ill-fame by a company of Marats and every man, woman and child within it will be arrested and sent to Paris as undesirable inhabitants of this most moral city: in Paris they will be tried as malefactors or evil-doers – cut-throats, thieves, what? and deported as convicts to Cayenne, or else sent to the guillotine. The Kernogans among that herd! What sayest thou to that, little sister? Thy father, thy lover, hung as thieves! M. le Duc and Mademoiselle branded as convicts! 'Tis pleasant to think on, eh?'

Louise made no reply. She stood looking at her brother, her pale, red-rimmed eyes seemed to drink in every word that he uttered, while her bony hand wandered mechanically across and across her forehead as if in a pathetic endeavour to clear the brain from everything save of the satisfying thoughts which this prospect of revenge had engendered.

Chauvelin's gentle voice broke in on her meditations. 'In the meanwhile,' he said placidly, 'remember my warning, citizen Martin-Roget. There are passing clever and mighty agencies at work, even at this hour, to wrest your prey from you. How will you convey the wench to the Rat Mort? Carrier has warned you of spies – but I have warned you against a crowd of English adventurers far more dangerous than an army of spies. Three pairs of eyes – probably more, and one pair the keenest in Europe – will be on the watch to seize upon the woman and to carry her off under your very nose.'

Martin-Roget uttered a savage oath.

'That brute Carrier has left me in the lurch,' he said roughly. 'I don't believe in your nightmares and your English adventurers, still it would have been better if I could have had the woman conveyed to the tavern under armed escort.'

'Armed escort has been denied you, and anyway it would not be much use. You and I, citizen Martin-Roget, must act independently of Carrier. Your friends down there,' he added, indicating the street with a jerk of the head, 'must redouble their watchfulness. The village lads of Vertou are of a truth no match intellectually with our English adventurers, but they have vigorous fists in case there is an attack on the wench while she walks across to the Rat Mort.'

'It would be simpler,' here interposed Louise roughly, 'if we were to knock the wench on the head and then let the lads carry her across.'

'It would not be simpler,' retorted Chauvelin drily, 'for Carrier might at any moment turn against us. Commandant Fleury with half a company of Marats will be posted round the Rat Mort, remember. They may interfere with the lads and arrest them and snatch the wench from us, when all our plans may fall to the ground...one never knows what double game Carrier may be playing. No! no! the girl must not be dragged or carried to the Rat Mort, She must walk into the trap of her own free will.'

'But name of a dog! how is it to be done?' ejaculated Martin-Roget, and he brought his clenched fist crashing down upon the table. 'The woman will not follow me – or Louise either – anywhere willingly.'

'She must follow a stranger then – or one whom she thinks a stranger – someone who will have gained her confidence...'

'Impossible.'

'Oh! nothing is impossible, citizen,' rejoined Chauvelin blandly.

'Do you know a way then?' queried the other with a sneer.

'I think I do. If you will trust me that is – '

'I don't know that I do. Your mind is so intent on those English adventurers, you are like as not to let the aristos slip through your fingers.'

'Well, citizen,' retorted Chauvelin imperturbably, will you take the risk of conveying the fair Yvonne to the Rat Mort by twelve o'clock tonight? I have very many things to see to, I confess that I should be glad if you will ease me from that responsibility.'

'I have already told you that I see no way,' retorted Martin-Roget with a snarl.

'Then why not let me act?'

'What are you going to do?'

'For the moment I am going for a walk on the quay and once more will commune with the north-west wind.'

'Tshaw!' ejaculated Martin-Roget savagely.

'Nay, citizen,' resumed Chauvelin blandly, 'the winds of heaven are excellent counsellors. I told you so just now and you agreed with me. They blow away the cobwebs of the mind and clear the brain for serious thinking. You want the Kernogan girl to be arrested inside the Rat Mort and you see no way of conveying her thither save by the use of violence, which for obvious reasons is to be deprecated: Carrier, for equally obvious reasons, will not have her taken to the place by force. On the other hand you admit that the wench would not follow you willingly – Well, citizen, we must find a way out of that impasse, for it is too unimportant an one to stand in the way of our plans: for this I must hold a consultation with the north-west wind.'

'I won't allow you to do anything without consulting me.'

'Am I likely to do that? To begin with I shall have need of your co-operation and that of the citizeness.'

'In that case...' muttered Martin-Roget grudgingly. 'But remember,' he added with a return to his usual self-assured manner, 'remember that Yvonne and her father belong to me and not to you. I brought them into Nantes for mine own purposes – not for yours. I will not have my revenge jeopardized so that your schemes may be furthered.'

'Who spoke of my schemes, citizen Martin-Roget?' broke in Chauvelin with perfect urbanity. 'Surely not I? What am I but an humble tool in the service of the Republic?...a tool that has proved useless – a failure, what? My only desire is to help you to the best of my abilities. Your enemies are the enemies of the Republic: my ambition is to help you in destroying them.'

For a moment longer Martin-Roget hesitated: he abominated this suggestion of becoming a mere instrument in the hands of this man whom he still would have affected to despise – had he dared. But here came the difficulty: he no longer dared to despise Chauvelin. He felt the strength of the man – the clearness of his intellect, and though he – Martin-Roget – still chose to disregard every warning in connection with the English spies, he could not wholly divest his mind from the possibility of their presence in Nantes. Carrier's scheme was so magnificent, so satisfying, that the ex-miller's son was ready to humble his pride and set his arrogance aside in order to see it carried through successfully.

So after a moment or two, despite the fact that he positively ached to shut Chauvelin out of the whole business, Martin-Roget gave a grudging assent to his proposal.

'Very well!' he said, 'you see to it. So long as it does not interfere with my plans...'

'It can but help them,' rejoined Chauvelin suavely. 'If you will act as I shall direct I pledge you my word that the wench will walk to the Rat Mort of her free will and at the hour when you want her. What else is there to say?'

'When and where shall we meet again?'

'Within the hour I will return here and explain to you and to the citizeness what I want you to do. We will get the aristos inside the Rat Mort, never fear; and after that I think that we may safely leave Carrier to do the rest, what?'

He picked up his hat and wrapped his mantle round him. He took no further heed of Martin-Roget or of Louise, for suddenly he had felt the crackling of crisp paper inside the breast-pocket of his coat and in a moment the spirit of the man had gone a-roaming out of the narrow confines of this squalid abode. It had crossed the English Channel and wandered once more into a brilliantly-lighted ball-room where an exquisitely dressed dandy declaimed inanities and doggerel rhymes for the delectation of a flippant assembly: it heard once more the lazy, drawling speech, the inane, affected laugh, it caught the glance of a pair of lazy, grey eyes fixed mockingly upon him. Chauvelin's thin claw-like hand went back to his pocket: it felt that packet of papers, it closed over it like a vulture's talon does upon a prey. He no longer heard Martin-Roget's obstinate murmurings, he no longer felt himself to be the disgraced, humiliated servant of the State: rather did he feel once more the master, the leader, the successful weaver of an hundred clever intrigues. The enemy who had baffled him so often had chosen once more to throw down the glove of mocking defiance. So be it! The battle would be fought this night – a decisive one – and long live the Republic and the power of the people!

With a curt nod of the head Chauvelin turned on his heel and without waiting for Martin-Roget to follow him, or for Louise to light him on his way, he strode from the room, and out of the house, and had soon disappeared in the darkness in the direction of the quay.

5

Once more free from the encumbering companionship of Martin-Roget, Chauvelin felt free to breathe and to think. He, the obscure and impassive servant of the Republic, the cold-blooded Terrorist who had gone through every phase of an exciting career without moving a muscle of his grave countenance, felt as if every one of his arteries was on fire. He strode along the quay in the teeth of the north-westerly wind, grateful for the cold blast which lashed his face and cooled his throbbing temples.

The packet of papers inside his coat seemed to sear his breast.

Before turning to go along the quay he paused, hesitating for a moment what he would do. His very humble lodgings were at the far end of the town, and every minute of time was precious. Inside Le Bouffay, where he had a small room allotted to him as a minor representative in Nantes of the Committee of Public Safety, there was the ever present danger of prying eyes.

On the whole – since time was so precious – he decided on returning to Le Bouffay. The concierge and the clerk fortunately let him through without those official delays which he – Chauvelin – was wont to find so galling ever since his disgrace had put a bar against the opening of every door at the bare mention of his name or the display of his tricolour scarf.

He strode rapidly across the hall: the men on guard eyed him with lazy indifference as he passed. Once inside his own sanctum he looked carefully around him; he drew the curtain closer across the window and dragged the table and a chair well away from the range which might be covered by an eye at the keyhole. It was only when he had thoroughly assured himself that no searching eye or inquisitive ear could possibly be watching over him that he at last drew the precious packet of papers from his pocket. He undid the red ribbon which held it together and spread the papers out on the table before him. Then he examined them carefully one by one.

As he did so an exclamation of wrath or of impatience escaped him from time to time, once he laughed – involuntarily – aloud.

The examination of the papers took him some time. When he had finished he gathered them all together again, retied the bit of ribbon round them and slipped the packet back into the pocket of his coat. There was a look of grim determination on his face, even though a bitter sigh escaped his set lips.

'Oh! for the power,' he muttered to himself, 'which I had a year ago! for the power to deal with mine enemy myself. So you have come to Nantes, my valiant Sir Percy Blakeney?' he added while a short, sardonic laugh escaped his thin, set lips: 'and you are determined that I shall know how and why you came! Do you reckon, I wonder, that I have no longer the power to deal with you? Well!....'

He sighed again but with more satisfaction this time.

'Well!....' he reiterated with obvious complacency. 'Unless that oaf Carrier is a bigger fool than I imagine him to be I think I have you this time, my elusive Scarlet Pimpernel.'

4

The Net

It was not an easy thing to obtain an audience of the great proconsul at this hour of the night, nor was Chauvelin, the disgraced servant of the Committee of Public Safety, a man to be considered. Carrier, with his love of ostentation and of tyranny, found great delight in keeping his colleagues waiting upon his pleasure, and he knew that he could trust young Jacques Lalouët to be as insolent as any tyrant's flunkey of yore.

'I must speak with the proconsul at once,' had been Chauvelin's urgent request of Fleury, the commandant of the great man's bodyguard.

'The proconsul dines at this hour,' had been Fleury's curt reply.

' 'Tis a matter which concerns the welfare and the safety of the State!'

'The proconsul's health is the concern of the State too, and he dines at this hour and must not be disturbed.'

'Commandant Fleury!' urged Chauvelin, 'you risk being implicated in a disaster. Danger and disgrace threaten the proconsul and all his adherents. I must speak with citizen Carrier at once.'

Fortunately for Chauvelin there were two keys which, when all else failed, were apt to open the doors of Carrier's stronghold: the key of fear and that of cupidity. He tried both and succeeded. He bribed and he threatened he endured Fleury's brutality and Lalouët's impertinence but he got his way. After an hour's weary waiting and ceaseless parleyings he was once more ushered into the antechamber where he had sat earlier in the day. The doors leading to the inner sanctuary were open. Young Jacques Lalouët stood by them on guard. Carrier, fuming and raging at having been disturbed, vented his spleen and ill-temper on Chauvelin.

'If the news that you bring me is not worth my consideration,' he cried savagely, 'I'll send you to moulder in Le Bouffay or to drink the waters of the Loire.'

Chauvelin silent, self-effaced, allowed the flood of the great man's wrath to spend itself in threats. Then he said quietly:

'Citizen proconsul I have come to tell you that the English spy, who is called the Scarlet Pimpernel, is now in Nantes. There is a reward of twenty thousand francs for his capture and I want your help to lay him by the heels.'

Carrier suddenly paused in his ravings. He sank into a chair and a livid hue spread over his face.

'It's not true!' he murmured hoarsely.

'I saw him – not an hour ago...'

'What proof have you?'

'I'll show them to you – but not across this threshold. Let me enter, citizen proconsul, and close your sanctuary doors behind me rather than before. What I have come hither to tell you, can only be said between four walls.'

'I'll make you tell me,' broke in Carrier in a raucous voice, which excitement and fear caused almost to choke in his throat. 'I'll make you...curse you for the traitor that you are... Curse you!' he cried more vigorously, 'I'll make you speak. Will you shield a spy by your silence, you miserable traitor? If you do I'll send you to rot in the mud of the Loire with other traitors less accursed than yourself.'

'If you only knew,' was Chauvelin's calm rejoinder to the other's ravings, 'how little I care for life. I only live to be even one day with an enemy whom I hate. That enemy is now in Nantes, but I am like a bird of prey whose wings have been clipped. If you do not help me mine enemy will again go free – and death in that case matters little or nothing to me.'

For a moment longer Carrier hesitated. Fear had gripped him by the throat. Chauvelin's earnestness seemed to vouch for the truth of his assertion, and if this were so – if those English spies were indeed in Nantes – then his own life was in deadly danger. He – like everyone of those bloodthirsty tyrants who had misused the sacred names of Fraternity and of Equality – had learned to dread the machinations of those mysterious Englishmen and of their unconquerable leader. Popular superstition had it that they were spies of the English Government and that they were not only bent on saving traitors from well-merited punishment but that they were hired assassins paid by Mr Pitt to murder every faithful servant of the Republic. The name of the Scarlet Pimpernel, so significantly uttered by Chauvelin, had turned Carrier's sallow cheeks to a livid hue. Sick with terror now he called Lalouët to him. He clung to the boy with both arms as to the one being in this world whom he trusted.

'What shall we do, Jacques?' he murmured hoarsely, 'shall we let him in?'

The boy roughly shook himself free from the embrace of the great proconsul.

'If you want twenty thousand francs,' he said with a dry laugh, 'I should listen quietly to what citizen Chauvelin has to say.'

Terror and rapacity were ranged on one side against inordinate vanity. The thought of twenty thousand francs made Carrier's ugly mouth water. Money was over scarce these days: also the fear of assassination was a spectre which haunted him at all hours of the day and night. On the other hand he positively worshipped the mystery wherewith he surrounded himself. It had been his boast for some time now that no one save the chosen few had crossed the threshold of his private chamber: and he was miserably afraid not only of Chauvelin's possible evil intentions, but also that this despicable ex-aristo and equally despicable failure would boast in the future of an ascendancy over him.

He thought the matter over for fully five minutes, during which there was dead silence in the two rooms – silence only broken by the stertorous breathing of that wretched coward, and the measured ticking of the fine Buhl clock behind him. Chauvelin's pale eyes were fixed upon the darkness, through which he could vaguely discern the uncouth figure of the proconsul, sprawling over his desk. Which way would his passions sway him? Chauvelin as he watched and waited felt that his habitual self-control was perhaps more severely taxed at this moment than it had ever been before. Upon the swaying of those passions, the passions of a man infinitely craven and infinitely base, depended all his – Chauvelin's – hopes of getting even at last with a daring and resourceful foe. Terror and rapacity were the counsellors which ranged themselves on the side of his schemes, but mere vanity and caprice fought a hard battle too.

In the end it was rapacity that gained the victory. An impatient exclamation from young Lalouët roused Carrier from his sombre brooding and hastened on a decision which was destined to have such momentous consequences for the future of both these men.

'Introduce citizen Chauvelin in here, Lalouët,' said the proconsul grudgingly. 'I will listen to what he has to say.'

2

Chauvelin crossed the threshold of the tyrant's sanctuary, in no way awed by the majesty of that dreaded presence or confused by the air of mystery which hung about the room.

He did not even bestow a glance on the multitudinous objects of art and the priceless furniture which littered the tiger's lair. His pale face remained quite expressionless as he bowed solemnly before Carrier and then took the chair which was indicated to him. Young Lalouët fetched a candelabra from the anteroom and carried it into the audience chamber: then he closed the communicating doors. The candelabra he placed on a console-table immediately behind Carrier's desk and chair, so that the latter's face remained in complete shadow, whilst the light fell full upon Chauvelin.

'Well! what is it?' queried the proconsul roughly. 'What is this story of English spies inside Nantes? How did they get here? Who is responsible for keeping such rabble out of our city? Name of a dog, but someone has been careless of duty! and carelessness these days is closely allied to treason.'

He talked loudly and volubly – his inordinate terror causing the words to come tumbling, almost incoherently, out of his mouth. Finally he turned on Chauvelin with a snarl like an angry cat:

'And how comes it, citizen,' he added savagely, 'that you alone here in Nantes are acquainted with the whereabouts of those dangerous spies?'

'I caught sight of them,' rejoined Chauvelin calmly, this afternoon after I left you. I knew we should have them here, the moment citizen Martin-Roget brought the Kernogans into the city. The woman is the wife of one of them.'

'Curse that blundering fool Martin-Roget for bringing that rabble about our ears, and those assassins inside our gates.'

'Nay! Why should you complain, citizen proconsul,' rejoined Chauvelin in his blandest manner. 'Surely you are not going to let the English spies escape this time? And if you succeed in laying them by the heels – there where everyone else has failed – you will have earned twenty thousand francs and the thanks of the entire Committee of Public Safety.'

He paused: and young Lalouët interposed with his impudent laugh:

'Go on, citizen Chauvelin,' he said, 'if there is twenty thousand francs to be made out of this game, I'll warrant that the proconsul will take a hand in it – eh, Carrier?'

And with the insolent familiarity of a terrier teasing a grizzly he tweaked the great man's ear.

Chauvelin in the meanwhile had drawn the packet of papers from his pocket and untied the ribbon that held them together. He now spread the papers out on the desk.

'What are these?' queried Carrier.

'A few papers,' replied Chauvelin, 'which one of your Marats, Paul Friche by name, picked up in the wake of the Englishmen. I caught sight of them in the far distance, and sent the Marats after them. For awhile Paul Friche kept on their track, but after that they disappeared in the darkness.'

'Who were the senseless louts,' growled Carrier, 'who allowed a pack of foreign assassins to escape? I'll soon make them disappear…in the Loire.'

'You will do what you like about that, citizen Carrier,' retorted Chauvelin drily; 'in the meanwhile you would do well to examine these papers.'

He sorted these out, examined them one by one, then passed them across to Carrier. Lalouët, impudent and inquisitive, sat on the corner of the desk, dangling his legs. With scant ceremony he snatched one paper after another out of Carrier's hands and examined them curiously.

'Can you understand all this gibberish?' he asked airily. 'Jean-Baptiste, my friend, how much English do you know?'

'Not much,' replied the proconsul, 'but enough to recognize that abominable doggerel rhyme which has gone the round of the Committees of Public Safety throughout the country.'

'I know it by heart,' rejoined young Lalouët. 'I was in Paris once, when citizen Robespierre received a copy of it. Name of a dog!' added the youngster with a coarse laugh, 'how he cursed!'

It is doubtful however if citizen Robespierre did on that occasion curse quite so volubly as Carrier did now.

'If I only knew why that *satané* Englishman throws so much calligraphy about,' he said, 'I would be easier in my mind. Now this senseless rhyme... I don't see...'

'Its importance?' broke in Chauvelin quietly. 'I dare say not. On the face of it, it appears foolish and childish: but it is intended as a taunt and is really a poor attempt at humour. They are a queer people these English. If you knew them as I do, you would not be surprised to see a man scribbling off a cheap joke before embarking on an enterprise which may cost him his head.'

'And this inane rubbish is of that sort,' concluded young Lalouët. And in his thin high treble he began reciting:

> 'We seek him here;
> We seek him there!
> Those Frenchies seek him everywhere.
> Is he in heaven?
> Is he in h–ll ?
> That demmed elusive Pimpernel?'

'Pointless and offensive,' he said as he tossed the paper back on the table.

'A cursed aristo that Englishman of yours,' growled Carrier. 'Oh! when I get him...'

He made an expressive gesture which made Lalouët laugh.

'What else have we got in the way of documents, citizen Chauvelin?' he asked.

'There is a letter,' replied the latter.

'Read it,' commanded Carrier. 'Or rather translate it as you read. I don't understand the whole of the gibberish.'

And Chauvelin, taking up a sheet of paper which was covered with neat, minute writing, began to read aloud, translating the English into French as he went along:

' "Here we are at last, my dear Tony! Didn't I tell you that we can get in anywhere despite all precautions taken against us!" '

'The impudent devils!' broke in Carrier.

– ' "Did you really think that they could keep us out of Nantes while Lady Anthony Dewhurst is a prisoner in their hands." '

'Who is that?'
'The Kernogan woman. As I told you just now, she is married to an Englishman who is named Dewhurst and who is one of the members of that thrice cursed League.'
Then he continued to read:

' "And did you really suppose that they would spot half a dozen English gentlemen in the guise of peat-gatherers, returning at dusk and covered with grime from their work? Not like, friend Tony! Not like! If you happen to meet mine engaging friend M. Chambertin before I have that privilege myself tell him I pray you, with my regards, that I am looking forward to the pleasure of making a long nose at him once more. Calais, Boulogne, Paris – now Nantes – the scenes of his triumphs multiply exceedingly." '

'What in the devil's name does all this mean?' queried Carrier with an oath.
'You don't understand it?' rejoined Chauvelin quietly.
'No. I do not.'
'Yet I translated quite clearly.'

'It is not the language that puzzles me. The contents seem to me such drivel. The man wants secrecy, what? He is supposed to be astute, resourceful, above all mysterious and enigmatic. Yet he writes to his friend – matter of no importance between them, recollections of the past, known to them both – and threats for the future, equally futile and senseless. I cannot reconcile it all. It puzzles me.'

'And it would puzzle me,' rejoined Chauvelin, while the ghost of a smile curled his thin lips, 'did I not know the man. Futile? Senseless, you say? Well, he does futile and senseless things one moment and amazing deeds of personal bravery and of astuteness the next. He is three parts a braggart too. He wanted you, me – all of us to know how he and his followers succeeded in eluding our vigilance and entered our closely-guarded city in the guise of grimy peat-gatherers. Now I come to think of it, it was easy enough for them to do that. Those peat-gatherers who live inside the city boundaries return from their work as the night falls in. Those cursed English adventurers are passing clever at disguise – they are born mountebanks the lot of them. Money and impudence they have in plenty. They could easily borrow or purchase some filthy rags from the cottages on the dunes, then mix with the crowd on its return to the city. I dare say it was cleverly done. That Scarlet Pimpernel is just a clever adventurer and nothing more. So far his marvellous good luck has carried him through. Now we shall see.'

Carrier had listened in silence. Something of his colleague's calm had by this time communicated itself to him too. He was no longer raving like an infuriated bull – his terror no longer made a half-cringing, wholly savage brute of him. He was sprawling across the desk – his arms folded, his deep-set eyes studying closely the well-nigh inscrutable face of Chauvelin. Young Lalouët too had lost something of his impudence. That mysterious spell which seemed to emanate from the elusive personality of the bold English adventurer had been cast over these two callous, bestial natures, humbling their arrogance and making them feel that here was no ordinary situation to be dealt with by smashing, senseless hitting and the spilling of innocent blood. Both felt instinctively too that this man Chauvelin, however wholly he may have failed in the past, was nevertheless still the only man who might grapple successfully with the elusive and adventurous foe.

'Are you assuming, citizen Chauvelin,' queried Carrier after awhile, 'that this packet of papers was dropped purposely by the Englishman, so that it might get into our hands?'

'There is always such a possibility,' replied Chauvelin drily. 'With that type of man one must be prepared to meet the unexpected.'

'Then go on, citizen Chauvelin. What else is there among those *satané* papers?'

'Nothing further of importance. There is a map of Nantes, and one of the coast and of Le Croisic. There is a cutting from *Le Moniteur* dated last September, and one from the *London Gazette* dated three years ago. The *Moniteur* makes reference to the production of *Athalie* at the Théâtre Molière, and the *London Gazette* to the sale of fat cattle at an Agricultural Show. There is a receipted account from a London tailor for two hundred pounds worth of clothes supplied, and one from a Lyons mercer for an hundred francs worth of silk cravats. Then there is the one letter which alone amidst all this rubbish appears to be of any consequence...'

He took up the last paper: his hand was still quite steady.

'Read the letter,' said Carrier.

'It is addressed in the English fashion to Lady Anthony Dewhurst,' continued Chauvelin slowly, 'the Kernogan woman you know, citizen. It says:

' "Keep up your courage. Your friends are inside the city and on the watch. Try the door of your prison every evening at one hour before midnight. Once you will find

207

it yield. Slip out and creep noiselessly down the stairs. At the bottom a friendly hand will be stretched out to you. Take it with confidence – it will lead you to safety and to freedom. Courage and secrecy." '

Lalouët had been looking over his shoulder while he read: now he pointed to the bottom of the letter.

'And there is the device,' he said, 'we have heard so much about of late – a five-petalled flower drawn in red ink...the Scarlet Pimpernel, I presume.'

'Aye! the Scarlet Pimpernel,' murmured Chauvelin, 'as you say! Braggadocio on his part or accident, his letters are certainly in our hands now and will prove – must prove, the tool whereby we can be even with him once and for all.'

'And you, citizen Chauvelin,' interposed Carrier with a sneer, 'are mighty lucky to have me to help you this time. I am not going to be fooled, as Candeille and you were fooled last September, as you were fooled in Calais and Héron in Paris. I shall be seeing this time to the capture of those English adventurers.'

'And that capture should not be difficult,' added Lalouët with a complacent laugh. 'Your famous adventurer's luck hath deserted him this time: an all-powerful proconsul is pitted against him and the loss of his papers hath destroyed the anonimity on which he reckons.'

Chauvelin paid no heed to the fatuous remarks.

How little did this flippant young braggart and this coarse-grained bully understand the subtle workings of that same adventurer's brain! He himself – one of the most astute men of the day – found it difficult. Even now – the losing of those letters in the open streets of Nantes – it was part of a plan. Chauvelin could have staked his head on that – a part of a plan for the liberation of Lady Anthony Dewhurst – but what plan? – what plan?

He took up the letter which his colleague had thrown down: he fingered it, handled it, letting the paper crackle through his fingers, as if he expected it to yield up the secret which it contained. The time had come – of that he felt no doubt – when he could at last be even with his enemy. He had endured more bitter humiliation at the hands of this elusive Pimpernel than he would have thought himself capable of bearing a couple of years ago. But the time had come at last – if only he kept his every faculty on the alert, if Fate helped him and his own nerves stood the strain. Above all if this blundering, self-satisfied Carrier could be reckoned on!...

There lay the one great source of trouble! He – Chauvelin – had no power: he was disgraced – a failure – a nonentity to be sneered at. He might protest, entreat, wring his hands, weep tears of blood and not one man would stir a finger to help him: this brute who sprawled here across his desk would not lend him half a dozen men to enable him to lay by the heels the most powerful enemy the Government of the Terror had ever known. Chauvelin inwardly ground his teeth with rage at his own impotence, at his own dependence on this clumsy lout, who was at this moment possessed of powers which he himself would give half his life to obtain.

But on the other hand he did possess a power which no one could take from him – the power to use others for the furtherance of his own aims – to efface himself while others danced as puppets to his piping. Carrier had the power: he had spies, Marats, prison-guards at his disposal. He was greedy for the reward, and cupidity and fear would make of him a willing instrument. All that Chauvelin need do was to use that instrument for his own ends. One would be the head to direct, the other – a mere insentient tool.

From this moment onwards every minute, every second and every fraction of a second would be full of portent, full of possibilities. Sir Percy Blakeney was in Nantes with at least three or four members of his League: he was at this very moment taxing every fibre of his resourceful brain in order to devise a means whereby he could rescue his friend's wife from the fate which was awaiting her: to gain this end he would dare everything, risk everything – risk and dare a great deal more than he had ever dared and risked before.

Chauvelin was finding a grim pleasure in reviewing the situation, in envisaging the danger of failure which he knew lay in wait for him, unless he too was able to call to his aid all the astuteness, all the daring, all the resource of his own fertile brain. He studied his colleague's face keenly – that sullen, savage expression in it, the arrogance, the blundering vanity. It was terrible to have to humour and fawn to a creature of that stamp when all one's hopes, all one's future, one's ideals and the welfare of one's country were at stake.

But this additional difficulty only served to whet the man's appetite for action. He drew in a long breath of delight, like a captive who first after many days and months of weary anguish scents freedom and ozone. He straightened out his shoulders. A gleam of triumph and of hope shot out of his keen pale eyes. He studied Carrier and he studied Lalouët and he felt that he could master them both – quietly, diplomatically, with subtle skill that would not alarm the proconsul's rampant self-esteem: and whilst this coarse-fibred brute gloated in anticipatory pleasure over the handling of a few thousand francs, and whilst Martin-Roget dreamed of a clumsy revenge against one woman and one man who had wronged him four years ago, he – Chauvelin – would pursue his work of striking at the enemy of the Revolution – of bringing to his knees the man who spent life and fortune in combating its ideals and in frustrating its aims. The destruction of such a foe was worthy a patriot's ambition.

On the other hand some of Carrier's bullying arrogance had gone. He was terrified to the very depths of his cowardly heart, and for once he was turning away from his favourite Jacques Lalouët and inclined to lean on Chauvelin for advice. Robespierre had been known to tremble at sight of that small scarlet device, how much more had he – Carrier – cause to be afraid. He knew his own limitations and he was terrified of the assassin's dagger. As Marat had perished, so he too might end his days, and the English spies were credited with murderous intentions and superhuman power. In his innermost self Carrier knew that despite countless failures Chauvelin was mentally his superior, and though he never would own to this and at this moment did not attempt to shed his overbearing manner, he was watching the other keenly and anxiously, ready to follow the guidance of an intellect stronger than his own.

3

At last Carrier elected to speak.

'And now, citizen Chauvelin,' he said, 'we know how we stand. We know that the English assassins are in Nantes. The question is how are we going to lay them by the heels?'

Chauvelin gave him no direct reply. He was busy collecting his precious papers together and thrusting them back into the pocket of his coat. Then he said quietly:

'It is through the Kernogan woman that we can get hold of him.'

'How?'

'Where she is, there will the Englishmen be. They are in Nantes for the sole purpose of getting the woman and her father out of your clutches...'

'Then it will be a fine haul inside the Rat Mort,' ejaculated Carrier with a chuckle. 'Eh, Jacques, you young scamp? You and I must go and see that, what? You have been complaining that life was getting monotonous. Drownages – Republican marriages! They have all palled in their turn on your jaded appetite... But the capture of the English assassins, eh?...of that League of the Scarlet Pimpernel which has even caused citizen Robespierre much uneasiness – that will stir up your sluggish blood, you lazy young vermin!... Go on, go on, citizen Chauvelin, I am vastly interested!'

He rubbed his dry, bony hands together and cackled with glee. Chauvelin interposed quietly:

'Inside the Rat Mort, eh, citizen?' he queried. 'Why, yes. Citizen Martin-Roget means to convey the Kernogan woman to the Rat Mort, doesn't he?'

'He does.'

'And you say that where the Kernogan woman is there the Englishmen will be...'

'The inference is obvious.'

'Which means ten thousand francs from that fool Martin-Roget for having the wench and her father arrested inside the Rat Mort! and twenty thousand for the capture of the English spies.... Have you forgotten, citizen Chauvelin,' he added with a raucous cry of triumph, 'that Commandant Fleury has my orders to make a raid on the Rat Mort this night with half a company of my Marats, and to arrest everyone whom they find inside?'

'The Kernogan wench is not at the Rat Mort yet,' quoth Chauvelin drily, 'and you have refused to lend a hand in having her conveyed thither.'

'I can't do it, my little Chauvelin,' rejoined Carrier, somewhat sobered by this reminder. 'I can't do it...you understand...my Marats taking an aristo to a house of ill-fame where presently I have her arrested it won't do...it won't do...you don't know how I am spied upon just now... It really would not do... I can't be mixed up in that part of the affair. The wench must go to the Rat Mort of her own free will, or the whole plan falls to the ground... That fool Martin-Roget must think of a way...it's his affair, after all. He must see to it... Or you can think of a way,' he added, assuming the coaxing ways of a tiger-cat; 'you are so clever, my little Chauvelin.'

'Yes,' replied Chauvelin quietly, 'I can think of a way. The Kernogan wench shall leave the house of citizeness Adet and walk into the tavern of the Rat Mort of her own free will. Your reputation, citizen Carrier,' he added without the slightest apparent trace of a sneer, 'your reputation shall be safeguarded in this matter. But supposing that in the interval of going from the one house to the other the English adventurer succeeds in kidnapping her...'

'Pah! is that likely?' quoth Carrier with a shrug of the shoulders.

'Exceedingly likely, citizen; and you would not doubt it if you knew this Scarlet Pimpernel as I do. I have seen him at his nefarious work. I know what he can do. There is nothing that he would not venture...there are few ventures in which he does not succeed. He is as strong as an ox, as agile as a cat. He can see in the dark and he can always vanish in a crowd. Here, there and everywhere, you never know where he will appear. He is a past master in the art of disguise and he is a born mountebank. Believe me, citizen, we shall want all the resources of our joint intellects to frustrate the machinations of such a foe.'

Carrier mused for a moment in silence.

'H'm!' he said after awhile, and with a sardonic laugh. 'You may be right, citizen Chauvelin. You have had experience with the rascal...you ought to know him. We won't leave anything to chance – don't be afraid of that. My Marats will be keen on the capture. We'll promise Commandant Fleury a thousand francs for himself and another thousand to be distributed among his men if we lay hands on the English assassins tonight. We'll leave nothing to chance,' he reiterated with an oath.

'In which case, citizen Carrier, you must on your side agree to two things,' rejoined Chauvelin firmly.

'What are they?'

'You must order Commandant Fleury to place himself and half a company of his Marats at my disposal.'

'What else?'

'You must allow them to lend a hand if there is an attempt to kidnap the Kernogan wench while she is being conveyed to the Rat Mort...'

Carrier hesitated for a second or two, but only for form's sake: it was his nature whenever he was forced to yield to do so grudgingly.

'Very well!' he said at last. 'I'll order Fleury to be on the watch and to interfere if there is any street-brawling outside or near the Rat Mort. Will that suit you?'

'Perfectly. I shall be on the watch too – somewhere close by… I'll warn Commandant Fleury if I suspect that the English are making ready for a coup outside the tavern. Personally I think it unlikely – because the duc de Kernogan will be inside the Rat Mort all the time, and he too will be the object of the Englishmen's attacks on his behalf. Citizen Martin-Roget too has about a score or so of his friends posted outside his sister's house: they are lads from his village who hate the Kernogans as much as he does himself. Still! I shall feel easier in my mind now that I am certain of Commandant Fleury's co-operation.'

'Then it seems to me that we have arranged everything satisfactorily, what?'

'Everything, except the exact moment when Commandant Fleury shall advance with his men to the door of the tavern and demand admittance in the name of the Republic.'

'Yes, he will have to make quite sure that the whole of our quarry is inside the net, eh?…before he draws the strings…or all our pretty plans fall to nought.'

'As you say,' rejoined Chauvelin, 'we must make sure. Supposing therefore that we get the wench safely into the tavern, that we have her there with her father, what we shall want will be someone in observation – someone who can help us to draw our birds into the snare just when we are ready for them. Now there is a man whom I have in my mind: he hath name Paul Friche and is one of your Marats – a surly, ill-conditioned giant…he was on guard outside Le Bouffay this afternoon… I spoke to him…he would suit our purpose admirably.'

'What do you want him to do?'

'Only to make himself look as like a Nantese cut-throat as he can...'

'He looks like one already,' broke in Jacques Lalouët with a laugh.

'So much the better. He'll excite no suspicion in that case in the minds of the frequenters of the Rat Mort. Then I'll instruct him to start a brawl – a fracas – soon after the arrival of the Kernogan wench. The row will inevitably draw the English adventurers hot-haste to the spot, either in the hope of getting the Kernogans away during the *mêlée* or with a view to protecting them. As soon as they have appeared upon the scene, the half company of the Marats will descend on the house and arrest everyone inside it.'

'It all sounds remarkably simple,' rejoined Carrier, and with a leer of satisfaction he turned to Jacques Lalouët. 'What think you of it, citizen?' he asked.

'That it sounds so remarkably simple,' replied young Lalouët, 'that personally I should be half afraid...'

'Of what?' queried Chauvelin blandly.

'If you fail, citizen Chauvelin...'

'Impossible!'

'If the Englishmen do not appear?'

'Even so the citizen proconsul will have lost nothing. He will merely have failed to gain the twenty thousand francs. But the Kernogans will still be in his power and citizen Martin-Roget's ten thousand francs are in any case assured.'

'Friend Jean-Baptiste,' concluded Lalouët with his habitual insolent familiarity, 'you had better do what citizen Chauvelin wants. Ten thousand francs are good...and thirty better still. Our privy purse has been empty far too long, and I for one would like the handling of a few brisk notes.'

'It will only be twenty-eight, citizen Lalouët,' interposed Chauvelin blandly, 'for Commandant Fleury will want one thousand francs and his men another thousand to stimulate their zeal. Still! I imagine that these hard times twenty-eight thousand francs are worth fighting for.'

'You seem to be fighting and planning and scheming for nothing, citizen Chauvelin,' retorted young Lalouët with a sneer. 'What are you going to gain, I should like to know, by the capture of that dare-devil Englishman?'

'Oh!' replied Chauvelin suavely, 'I shall gain the citizen proconsul's regard, I hope – and yours too, citizen Lalouët. I want nothing more except the success of my plan.'

Young Lalouët jumped down to his feet. He shrugged his shoulders and through his fine eyes shot a glance of mockery and scorn on the thin, shrunken figure of the Terrorist.

'How you do hate that Englishman, citizen Chauvelin,' he said with a light laugh.

4

Carrier having fully realized that he in any case stood to make a vast sum of money out of the capture of the band of English spies, gave his support generously to Chauvelin's scheme. Fleury, summoned into his presence, was ordered to place himself and half a company of Marats at the disposal of citizen Chauvelin. He demurred and growled like a bear with a sore head at being placed under the orders of a civilian, but it was not easy to run counter to the proconsul's will. A good deal of swearing, one or two overt threats and the citizen commandant was reduced to submission, The promise of a thousand francs, when the reward for the capture of the English spies was paid out by a grateful Government, overcame his last objections.

'I think you should rid yourself of that obstinate oaf,' was young Lalouët's cynical comment, when Fleury had finally left the audience chamber; 'he is too argumentative for my taste.'

Chauvelin smiled quietly to himself. He cared little what became of everyone of these Nantese louts once his great object had been attained.

'I need not trouble you further, citizen Carrier,' he said as he finally rose to take his leave. 'I shall have my hands full until I myself lay that meddlesome Englishman bound and gagged at your feet.'

The phrase delighted Carrier's insensate vanity. He was over-gracious to Chauvelin now.

'You shall do that at the Rat Mort, citizen Chauvelin,' he said with marked affability, 'and I myself will commend you for your zeal to the Committee of Public Safety.'

'Always supposing,' interposed Jacques Lalouët with his cynical laugh, 'that citizen Chauvelin does not let the whole rabble slip through his fingers.'

'If I do,' concluded Chauvelin drily, 'you may drag the Loire for my body tomorrow.'

'Oh!' laughed Carrier, 'we won't trouble to do that. Au revoir, citizen Chauvelin,' he added with one of his grandiloquent gestures of dismissal, 'I wish you luck at the Rat Mort tonight.'

Jacques Lalouët ushered Chauvelin out. When he was finally left standing alone at the head of the stairs and young Lalouët's footsteps had ceased to resound across the floors of the rooms beyond, he remained quite still for awhile, his eyes fixed into vacancy, his face set and expressionless; and through his lips there came a long-drawn-out sigh of intense satisfaction.

'And now, my fine Scarlet Pimpernel,' he murmured softly, 'once more *à nous deux.*'

Then he ran swiftly down the stairs and a moment later was once more speeding toward Le Bouffay.

5

The Message of Hope

After Martin-Roget and Chauvelin had left her, Yvonne had sat for a long time motionless, almost unconscious. It seemed as if gradually, hour by hour, minute by minute, her every feeling of courage and of hope were deserting her. Three days now she had been separated from her father – three days she had been under the constant supervision of a woman who had not a single thought of compassion or of mercy for the 'aristocrat' whom she hated so bitterly.

At night, curled up on a small bundle of dank straw Yvonne had made vain efforts to snatch a little sleep. Ever since the day when she had been ruthlessly torn away from the protection of her dear milor, she had persistently clung to the belief that he would find the means to come to her, to wrest her from the cruel fate which her pitiless enemies had devised for her. She had clung to that hope throughout that dreary journey from dear England to this abominable city. She had clung to it even whilst her father knelt at her feet in an agony of remorse. She had clung to hope while Martin-Roget alternately coaxed and terrorized her, while her father was dragged away from her, while she endured untold misery, starvation, humiliation at the hands of Louise Adet: but now – quite unaccountably – that hope seemed suddenly to have fled from her, leaving her lonely and inexpressibly desolate. That small, shrunken figure which, wrapped in a dark mantle, had stood in the corner of the room watching her like a serpent watches its prey, had seemed like the forerunner of the fate with which Martin-Roget, gloating over her helplessness, had already threatened her.

She knew, of course, that neither from him, nor from the callous brute who governed Nantes, could she expect the slightest justice or mercy. She had been brought here by Martin-Roget not only to die, but to suffer grievously at his hands in return for a crime for which she personally was in no way responsible. To hope for mercy from him at the eleventh hour were worse than futile. Her already overburdened heart ached at thought of her father: he suffered all that she suffered, and in addition he must be tortured with anxiety for her and with remorse. Sometimes she was afraid that under the stress of desperate soul-agony he might perhaps have been led to suicide. She knew nothing of what had happened to him, where he was, nor whether privations and lack of food or sleep, together with Martin-Roget's threats, had by now weakened his morale and turned his pride into humiliating submission.

2

A distant tower-clock struck the evening hours one after the other. Yvonne for the past three days had only been vaguely conscious of time. Martin-Roget had spoken of a few hours' respite only, of the proconsul's desire to be soon rid of her. Well! this meant no doubt that the morrow would see the end of it all – the end of her life which such a brief while ago seemed so full of delight, of love and of happiness.

The end of her life! She had hardly begun to live and her dear milor had whispered to her such sweet promises of endless vistas of bliss.

Yvonne shivered beneath her thin gown. The north-westerly blast came in cruel gusts through the unglazed window and a vague instinct of self-preservation caused Yvonne to seek shelter in the one corner of the room where the icy draught did not penetrate quite so freely.

Eight, nine and ten struck from the tower-clock far away: she heard these sounds as in a dream. Tired, cold and hungry her vitality at that moment was at its lowest ebb – and, with her back resting against the wall she fell presently into a torpor-like sleep.

Suddenly something roused her, and in an instant she sat up – wide-awake and wide-eyed, everyone of her senses conscious and on the alert. Something had roused her – at first she could not say what it was – or remember. Then presently individual sounds detached themselves from the buzzing in her ears. Hitherto the house had always been so still; except on the isolated occasions when Martin-Roget had come to visit her and his heavy tread had caused every loose board in the tumble-down house to creak, it was only Louise Adet's shuffling footsteps which had roused the dormant echoes, when she crept upstairs either to her own room, or to throw a piece of stale bread to her prisoner.

But now – it was neither Martin-Roget's heavy footfall nor the shuffling gait of Louise Adet which had roused Yvonne from her trance-like sleep. It was a gentle, soft, creeping step which was slowly, cautiously mounting the stairs. Yvonne crouching against the wall could count every tread – now and then a board creaked – now and then the footsteps halted.

Yvonne, wide-eyed, her heart stirred by a nameless terror was watching the door.

The piece of tallow-candle flickered in the draught. Its feeble light just touched the remote corner of the room. And Yvonne heard those soft, creeping footsteps as they reached the landing and came to a halt outside the door.

Every drop of blood in her seemed to be frozen by terror: her knees shook: her heart almost stopped its beating.

Under the door something small and white had just been introduced – a scrap of paper; and there it remained – white against the darkness of the unwashed boards – a mysterious message left here by an unknown hand, whilst the unknown footsteps softly crept down the stairs again.

For awhile longer Yvonne remained as she was – cowering against the wall – like a timid little animal, fearful lest that innocent-looking object hid some unthought-of danger. Then at last she gathered courage. Trembling with excitement she raised herself to her knees and then on hands and knees – for she was very weak and faint – she crawled up to that mysterious piece of paper and picked it up.

Her trembling hand closed over it. With wide staring terror-filled eyes she looked all round the narrow room, ere she dared cast one more glance on that mysterious scrap of paper. Then she struggled to her feet and tottered up to the table. She sat down and with fingers numbed with cold she smoothed out the paper and held it close to the light, trying to read what was written on it.

Her sight was blurred. She had to pull herself resolutely together, for suddenly she felt ashamed of her weakness and her overwhelming terror yielded to feverish excitement.

The scrap of paper contained a message – a message addressed to her in that name of which she was so proud – the name which she thought she would never be allowed to bear again: Lady Anthony Dewhurst. She reiterated the words several times, her lips clinging lovingly to them – and just below them there was a small device, drawn in red ink...a tiny flower with five petals...

Yvonne frowned and murmured, vaguely puzzled – no longer frightened now: 'A flower...drawn in red...what can it mean?'

And as a vague memory struggled for expression in her troubled mind she added half aloud: 'Oh! if it should be...!'

But now suddenly all her fears fell away from her. Hope was once more knocking at the gates of her heart – vague memories had taken definite shape...the mysterious letter...the message of hope...the red flower...all were gaining significance. She stooped low to read the letter by the feeble light of the flickering candle. She read it through with her eyes first – then with her lips in a soft murmur, while her mind gradually took in all that it meant for her.

'Keep up your courage. Your friends are inside the city and on the watch. Try the door of your prison every evening at one hour before midnight. Once you will find it yield. Slip out and creep noiselessly down the stairs. At the bottom a friendly hand will be stretched out to you. Take it with confidence – it will lead you to safety and to freedom. Courage and secrecy.'

When she had finished reading, her eyes were swimming in tears. There was no longer any doubt in her mind about the message now, for her dear milor had so often spoken to her about the brave Scarlet Pimpernel who had risked his precious life many a time ere this, in order to render service to the innocent and the oppressed. And now, of a surety, this message came from him: from her dear milor and from his gallant chief. There was the small device – the little red flower which had so often brought hope to despairing hearts. And it was more than hope that it brought to Yvonne. It brought certitude and happiness, and a sweet, tender remorse that she should ever have doubted. She ought to have known all along that everything would be for the best: she had no right ever to have given way to despair. In her heart she prayed for forgiveness from her dear absent milor.

How could she ever doubt him? Was it likely that he would abandon her? – he and that brave friend of his whose powers were indeed magical. Why! she ought to have done her best to keep up her physical as well as her mental faculties – who knows? But perhaps physical strength might be of inestimable value both to herself and to her gallant rescuers presently.

She took up the stale brown bread and ate it resolutely. She drank some water and then stamped round the room to get some warmth into her limbs.

A distant clock had struck ten awhile ago – and if possible she ought to get an hour's rest before the time came for her to be strong and to act: so she shook up her meagre straw paillasse and lay down, determined if possible to get a little sleep – for indeed she felt that that was just what her dear milor would have wished her to do.

Thus time went by – waking or dreaming, Yvonne could never afterwards have said in what state she waited during that one long hour which separated her from the great, blissful moment. The bit of candle burnt low and presently died out. After that Yvonne remained quite still upon the straw, in total darkness: no light came in through the tiny window, only the cold north-westerly wind blew in in gusts. But of a surety the prisoner who was within sight of freedom felt neither cold nor fatigue now.

The tower-clock in the distance struck the quarters with dreary monotony.

3

The last stroke of eleven ceased to vibrate through the stillness of the winter's night.

Yvonne roused herself from the torpor-like state into which she had fallen. She tried to struggle to her feet, but intensity of excitement had caused a strange numbness to invade her limbs. She could hardly move. A second or two ago it had seemed to her that she heard a gentle scraping noise at the door – a drawing of bolts – the grating of a key in the lock – then again, soft, shuffling footsteps that came and went and that were not those of Louise Adet.

At last Yvonne contrived to stand on her feet; but she had to close her eyes and to remain quite still for awhile after that, for her ears were buzzing and her head swimming: she thought that she must fall if she moved and mayhap lose consciousness.

But this state of weakness only lasted a few seconds: the next she had groped her way to the door and her hand had found the iron latch. It yielded. Then she waited, calling up all her strength – for the hour had come wherein she must not only think and act for herself, but think of every possibility which might occur, and act as she imagined her dear lord would require it of her.

She pressed the clumsy iron latch further: it yielded again, and anon she was able to push open the door.

Excited yet confident she tip-toed out of the room. The darkness – like unto pitch – was terribly disconcerting. With the exception of her narrow prison Yvonne had only once seen the interior of the house and that was when, half fainting, she had been dragged across its threshold and up the stairs. She had therefore only a very vague idea as to where the stairs lay and how she was to get about without stumbling.

Slowly and cautiously she crept a few paces forward, then she turned and carefully closed the door behind her. There was not a sound inside the house: everything was silent around her: neither footfall nor whisperings reached her straining ears. She felt about her with her hands, she crouched down on her knees: anon she discovered the head of the stairs.

Then suddenly she drew back, like a frightened hare conscious of danger. All the blood rushed back to her heart, making it beat so violently that she once more felt sick and faint. A sound – gentle as a breath – had broken that absolute and dead silence which up to now had given her confidence. She felt suddenly that she was no longer alone in the darkness – that somewhere close by there was someone – friend or foe – who was lying in watch for her – that somewhere in the darkness something moved and breathed.

The crackling of the paper inside her kerchief served to remind her that her dear milor was on the watch and that the blessed message had spoken of a friendly hand which would be stretched out to her and which she was enjoined to take with confidence. Reassured she crept on again, and anon a softly murmured: 'Hush – sh! – sh! – ' reached her ear. It seemed to come from down below – not very far – and Yvonne, having once more located the head of the stairs with her hands, began slowly to creep downstairs – softly as a mouse – step by step – but every time that a board creaked she paused, terrified, listening for Louise Adet's heavy footstep, for a sound that would mean the near approach of danger.

'Hush – sh – sh' came again as a gentle murmur from below and the something that moved and breathed in the darkness seemed to draw nearer to Yvonne.

A few more seconds of soul-racking suspense, a few more steps down the creaking stairs and she felt a strong hand laid upon her wrist and heard a muffled voice whisper in English:

'All is well! Trust me! Follow me!'

She did not recognize the voice, even though there was something vaguely familiar in its intonation. Yvonne did not pause to conjecture: she had been made happy by the very sound of the language which stood to her for every word of love she had ever heard: it restored her courage and her confidence in their fullest measure.

Obeying the whispered command, Yvonne was content now to follow her mysterious guide who had hold of her hand. The stairs were steep and winding – at a turn she perceived a feeble light at their foot down below. Up against this feeble light the form of her guide was silhouetted in a broad, dark mass. Yvonne could see nothing of him beyond the square outline of his shoulders and that of his sugar-loaf hat. Her mind now was thrilled with excitement and her fingers closed almost convulsively round his hand. He led her across Louise Adet's back kitchen. It was from here that the feeble light came – from a small oil-lamp which stood on the centre table. It helped to guide Yvonne and her mysterious friend to the bottom of the stairs, then across the kitchen to the front door, where again complete darkness reigned. But soon Yvonne – who was following blindly whithersoever she was led – heard the click of a latch and the grating of a door upon its hinges: a cold current of air caught her straight in the face. She could see nothing, for it seemed to be as dark out of doors as in: but she had the sensation of that open door, of a threshold to cross, of freedom and happiness beckoning to her straight out of the gloom. Within the next second or two she would be out of this terrible place, its squalid and dank walls would be behind her. On ahead in that thrice welcome obscurity her dear milor and his powerful friend were beckoning to her to come boldly on – their protecting arms were already stretched out for her; it seemed to her excited fancy as if the cold night-wind brought to her ears the echo of their endearing words.

She filled her lungs with the keen winter air: hope, happiness, excitement thrilled her every nerve.

'A short walk, my lady,' whispered the guide, still speaking in English; 'you are not cold?'

'No, no, I am not cold,' she whispered in reply. 'I am conscious of nothing save that I am free.'

'And you are not afraid?'

'Indeed, indeed I am not afraid,' she murmured fervently. 'May God reward you, sir, for what you do.'

Again there had been that certain something – vaguely familiar – in the way the man spoke which for the moment piqued Yvonne's curiosity. She did not, of a truth, know English well enough to detect the very obvious foreign intonation; she only felt that sometime in the dim and happy past she had heard this man speak. But even this vague sense of puzzlement she dismissed very quickly from her mind. Was she not taking everything on trust? Indeed hope and confidence had a very firm hold on her at last.

6

The Rat Mort

The guide had stepped out of the house into the street, Yvonne
following closely on his heels. The night was very dark and the
narrow little Carrefour de la Poissonnerie very sparsely lighted.
Somewhere overhead on the right, something groaned and
creaked persistently in the wind. A little further on a street
lanthorn was swinging aloft, throwing a small circle of dim,
yellowish light on the unpaved street below. By its fiftul
glimmer Yvonne could vaguely perceive the tall figure of her
guide as he stepped out with noiseless yet firm tread, his
shoulder brushing against the side of the nearest house as he
kept closely within the shadow of its high wall. The sight of his
broad back thrilled her. She had fallen to imagining whether
this was not perchance that gallant and all-powerful Scarlet
Pimpernel himself: the mysterious friend of whom her dear
milor so often spoke with an admiration that was akin to
worship. He too was probably tall and broad – for English
gentlemen were usually built that way; and Yvonne's over-
excited mind went galloping on the wings of fancy, and in her
heart she felt that she was glad that she had suffered so much,
and then lived through such a glorious moment as this.

Now from the narrow unpaved yard in front of the house the
guide turned sharply to the right. Yvonne could only distinguish
outlines. The streets of Nantes were familiar to her, and she

knew pretty well where she was. The lanthorn inside the clock tower of Le Bouffay guided her – it was now on her right – the house wherein she had been kept a prisoner these past three days was built against the walls of the great prison house. She knew that she was in the Carrefour de la Poissonnerie.

She felt neither fatigue nor cold, for she was wildly excited. The keen north-westerly wind searched all the weak places in her worn clothing and her thin shoes were wet through. But her courage up to this point had never once forsaken her. Hope and the feeling of freedom gave her marvellous strength, and when her guide paused a moment ere he turned the angle of the high wall and whispered hurriedly: 'You have courage, my lady?' she was able to answer serenely: 'In plenty, sir.'

She tried to peer into the darkness in order to realize whither she was being led. The guide had come to a halt in front of the house which was next to that of Louise Adet: it projected several feet in front of the latter: the thing that had creaked so weirdly in the wind turned out to be a painted sign, which swung out from an iron bracket fixed into the wall. Yvonne could not read the writing on the sign, but she noticed that just above it there was a small window dimly lighted from within.

What sort of a house it was Yvonne could not, of course, see. The frontage was dark save for narrow streaks of light which peeped through the interstices of the door and through the chinks of ill-fastened shutters on either side. Not a sound came from within, but now that the guide had come to a halt it seemed to Yvonne – whose nerves and senses had become preternaturally acute – that the whole air around her was filled with muffled sounds, and when she stood still and strained her ears to listen she was conscious right through the inky blackness of vague forms – shapeless and silent – that glided past her in the gloom.

2

'Your friends will meet you here,' the guide whispered as he pointed to the door of the house in front of him. 'The door is on the latch. Push it open and walk in boldly. Then gather up all your courage, for you will find yourself in the company of poor people, whose manners are somewhat rougher than those to which you have been accustomed. But though the people are uncouth, you will find them kind. Above all you will find that they will pay no heed to you. So I entreat you do not be afraid. Your friends would have arranged for a more refined place wherein to come and find you, but as you may well imagine they had no choice.'

'I quite understand, sir,' said Yvonne quietly, 'and I am not afraid.'

'Ah! that's brave!' he rejoined. 'Then do as I tell you. I give you my word that inside that house you will be perfectly safe until such time as your friends are able to get to you. You may have to wait an hour, or even two; you must have patience. Find a quiet place in one of the corners of the room and sit there quietly, taking no notice of what goes on around you. You will be quite safe, and the arrival of your friends is only a question of time.'

'My friends, sir?' she said earnestly, and her voice shook slightly as she spoke, 'are you not one of the most devoted friends I can ever hope to have? I cannot find the words now wherewith to thank you, but…'

'I pray you do not thank me,' he broke in gruffly, 'and do not waste time in parleying. The open street is none too safe a place for you just now. The house is.'

His hand was on the latch and he was about to push open the door, when Yvonne stopped him with a word.

'My father?' she whispered with passionate entreaty. 'Will you help him too?'

'M. le duc de Kernogan is as safe as you are, my lady,' he replied. 'He will join you anon. I pray you have no fears for him. Your friends are caring for him in the same way as they care for you.'

'Then I shall see him...soon?'

'Very soon. And in the meanwhile,' he added, 'I pray you to sit quite still and to wait events...despite anything you may see or hear. Your father's safety and your own – not to speak of that of your friends – hangs on your quiescence, your silence, your obedience.'

'I will remember, sir,' rejoined Yvonne quietly. 'I in my turn entreat you to have no fears for me.'

Even while she said this, the man pushed the door open.

3

Yvonne had meant to be brave. Above all she had meant to be obedient. But even so, she could not help recoiling at sight of the place where she had just been told she must wait patiently and silently for an hour, or even two.

The room into which her guide now gently urged her forward was large and low, only dimly lighted by an oil-lamp which hung from the ceiling and emitted a thin stream of black smoke and evil smell. Such air as there was, was foul and reeked of the fumes of alcohol and charcoal, of the smoking lamp and of rancid grease. The walls had no doubt been whitewashed once, now they were of a dull greyish tint, with here and there hideous stains of red or the marks of a set of greasy fingers. The plaster was hanging in strips and lumps from the ceiling; it had fallen away in patches from the walls where it displayed the skeleton laths beneath. There were two doors in the wall immediately facing the front entrance, and on each side of the latter there was a small window, both insecurely shuttered. To Yvonne the whole place appeared unspeakably squalid and noisome. Even as she entered her ears caught the sound of hideous muttered blasphemy, followed by quickly suppressed hoarse and mirthless laughter and the piteous cry of an infant at the breast.

There were perhaps sixteen to twenty people in the room – amongst them a goodly number of women, some of whom had tiny, miserable atoms of humanity clinging to their ragged skirts. A group of men in tattered shirts, bare shins and sabots stood in the centre of the room and had apparently been in conclave when the entrance of Yvonne and her guide caused them to turn quickly to the door and to scan the new-comers with a furtive, suspicious look which would have been pathetic had it not been so full of evil intent. The muttered blasphemy had come from this group; one or two of the men spat upon the ground in the direction of the door, where Yvonne instinctively had remained rooted to the spot.

As for the women, they only betrayed their sex by the ragged clothes which they wore: there was not a face here which had on it a single line of softness or of gentleness: they might have been old women or young: their hair was of a uniform, nondescript colour, lank and unkempt, hanging in thin strands over their brows; their eyes were sunken, their cheeks either flaccid or haggard – there was no individuality amongst them – just one uniform sisterhood of wretchedness which had already gone hand in hand with crime.

Across one angle of the room there was a high wooden counter like a bar, on which stood a number of jugs and bottles, some chunks of bread and pieces of cheese, and a collection of pewter mugs. An old man and a fat, coarse-featured, middle-aged woman stood behind it and dispensed various noxious-looking liquors. Above their heads upon the grimy, tumble-down wall the Republican device 'Liberté! Egalité! Fraternité!' was scrawled in charcoal in huge characters, and below it was scribbled the hideous doggerel which an impious mind had fashioned last autumn on the subject of the martyred Queen.

4

Yvonne had closed her eyes for a moment as she entered; now she turned appealingly toward her guide.

'Must it be in here?' she asked.

'I am afraid it must,' he replied with a sigh. 'You told me that you would be brave.'

She pulled herself together resolutely. 'I will be brave,' she said quietly.

'Ah! that's better,' he rejoined. 'I give you my word that you will be absolutely safe in here until such time as your friends can get to you. I entreat you to gather up your courage. I assure you that these wretched people are not unkind: misery – not unlike that which you yourself have endured – has made them what they are. No doubt we should have arranged for a better place for you wherein to await your friends if we had the choice. But you will understand that your safety and our own had to be our paramount consideration, and we had no choice.'

'I quite understand, sir,' said Yvonne valiantly, 'and am already ashamed of my fears.'

And without another word of protest she stepped boldly into the room.

For a moment or two the guide remained standing on the threshold, watching Yvonne's progress. She had already perceived an empty bench in the furthest angle of the room, up against the door opposite, where she hoped or believed that she could remain unmolested while she waited patiently and in silence as she had been ordered to do. She skirted the groups of men in the centre of the room as she went, but even so she felt more than she heard that muttered insults accompanied the furtive and glowering looks wherewith she was regarded. More than one wretch spat upon her skirts on the way.

But now she was in no sense frightened, only wildly excited; even her feeling of horror she contrived to conquer. The knowledge that her own attitude, and above all her obedience, would help her gallant rescuers in their work gave her enduring strength. She felt quite confident that within an hour or two she would be in the arms of her dear milor who had risked his life in order to come to her. It was indeed well worthwhile to have suffered as she had done, to endure all that she might yet have to endure, for the sake of the happiness which was in store for her.

She turned to give a last look at her guide – a look which was intended to reassure him completely as to her courage and her obedience: but already he had gone and had closed the door behind him, and quite against her will the sudden sense of loneliness and helplessness clutched at her heart with a grip that made it ache. She wished that she had succeeded in catching sight of the face of so valiant a friend: the fact that she was safely out of Louise Adet's vengeful clutches was due to the man who had just disappeared behind that door. It would be thanks to him presently if she saw her father again. Yvonne felt more convinced than ever that he was the Scarlet Pimpernel – milor's friend – who kept his valiant personality a mystery, even to those who owed their lives to him. She had seen the outline of his broad figure, she had felt the touch of his hand. Would she recognize these again when she met him in England in the happy days that were to come? In any case she thought that she would recognize the voice and the manner of speaking, so unlike that of any English gentleman she had known.

5

The man who had so mysteriously led Yvonne de Kernogan from the house of Louise Adet to the Rat Mort, turned away from the door of the tavern as soon as it had closed on the young girl, and started to go back the way he came.

At the angle formed by the high wall of the tavern he paused; a moving form had detached itself from the surrounding gloom and hailed him with a cautious whisper:

233

'Hist! citizen Martin-Roget, is that you?'

'Yes.'

'Everything just as we anticipated?'

'Everything.'

'And the wench safely inside?'

'Quite safely.'

The other gave a low cackle, which might have been intended for a laugh.

'The simplest means,' he said, 'are always the best.'

'She never suspected me. It was all perfectly simple. You are a magician, citizen Chauvelin,' added Martin-Roget grudgingly. 'I never would have thought of such a clever ruse.'

'You see,' rejoined Chauvelin drily, 'I graduated in the school of a master of all ruses – a master of daring and a past master in the art of mimicry. And hope was our great ally – the hope that never forsakes a prisoner – that of getting free. Your fair Yvonne had boundless faith in the power of her English friends, therefore she fell into our trap like a bird.'

'And like a bird she shall struggle in vain after this,' said Martin-Roget slowly. 'Oh! that I could hasten the flight of time – the next few minutes will hang on me like hours. And I wish too it were not so bitterly cold,' he added with a curse; 'this north-westerly wind has got into my bones.'

'On to your nerves, I imagine, citizen,' retorted Chauvelin with a laugh; 'for my part I feel as warm and comfortable as on a lovely day in June.'

'Hark! Who goes there?' broke in the other man abruptly, as a solitary moving form detached itself from the surrounding inky blackness and the sound of measured footsteps broke the silence of the night.

'Quite in order, citizen!' was the prompt reply.

The shadowy form came a step or two further forward.

'Is it you, citizen Fleury?' queried Chauvelin.

'Himself, citizen,' replied the other.

The men had spoken in a whisper. Fleury now placed his hand on Chauvelin's arm.

'We had best not stand so close to the tavern,' he said, 'the night-hawks are already about and we don't want to scare them.'

He led the others up the yard, then into a very narrow passage which lay between Louise Adet's house and the Rat Mort and was bordered by the high walls of the houses on either side.

'This is a blind alley,' he whispered. 'We have the wall of Le Bouffay in front of us: the wall of the Rat Mort is on one side and the house of the citizeness Adet on the other. We can talk here undisturbed.'

Overhead there was a tiny window dimly lighted from within. Chauvelin pointed up to it.

'What is that?' he asked.

'An aperture too small for any human being to pass through,' replied Fleury drily. 'It gives on a small landing at the foot of the stairs. I told Friche to try and manoeuvre so that the wench and her father are pushed in there out of the way while the worst of the fracas is going on. That was your suggestion, citizen Chauvelin.'

'It was. I was afraid the two aristos might get spirited away while your men were tackling the crowd in the tap-room. I wanted them put away in a safe place.'

'The staircase is safe enough,' rejoined Fleury, 'it has no egress save that on the tap-room and only leads to the upper story and the attic. The house has no back entrance – it is built against the wall of Le Bouffay.'

'And what about your Marats, citizen commandant?'

'Oh! I have them all along the street – entirely under cover but closely on the watch – half a company and all keen after the game. The thousand francs you promised them has stimulated their zeal most marvellously, and as soon as Paul Friche in there has whipped up the tempers of the frequenters of the Rat Mort, we shall be ready to rush the place and I assure you, citizen Chauvelin that only a disembodied ghost – if there be one in the place – will succeed in evading arrest.'

'Is Paul Friche already at his post then?'

'And at work – or I'm much mistaken,' replied Fleury as he suddenly gripped Chauvelin by the arm.

For just at this moment the silence of the winter's night was broken by loud cries which came from the interior of the Rat Mort – voices were raised to hoarse and raucous cries – men and women all appeared to be shrieking together, and presently there was a loud crash as of overturned furniture and broken glass.

'A few minutes longer, citizen Fleury,' said Chauvelin, as the commandant of the Marats turned on his heel and started to go back to the Carrefour de la Poissonnerie.

'Oh yes!' whispered the latter, 'we'll wait awhile longer to give the Englishmen time to arrive on the scene. The coast is clear for them – my Marats are hidden from sight behind the doorways and shop-fronts of the houses opposite. In about three minutes from now I'll send them forward.'

'And good luck to your hunting, citizen,' whispered Chauvelin in response.

Fleury very quickly disappeared in the darkness and the other two men followed in his wake. They hugged the wall of the Rat Mort as they went along and its shadow enveloped them completely: their shoes made no sound on the unpaved ground. Chauvelin's nostrils quivered as he drew the keen, cold air into his lungs and faced the north-westerly blast which at this moment also lashed the face of his enemy. His keen eyes tried to pierce the gloom, his ears were strained to hear that merry peal of laughter which in the unforgettable past had been wont to proclaim the presence of the reckless adventurer. He knew – he felt – as certainly as he felt the air which he breathed, that the man whom he hated beyond everything on earth was somewhere close by, wrapped in the murkiness of the night –

thinking, planning, intriguing, pitting his sharp wits, his indomitable pluck, his impudent dare-devilry against the sure and patient trap which had been set for him.

Half a company of Marats in front – the walls of Le Bouffay in the rear! Chauvelin rubbed his thin hands together!

'You are not a disembodied ghost, my fine Scarlet Pimpernel,' he murmured, 'and this time I really think – '

7

The Fracas in the Tavern

Yvonne had settled herself in a corner of the tap-room on a bench and had tried to lose consciousness of her surroundings.

It was not easy! Glances charged with rancour were levelled at her dainty appearance – dainty and refined despite the look of starvation and of weariness on her face and the miserable state of her clothing – and not a few muttered insults waited on those glances.

As soon as she was seated Yvonne noticed that the old man and the coarse, fat woman behind the bar started an animated conversation together, of which she was very obviously the object, for the two heads – the lean and the round – were jerked more than once in her direction. Presently the man – it was George Lemoine, the proprietor of the Rat Mort – came up to where she was sitting: his lank figure was bent so that his lean back formed the best part of an arc, and an expression of mock deference further distorted his ugly face.

He came up quite close to Yvonne and she found it passing difficult not to draw away from him, for the leer on his face was appalling: his eyes, which were set very near to his hooked nose, had a horrible squint, his lips were thick and moist, and his breath reeked of alcohol.

'What will the noble lady deign to drink?' he now asked in an oily, suave voice.

And Yvonne, remembering the guide's admonitions, contrived to smile unconcernedly into the hideous face.

'I would very much like some wine,' she said cheerfully, 'but I am afraid that I have no money wherewith to pay you for it.'

The creature with a gesture of abject humility rubbed his greasy hands together.

'And may I respectfully ask,' he queried blandly, 'what are the intentions of the noble lady in coming to this humble abode, if she hath no desire to partake of refreshments?'

'I am expecting friends,' replied Yvonne bravely; 'they will be here very soon, and will gladly repay you lavishly for all the kindness which you may be inclined to show to me the while.'

She was very brave indeed and looked this awful misshapen specimen of a man quite boldly in the face: she even contrived to smile, though she was well aware that a number of men and women – perhaps a dozen altogether – had congregated in front of her in a compact group around the landlord, that they were nudging one another and pointing derisively – malevolently – at her. It was impossible, despite all attempts at valour, to mistake the hostile attitude of these people. Some of the most obscene words, coined during these last horrible days of the Revolution, were freely hurled at her, and one woman suddenly cried out in a shrill treble:

'Throw her out, citizen Lemoine! We don't want spies in here!'

'Indeed, indeed,' said Yvonne as quietly as she could, 'I am no spy. I am poor and wretched like yourselves and desperately lonely, save for the kind friends who will meet me here anon.'

'Aristos like yourself!' growled one of the men. 'This is no place for you or for them.'

'No! No! This is no place for aristos,' cried one of the women in a voice which many excesses and many vices had rendered hoarse and rough. 'Spy or not, we don't want you in here. Do we?' she added as with arms akimbo she turned to face those of her own sex, who behind the men had come up in order to see what was going on.

'Throw her out, Lemoine,' reiterated a man who appeared to be an oracle amongst the others.

'Please! please let me stop here!' pleaded Yvonne; 'if you turn me out I shall not know what to do: I shall not know where to meet my friends…'

'Pretty story about those friends,' broke in Lemoine roughly. 'How do I know if you're lying or not?'

From the opposite angle of the room, the woman behind the bar had been watching the little scene with eyes that glistened with cupidity. Now she emerged from behind her stronghold of bottles and mugs and slowly waddled across the room. She pushed her way unceremoniously past her customers, elbowing men, women and children vigorously aside with a deft play of her large, muscular arms. Having reached the forefront of the little group she came to a standstill immediately in front of Yvonne, and crossing her mighty arms over her ponderous chest she eyed the 'aristo' with unconcealed malignity.

'We do know that the slut is lying – that is where you make the mistake, Lemoine. A slut, that's what she is – and the friend whom she's going to meet…? Well!' she added, turning with an ugly leer toward the other women, 'we all know what sort of friend that one is likely to be, eh, mesdames? Bringing evil fame on this house, that's what the wench is after…so as to bring the police about our ears… I wouldn't trust her, not another minute. Out with you and at once – do you hear?…this instant… Lemoine has parleyed quite long enough with you already!'

Despite all her resolutions Yvonne was terribly frightened. While the hideous old hag talked and screamed and waved her coarse, red arms about, the unfortunate young girl with a great effort of will, kept repeating to herself: 'I am not frightened – I must not be frightened. He assured me that these people would do me no harm…' But now when the woman had ceased speaking there was a general murmur of:

'Throw her out! Spy or aristo we don't want her here!' whilst some of the men added significantly: 'I am sure that she is one of Carrier's spies and in league with his Marats! We shall have those devils in here in a moment if we don't look out! Throw her out before she can signal to the Marats!'

Ugly faces charged with hatred and virulence were thrust threateningly forward – one or two of the women were obviously looking forward to joining in the scramble, when this 'stuck-up wench' would presently be hurled out into the street.

'Now then, my girl, out you get,' concluded the woman Lemoine, as with an expressive gesture she proceeded to roll her sleeves higher up her arm. She was about to lay her dirty hands on Yvonne, and the poor girl was nearly sick with horror, when one of the men – a huge, coarse giant, whose muscular torso, covered with grease and grime showed almost naked through a ragged shirt which hung from his shoulders in strips – seized the woman Lemoine by the arm and dragged her back a step or two away from Yvonne.

'Don't be a fool, *petite mère*,' he said, accompanying this admonition with a blasphemous oath. 'Slut or no, the wench may as well pay you something for the privilege of staying here. Look at that cloak she's wearing – the shoe-leather on her feet. Aren't they worth a bottle of your sour wine?'

'What's that to you, Paul Friche?' retorted the woman roughly, as with a vigorous gesture she freed her arm from the man's grasp. 'Is this my house or yours?'

'Yours, of course,' replied the man with a coarse laugh and a still coarser jest, 'but this won't be the first time that I have saved you from impulsive folly. Yesterday you were for harbouring a couple of rogues who were Marats in disguise: if I hadn't given you warning, you would now have swallowed more water from the Loire than you would care to hold. But for me two days ago you would have received the goods pinched by Ferté out of Balaze's shop, and been thrown to the fishes in consequence for the entertainment of the proconsul and his friends. You must admit that I've been a good friend to you before now.'

'And if you have, Paul Friche,' retorted the hag obstinately, 'I paid you well for your friendship, both yesterday and the day before, didn't I?'

'You did,' assented Friche imperturbably. 'That's why I want to serve you again tonight.'

'Don't listen to him, *petite mère*,' interposed one or two out of the crowd. 'He is a white-livered skunk to talk to you like that.'

'Very well! Very well!' quoth Paul Friche, and he spat vigorously on the ground in token that henceforth he divested himself from any responsibility in this matter, 'don't listen to me. Lose a benefit of twenty, perhaps forty francs for the sake of a bit of fun. Very well! Very well!' he continued as he turned and slouched out of the group to the further end of the room, where he sat down on a barrel. He drew the stump of a clay pipe out of the pocket of his breeches, stuffed it into his mouth, stretched his long legs out before him and sucked away at his pipe with complacent detachment. 'I didn't know,' he added with biting sarcasm by way of a parting shot, 'that you and Lemoine had come into a fortune recently and that forty or fifty francs are nothing to you now.'

'Forty or fifty? Come! come!' protested Lemoine feebly.

2

Yvonne's fate was hanging in the balance. The attitude of the small crowd was no less threatening than before, but immediate action was withheld while the Lemoines obviously debated in their minds what was best to be done. The instinct to 'have at' an aristo with all the accumulated hatred of many generations was warring with the innate rapacity of the Breton peasant.

'Forty or fifty?' reiterated Paul Friche emphatically. 'Can't you see that the wench is an aristo escaped out of Le Bouffay or the entrepôt?' he added contemptuously.

'I know that she is an aristo,' said the woman, 'that's why I want to throw her out.'

'And get nothing for your pains,' retorted Friche roughly. 'If you wait for her friends we may all of us get as much as twenty francs each to hold our tongues.'

'Twenty francs each...' The murmur was repeated with many a sigh of savage gluttony, by everyone in the room – and repeated again and again – especially by the women.

'You are a fool Paul Friche...' commented Lemoine. 'A fool am I?' retorted the giant. 'Then let me tell you, that 'tis you who are a fool and worse. I happen to know,' he added as he once more rose and rejoined the group in the centre of the room, 'I happen to know that you and everyone here is heading straight for a trap arranged by the Committee of Public Safety, whose chief emissary came into Nantes awhile ago and is named Chauvelin. It is a trap which will land you all in the criminal dock first and on the way to Cayenne or the guillotine afterwards. This place is surrounded with Marats, and orders have been issued to them to make a descent on this place, as soon as papa Lemoine's customers are assembled. There are two members of the accursed company amongst us at the present moment...'

He was standing right in the middle of the room, immediately beneath the hanging lamp. At his words – spoken with such firm confidence, as one who knows and is therefore empowered to speak – a sudden change came over the spirit of the whole assembly. Everything was forgotten in the face of this new danger – two Marats, the sleuth-hounds of the proconsul – here present, as spies and as informants! Every face became more haggard – every cheek more livid. There was a quick and furtive scurrying toward the front door.

'Two Marats here?' shouted one man, who was bolder than the rest. 'Where are they?'

Paul Friche, who towered above his friends, stood at this moment quite close to a small man, dressed like the others in ragged breeches and shirt, and wearing the broad-brimmed hat usually affected by the Breton peasantry.

'Two Marats? Two spies?' screeched a woman. 'Where are they?'

'Here is one,' replied Paul Friche with a loud laugh: and with his large grimy hand he lifted the hat from his neighbour's head and threw it on the ground; 'and there,' he added as with long, bony finger he pointed to the front door, where another man – a square-built youngster with tow-coloured hair somewhat resembling a shaggy dog – was endeavouring to effect a surreptitious exit, 'there is the other; and he is on the point of slipping quietly away in order to report to his captain what he has seen and heard at the Rat Mort. One moment, citizen,' he added, and with a couple of giant strides he too had reached the door; his large rough hand had come down heavily on the shoulder of the youth with the tow-coloured hair, and had forced him to veer round and to face the angry, gesticulating crowd.

'Two Marats! Two spies!' shouted the men. 'Now we'll soon settle their little business for them!'

'Marat yourself,' cried the small man who had first been denounced by Friche. 'I am no Marat, as a good many of you here know. Maman Lemoine,' he added pleading, 'you know me. Am I a Marat?'

But the Lemoines – man and wife – at the first suggestion of police had turned a deaf ear to all their customers. Their own safety being in jeopardy they cared little what happened to anybody else. They had retired behind their counter and were in close consultation together, no doubt as to the best means of escape if indeed the man Paul Friche spoke the truth.

'I know nothing about him,' the woman was saying, 'but he certainly was right last night about those two men who came ferreting in here – and last week too…'

'Am I a Marat, maman Lemoine?' shouted the small man as he hammered his fists upon the counter. 'For ten years and more I have been a customer in this place and...'

'Am I a Marat?' shouted the youth with the tow-coloured hair addressing the assembly indiscriminately. 'Some of you here know me well enough. Jean Paul, you know – Ledouble, you too ...'

'Of course! Of course I know you well enough, Jacques Leroux,' came with a loud laugh from one of the crowd 'Who said you were a Marat?'

'Am I a Marat, maman Lemoine?' reiterated the small man at the counter.

'Oh! leave me alone with your quarrels,' shouted the woman Lemoine in reply. 'Settle them among yourselves.'

'Then if Jacques Leroux is not a Marat,' now came in a bibulous voice from a distant corner of the room, 'and this compeer here is known to maman Lemoine, where are the real Marats who according to this fellow Friche, whom we none of us know, are spying upon us?'

'Yes! where are they?' suggested another. 'Show 'em to us, Paul Friche, or whatever your accursed name happens to be.'

'Tell us where you come from yourself,' screamed the woman with the shrill treble, 'it seems to me quite possible that you're a Marat yourself.'

This suggestion was at once taken up.

'Marat yourself!' shouted the crowd, and the two men who a moment ago had been accused of being spies in disguise shouted louder than the rest: 'Marat yourself!'

3

After that, pandemonium reigned.

The words 'police' and 'Marats' had aroused the terror of all these night-hawks, who were wont to think themselves immune inside their lair: and terror is at all times an evil counsellor. In the space of a few seconds confusion held undisputed sway. Everyone screamed, waved arms, stamped feet, struck out with heavy bare fists at his nearest neighbour. Everyone's hand was against everyone else.

'Spy! Marat! Informer!' were the three words that detached themselves most clearly from out the babel of vituperations freely hurled from end to end of the room.

The children screamed, the women's shrill or hoarse treble mingled with the cries and imprecations of the men.

Paul Friche had noted that the turn of the tide was against him, long before the first naked fist had been brandished in his face. Agile as a monkey he had pushed his way through to the bar, and placing his two hands upon it, with a swift leap he had taken up a sitting position in the very middle of the table amongst the jugs and bottles, which he promptly seized and used as missiles and weapons, whilst with his dangling feet encased in heavy sabots he kicked out vigorously and unceasingly against the shins of his foremost assailants.

He had the advantage of position and used it cleverly. In his right hand he held a pewter mug by the handle and used it as a swivel against his aggressors with great effect.

'The Loire for you – you blackmailer! liar! traitor!' shouted some of the women who, bolder than the men, thrust shaking fists at Paul Friche as closely as that pewter mug would allow.

'Break his jaw before he can yell for the police,' admonished one of the men from the rear, 'before he can save his own skin.'

But those who shouted loudest had only their fists by way of weapon and Paul Friche had mugs and bottles, and those sabots of his kicked out with uncomfortable agility.

'Break my jaw will you,' he shouted every time that a blow from the mug went home, 'a spy am I? Very well then, here's for you, Jacques Leroux; go and nurse your cracked skull at home. You want a row?' he added hitting at a youth who brandished a heavy fist in his face, 'well! you shall have it and as much of it as you like! as much of it as will bring the patrols of police comfortably about your ears.'

Bang! went the pewter mug crashing against a man's hard skull! Bang went Paul Friche's naked fist against the chest of another. He was a hard hitter and swift.

The Lemoines from behind their bar shouted louder than the rest, doing as much as their lungs would allow them in the way of admonishing, entreating, protesting – cursing everyone for a set of fools who were playing straight into the hands of the police.

'Now then! Now then, children, stop that bellowing, will you? There are no spies here Paul Friche was only having his little joke! We all know one another, what?'

'Camels!' added Lemoine more forcibly. 'They'll bring the patrols about our ears for sure.'

Paul Friche was not by any means the only man who was being vigorously attacked. After the first two or three minutes of this kingdom of pandemonium, it was difficult to say who was quarrelling with whom. Old grudges were revived, old feuds taken up there, where they had previously been interrupted. Accusations of spying were followed by abuse for some past wrong of black-legging or cheating a confrère. The temperature of the room became suffocating. All these violent passions seething within these four walls seemed to become tangible and to mingle with the atmosphere already surcharged with the fumes of alcohol, of tobacco and of perspiring humanity. There was many a black-eye already, many a contusion: more than one knife – surreptitiously drawn – was already stained with red.

4

There was also a stampede for the door. One man gave the signal. Seeing that his mates were wasting precious time by venting their wrath against Paul Friche and then quarrelling among themselves, he hoped to effect an escape ere the police came to stop the noise. No one believed in the place being surrounded. Why should it be? The Marats were far too busy hunting up rebels and aristos to trouble much about the Rat Mort and its customers, but it was quite possible that a brawl would bring a patrol along, and then 'ware the *police correction-nelle* and the possibility of deportation or worse. Retreat was undoubtedly safer while there was time. One man first: then one or two more on his heels, and those among the women who had children in their arms or clinging to their skirts: they turned stealthily to the door – almost ashamed of their cowardice, ashamed lest they were seen abandoning the field of combat.

It was while confusion reigned unchecked that Yvonne – who was cowering, frankly terrified at last, in the corner of the room, became aware that the door close beside her – the door situated immediately opposite the front entrance – was surreptitiously opened. She turned quickly to look – for she was like a terror-stricken little animal now – one that scents and feels and fears danger from every quarter round. The door was being pushed open very slowly by what was still to Yvonne an unseen hand. Somehow that opening door fascinated her: for the moment she forgot the noise and the confusion around her.

Then suddenly with a great effort of will she checked the scream which had forced itself up to her throat.

'Father!' was all that she contrived to say in a hoarse and passionate murmur.

Fortunately as he peered cautiously round the room, M. le duc caught sight of his daughter. She was staring at him – wide-eyed, her lips bloodless, her cheeks the colour of ashes. He looked but the ghost now of that proud aristocrat who little more than a week ago was the centre of a group of courtiers round the person of the heir to the English throne. Starved, emaciated, livid, he was the shadow of his former self, and there was a haunted look in his purple-rimmed eyes which spoke with pathetic eloquence of sleepless nights and of a soul tortured with remorse.

Just for the moment no one took any notice of him – everyone was shrieking, everyone was quarrelling, and M. le duc, placing a finger to his lips, stole cautiously round to his daughter. The next instant they were clinging to one another, these two, who had endured so much together – he the father who had wrought such an unspeakable wrong, and she the child who was so lonely, so forlorn and almost happy in finding someone who belonged to her, someone to whom she could cling.

'Father, dear! what shall we do?' Yvonne murmured, for she felt the last shred of her fictitious courage oozing out of her, in face of this awful lawlessness which literally paralyzed her thinking faculties.

'Sh! dear!' whispered M. le duc in reply. 'We must get out of this loathsome place while this hideous row is going on. I heard it all from the filthy garret up above, where those devils have kept me these three days. The door was not locked... I crept downstairs... No one is paying heed to us... We can creep out. Come.'

But at the suggestion, Yvonne's spirits, which had been stunned by the events of the past few moments, revived with truly mercurial rapidity.

'No! no! dear,' she urged. 'We must stay here... You don't know... I have had a message – from my own dear milor – my husband...he sent a friend to take me out of the hideous prison where that awful Pierre Adet was keeping me – a friend who assured me that my dear milor was watching over me...he brought me to this place – and begged me not to be frightened...but to wait patiently...and I must wait, dear... I must wait!'

She spoke rapidly in whispers and in short jerky sentences. M. le duc listened to her wide-eyed, a deep line of puzzlement between his brows. Sorrow, remorse, starvation, misery had in a measure numbed his mind. The thought of help, of hope, of friends could not penetrate into his brain.

'A message,' he murmured inanely, 'a message. No! no! my girl, you must trust no one... Pierre Adet... Pierre Adet is full of evil tricks – he will trap you...he means to destroy us both... he has brought you here so that you should be murdered by these ferocious devils.'

'Impossible, father dear,' she said, still striving to speak bravely. 'We have both of us been all this while in the power of Pierre Adet; he could have had no object in bringing me here tonight.'

But the father who had been an insentient tool in the schemes of that miserable intriguer, who had been the means of bringing his only child to this terrible and deadly pass – the man who had listened to the lying counsels and proposals of his own most bitter enemy, could only groan now in terror and in doubt.

'Who can probe the depths of that abominable villain's plans,' he murmured vaguely.

In the meanwhile the little group who had thought prudence the better part of valour had reached the door. The foremost man amongst them opened it and peered cautiously out into the darkness. He turned back to those behind him, put a finger to his lip and beckoned to them to follow him in silence.

'Yvonne, let us go!' whispered the duc, who had seized his daughter by the hand.

'But father...'

'Let us go!' he reiterated pitiably. 'I shall die if we stay here!'

'It won't be for long, father dear,' she entreated; 'if milor should come with his friend, and find us gone, we should be endangering his life as well as our own.'

'I don't believe it,' he rejoined with the obstinacy of weakness. 'I don't believe in your message...how could milor or anyone come to your rescue, my child?... No one knows that you are here, in this hell in Nantes.'

Yvonne clung to him with the strength of despair. She too was as terrified as any human creature could be and live, but terror had not altogether swept away her belief in that mysterious message, in that tall guide who had led her hither, in that scarlet device – the five-petalled flower which stood for everything that was most gallant and most brave.

She desired with all her might to remain here – despite everything, despite the awful brawl that was raging round her and which sickened her, despite the horror of the whole thing – to remain here and to wait. She put her arms round her father: she dragged him back every time that he tried to move. But a sort of unnatural strength seemed to have conquered his former debility. His attempts to get away became more and more determined and more and more febrile.

'Come, Yvonne! we must go!' he continued to murmur intermittently and with ever-growing obstinacy. 'No one will notice us... I heard the noise from my garret upstairs... I crept down... I knew no one would notice me... Come – we must go...now is our time.'

'Father dear, whither could we go? Once in the streets of Nantes what would happen to us?'

'We can find our way to the Loire!' he retorted almost brutally. He shook himself free from her restraining arms and gripped her firmly by the hand. He tried to drag her toward the door, whilst she still struggled to keep him back. He had just caught sight of the group of men and women at the front door: their leader was standing upon the threshold and was still peering out into the darkness.

But the next moment they all came to a halt: what their leader had perceived through the darkness did not evidently quite satisfy him: he turned and held a whispered consultation with the others. M. le duc strove with all his might to join in with that group. He felt that in its wake would lie the road to freedom. He would have struck Yvonne for standing in the way of her own safety.

'Father dear,' she contrived finally to say to him, 'if you go hence, you will go alone. Nothing will move me from here, because I know that milor will come.'

'Curse you for your obstinacy,' retorted the duc, 'you jeopardize my life and yours.'

Then suddenly from the angle of the room where wrangling and fighting were at their fiercest, there came a loud call:

'Look out, père Lemoine, your aristos are running away. You are losing your last chance of those fifty francs.'

It was Paul Friche who had shouted. His position on the table was giving him a commanding view over the heads of the threatening, shouting, perspiring crowd, and he had just caught sight of M. le duc dragging his daughter by force toward the door.

'The authors of all this pother,' he added with an oath, 'and they will get away whilst we have the police about our ears.'

'Name of a name of a dog,' swore Lemoine from behind his bar, 'that shall not be. Come along, maman, let us bring those aristos along here. Quick now.'

It was all done in a second. Lemoine and his wife, with the weight and authority of the masters of the establishment, contrived to elbow their way through the crowd. The next moment Yvonne felt herself forcibly dragged away from her father.

'This way, my girl, and no screaming,' a bibulous voice said in her ear, 'no screaming, or I'll smash some of those front teeth of yours. You said some rich friends were coming along for you presently. Well then! come and wait for them out of the crowd.'

Indeed Yvonne had no desire to struggle or to scream. Salvation she thought had come to her and to her father in this rough guise. In another moment mayhap he would have forced her to follow him, to leave milor in the lurch, to jeopardize for ever every chance of safety.

'It is all for the best, father dear,' she managed to cry out over her shoulder, for she had just caught sight of him being seized round the shoulders by Lemoine and heard him protesting loudly:

'I'll not go! I'll not go! Let me go!' he shouted hoarsely. 'My daughter! Yvonne! Let me go! You devil!'

But Lemoine had twice the vigour of the duc de Kernogan, nor did he care one jot about the other's protests. He hated all this row inside his house, but there had been rows in it before and he was beginning to hope that nothing serious would come of it. On the other hand, Paul Friche might be right about these aristos; there might be forty or fifty francs to be made out of them, and in any case they had one or two things upon their persons which might be worth a few francs – and who knows? they might even have something in their pockets worth taking.

This hope and thought gave Lemoine additional strength, and seeing that the aristo struggled so desperately, he thought to silence him by bringing his heavy fist with a crash upon the old man's head.

'Yvonne! *A moi*!' shouted M. le duc ere he fell back senseless.

That awful cry, Yvonne heard it as she was being dragged through the noisome crowd. It mingled in her ear with the other awful sounds – the oaths and blasphemies which filled the air with their hideousness. It died away just as a formidable crash against the entrance door suddenly silenced every cry within.

'All hands up!' came with a peremptory word of command from the doorway.

'Mercy on us!' murmured the woman Lemoine, who still had Yvonne by the hand, 'we are undone this time.'

There was a clatter and grounding of arms – a scurrying of bare feet and sabots upon the floor, the mingled sounds of men trying to fly and being caught in the act and hurled back: screams of terror from the women, one or two pitiable calls, a few shrill cries from frightened children, a few dull thuds as of

253

human bodies falling... It was all so confused, so unspeakably horrible. Yvonne was hardly conscious. Near her someone whispered hurriedly:

'Put the aristos away somewhere, maman Lemoine...the whole thing may only be a scare...the Marats may only be here about the aristos...they will probably leave you alone if you give them up...perhaps you'll get a reward... Put them away till some of this row subsides... I'll talk to Commandant Fleury if I can.'

Yvonne felt her knees giving way under her. There was nothing more to hope for now – nothing. She felt herself lifted from the ground – she was too sick and faint to realize what was happening: through the din which filled her ears she vainly tried to distinguish her father's voice again.

5

A moment or two later she found herself squatting somewhere on the ground. How she got here she did not know – where she was she knew still less. She was in total darkness. A fusty, close smell of food and wine gave her a wretched feeling of nausea – her head ached intolerably, her eyes were hot, her throat dry: there was a constant buzzing in her ears.

The terrible sounds of fighting and screaming and cursing, the crash of broken glass and overturned benches came to her as through a partition – close by but muffled.

In the immediate nearness all was silence and darkness.

8

The English Adventurers

It was with that muffled din still ringing in her ear and with the conception of all that was going on, on the other side of the partition, standing like an awesome spectre of evil before her mind, that Yvonne woke to the consciousness that her father was dead.

He lay along the last half-dozen steps of a narrow wooden staircase which had its base in the narrow, cupboard-like landing on to which the Lemoines had just thrust them both. Through a small heart-shaped hole cut in the door of the partition-wall, a shaft of feeble light struck straight across to the foot of the stairs: it lit up the recumbent figure of the last of the ducs de Kernogan, killed in a brawl in a house of evil fame.

Weakened by starvation, by the hardships of the past few days, his constitution undermined by privations and mayhap too by gnawing remorse, he had succumbed to the stunning blow dealt to him by a half drunken brute. His cry: 'Yvonne! *A moi!*' was the last despairing call of a soul racked with remorse to the daughter whom he had so cruelly wronged.

When first that feeble shaft of light had revealed to her the presence of that inert form upon the steps, she had struggled to her feet and – dazed – had tottered up to it. Even before she had touched the face, the hands, before she had bent her ear to the half-closed mouth and failed to catch the slightest breath, she knew the full extent of her misery. The look in the wide-open eyes did not terrify her, but they told her the truth, and since then she had cowered beside her dead father on the bottom step of the narrow stairs, her fingers tightly closed over that one hand which never would be raised against her.

An unspeakable sense of horror filled her soul. The thought that he – the proud father, the haughty aristocrat, should lie like this and in such a spot, dragged in and thrown down – no doubt by Lemoine – like a parcel of rubbish and left here to be dragged away again and thrown again like a dog into some unhallowed ground – that thought was so horrible, so monstrous, that at first it dominated even sorrow. Then came the heartrending sense of loneliness. Yvonne Dewhurst had endured so much these past few days that awhile ago she would have affirmed that nothing could appal her in the future. But this was indeed the awful and overwhelming climax to what had already been a surfeit of misery.

This! she, Yvonne, cowering beside her dead father, with no one to stand between her and any insult, any outrage which might be put upon her, with nothing now but a few laths between her and that yelling, screeching mob outside.

Oh! the loneliness! the utter, utter loneliness!

She kissed the inert hand, the pale forehead: with gentle, reverent fingers she tried to smoothe out those lines of horror and of fear which gave such a pitiful expression to the face. Of all the wrongs which her father had done her she never thought for a moment. It was he who had brought her to this terrible pass: he who had betrayed her into the hands of her deadliest enemy: he who had torn her from the protecting arms of her dear milor and flung her and himself at the mercy of a set of inhuman wretches who knew neither compunction nor pity.

But all this she forgot, as she knelt beside the lifeless form – the last thing on earth that belonged to her – the last protection to which she might have clung.

2

Out of the confusion of sounds which came – deadened by the intervening partition – to her ear, it was impossible to distinguish anything very clearly. All that Yvonne could do, as soon as she had in a measure collected her scattered senses, was to try and piece together the events of the last few minutes – minutes which indeed seemed like days and even years to her.

Instinctively she gave to the inert hand which she held an additional tender touch. At any rate her father was out of it all. He was at rest and at peace. As for the rest, it was in God's hands. Having only herself to think of now, she ceased to care what became of her. He was out of it all: and those wretches after all could not do more than kill her. A complete numbness of senses and of mind had succeeded the feverish excitement of the past few hours: whether hope still survived at this moment in Yvonne Dewhurst's mind it were impossible to say. Certain it is that it lay dormant – buried beneath the overwhelming misery of her loneliness.

She took the fichu from her shoulders and laid it reverently over the dead man's face: she folded the hands across the breast. She could not cry: she could only pray, and that quite mechanically.

The thought of her dear milor, of his clever friend, of the message which she had received in prison, of the guide who had led her to this awful place, was relegated – almost as a memory – in the furthermost cell of her brain.

3

But after awhile outraged nature, still full of vitality and of youth, re-asserted itself. She felt numb and cold and struggled to her feet. From somewhere close to her a continuous current of air indicated the presence of some sort of window. Yvonne, faint with the close and sickly smell, which even that current failed to disperse, felt her way all round the walls of the narrow landing.

The window was in the wall between the partition and the staircase, it was small and quite low down. It was crossed with heavy iron bars. Yvonne leaned up against it, grateful for the breath of pure air.

For awhile yet she remained unconscious of everything save the confused din which still went on inside the tavern, and at first the sounds which came through the grated window mingled with those on the other side of the partition. But gradually as she contrived to fill her lungs with the cold breath of heaven, it seemed as if a curtain was being slowly drawn away from her atrophied senses.

Just below the window two men were speaking. She could hear them quite distinctly now – and soon one of the voices – clearer than the other – struck her ear with unmistakable familiarity.

'I told Paul Friche to come out here and speak to me,' Yvonne heard that same voice say.

'Then he should be here,' replied the other, 'and if I am not mistaken…'

There was a pause, and then the first voice was raised again.

'Halt! Is that Paul Friche?'

'At your service, citizen,' came in reply.

'Well! Is everything working smoothly inside?'

'Quite smoothly; but your Englishmen are not there.'

'How do you know?'

'Bah! I know most of the faces that are to be found inside the Rat Mort at this hour: there are no strangers among them.'

The voice that had sounded so familiar to Yvonne was raised now in loud and coarse laughter.

'Name of a dog! I never for a moment thought that there were any Englishmen about. Citizen Chauvelin was suffering from nightmare.'

'It is early yet,' came in response from a gentle bland voice, 'you must have patience, citizen.'

'Patience? Bah!' ejaculated the other roughly. 'As I told you before 'tis but little I care about your English spies. 'Tis the Kernogans I am interested in. What have you done with them, citizen?'

'I got that blundering fool Lemoine to lock them up on the landing at the bottom of the stairs.'

'Is that safe?'

'Absolutely. It has no egress save into the tap-room and up the stairs, to the rooms above. Your English spies if they came now would have to fly in and out of those top windows ere they could get to the aristos.'

'Then in Satan's name keep them there awhile,' urged the more gentle, insinuating voice, 'until we can make sure of the English spies.'

'Tshaw! What foolery!' interjected the other, who appeared to be in a towering passion. 'Bring them out at once, citizen Friche...bring them out...right into the middle of the rabble in the tap-room... Commandant Fleury is directing the perquisition – he is taking down the names of all that cattle which he is arresting inside the premises – let the ci-devant duc de Kernogan and his exquisite daughter figure among the vilest cut-throats of Nantes.'

'Citizen, let me urge on you once more...' came in earnest persuasive accents from that gentle voice.

'Nothing!' broke in the other savagely. 'To h–ll with your English spies. It is the Kernogans that I want.'

Yvonne, half-crazed with horror, had heard the whole of this abominable conversation wherein she had not failed to recognize the voice of Martin-Roget or Pierre Adet, as she now knew him to be. Who the other two men were she could easily conjecture. The soft bland voice she had heard twice during these past few days, which had been so full of misery, of terror and of surprise: once she had heard it on board the ship which had taken her away from England and once again a few hours since, inside the narrow room which had been her prison. The third man who had subsequently arrived on the scene was that coarse and grimy creature who had seemed to be the moving evil spirit of that awful brawl in the tavern.

What the conversation meant to her she could not fail to guess. Pierre Adet had by what he said made the whole of his abominable intrigue against her palpably clear. Her father had been right, after all. It was Pierre Adet who through some clever trickery had lured her to this place of evil. How it was all done she could not guess. The message…the device…her walk across the street…the silence…the mysterious guide…which of these had been the trickery?…which had been concocted by her enemy?…which devised by her dear milor?

Enough that the whole thing was a trap, a trap all the more hideous as she, Yvonne, who would have given her heart's blood for her beloved, was obviously the bait wherewith these friends meant to capture him and his noble chief. They knew evidently of the presence of the gallant Scarlet Pimpernel and his band of heroes here in Nantes – they seemed to expect their appearance at this abominable place tonight. She, Yvonne, was to be the decoy which was to lure to this hideous lair those noble eagles who were still out of reach.

And if that was so – if indeed her beloved and his valiant friends had followed her hither, then some part of the message of hope must have come from them or from their chief…and milor and his friend must even now be somewhere close by, watching their opportunity to come to her rescue…heedless of the awful danger which lay in wait for them…ignorant mayhap of the abominable trap which had been so cunningly set for them by these astute and ferocious brutes.

Yvonne a prisoner in this narrow space, clinging to the bars of what was perhaps the most cruel prison in which she had yet been confined, bruised her hands and arms against those bars in a wild desire to get out. She longed with all her might to utter one long, loud and piercing cry of warning to her dear milor not to come nigh her now, to fly, to run while there was yet time; and all the while she knew that if she did utter such a cry he would hurry hot-haste to her side. One moment she would have had him near – another she wished him an hundred miles away.

4

In the tap-room a more ordered medley of sounds had followed on the wild pandemonium of awhile ago. Brief, peremptory words of command, steady tramping of feet, loud harsh questions and subdued answers, occasionally a moan or a few words of protest quickly suppressed, came through the partition to Yvonne's straining ears.

'Your name?'

'Where do you live?'

'Your occupation?'

'That's enough. Silence. The next.'

'Your name?'

'Where do you live?'

Men, women and even children were being questioned, classified, packed off, God knew whither. Sometimes a child would cry, a man utter an oath, a woman shriek: then would come harsh orders delivered in a gruff voice, more swearing, the grounding of arms and more often than not a dull, flat sound like a blow struck against human flesh, followed by a volley of curses, or a cry of pain.

'Your name?'

'George Amédé Lemoine.'

'Where do you live?'

'In this house.'

'Your occupation?'

'I am the proprietor of the tavern, citizen. I am an honest man and a patriot. The Republic…'

'That's enough.'

'But I protest.'

'Silence. The next.'

All with dreary, ceaseless monotony: and Yvonne like a trapped bird was bruising her wings against the bars of her cage. Outside the window Chauvelin and Martin-Roget were still speaking in whispers – the fowlers were still watching for their prey. The third man had apparently gone away. What went on beyond the range of her prison window – out in the darkness of the night which Yvonne's aching eyes could not pierce – she, the miserable watcher, the bait set here to catch the noble game, could not even conjecture. The window was small and her vision was further obstructed by heavy bars. She could see nothing – hear nothing save those two men talking in whispers. Now and again she caught a few words:

'A little while longer, citizen...you lose nothing by waiting. Your Kernogans are safe enough. Paul Friche has assured you that the landing where they are now has no egress save through the tap-room, and to the floor above. Wait at least until Commandant Fleury has got the crowd together, after which he will send his Marats to search the house. It won't be too late then to lay hands on your aristos, if in the meanwhile...'

' 'Tis futile to wait,' here interrupted Martin-Roget roughly, 'and you are a fool, citizen, if you think that those Englishmen exist elsewhere than in your imagination.'

'Hark!' broke in the gentle voice abruptly and with forceful command.

And as Yvonne too in instinctive response to that peremptory call was further straining her every sense in order to listen, there came from somewhere, not very far away, right through the stillness of the night, a sound which caused her pulses to still their beating and her throat to choke with the cry which rose from her breast.

It was only the sound of a quaint and drawly voice saying loudly and in English:

'Egad, Tony! ain't you getting demmed sleepy?'

Just for the space of two or three seconds Yvonne had remained quite still while this unexpected sound sent its dulcet echo on the wings of the north-westerly blast. The next – stumbling in the dark – she had run to the stairs even while she heard Martin-Roget calling loudly and excitedly to Paul Friche.

One reverent pause beside her dead father, one mute prayer commending his soul to the mercy of his Maker, one agonized entreaty to God to protect her beloved and his friend, and then she ran swiftly up the winding steps.

At the top of the stairs, immediately in front of her, a door – slightly ajar – showed a feeble light through its aperture. Yvonne pushed the door further open and slipped into the room beyond. She did not pause to look round but went straight to the window and throwing open the ricketty sash she peeped out. For the moment she felt that she would gladly have bartered away twenty years of her life to know exactly whence had come that quaint and drawling voice. She leaned far out of the window trying to see. It gave on the side of the Rat Mort over against Louise Adet's house – the space below seemed to her to be swarming with men: there were hurried and whispered calls – orders were given to stand at close attention, whilst Martin-Roget had apparently been questioning Paul Friche, for Yvonne heard the latter declare emphatically:

'I am certain that it came either from inside the house or from the roof. And with your permission, citizen, I would like to make assurance doubly sure.'

Then one of the men must suddenly have caught sight of the vague silhouette leaning out of the window, for Martin-Roget and Friche uttered a simultaneous cry, whilst Chauvelin said hurriedly:

'You are right, citizen, something is going on inside the house.'

'What can we do?' queried Martin-Roget excitedly.

'Nothing for the moment but wait. The Englishmen are caught sure enough like rats in their holes.'

'Wait!' ejaculated Martin-Roget with a savage oath, 'wait! always wait! while the quarry slips through one's fingers.'

'It shall not slip through mine,' retorted Paul Friche. 'I was a steeple-jack by trade in my day: it won't be the first time that I have climbed the side of a house by the gutter-pipe. *A moi* Jean-Pierre,' he added, 'and may I be drowned in the Loire if between us two we do not lay those cursed English spies low.'

'An hundred francs for each of you,' called Chauvelin lustily, 'if you succeed.'

Yvonne did not think to close the window again. Vigorous shouting and laughter from below testified that that hideous creature Friche and his mate had put their project in immediate execution; she turned and ran down the stairs – feeling now like an animal at bay; by the time that she had reached the bottom, she heard a prolonged, hoarse cry of triumph from below and guessed that Paul Friche and his mate had reached the windowsill: the next moment there was a crash overhead of broken window-glass and of furniture kicked from one end of the room to the other, immediately followed by the sound of heavy footsteps running helter-skelter down the stairs.

Yvonne, half-crazed with terror, faint and sick, fell unconscious over the body of her father.

5

Inside the tap-room Commandant Fleury was still at work.

'Your name?'

'Where do you live?'

'Your occupation?'

The low room was filled to suffocation: the walls lined with Marats, the doors and windows which were wide open were closely guarded, whilst in the corner of the room, huddled together like bales of rubbish, was the human cattle that had been driven together, preparatory to being sent for trial to Paris in vindication of Carrier's brutalities against the city.

Fleury for form's sake made entries in a notebook – the whole thing was a mere farce – these wretched people were not likely to get a fair trial – what did the whole thing matter? Still! the commandant of the Marats went solemnly through the farce which Carrier had invented with a view to his own justification.

Lemoine and his wife had protested and been silenced: men had struggled and women had fought – some of them like wild cats – in trying to get away. Now there were only half a dozen or so more to docket. Fleury swore, for he was tired and hot.

'This place is like a pest-house,' he said.

Just then came the sound of that lusty cry of triumph from outside, followed by all the clatter and the breaking of window glass.

'What's that?' queried Fleury.

The heavy footsteps running down the stairs caused him to look up from his work and to call briefly to a sergeant of the Marats who stood beside his chair:

'Go and see what that *sacré* row is about,' he commanded. 'In there,' he added as he indicated the door of the landing with a jerk of the head.

But before the man could reach the door, it was thrown open from within with a vigorous kick from the point of a sabot, and Paul Friche appeared under the lintel with the aristo wench thrown over his shoulder like a sack of potatoes, his thick, muscular arms encircling her knees. His scarlet bonnet was cocked over one eye, his face was smeared with dirt, his breeches were torn at the knees, his shirt hung in strips from his powerful shoulders. Behind him his mate – who had climbed up the gutter-pipe into the house in his wake – was tottering under the load of the ci-devant duc de Kernogan's body which he had slung across his back and was holding on to by the wrists.

Fleury jumped to his feet – the appearance of these two men, each with his burden, caused him to frown with anger and to demand peremptorily: 'What is the meaning of this?'

'The aristos,' said Paul Friche curtly; 'they were trying to escape.'

He strode into the room, carrying the unconscious form of the girl as if it were a load of feathers. He was a huge, massive-looking giant: the girl's shoulders nearly touched the low ceiling as he swung forward facing the angry commandant.

'How did you get into the house? and by whose orders?' demanded Fleury roughly.

'Climbed in by the window, *pardi*,' retorted the man, 'and by the orders of citizen Martin-Roget.'

'A corporal of the Company Marat takes orders only from me; you should know that, citizen Friche.'

'Nay!' interposed the sergeant quickly, 'this man is not a corporal of the Company Marat, citizen commandant. As for Corporal Friche, why! he was taken to the infirmary some hours ago with a cracked skull, he…'

'Not Corporal Friche,' exclaimed Fleury with an oath, 'then who in the devil's name is this man?'

'The Scarlet Pimpernel, at your service, citizen commandant,' came loudly and with a merry laugh from the pseudo Friche.

And before either Fleury or the sergeant or any of the Marats could even begin to realize what was happening, he had literally bounded across the room, and as he did so he knocked against the hanging lamp which fell with a crash to the floor, scattering oil and broken glass in every direction and by its fall plunging the place into total darkness. At once there arose a confusion and medley of terrified screams, of piercing shrieks from the women and the children, and of loud imprecations from the men. These mingled with the hasty words of command, with quick orders from Fleury and the sergeant, with the grounding of arms and the tramping of many feet, and with the fall of human bodies that happened to be in the way of the reckless adventurer and his flight.

'He is through the door,' cried the men who had been there on guard.

'After him then!' shouted Fleury, 'Curse you all for cowards and for fools.'

The order had no need to be repeated. The confusion, though great, had only been momentary. Within a second or less, Fleury and his sergeant had fought their way through to the door, urging the men to follow.

'After him...quick!...he is heavily loaded...he cannot have got far...' commanded Fleury as soon as he had crossed the threshold. 'Sergeant, keep order within, and on your life see that no one else escapes.'

9

The Proconsul

From round the angle of the house Martin-Roget and Chauvelin were already speeding along at a rapid pace.

'What does it all mean?' queried the latter hastily.

'The Englishman – with the wench on his back? have you seen him?'

'Malediction! what do you mean?'

'Have you seen him?' reiterated Fleury hoarsely.

'No.'

'He couldn't have passed you?'

'Impossible.'

'Then unless some of us here have eyes like cats that limb of Satan will get away. On to him my men,' he called once more. 'Can you see him?'

The darkness outside was intense. The north-westerly wind was whistling down the narrow street, drowning the sound of every distant footfall: it tore mercilessly round the men's heads, snatching the bonnets from off their heads, dragging at their loose shirts and breeches, adding to the confusion which already reigned.

'He went this way…' shouted one.

'No! that!' cried another.

'There he is!' came finally in chorus from several lusty throats. 'Just crossing the bridge.'

'After him,' cried Fleury, 'an hundred francs to the man who first lays hands on that devil.'

Then the chase began. The Englishman on ahead was unmistakable with that burden on his shoulder. He had just reached the foot of the bridge where a street lanthorn fixed on a tall bracket on the corner stone had suddenly thrown him into bold relief. He had less than an hundred metres start of his pursuers and with a wild cry of excitement they started in his wake.

He was now in the middle of the bridge – an unmistakable figure of a giant vaguely silhouetted against the light from the lanthorns on the further end of the bridge – seeming preternaturally tall and misshapen with that hump upon his back.

From right and left, from under the doorways of the houses in the Carrefour de la Poissonnerie the Marats who had been left on guard in the street now joined in the chase. Overhead windows were thrown open – the good burghers of Nantes, awakened from their sleep, forgetful for the nonce of all their anxieties, their squalor and their miseries, leaned out to see what this new kind of din might mean. From everywhere – it almost seemed as if some sprang out of the earth – men, either of the town-guard or Marats on patrol duty, or merely idlers and night-hawks who happened to be about, yielded to that primeval instinct of brutality which causes men as well as beasts to join in a pursuit against a fellow creature.

Fleury was in the rear of his posse, Martin-Roget and Chauvelin, walking as rapidly as they could by his side, tried to glean some information out of the commandant's breathless and scrappy narrative:

'What happened exactly?'

'It was the man Paul Friche...with the aristo wench on his back...and another man carrying the ci-devant aristo...they were the English spies...in disguise...they knocked over the lamp...and got away...'

'Name of a…'

'No use swearing, citizen Martin-Roget,' retorted Fleury as hotly as his agitated movements would allow. 'You and citizen Chauvelin are responsible for the affairs. It was you, citizen Chauvelin, who placed Paul Friche inside that tavern in observation – you told him what to do…'

'Well?'

'Paul Friche – the real Paul Friche – was taken to the infirmary some hours ago…with a cracked skull, dealt him by your Englishman, I've no doubt…'

'Impossible,' reiterated Chauvelin with a curse.

'Impossible? why impossible?'

'The man I spoke to outside Le Bouffay…'

'Was not Paul Friche.'

'He was on guard in the Place with two other Marats.'

'He was not Paul Friche – the others were not Marats.'

'Then the man who was inside the tavern?…'

'Was not Paul Friche.'

'…who climbed the gutter pipe…'

'Malediction!'

And the chase continued – waxing hotter every minute. The hare had gained slightly on the hounds – there were more than a hundred hot on the trail by now – having crossed the bridge he was on the Isle Feydeau, and without hesitating a moment he plunged at once into the network of narrow streets which cover the island in the rear of La Petite Hollande and the Hôtel de la Villestreux, where lodged Carrier, the representative of the people. The hounds after him had lost some ground by halting – if only for a second or two – first at the head of the bridge, then at the corners of the various streets, while they peered into the darkness to see which way had gone that fleet-footed hare.

'Down this way!'

'No! That!'

'There he goes!'

It always took a few seconds to decide, during which the man on ahead with his burden on his shoulder had time mayhap to reach the end of a street and to turn a corner and once again to plunge into darkness and out of sight. The street lanthorns were few in this squalid corner of the city, and it was only when perforce the running hare had to cross a circle of light that the hounds were able to keep hot on the trail.

'To the bridges for your lives!' now shouted Fleury to the men nearest to him. 'Leave him to wander on the island. He cannot come off it, unless he jumps into the Loire.'

The Marats – intelligent and ferociously keen on the chase – had already grasped the importance of this order: with the bridges guarded that fleet-footed Englishman might run as much as he liked, he was bound to be run to earth like a fox in his burrow. In a moment they had dispersed along the quays, some to one bridge-head, some to another – the Englishman could not double back now, and if he had already crossed to the Isle Gloriette, which was not joined to the left bank of the river by any bridge, he would be equally caught like a rat in a trap.

'Unless he jumps into the Loire,' reiterated Fleury triumphantly.

'The proconsul will have more excitement than he hoped for,' he added with a laugh. 'He was looking forward to the capture of the English spy, and in deadly terror lest he escaped. But now meseems that we shall run our fox down in sight of the very gates of la Villestreux.

Martin-Roget's thoughts ran on Yvonne and the duc.

'You will remember, citizen commandant,' he contrived to say to Fleury, 'that the ci-devant Kernogans were found inside the Rat Mort.'

Fleury uttered an exclamation of rough impatience. What did he, what did anyone care at this moment for a couple of aristos more or less when the noblest game that had ever fallen to the bag of any Terrorist was so near being run to earth? But

Chauvelin said nothing. He walked on at a brisk pace, keeping close to Commandant Fleury's side, in the immediate wake of the pursuit. His lips were pressed tightly together and a hissing breath came through his wide-open nostrils. His pale eyes were fixed into the darkness and beyond it, where the most bitter enemy of the cause which he loved was fighting his last battle against Fate.

2

'He cannot get off the island!' Fleury had said awhile ago. Well! there was of a truth little or nothing now between the hunted hare and capture. The bridges were well guarded: the island swarming with hounds, the Marats at their posts and the Loire an impassable barrier all round.

And Chauvelin, the most tenacious enemy man ever had, Fleury keen on a reward and Martin-Roget with a private grudge to pay off, all within two hundred yards behind him.

True for the moment the Englishman had disappeared. Burden and all, the gloom appeared to have swallowed him up. But there was nowhere he could go; mayhap he had taken refuge under a doorway in one of the narrow streets and hoped perhaps under cover of the darkness to allow his pursuers to slip past him and then to double back.

Fleury was laughing in the best of humours. He was gradually collecting all the Marats together and sending them to the bridge-heads under the command of their various sergeants. Let the Englishman spend the night on the islands if he had a mind. There was a full company of Marats here to account for him as soon as he attempted to come out in the open.

The idlers and night-hawks as well as the municipal town-guard continued to run excitedly up and down the streets – sometimes there would come a lusty cry from a knot of pursuers who thought they spied the Englishman through the darkness, at others there would be a call of halt, and feverish consultation held at a street corner as to the best policy to adopt.

The town-guard, jealous of the Marats, were pining to lay hands on the English spy for the sake of the reward. Fleury, coming across their provost, called him a fool for his pains.

'My Marats will deal with the English spies, citizen,' he said roughly, 'he is no concern of yours.'

The provost demurred: an altercation might have ensued when Chauvelin's suave voice poured oil on the troubled waters.

'Why not,' he said, 'let the town-guard continue their search on the island, citizen commandant? The men may succeed in digging our rat out of his hole and forcing him out into the open all the sooner. Your Marats will have him quickly enough after that.'

To this suggestion the provost gave a grudging assent. The reward when the English spy was caught could be fought for later on. For the nonce he turned unceremoniously on his heel, and left Fleury cursing him for a meddlesome busybody.

'So long as he and his rabble does not interfere with my Marats,' growled the commandant.

'Will you see your sergeants citizen?' queried Chauvelin tentatively. 'They will have to keep very much on the alert, and will require constant prodding to their vigilance. If I can be of any service…'

'No,' retorted Fleury curtly, 'you and citizen Martin-Roget had best try and see the proconsul and tell him what we have done.'

'He'll be half wild with terror when he hears that the English spy is at large upon the island.'

'You must pacify him as best you can. Tell him I have a score of Marats at every bridge-head and that I am looking personally to every arrangement. There is no escape for the devil possible save by drowning himself and the wench in the Loire.'

3

Chauvelin and Martin-Roget turned from the quay on to the Petite Hollande – the great open ground with its converging row of trees which ends at the very apex of the Isle of Feydeau. Opposite to them at the further corner of the Place was the Hôtel de la Villestreux. One or two of the windows in the hotel were lighted from within. No doubt the proconsul was awake, trembling in the remotest angle of his lair, with the spectre of assassination rampant before him – aroused by the continued disturbance of the night, by the feverishness of this man-hunt carried on almost at his gates.

Even through the darkness it was easy to perceive groups of people either rushing backwards and forwards on the Place or congregating in groups under the trees. Excitement was in the air. It could be felt and heard right through the soughing of the north-westerly wind which caused the bare branches of the trees to groan and to crackle, and the dead leaves, which still hung on the twigs, to fly wildly through the night.

In the centre of the Place two small lights, gleaming like eyes in the midst of the gloom, betrayed the presence of the proconsul's coach, which stood there as always, ready to take him away to a place of safety – away from this city where he was mortally hated and dreaded...whenever the spectre of terror became more insistent than usual, and drove him hence out of his stronghold. The horses were pawing the frozen ground and champing their bits – the steam from their nostrils caught the rays of the carriage lamps, which also lit up with a feeble flicker the vague outline of the coachman on his box and of the postilion rigid in his saddle.

The citizens of Nantes were never tired of gaping at the carriage – a huge C-springed barouche – at the coachman's fine caped coat of bottle-green cloth and at the horses with their handsome harness set off with heavy brass bosses: they never tired of bandying words with the successive coachmen as they mounted their box and gathered up the reins, or with the postilions who loved to crack their whips and to appear smart and well-groomed, in the midst of the squalor which reigned in the terror-stricken city. They were the guardians of the mighty proconsul; on their skill, quickness and presence of mind might depend his precious life.

Even when the shadow of death hangs over an entire community, there will be some who will stand and gape and crack jokes at an uncommon sight.

And now when the pall of night hung over the abode of the man-tiger and his lair, and wrapped in its embrace the hunted and the hunters, there still was a knot of people standing round the carriage – between it and the hotel – gazing with lack-lustre eyes on the costly appurtenances wherewith the representative of a wretched people loved to surround himself. They could only see the solid mass of the carriage and of the horses, but they could hear the coachman clicking with his tongue and the postilion cracking his whip, and these sights broke the absolute dreary monotony of their lives.

It was from behind this knot of gaffers that there rose gradually a tumult as of a man calling out in wrath and lashing himself into a fury. Chauvelin and Martin-Roget were just then crossing La Petite Hollande from one bank of the river to the other: they were walking rapidly towards the hotel, when they heard the tumult which presently culminated in a hoarse cry and a volley of oaths.

'My coach! my coach at once...Lalouët, don't leave me... Curse you all for a set of cowardly oafs... My coach I say...'

'The proconsul,' murmured Chauvelin as he hastened forward, Martin-Roget following closely on his heels.

By the time that they had come near enough to the coach to distinguish vaguely in the gloom what was going on, people came rushing to the same spot from end to end of the Place. In a moment there was quite a crowd round the carriage, and the two men had much ado to push their way through by a vigorous play of their elbows.

'Citizen Carrier!' cried Chauvelin at the top of his voice, trying to dominate the hubbub, 'one minute... I have excellent news for you...the English spy...'

'Curse you for a set of blundering fools,' came with a husky cry from out the darkness, 'you have let that English devil escape... I knew it... I knew it...the assassin is at large...the murderer...my coach at once...my coach... Lalouët – do not leave me.'

Chauvelin had by this time succeeded in pushing his way to the forefront of the crowd: Martin-Roget, tall and powerful, had effectually made a way for him. Through the dense gloom he could see the misshapen form of the proconsul, wildly gesticulating with one arm and with the other clinging convulsively to young Lalouët who already had his hand on the handle of the carriage door.

With a quick, resolute gesture Chauvelin stepped between the door and the advancing proconsul.

'Citizen Carrier,' he said with calm determination, 'on my oath there is no cause for alarm. Your life is absolutely safe... I entreat you to return to your lodgings...'

To emphasize his words he had stretched out a hand and firmly grasped the proconsul's coat sleeve. This gesture, however, instead of pacifying the apparently terror-stricken maniac, seemed to have the effect of further exasperating his insensate fear. With a loud oath he tore himself free from Chauvelin's grasp.

'Ten thousand devils,' he cried hoarsely, 'who is this fool who dares to interfere with me? Stand aside man...stand aside or...'

And before Chauvelin could utter another word or Martin-Roget come to his colleague's rescue, there came the sudden sharp report of a pistol; the horses reared, the crowd was scattered in every direction, Chauvelin was knocked over by a smart blow on the head whilst a vigorous drag on his shoulder alone saved him from falling under the wheels of the coach.

Whilst confusion was at its highest, the carriage door was closed to with a bang and there was a loud, commanding cry hurled through the window at the coachman on his box.

'*En avant*, citizen coachman! Drive for your life! through the Savenay gate. The English assassins are on our heels.'

The postilion cracked his whip. The horses, maddened by the report, by the pushing, jostling crowd and the confused cries and screams around, plunged forward, wild with excitement. Their hoofs clattered on the hard road. Some of the crowd ran after the coach across the Place, shouting lustily: 'The proconsul! the proconsul!'

Chauvelin – dazed and bruised – was picked up by Martin-Roget.

'The cowardly brute!' was all that he said between his teeth, 'he shall rue this outrage as soon as I can give my mind to his affairs. In the meanwhile...'

The clatter of the horses' hoofs was already dying away in the distance. For a few seconds longer the rattle of the coach was still accompanied by cries of 'The proconsul! the proconsul!' Fleury at the bridge-head, seeing and hearing its approach, had only just time to order his Marats to stand at attention. A salvo should have been fired when the representative of the people, the high and mighty proconsul, was abroad, but there was no time for that, and the coach clattered over the bridge at breakneck speed, whilst Carrier with his head out of the window was hurling anathemas and insults at Fleury for having allowed the paid spies of that cursed British Government to threaten the life of a representative of the people.

'I go to Savenay,' he shouted just at the last, 'until that assassin has been thrown in the Loire. But when I return...look to yourself Commandant Fleury.'

Then the carriage turned down the Quai de la Fosse and a few minutes later was swallowed up by the gloom.

BARONESS ORCZY

4

Chauvelin, supported by Martin-Roget, was hobbling back across the Place. The crowd was still standing about, vaguely wondering why it had got so excited over the departure of the proconsul and the rattle of a coach and pair across the bridge, when on the island there was still an assassin at large – an English spy, the capture of whom would be one of the great events in the chronicles of the city of Nantes.

'I think,' said Martin-Roget, 'that we may as well go to bed now, and leave the rest to Commandant Fleury. The Englishman may not be captured for some hours, and I for one am over-fatigued.'

'Then go to bed an you desire, citizen Martin-Roget,' retorted Chauvelin drily, 'I for one will stay here until I see the Englishman in the hands of Commandant Fleury.'

'Hark,' interposed Martin-Roget abruptly. 'What was that?'

Chauvelin had paused even before Martin-Roget's restraining hand had rested on his arm. He stood still in the middle of the Place and his knees shook under him so that he nearly fell prone to the ground.

'What is it?' reiterated Martin-Roget with vague puzzlement. 'It sounds like young Lalouët's voice.'

Chauvelin said nothing. He had forgotten his bruises: he no longer hobbled – he ran across the Place to the front of the hotel whence the voice had come which was so like that of young Lalouët.

The youngster – it was undoubtedly he – was standing at the angle of the hotel: above him a lanthorn threw a dim circle of light on his bare head with its mass of dark curls, and on a small knot of idlers with two or three of the town-guard amongst them. The first words spoken by him which Chauvelin distinguished quite clearly were:

278

'You are all mad...or else drunk... The citizen proconsul is upstairs in his room... He has just sent me down to hear what news there is of the English spies...'

5

No one made reply. It seemed as if some giant and spectral hand had passed over this mass of people and with its magic touch had stilled their turbulent passions, silenced their imprecations and cooled their ardour – and left naught but a vague fear, a subtle sense of awe as when something unexplainable and supernatural has manifested itself before the eyes of men.

From far away the roll of coach wheels rapidly disappearing in the distance alone broke the silence of the night.

'Is there no one here who will explain what all this means?' queried young Lalouët, who alone had remained self-assured and calm, for he alone knew nothing of what had happened. 'Citizen Fleury, are you there?'

Then as once again he received no reply, he added peremptorily:

'Hey! someone there! Are you all louts and oafs that not one of you can speak?'

A timid voice from the rear ventured on explanation.

'The citizen proconsul was here a moment ago... We all saw him, and you citizen Lalouët were with him...'

An imprecation from young Lalouët silenced the timid voice for the nonce...and then another resumed the halting narrative:

'We all could have sworn that we saw you, citizen Lalouët, also the citizen proconsul... He got into his coach with you... you...that is...they have driven off...'

'This is some awful and treacherous hoax,' cried the youngster now in a towering passion; 'the citizen proconsul is upstairs in bed, I tell you...and I have only just come out of the hotel...! Name of a name of a dog! am I standing here or am I not?'

Then suddenly he bethought himself of the many events of the day which had culminated in this gigantic feat of leger-de-main.

'Chauvelin!' he exclaimed. 'Where in the name of h–ll is citizen Chauvelin?'

But Chauvelin for the moment could nowhere be found. Dazed, half-unconscious, wholly distraught, he had fled from the scene of his discomfiture as fast as his trembling knees would allow. Carrier searched the city for him high and low, and for days afterwards the soldiers of the Compagnie Marat gave aristos and rebels a rest: they were on the look-out for a small, wizened figure of a man – the man with the pale, keen eyes who had failed to recognize in the pseudo Paul Friche, in the dirty, out-at-elbows *sans-culotte* – the most exquisite dandy that had ever graced the salons of Bath and of London: they were searching for the man with the acute and sensitive brain who had failed to scent in the pseudo-Carrier and the pseudo-Lalouët his old and arch enemy Sir Percy Blakeney and the charming wife of my lord Anthony Dewhurst.

10

Lord Tony

A quarter of an hour later citizen-commandant Fleury was at last ushered into the presence of the proconsul and received upon his truly innocent head the full torrent of the despot's wrath. But Martin-Roget had listened to the counsels of prudence: for obvious reasons he desired to avoid any personal contact for the moment with Carrier, whom fear of the English spies had made into a more abject and more craven tyrant than ever before. At the same time he thought it wisest to try and pacify the brute by sending him the ten thousand francs – the bribe agreed upon for his help in the undertaking which had culminated in such a disastrous failure.

At the self-same hour whilst Carrier – fuming and swearing – was for the hundredth time uttering that furious "How?" which for the hundredth time had remained unanswered, two men were taking leave of one another at the small postern gate which gives on the cemetery of St Anne. The taller and younger one of the two had just dropped a heavy purse into the hand of the other. The latter stooped and kissed the kindly hand.

'Milor,' he said, 'I swear to you most solemnly that M. le duc de Kernogan will rest in peace in hallowed ground. M. le *curé* de Vertou – ah! he is a saint and a brave man, milor – comes over whenever he can prudently do so and reads the offices for the dead – over those who have died as Christians, and there is a piece of consecrated ground out here in the open which those fiends of Terrorists have not discovered yet.'

'And you will bury M. le duc immediately,' admonished the younger man, 'and apprise M. le *curé* of what has happened.'

'Aye! aye! I'll do that, milor, within the hour. Though M. le duc was never a very kind master to me in the past, I cannot forget that I served him and his family for over thirty years as coachman. I drove Mlle. Yvonne in the first pony-cart she ever possessed. I drove her – ah! that was a bitter day! – her and M. le duc when they left Kernogan never to return. I drove Mlle. Yvonne on that memorable night when a crowd of miserable peasants attacked her coach, and that brute Pierre Adet started to lead a rabble against the château. That was the beginning of things, milor. God alone knows what has happened to Pierre Adet. His father Jean was hanged by order of M. le duc. Now M. le duc is destined to lie in a forgotten grave. I serve this abominable Republic by digging graves for her victims. I would be happier, I think, if I knew what had become of Mlle. Yvonne.'

'Mlle. Yvonne is my wife, old friend,' said the younger man softly. 'Please God she has years of happiness before her, if I succeed in making her forget all that she has suffered.'

'Amen to that, milor!' rejoined the man fervently. 'Then I pray you tell the noble lady to rest assured. Jean-Marie – her old coachman whom she used to trust implicitly in the past – will see that M. le duc de Kernogan is buried as a gentleman and a Christian should be.'

'You are not running too great a risk by this, I hope, my good Jean-Marie,' quoth Lord Tony gently.

'No greater risk, milor,' replied Jean-Marie earnestly, 'than the one which you ran by carrying my old master's dead body on your shoulders through the streets of Nantes.'

'Bah! that was simple enough,' said the younger man, 'the hue and cry is after higher quarry tonight. Pray God the hounds have not run the noble game to earth.'

Even as he spoke there came from far away through the darkness the sound of a fast trotting pair of horses and the rumble of coach-wheels on the unpaved road.

'There they are, thank God!' exclaimed Lord Tony, and the tremor in his voice alone betrayed the torturing anxiety which he had been enduring, ever since he had seen the last both of his adored young wife and of his gallant chief in the squalid taproom of the Rat Mort.

With the dead body of Yvonne's father on his back he had quietly worked his way out of the tavern in the wake of his chief. He had his orders, and for the members of that gallant League of the Scarlet Pimpernel there was no such word as 'disobedience' and no such word as 'fail.' Through the darkness and through the tortuous streets of Nantes Lord Anthony Dewhurst – the young and wealthy exquisite, the hero of an hundred fâtes and galas in Bath, in London – staggered under the weight of a burden imposed upon him only by his loyalty and a noble sense of self-prescribed discipline – and that burden the dead body of the man who had done him an unforgiveable wrong. Without a thought of revolt he had obeyed – and risked his life and worse in the obedience.

The darkness of the night was his faithful handmaiden, and the excitement of the chase after the other quarry had fortunately drawn every possible enemy from his track. He had set his teeth and accomplished his task, and even the deathly anxiety for the wife whom he idolized had been crushed, under the iron heel of a grim resolve. Now his work was done, and from far away he heard the rattle of the coach-wheels which were bringing his beloved nearer and nearer to him.

Five minutes longer and the coach came to a halt. A cheery voice called out gaily:

'Tony! are you there?'

'Percy!' exclaimed the young man.

Already he knew that all was well. The gallant leader, the loyal and loving friend, had taxed every resource of a boundlessly fertile brain in order to win yet another wreath of immortal laurels for the League which he commanded, and the very tone of his merry voice proclaimed the triumph which had crowned his daring scheme.

The next moment Yvonne lay in the arms of her dear milor. He had stepped into the carriage, even while Sir Percy climbed nimbly on the box and took the reins from the bewildered coachman's hands.

'Citizen proconsul...' murmured the latter, who of a truth thought that he was dreaming.

'Get off the box, you old noodle,' quoth the pseudo-proconsul peremptorily. 'Thou and thy friend the postilion will remain here in the road, and on the morrow you'll explain to whomsoever it may concern that the English spy made a murderous attack on you both and left you half dead outside the postern gate of the cemetery of St. Anne. Here,' he added as he threw a purse down to the two men – who half-dazed and overcome by superstitious fear had indeed scrambled down, one from his box, the other from his horse – 'there's a hundred francs for each of you in there, and mind you drink to the health of the English spy and the confusion of your brutish proconsul.'

There was no time to lose: the horses – still very fresh – were fretting to start.

'Where do we pick up Hastings and Ffoulkes?' asked Sir Percy Blakeney finally as he turned toward the interior of the barouche, the hood of which hid its occupants from view.

'At the corner of the rue de Gigan,' came the quick answer. 'It is only two hundred metres from the city gate. They are on the look out for you.'

'Ffoulkes shall be postilion,' rejoined Sir Percy with a laugh, 'and Hastings sit beside me on the box. And you will see how at the city gate and all along the route soldiers of the guard will salute the equipage of the all-powerful proconsul of Nantes. By Gad!' he added under his breath, 'I've never had a merrier time in all my life – not even when...'

He clicked his tongue and gave the horses their heads – and soon the coachman and the postilion and Jean-Marie the gravedigger of the cemetery of St. Anne were left gaping out into the night in the direction where the barouche had so quickly disappeared.

'Now for Le Croisic and the *Day-Dream*,' sighed the daring adventurer contentedly, '...and for Marguerite!' he added wistfully.

2

Under the hood of the barouche Yvonne, wearied but immeasurably happy, was doing her best to answer all her dear milor's impassioned questions and to give him a fairly clear account of that terrible chase and flight through the streets of the Isle Feydeau.

'Ah, milor, how can I tell you what I felt when I realized that I was being carried along in the arms of the valiant Scarlet Pimpernel? A word from him and I understood. After that I tried to be both resourceful and brave. When the chase after us was at its hottest we slipped into a ruined and deserted house. In a room at the back there were several bundles of what looked like old clothes. "This is my store-house," milor said to me; "now that we have reached it we can just make long noses at the whole pack of bloodhounds." He made me slip into some boy's clothes which he gave me, and whilst I donned these he disappeared. When he returned I truly did not recognize him. He looked horrible, and his voice...! After a moment or two he laughed, and then I knew him. He explained to me the rôle which I was to play, and I did my best to obey him in everything. But oh! I hardly lived while we once more emerged into the open street and then turned into the great Place which was full – oh full! – of people. I felt that at every moment we might be suspected. Figure to yourself, my dear milor…'

What Yvonne Dewhurst was about to say next will never be recorded. My lord Tony had closed her lips with a kiss.

BARONESS ORCZY

THE ELUSIVE PIMPERNEL

In this, the sequel to *The Scarlet Pimpernel*, French agent and chief spy-catcher Chauvelin is as crafty as ever, but Sir Percy Blakeney is more than a match for his arch-enemy. Meanwhile the beautiful Marguerite remains wholly devoted to Sir Percy, her husband. Cue more swashbuckling adventures as Sir Percy attempts to smuggle French aristocrats out of the country to safety.

THE LAUGHING CAVALIER

The year is 1623, the place Haarlem in the Netherlands. Diogenes – the first Sir Percy Blakeney, the Scarlet Pimpernel's ancestor – and his friends Pythagoras and Socrates defend justice and the royalist cause. The famous artist Frans Hals also makes an appearance in this historical adventure: Orczy maintains that Hals' celebrated portrait *The Laughing Cavalier* is actually a portrayal of the Scarlet Pimpernel's ancestor.

BARONESS ORCZY

THE LEAGUE OF THE SCARLET PIMPERNEL

More adventures amongst the terrors of revolutionary France. No one has uncovered the identity of the famous Scarlet Pimpernel – no one except his wife Marguerite and his arch-enemy, citizen Chauvelin. Sir Percy Blakeney is still at large, however, evading capture...

LEATHERFACE

The Prince saw a 'figure of a man, clad in dark, shapeless woollen clothes wearing a hood of the same dark stuff over his head and a leather mask over his face'. The year is 1572 and the Prince of Orange is at Mons under night attack from the Spaniards. However Leatherface raises the alarm in the nick of time. The mysterious masked man has vowed to reappear – when his Highness' life is in danger. Who is Leatherface? And when will he next be needed?

BARONESS ORCZY

THE SCARLET PIMPERNEL

A group of titled Englishmen, under the leadership of a mysterious man, valiantly aid condemned aristocrats in their escape from Paris to England during the French Revolution. Their leader is the Scarlet Pimpernel – a man whose audacity and clever disguises foil the villainous agent Chauvelin. Who is he and can he keep one step ahead of the revolutionaries?

THE TRIUMPH OF THE SCARLET PIMPERNEL

It is Paris, 1794, and Robespierre's revolution is inflicting its reign of terror. The elusive Scarlet Pimpernel is still at large – so far. But the sinister agent Chauvelin has taken prisoner his darling Marguerite. Will she act as a decoy and draw the Scarlet Pimpernel to the enemy? And will our dashing hero evade capture and live to enjoy a day 'when tyranny was crushed and men dared to be men again'?

OTHER TITLES BY BARONESS ORCZY AVAILABLE DIRECT FROM HOUSE OF STRATUS

Quantity		£	$(US)	$(CAN)	€
☐	THE ADVENTURES OF THE SCARLET PIMPERNEL	6.99	12.95	19.95	13.50
☐	BY THE GODS BELOVED	6.99	12.95	19.95	13.50
☐	THE CASE OF MISS ELLIOTT	6.99	12.95	19.95	13.50
☐	ELDORADO	6.99	12.95	19.95	13.50
☐	THE ELUSIVE PIMPERNEL	6.99	12.95	19.95	13.50
☐	THE FIRST SIR PERCY	6.99	12.95	19.95	13.50
☐	I WILL REPAY	6.99	12.95	19.95	13.50
☐	LADY MOLLY OF SCOTLAND YARD	6.99	12.95	19.95	13.50
☐	THE LAUGHING CAVALIER	6.99	12.95	19.95	13.50
☐	THE LEAGUE OF THE SCARLET PIMPERNEL	6.99	12.95	19.95	13.50
☐	LEATHERFACE	6.99	12.95	19.95	13.50
☐	MAM'ZELLE GUILLOTINE	6.99	12.95	19.95	13.50
☐	THE OLD MAN IN THE CORNER	6.99	12.95	19.95	13.50
☐	PIMPERNEL AND ROSEMARY	6.99	12.95	19.95	13.50
☐	THE SCARLET PIMPERNEL	8.99	13.95	20.95	15.00
☐	SIR PERCY HITS BACK	6.99	12.95	19.95	13.50
☐	SIR PERCY LEADS THE BAND	6.99	12.95	19.95	13.50
☐	THE TRIUMPH OF THE SCARLET PIMPERNEL	8.99	13.95	20.95	15.00
☐	UNRAVELLED KNOTS	6.99	12.95	19.95	13.50
☐	THE WAY OF THE SCARLET PIMPERNEL	6.99	12.95	19.95	13.50

ALL HOUSE OF STRATUS BOOKS ARE AVAILABLE FROM GOOD BOOKSHOPS OR DIRECT FROM THE PUBLISHER:

Internet: www.houseofstratus.com including synopses and features.

Email: sales@houseofstratus.com
info@houseofstratus.com
(please quote author, title and credit card details.)

Tel: Order Line
0800 169 1780 (UK)
1 800 724 1100 (USA)
International
+44 (0) 1845 527700 (UK)
+01   845 463 1100 (USA)

Fax: +44 (0) 1845 527711 (UK)
+01   845 463 0018 (USA)
(please quote author, title and credit card details.)

Send to: House of Stratus Sales Department   House of Stratus Inc.
Thirsk Industrial Park   2 Neptune Road
York Road, Thirsk   Poughkeepsie
North Yorkshire, YO7 3BX   NY 12601
UK   USA

PAYMENT

Please tick currency you wish to use:

☐ £ (Sterling)　☐ $ (US)　☐ $ (CAN)　☐ € (Euros)

Allow for shipping costs charged per order plus an amount per book as set out in the tables below:

CURRENCY/DESTINATION

	£(Sterling)	$(US)	$(CAN)	€(Euros)
Cost per order				
UK	1.50	2.25	3.50	2.50
Europe	3.00	4.50	6.75	5.00
North America	3.00	3.50	5.25	5.00
Rest of World	3.00	4.50	6.75	5.00
Additional cost per book				
UK	0.50	0.75	1.15	0.85
Europe	1.00	1.50	2.25	1.70
North America	1.00	1.00	1.50	1.70
Rest of World	1.50	2.25	3.50	3.00

PLEASE SEND CHEQUE OR INTERNATIONAL MONEY ORDER
payable to: HOUSE OF STRATUS LTD or HOUSE OF STRATUS INC. or card payment as indicated

STERLING EXAMPLE

Cost of book(s):..................... Example: 3 x books at £6.99 each: £20.97

Cost of order: .... Example: £1.50 (Delivery to UK address)

Additional cost per book:............... Example: 3 x £0.50: £1.50

Order total including shipping:........... Example: £23.97

VISA, MASTERCARD, SWITCH, AMEX:

☐☐☐☐☐☐☐☐☐☐☐☐☐☐☐☐☐☐☐

Issue number (Switch only):

☐☐☐

Start Date: ☐☐/☐☐　　**Expiry Date:** ☐☐/☐☐

Signature: _____

NAME: _____

ADDRESS: _____

COUNTRY: _____

ZIP/POSTCODE: _____

Please allow 28 days for delivery. Despatch normally within 48 hours.

Prices subject to change without notice.
Please tick box if you do not wish to receive any additional information. ☐

House of Stratus publishes many other titles in this genre; please check our website (**www.houseofstratus.com**) for more details.